# SLANT

*a novel by*

## Scout Larken Link

# SLANT

## Scout Larken Link

ISBN 978-1-934894-62-0
LITERARY FICTION

CREDITS:
The historic physio-graphic diagram (modified on the back cover) was
originally created by Kentucky Geological Survey.

Front / back cover photos and inside maps of SLANT and TRS were created by the author.

Kentucky Foundation for Women (founded in1985 by feminist philanthropist Sallie Bingham)
generously provided grant funding during the writing, which propelled completion of the first
full draft. The author is grateful to KFW for this and other artistic support over the years.

A few segments of this book were previously published in slightly different versions.

Published in Kentucky by

*dedicated to*
*my three favorite* EVAs
*& my essential* ANNE

*humble thanx go to my first-draft readers,* ERIN, DEBBIE & JENNY,
*and to my son,* TOBY,
*in gratitude for valuable feedback and enthusiastic support from you all*

"The vision of Christ that thou dost see
is my vision's greatest enemy."
—*WILLIAM BLAKE*


"That night, that year of now done darkness
I wretch lay wrestling with (my God!) my God."
—*GERARD MANLEY HOPKINS*


"Those who can be made to believe absurdities
can be made to commit atrocities."
—*VOLTAIRE*

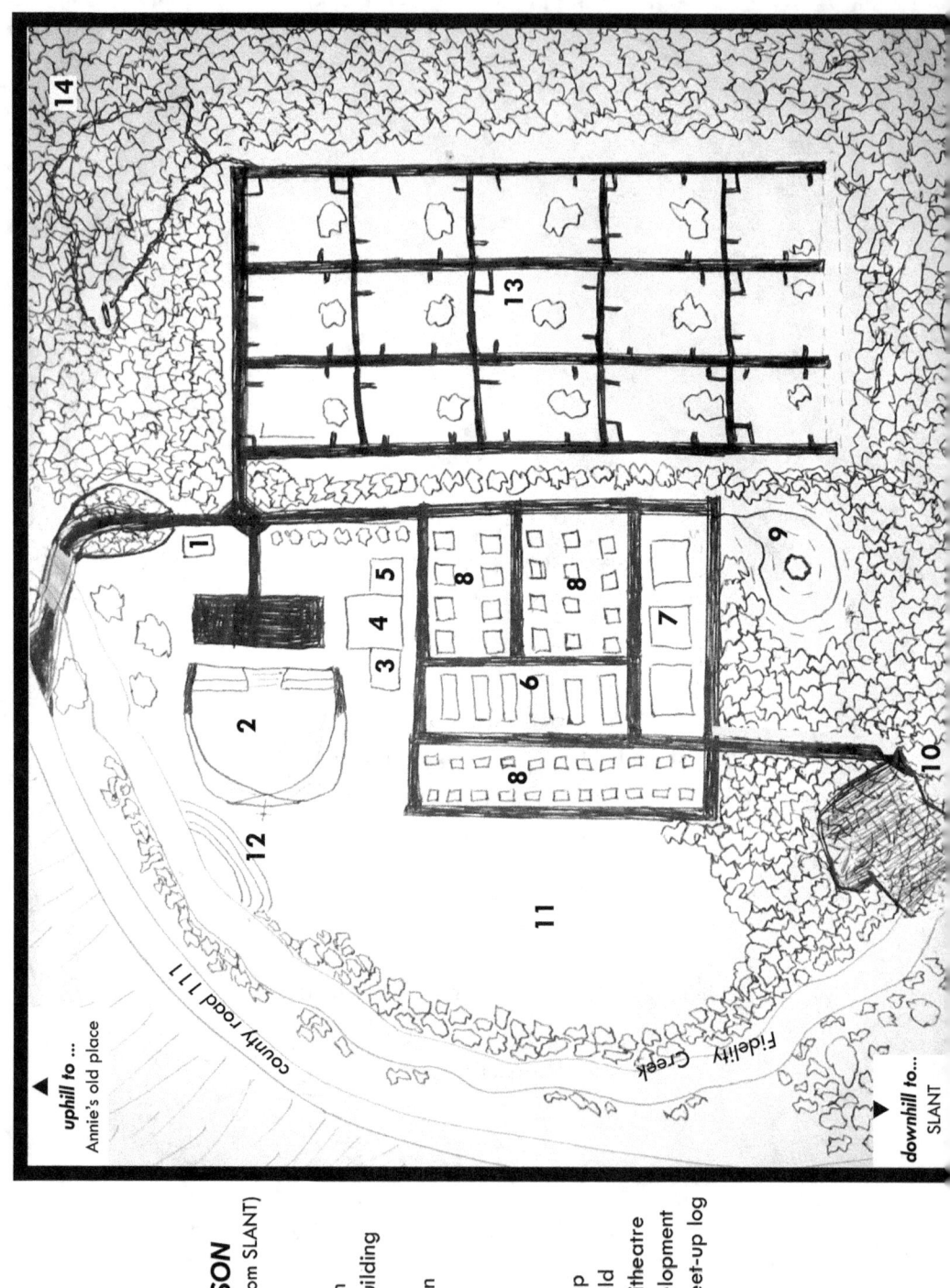

**Map of**
**THE RISING SON**
(church camp uphill from SLANT)

1 Guard shack
2 Chapel / Pavilion
3 Administration building
4 Dining Hall
5 Tea Party canteen
6 Bunkhouses
7 Dormitories
8 Small cabins
9 Fire circle
10 Illegal toxic dump
11 Sloping open field
12 Baptismal amphitheatre
13 Phase One development
14 Nick & Sam's meet-up log

uphill to ...
Annie's old place

downhill to....
SLANT

county road 111

Fidelity Creek

# Map of
# SLANT
(high on Barrel Chute Knob)

1 The Jimmies (the big house)
2 The General (old juke joint)
3 Craft Cabin
4 Horse's bench
5 Gazebo
6 Heart-Headed
7 Campground & picnic area
8 Billings boys' house
9 Billings' Fix-It Shop
10 Wilma Carl
11 Turk & Turner
12 Dick's place
13 Horse's trailer
14 Alec's treehouse
15 Pair Square
16 Meddy
17 Farnsley
18 Tractor Girl
19 Bard
20 Joy
21 Nooner
22 Juny
23 Willie & Iwana
24 Tomlah (Cora's house)
25 Jorge

Fidelity Creek

Whisper

community garden

pond

community garden

community garden

orchard

county road

Barrel Chute Knob Trailhead

uphill to ...
TRS church camp

downhill to ...
TG's bonsai farm
post office
city / mega-church

# SLANT

# The Freakin' Garden of Eden

TRACTOR GIRL HAS ONE HELL OF A COMMUTE. Every day she juices herself some fresh fruit and protein powder into a morning smoothie, packs a generous lunch and leaves the cozy confines of her cottage in SLANT. Rain or shine, she walks peacefully and purposefully past Meddy's shelter to the particular place along the edge of Fidelity Creek where she stows her kayak, which she named Whisper. She'd attached a couple of crude wooden braces to tree stumps; onto these she lashes the boat, upside down, when she isn't using it. At least five mornings every week from late winter until late fall Tractor Girl lifts Whisper off its dry dock and slides it expertly into the waters of Fidelity. Then, downstream she floats. Her morning trip might find her in joy or wonder or peace … or all three at once in a brilliant confluence that she experiences as quiet ecstasy.

*Fidelity is a good old girl,* she thought this morning, resting her paddle across her thighs and watching the water quietly unzip for her little craft. Going downstream isn't nearly as much a chore as paddling home, but Tractor Girl is in excellent physical condition, so she handles the round trip easily day after day. Still, because she loves being on the water, she often takes her time going down, using the paddle only as a rudder when needed, letting the lethargic current, fed by the cumulative trickle of an uphill spring, get her there in its own good time.

Fidelity has no whitewater. In fact, the lazy waterway's most extreme curves have carved out big pools that are effective in retarding the water's speed. The creek's bed is four to six feet deep on average, so no portage is required at any point between SLANT and Tractor Girl's daily destination. In the afternoon she paddles against the gentle current, back upstream to SLANT. Upstream is, of course, uphill, but the creek meanders so much back and forth along the side of the knob that it never feels too steep either going down or coming back.

Tractor Girl is particularly fond of the birds living along Fidelity. They whistle and chirrup in generous rhythmic proportion, offering atmospheric trills in a code no human fully fathoms. She's pleased enough to receive the creatures' tunes by proximity. Being in their musical company always makes Tractor Girl smile.

It takes her about twenty minutes to get from SLANT to her bonsai farm where she works—because of the knob's elevation, it takes nearly twice that long to get back home—and she looks forward to both directions of the going every single day, drizzle or beam. Even if the birds are hiding out from a downpour, there's the flora to notice, the scene constantly changing. Whoever once said *it's never the same river twice* was a genius. Daily she watches this fluid glory of Mother Nature go through variants of its cycles. Seasons dramatically change, yes, but it's the subtle daily variables that seem to her most remarkable: a limb lowering today more than yesterday because of the ripening of its fruit or the burgeoning of its garment of leaves; the displacement of reeds in the shallows after a windstorm; creatures finding new places to nest or to rest; blooms that weren't there last week, or the absence of something that had been.

Oh, it is indeed a sweet commute. Possibly the best part of her day. Not that she doesn't love where she's headed, of course.

The deep truth of Tractor Girl is this: no matter which direction she and Whisper travel on Fidelity, she consciously opens herself to bliss. Paddling to the kind of work that fills her up with anticipation and calm, or headed back home, saturated with well-earned sweat and sweet satis-faction, it's all the same to her. She has learned to love her life. And this is welcomed news, for loving her life hasn't always been the case.

Tractor Girl—called Hannaleigh as a child—had come up through some pretty rough circumstances. Her father had suffered an undiagnosed mental illness, and it would make him suddenly mean in ways that she and her mother never did understand, no matter how they tried. He had absolutely no patience, yet demanded it of them. Every hour of her childhood had been a test that she could not pass. Every week a chore. Every year a punishment.

This daily commute, then, became an adult tonic that soothed the chronic distress her childhood had left her burdened with. For that matter, it quieted much of the later loss and disappointment in her life, as well. She has, after long and intense care, come to terms with her Complex PTSD and, mostly, manages it well. Water is a sure factor in her recovery.

The creek on this tranquil Tuesday morning was a little brighter than usual, and it reminded Tractor Girl that sunrise was occurring earlier each morning now. That would account for the recent perk-up of the twelve-inch trees whose pots sat row upon row on wide, level swaths of black ground-cloth defining the working part of her bonsai farm. *Those fellas are catching a few minutes more sun each day, and it's got 'em revved up like naughty little boys with spring fever,* she thought. This made her chuckle aloud to herself, something she had never done before finding her home in SLANT.

Nearing trip's end, she always looked forward to gliding her kayak under the swimming-hole-rope and then stepping onto the sacred bottom ground of the bonsai farm. There would be good work to do. She relished caring for things that returned only peace and fruitfulness for her labors. She liked to start the little trees on their way, from cuttings, roots or seeds. And she liked healing them when they were in trouble, just as the creek healed her.

Fidelity was mostly shady, but once off it Tractor Girl stepped into full sun slicing in toward the water from the other edge of the bonsai farm. She was dressed for the heat, her shorts rolled up, tank top tied high about her ribcage. She had one of those neck bandannas with a sewn-in pouch containing a gelled substance that, when soaked in the waters of Fidelity and then tied around her neck, kept her cool for a couple hours at a time. Her headgear rotated between a do-rag, a safari hat with a stiff, wide brim, and a cherished Boston Red Sox ball cap with a raggedy visor— sun-bleached more grey now than blue, but that made her love it all the more, for it reminded her that she'd had it as long she'd had independence and, by now, that was a good long time. In cooler weather, she wore khaki work pants and, sometimes, a holey old sweater that once had been her great-mamaw's, a woman who had been able to grow almost anything. Tractor Girl considered that sweater a talisman when she was at work on the bonsais at the beginning and end of the growing season. Year round she wore outback boots and socks, except when she pulled them off for cooling dips in the creek. She had bought the rugged boots on her only trip to Alice Springs, years ago. "Good old Rossi's," the clerk had called them. Sturdily made; not too expensive. When she boarded Qantas for her lengthy return to the U.S., she was wearing those boots. Had worn them almost daily ever since.

This morning, after landing and pulling on her boots, she supplied water and nutrients to everybody lined up on the tarps. Then, she resumed working on the particular row of tiny trees that she'd been shaping, pot by pot, since earlier in the week. She reached into her hip pocket, pulled out a pair of nippers and some fine wire, and smiled at the section of the row she had worked on yesterday. She thought those plucky plants seemed to stand a little taller in their small pots, a little more proud of their buff new looks. She grinned at them, then turned her attention to the remainder of the row. "You girls ready for your spa treatment?" She kneeled to her labor.

Gazelle had once—long ago now—asked Tractor Girl how she could take a wild-looking bush and make a perfect little wind-swept tree emerge from such a ragged starter clump. Tractor Girl had simply said, "I just look at the plant and cut away everything that doesn't belong."

"But can you really see the shape lurking inside a scruffy shrub before you start snipping things away?" Gazelle's curiosity had seemed sincere at the time.

"Well, sure," Tractor Girl had said, rotating a pot before her, gazing at the tiny plant purposefully. Then she had turned to Gazelle and with a sudden puzzled look asked, "Can't you?"

Was a time when Tractor Girl often thought of her wife *(ex-wife? how could that be?)* while she worked. It had never occurred to her, back in those happy days, to wonder whether Gazelle likewise had had sweet thoughts of her. Just seemed like a given. Well, those days were gone, as the gaping hole in Tractor Girl's chest constantly reminded her.

In late-morning the heat started to build on the football-field-sized clearing along the creek bottom. Tractor Girl worked her way down about a third of one of the long rows of pots. She always took her time, making sure each of the little plants got a good manicure, for they would have to wait several weeks before their turn came around again.

By early afternoon, the sun began crawling down the slope, spreading light and health on the treetops and clearings in and around this side of Barrel Chute Knob. Tractor Girl found that if she took her lunch and siesta around noon, she'd be able to cross over to the other edge of the field and work in the increasing slant of shade accumulating on that side until mid-afternoon.

In summer, she usually started her paddle back up Fidelity against the gentle current around three, three-thirty, because by then the grid's dark tarps were unbearable, even those in the shade. Today, she thought a quick swim might be just the thing before launching her kayak homeward.

"Where d'ya think you're a-goin'?" The voice was male, quiet, and had an edge of suggestiveness in it. She was jarred only for a second.

"What's it to ya?" she shot back. She wasn't afraid.

"Most folks don't git off work 'til five," the voice said. A man stepped out of a birch grove. "You think you're special or something?"

"Noop," Tractor Girl said. She bent over to pull off her work boots and socks. "I think I'm the boss."

Nooner laughed. "That's good enough for me," he said, unhooking a canteen from his belt and holding it out.

"Thanks, man," Tractor Girl said. She swallowed a long pull of the water, then poured a dribble onto the top of her head before she handed it back.

"You've sure got the spread lookin' good down here," Nooner said. He turned a slow arc, surveying the layout of the bonsai farm: dark ground-cloth strips forming the gigantic, rectangular grid, pots holding bonsai trees aligned according to size in meticulous rows everywhere. "I'll admit I never noticed before, but I'm guessing *both* your thumbs must be green.

Lemme see."

Tractor Girl grinned, gave him a matched pair of thumbs-up.

Stepping to creek's edge, she couldn't wait to put her feet into that water, cool and spring-fed and making its perpetual way down from its source up above SLANT. Water was a great leveler of people, places and things. Tractor Girl believed on that.

"You know what Confucius said?" she asked.

Nooner shook his head, waited.

"Said, 'Everything flows on and on like this river, without pause, day and night.'"

Nooner took in the moving water below them, first downstream, then up. His eyes felt most easy when it was water he was looking at. "Smart man, that Confucius," he said. "Time's the only flow there is, when you get right down to it."

Tractor Girl nodded agreement, waded quietly into the water from its shallow shore below the bank, bent her knees and leaned backward to dunk herself in the cool. When she stood again in a waist-deep spot, she shook the water off her head and lifted her hands out to her sides. Droplets fell from her fingers like tiny clear pebbles, but when they hit the water's surface they melded with it on contact; no longer separate bits of water, they became one with the whole. She didn't have words to describe how seeing that made her feel.

Nooner, his gaze locked on the rarely seen Indigo Bunting until it took wing and shot into denser growth, broke his reverie first. "Say," he said. "When you gonna pitch another one of them throw-downs down here, TG? We ain't had us a big time like that since our last shindig."

Tractor Girl heard him, but it took a few seconds for her to reply. Having also spotted the bright blue flash of her favorite bird, she found the act of coaxing her mind to rejoin the world to be a strange and diffi-cult effort. Not unusual for her. Without turning back to face him, she answered, "You thinking it's about time, Nooner?"

"I'm thinkin' with all the changes up there at TRS, we're gonna be needin' something of a steam valve, lest *some* of us get so worked up we blow our tops."

She turned back toward him. Something in his voice was worrying, but she decided this day wasn't the time to pursue it. "Well then, why don't you and me get on that plan right now," she finally said. "When's good for you?"

"We prolly shoulda done it this spring at Equinox," said he, "but we missed that one. Solstice comin'—why don't we shoot for that?"

"Perfect," Tractor Girl said, wading back to her kayak. "Reckon we can get people here? They don't seem to mind the trip downhill, but they get to dreading having to climb or paddle back up. Might make for a convenient excuse to skip out altogether."

"Naw. Food, music and a big bonfire? They'll come," he said. "Always do."

She shook more water off her hands, reached for her work boots, dropped them into the little boat's rear hatch and secured it. "Hope so," she said.

"Maybe Earl'n'em'll make a sugarhead run between now and then. Folks get wind of moonshine on the premises, that oughta bring 'em gallopin' down this old knob."

"All right then," she said, slipping Whisper into the creek. "Solstice it is." She waded in the shallow and guided the kayak toward her. "We'll call it 'SLANT's Sizzling Summer Solstice Supper' this time. Let's make it a potluck. You and me supply the cold beer and sweet tea?"

The details, they knew, would work themselves out before the day arrived. Other people would organize other parts of the preparations. All Nooner and TG had to do was get the idea rolling, inform Mayor Sheepwater, and turn loose the SLANT party line. It'd sort itself out from there.

Nooner's tone turned a bit more serious when he gestured in the direction of a nearby shed's roof extension, a sort of carport under which Tractor Girl parked the bonsai farm's pickup truck—a beloved, formerly-white, 1978 three-on-the-tree F-100 that she had long ago named *Towanda*. "Ever had any vandalism down here?" he asked.

"Noop, never have," she said. "Why? You aware of somethin' I oughta be prepared for?"

"I'd just keep one eye open," he said. "I'm not likin' what I'm seein' up at that church camp. *Under New Management* ain't the half of it."

"Oh?"

"Somethin's not right up there, is all I'm sayin'," Nooner said.

"Well, when you figure it out, let me know, will you? I mean, I've got a vested interest in what's going on up and down Fidelity."

"You bet, TG. Top of my list. But don't you fret," he advised. He gestured toward her hands. "Just keep on doin' what those magic green thumbs of yours do best." His gaze swept again over the immaculate rows of tiny potted trees. "Damn, it's unbelievable," he said. "To think that I get to live right upstream from the freakin' Garden of Eden."

"That name's taken, I heard," Tractor Girl said, grinning, "but if I'm ever forced to put a label on this place, I'll take that one under advisement." She shook water off one foot, positioned her kayak, settled easily into the cockpit and unclipped her paddle from its starboard side. "Reckon I better go with the flow," she said, pushing off.

"Or against it, as the case may be," said Nooner.

She grinned.

"Have a good trip," Nooner said. "See you topside."

"Not if I see you first!" She chuckled, paddled several strokes, then had a second thought that urged her to call back toward the creek bank. "Hey, Nooner, check that latch on my gate going out to the road, will you?"

"You bet, skipper." Nooner gave her a mock salute and spun smartly on his heel. Then he ambled toward his pickup.

She lifted her chin toward him with an affirmative jerk, and turned her attention to the task at hand: digging in against Fidelity's lazy current to begin her leisurely ascent.

Life was, indeed, good on the knob. Little did she know, all that would soon change.

# Meditate Toward Solutions

I NEED TO HIT THE CUSHION. BAD. That's because what I have to be, before this telling, is securely centered, fully focused. Maybe if I meditate, empty my mind, I'll be ready to channel this story as it wants to be told—and keep myself mostly out of its way. I intend to try. They don't call me The Bard for nothing. And on behalf of every last SLANTer, this account will require my best effort.

Here's the deal. I hold an interesting position in this community, for I am SLANT's keeper of stories. You heard that right. I've mercifully been allowed to live a life perfectly suited to my talents. I tell stories. I recite poems. Some I have told to one person at a time, or two, or a porch full. Some I have told to the whole of SLANT all at once. It's who I've been, who I am. No matter where I go or what I do, it's who I'll always be. I'm one of those curious types who observe and make meaning, one of those who uncover obscure lessons and simplify the complexities of human living (or complicate the simplicities). This old boy is a universal citizen landed in a place that has uniquely valued wordsmiths so much that they honored one (me!) with a magical title: Resident Bard.

I write. I tell. But I listen, too. That's because one of my jobs is to chronicle all things SLANT. It's an interesting function, archiving SLANT's collective memory. You might say I'm a journalist without a news outlet, an editor that never goes formally to press. Nevertheless, I have filled pages, spoken volumes, heard epics, recorded memories. The narratives I collect and interpret are both instructive and entertaining—at least I hope so, for those have always been my aims. The fact that SLANT, from its genesis, insisted on having a Resident Bard tells you much more about the whole of us than it does about the individual me.

But I digress. And if I know me, there'll be plenty of digressions, side roads and tangents. Like Fidelity Creek, this story meanders as it likes. Your best approach? Relax. Give yourself permission to enjoy the flow. Open your internal viewfinder. Broaden your assumptions. Don't shy from brutal truth. (And don't say I didn't warn you!)

If I know anything at all, I know it's not easy to tell other people's

stories—far less easy than telling your own, particularly if you're committed to doing a story justice. Telling can be a dangerous undertaking. But
I'm here to try because I've faith in the storytelling process—including
the gathering, including the telling, including the listening, including the
thinking going on within both teller and listener and, most valuable, *their*
*collaboration* in the process.

I vow that I'll pull no punches. I'll give you everything as honestly
as I can; I don't know any other way to do it.

Here's what I propose, in case you'd care to know: I'm going to tell
you one big story about two small places—noticeably different from one
another in purpose and design, though geographically they are only a few
miles apart as the crow flies—and I'm going to use myriad little stories
to get that done. Lots of small stories because every single person, alive
or dead, *is* a story ... is, in fact, a series of stories going forward and
backward.

And places are stories too. You'll see.

This one, to be clear, is a story that mostly has already happened,
in all of its parts and pieces. It's not the first, last or only story of this
place, but it's a significant slice of a continuum that documents our living
here. Like all humans, we've known struggles and we've known joys, both
individually and collectively. We've questioned; we've discovered enlightenment; we've uncovered truths and lies and values and meaning. In other
words, we've *lived*. Looking back on it all, I find this fascinating, revealing—a study in community, politics, religion, culture, conflict, passion.
Here's hoping you too find worth in our stories. We're walking this world
together, after all. Might as well learn some useful lessons, dive into some
productive thinking along the way. What I'm saying is: if we're not about
*making meaning* out of the randomness and chaos, then what's the damned
point?

As a matter of principle and accuracy, it's important that many voices
contribute to this telling. And so it will be. A writer, regardless of what
you've been told, is not an island, for one person does not a community
make. Mine is a functional and artistic role in the life of my tribe, SLANT—
I attempt to coalesce the many stories of these people in this place.

*E pluribus unum*, and all that jive.

So there's Top Notch Annie (passed on, bless her soul) and Alec and
Horse—they self-marginalized and mused as loners. Nooner and Meddy
and Joy conversed and theorized as neighbors. The Jimmies dreamed as
peers. The artists, Juny and Willie and Birdie and Tractor Girl and I, well,
we communicate through our respective art forms. Mayor Sheepwater has
always spoken softly, listened well and mediated brilliantly in a homespun
manner from deep within his hyper-simple intuition. The Billings boys
use few words, but their work creates the practical art of function and

comfort for us all. Jorge builds things; Dick collects things. Wilma Carl's family arrange for supplies to meet our needs.

These are but a few of us. So many voices. And not just here in SLANT. There are significant uphill voices too, from the place called The Rising Son. There are even a few downhill voices in this gumbo.

My work, concisely put, is anchored in assembling voices—all these and more. And it's centered right there in your brain, too, as you receive them. You're the interpreter who matters most, because if a story doesn't work for you (the reader, the listener) then perhaps it doesn't work at all.

Notice that you're hearing me make no promises about chronology!

Here's some free advice, should you want it: if you're assuming a chronological narrative that's more about *what happens in what order* than it's about *fully who it happens to* and *how it affects them*, might I suggest that you consider suspending any plot-driven expectations you may be unintentionally harboring. Up to you, though. The story unspools. The Bard will abide.

Now, what you're wondering is how I came to know these particular tales and histories and moments and conversations and events. Did I get my information firsthand, or did I pick it up farther from the tree? Are these stories real, or did I imagine them? Am I a believer in myth, or a believer in truth, or a believer in nothing? Will I stay neutral, or take sides? Do I believe we have the greater responsibility to each other, or to ourselves?

The answer to everything you ask is Yes.

# Be Ready

MAYBE IT WAS THE MUSHROOMS. Memory does not always serve well when mixed with psychedelic substances. The Jimmies told slightly different accounts of how the community of SLANT was established, that event having occurred notably ahead of the current arc of cultural history. Nevertheless, it went something like this....

The Cuban Missile Crisis, as Americans call it, happened in the fall of 1962. The whole of the United States and everyone in it were stressed completely out by our continued engagement in the post-World War II Cold War in opposition to the Soviets and their allies. School children were required to participate in frightening "duck-and-cover" Civil Defense drills on command (preferably right in the middle of arithmetic class, although that hardly ever happened)—as if hiding under a wooden desk, one hand cupped over the back of the neck, would protect anyone of any age from an incoming nuclear warhead. Yet people believed all manner of crazy things back then. A very high percentage of Americans in those years still trusted their government. (It's a fact; you could look it up.)

Beyond the school drills, citizens in Kentucky and California and Texas and Massachusetts and Arkansas and the Dakotas and Wisconsin and Georgia and every-damn-where else were being indoctrinated in a permeating sort of us-against-them civic religion. These days, citizens of a certain age who aren't still lying to themselves know that Time has proven the "Cuba situation" to be Round One in an escalation of sinister brainwashing that has today become a political art form: duck-and-cover was theatre in its day, much like TSA screening in airports is theatre today. Do such theatrics *actually* make people safer? Perhaps it fools those still naïve enough to trust that someone "up there" (in government or in the clouds) is looking out for them. For the rest of us though, political drama and the implied threat of imminent danger only make us feel worse, more stressed out, more vulnerable and fearful and helpless. Not because of the lies alone, but because of (A) the people with sinister motives who *deliver* the lies and (B) those who in ignorance or complicity *believe* the lies.

Lying is a plague on human existence. I must state this bluntly because it is a blunt fact. But you already know it. As the decades have passed and our democracy has become compromised from within, we have all witnessed the dangers of compulsive lying, both politically and personally. But it's what we're up against, especially these days. Here I remind you that in 1959 it was reported that Soviet leader Nikita Khrushchev proclaimed, "We will take America without firing a shot. We do not have to invade the U.S. We will destroy you from within...."

Admit it: many of us are terrified that we're watching this prophecy unfold in the 21st century, in large part because corruption, dishonesty, raw greed and sneaky foreign influence have become prevalent in the leadership of one of the major political parties in our country. Not surprisingly, that's the party that enables half-truths, mistruths and outright lies, wraps itself in the flag and beats down individual rights with a flaming cross.

Here's something you should know, if you don't already: over the past few years, our nation has witnessed the activation of true-to-form strategies employed by the kinds of despots who, historically, have over-thrown democratic republics and installed authoritarianism in their place. Such coups happen with imperceptible stealth. Bit by bit. Until it's too late. Could American democracy experience the proverbial *death by a thousand cuts?* It's not looking good.

We're aware of widely used technologies these days that, in spite of their claims to bring us together, are tearing us down, breaking us apart as a nation. Was a time when "can't see the forest for the trees" was a commonly understood platitude. A more appropriate one these days is "can't see the truth for the screens."

Anyway, in such an oppressive atmosphere, neither freedom *of* nor freedom *from* religious dogma are protected, especially in the face of so-called Christian Nationalism. In such a dangerous climate, patriotism has no functioning definition. Until recently, too many Americans simply never believed that the threat of an authoritarian regime could happen here. We take our liberty for granted. We have (for far too long) seen our nation as too big and too strong to fail. Like the schoolchildren we once were, we assiduously assume that those proverbial "checks and balances" actually work, because they are constitutionally ordained by separation of powers split among three co-equal branches in our governing system.

But assumption, these days, just isn't good enough.

Laws and norms are essential to governing. Some people don't want to govern, though. They only want to rule. And the way they want to rule is by breaking all the rules. So, when laws are ignored or, worse, flouted outright, that's when we know we're in peril.

We are in peril.

At some point, we citizens became civically complacent. We've been neither fully aware nor adequately prepared to defend our democracy vigorously from *internal* attacks. Which, alas, is precisely what Khrushchev predicted.

Are we waking up? Possibly. Is it too late? Most likely.

But enough digression. You came here for a story. Yet here I go, wading into minutiae. Providing broad-stroke background. Detailing philosophical context both prior to and following the founding of SLANT. Remember, you can't say I haven't warned you! Context is necessary, and it's all very interesting. But the story's the thing. And so are the people in it.

So, yes, we went through all that Cold War terror in mid-20th century, even though there was scarcely a missile in existence in 1962 that, fired from Cuba, could land much farther away than a handful of cities in Florida and maybe the Southeast region (the super long-range ICBMs being a couple of decades into the future). But even in that era of naiveté, U.S. citizens didn't yet accept that their government would do *anything*, ethical or not, to gin up scenarios built on irrational fear just to manipulate us. This was probably the infancy of the kind of thing that today we label "conspiracy theory," which is another of the most dangerous components of contemporary living, my opinion. Far too many folks allow unfounded and outlandish conspiracies to take up too much real estate in their brains. I trust you are not one of those people. Thankfully, we don't all have to think exactly alike to enjoy a good tale well told. So, buckle up or walk away—makes no nevermind to me. This story, my friends, has begun—began, in fact, decades ago.

During that long ago October it was the extreme southeastern U.S. that was in imminent danger; however, even people deep in the heartland and far to the west coast were terrified of being fried or obliterated or maimed or orphaned. Those missiles were being prepared for nuclear warheads, so if the crisis had been fully realized (history teaches us that it was not, of course), radioactive fallout could have been carried well beyond the blast sites to affect millions and millions of American citizens. And an escalated war would have been much, much worse. People weren't wrong to worry.

The 1962 Cuban Missile Crisis did indeed explode into a global political event, no matter how you prefer to slice-and-dice it. All the world's nations were holding their collective breath to see how this tense standoff would end—or whether it would lead to actual worldwide war, which no one wanted.

Russia and China call it The Caribbean Crisis. Cuba calls it The October Crisis. Poor old Mother Nature must have been a fright. If she had a face like ours, her eyebrows would surely have been up to her hairline for a few weeks that autumn as she watched the mess unfold. Knowing how thoroughly humans usually fuck things up, I'd say she was probably hoping for the best but urgently preparing for the worst.

Anyway, The Jimmies had gotten fed up with the stress and spin and fear and bombast that permeated the behavior of both the general populace and all the governments who had involved themselves. Because The Jimmies (A) had been paying attention and (B) had recently been reading some especially radical underground poets and philosophers, they were among the first wave of skeptics in a youth-led revolution that soon became America's next big culture war.

That, and they had been doing mushrooms. Of course.

So it was in the middle of this anxious Cold War standoff that The Jimmies decided the only thing to do was to drop out of society as they knew it. This was at least a half-decade before "dropping out" or "getting back to the land" became the faddish thing to do. The Jimmies were barely out of college, hadn't been married long, but they were well-fixed White trust-fund babies who had already come of age and so could afford to do whatever they wanted with the rest of their privileged lives. Interestingly, the *means* by which those capitalist fortunes had been amassed by their forebears (with whom the younger set were cordial in spite of a near complete lack of any mutual political respect between the generations) were under-emphasized, wrapped in a convenient silence that would have been resented by a life partner who hadn't come from a similar background. In other words, neither of The Jimmies wanted to talk about having money, much less the possibly unpalatable sources from which their families had gained said fortunes. This was just one more way in which The Jimmies were perfectly compatible with one another.

I'll just say they had money. Lots of it. And having money aplenty, they bummed around the country for a while, seeing what there was to see, experiencing what their generation was getting turned on to. Granted, this was a sliver in time wedged between the Beats and the Hippies—more Newport Folk than Woodstock. But still. Change always has its slow pivots.

The version I heard went something like this. On a whim one day in 1964 (after the Cuban Crisis, and after that successfully diplomatic U.S. president was assassinated, leaving us all in the throes of yet another national trauma), The Jimmies—filled with (A) a political fear they didn't know whether or not was legitimate and (B) an intense and growing loathing for everything associated with government—drove up into the western rim of the deeply rural Knobs region of Kentucky. They pulled off at an abandoned wide spot along a narrow county road, parked in that isolated and elevated place with a view, did the extra mushrooms they possessed, and immediately experienced a shared vision. A parcel of land revealed itself, several hundred acres in size, bordered by a beautiful little creek. Though they wouldn't know it until later when they entered the land for a closer look, on its wooded slope sat several modest frame buildings—a large, well-porched farmhouse, plus several shanties, some as small as one room, built on stilts to fit the knob's contours. These had been long ago occupied by farm families, sharecroppers and hired-hands. Several barns and outbuildings there were, too, and a series of neglected lanes and paths curving and curling all through the uneven land. There were a few fallow and sloping fields, fences, wells and ponds, along with the *coup de gras:* an abandoned juke joint that had outgrown its time and was standing in forlorn disrepair, just waiting to be loved back into shape.

Don't be mistaken—this was no drug-induced mirage. It was real land *FOR SALE BY OWNER*, right over there across the road from where the disillusioned pair of lovebirds sat on the sun-warmed hood of their beloved Dodge Dart droptop.

And so it was that the cumulative effect of the mushrooms may or may not have become a deeper part of the developing karma in that scene, for one of The Jimmies (either Jimi or Jimmy, a point entirely lost to history because both later claimed to have been the one) pointed out (A) the remarkable geography within which they found themselves, coupled with (B) the heavily-weathered language on the side of the pitiful, run-down juke joint, and noted (C) how the two converged to mirror perfectly the tenor of the times.

That is to say, (1) the Knobs (The Jimmies and their car were perched in the side of a knob called Barrel Chute) are sudden, up-sloping cones surrounded by flats; (2) The Jimmies (and all us other U.S. inhabitants) were feeling more politically and culturally off-kilter than we ever had felt before; and (3) only a handful of the weathered-away crudely-painted letters in the juke's original name (*Seven Lanterns Tavern*) could still be read: The S from Seven, the L-A-N from Lanterns, and the T from Tavern.

It was a moment that was half "Eureka!" and half "That's odd." But the obvious connections couldn't, in The Jimmies' melded state of height-ened mindfulness, be ignored.

When they noticed that the building's only remaining letters spelled the word *SLANT*, Jimi had been particularly tickled. About one thing she is to this day certain: not three years prior it had been *her* Memphis banker grandfather—having observed (as long as he could stand to in polite silence) the unconventional ways she and her young peers lived, reasoned, talked and apparently believed—who had blurted out to her in exasperation, "Honey, I worry about you. Aren't you ever going to settle down and *try?* From what I can tell, you and that group you run with, y'all seem to function *at a slant* all the time." What had confused Grandfather further was the pure delight with which she accepted his unsolicited but insightful commentary on her chosen way of life—to her *it had been a compliment!*

A thousand days or so had passed since that offhand comment made by her beloved forebear, who adored her in spite of her weirdness and whom she cherished in spite of his greed, yet she had never forgotten his choice of word, for *slant* was a perfect fit for the way many of us rebels lived in those halcyon days. She loved the feel of the word *slant* on her tongue and in her brain. Because that indeed was how our generation saw things and lived things and understood things, Jimi was delighted that *here it was*—manifest in front of her very eyes on a barely populated knob in, of all places, rural Kentucky.

*It's not the end of the world,* said Jimmy, *but I'm pretty sure I can see it from here!*

And so, after they had walked the land and seen what there was to see in all its crumbling glory, The Jimmies sat, backs again against the windshield of an ugly lovable car, smoking weed, feeling the mushrooms, knowing they were but two of many people who weren't a good fit within that fearful and dangerous culture of their parents' and grandparents' making. The couple relaxed together into a *FOR SALE BY OWNER* dream that felt like it could actually come true.

*We're going to buy this land,* Jimmy told Jimi (or Jimi told Jimmy, depending on whose version you believe). *We're going to create a safe place far from the madness. We're going to share it with others who will need and appreciate it as much as we do.*

*And this place will be called SLANT,* the other Jimi (or Jimmy) proclaimed.

Eventually, one of them blew a smoke ring from her (or his) clove cigarette toward the property in question, and they both later reported having witnessed it perfectly encircle the letters *S-LAN-T* on the side of yon dilapidated building ... and hang suspended there a moment in the foreground—the perfect frame for the perfect future.

Before the season was gone, SLANT was theirs.

Once their fellow SLANTers had begun joining The Jimmies' venture, populating SLANT either by inhabiting the existing little abodes or creating new ones, SLANT became a real live, honest-to-goodness community. Over time, SLANTers adapted whatever was already there or they carefully created what they needed, causing as little impact as possible to the property. Eventually, along with homes and campers, there grew a central meeting place, workshops and a gazebo used (among other ways) as a music stage. Application for a U.S. post office had been discussed briefly at some point but was ultimately deemed out of the question for a community of people who had dropped out and did not want to garner attention from the fucking Establishment.

The legend of our village's founding has been told many times at the community's annual Come Together. At the end of each retelling,

*SLANT*, everyone agrees, is *THE perfect name.* For as time passes, we've found that, with the knob's geography as a metaphor, we are all indeed more than satisfied to live life always at odd angles, in creative and uncounted ways.

Besides, the only other possibility for our place name might have been something like SERENDIPITY, but that would be just way too hard to pronounce under the influence.

# To Experience Is To Understand

THE OLDER I GROW, THE LESS I KNOW. Now, I realize I'm not the only person who has expressed this idea in some form or other. And I'm not the only person who has struggled mightily to accept the truth of it, either.

There's nothing unique about being a smartass in youth who becomes humbled by age. Happens to us all. Only those too arrogant to learn will continue to fight (with ultimate lack of success) against their own inevitable irrelevance. Old folks look ridiculous when they try unconvincingly to hang onto youth well beyond its "use by" date. The rest of us codgers on the other hand—we find a way to relax into aging and irrelevance and irreverence and the like, even when said relaxation is finally forced upon us in numerous humiliating ways. We are hard-headed, some of us, but Time is harder-headed and cannot be slowed or stopped or beaten to a pulp.

But how do we learn this crucial lesson? For my part, I'll admit that I have both experienced and witnessed a combination of instructive acts, personal and communal: hard knocks, rudeness, luck (good and bad), the joyful love of real friends, being betrayed by people I trusted entirely, giving and receiving small and large kindnesses, memorable encounters with strangers, lessons from books and films, and Experience Its Own Self (mine, plus reports of others'). Mostly, though, I've learned about my own irrelevance and its gift of perfect freedom in various ways—from observing my past and present, and combining that with what I see in the experiences of those who are further along than I am. Evolution of character should occur shortly after this "giving over," if it is to occur at all. I'm not a believer in much, but I will not deny that *change* (good and bad) is the only constant. In these philosophical ways, my friend Meddy and I have always had much in common.

"Bard, fella, you're too damned easy," she once told me. But I'm not. I'm just the opposite. It takes a lot to convince me of anything. (Talk about a rock for a noggin!) Once I "get" a thing, though, I've got it for solid good.

By way of illustration, it took me for-damned-ever but I finally decided at some point that I'm not afraid anymore. This is huge. We are, all of us, driven by fear nearly all the way through this trip that most people so off-handedly call Life—that is to say, we are mostly motivated by fear of losing something: breath, money, status, salvation, senses, love, loved ones, companionship, likeability, power, property, esteem, our art, mobility, control, autonomy ... *something*.

But I'm so goddamn done with fear. Fear can kiss my rosy red! It'll keep showing up, no doubt, but I'll keep facing it down, I reckon.

Now, I do know one thing for a natural fact—the best thing that ever happened to me was falling entirely by accident into the one place (SLANT) where I found people of all stripes, each of whom taught me their best stuff merely by example. All I had to do was pay attention to their very ways of Thinking and Living. I learned some more by hearing stories of folks who had once also Lived. The rest, I've been prone to imagine ... and aspire to.

One small, powerful lesson is this: some of our fears stem from knowing our pasts, and some come from *not* knowing our futures. But I say Fear is a big old unwieldy boulder we struggle to lift and carry everywhere we go. You got a river of fate to cross, you'll find you can't swim carrying a boulder. Fear will take you down and end you. So that's why I'm through with it, I reckon. Been feeling fortunate that I finally figured that out.

Too, this old storytelling nerd becomes more a student every day—especially as I age, even as I diminish physically, certainly as my memory flickers. I want to learn how to be ready for what's next, yet I don't worry about not knowing what exactly that's going to be. Talk about change! I once numbered among the most frightened guys on the planet. Everything scared me. And that kept me from my own potential. I was at times paralyzed by fear, especially fear of the unknown—which is a control thing, I reckon. But no more. Fear or the absence of fear, those are things we're taught. I've learned that *un*-teaching ourselves is as good a thing as teaching ourselves. We can change, and we should. Stagnation is putrid.

Anyway ....

Two other things I've learned: places shape people, and people shape places. On Barrel Chute Knob, that's as true a truth as I've ever been privileged to observe. The place itself is fascinating, and so are the folks who've landed in it. It's up to you to offer eyes and ears and a mind open enough to deep-mine our history for meaning.

But you don't have to take my word for it—that's why we have stories.

# From Many, One

ALEC WAS OFF THE GRID. Not just in the way he lived. In the way his mind worked.

Alec lived in the margins in nearly every sense. Economically. Emotionally. Psychologically. Socially.

Even his physical home was in the margins, geographically—it was a treehouse, centered on a camo-tarp-enclosed eight-by-eight platform built onto several massive limbs that overhung Fidelity Creek upstream from SLANT and near the border that separated it from the fringes of the property owned by that old church camp, last known as The Rising Son. Alec's treehouse had expanded over time so that, by now, its suspended flooring took as joists the larger overhanging limbs angling in from both banks to a point directly above the water at the creek's narrowest width. Two or three smaller platforms, constructed from discarded wooden pallets, branched off the original. The whole business moved gently atop wind currents, much like a boat bobs in a bay.

From quiet proximity, SLANTers kept a helpful eye out for Alec. Nothing pushy. On occasion, somebody would leave a meal or a snack for him to find, so he'd know we were here if he needed us. He, meanwhile, reasoned that he didn't belong to either community. "Not a joiner," he would say, if anyone had the opportunity to ask him. To prove it, he had built entrances to his home from both sides of the creek. And—always thinking!—*those entrances could cleverly be used as exits, too.* He thought this, then added, entirely internally (his mind being a fairly crowded place), *Dumbass! Don't think so loud.*

Alec had come to Barrel Chute Knob in much the same way others of we SLANTers had—looking for someplace remote from Civilized People who lived by someone's idea of The Rules. But Alec, in his usual way, had taken the escape concept to its extreme. As remotely located as they were, The Rising Son and SLANT were even too much civilization for him. He wanted to live *completely* alone. He named his treehouse community "Alec." Its official language was Alec, and Alecness described its culture to a *T*. Alec lived in Alec, and he was everyone in it. This was way too much responsibility and it stressed him out, but he did his best to play all the roles. He tried to take them one at a time, but sometimes they sort of piled up. At these times, Alec felt like he was a juggler who then felt like the person watching the juggler, yet realizing the juggler is, in fact, himself. Other times, he was the camera operator getting a shot of the juggler and the juggler's audience-of-one watching himself juggle. But then he would realize that in such a circumstance he had to be both *in* the shot and *shooting* the shot. Well, this sort of thing would usually cause a meltdown of one kind or another. Poor guy.

Back when Alec had been forced to live on the grid—culturally, mentally, economically—he would short out at times like these, because the thinking just got too complicated. Not that he couldn't NOT have complicated thoughts. Complicated was, in fact, the only kind of thinking he could do because of his seizures and severe OCD and the fractioned perspective of his psyche, not to mention the fact that he may or may not have been just a teeny-tiny bit schizophrenic. Whatever it was, Alec was neurodiverse as hell. Living off the grid, however, Alec didn't feel as likely to inconvenience other people or draw so much attention when his come-aparts occurred, which is why he stayed to himself. Solitude made him feel safer; he was less likely to be set off. Not being plugged-in, he realized, meant not having so much psychological "juice" with which to hurt himself—or be a bother to other people, for that matter. He preferred not to have all his strange selves on public display.

SLANT claimed Alec, but he didn't claim SLANT. Which was okay either way with SLANT, being too laid back to want to impose anything on anybody. But still.

The Rising Son, on the other hand, didn't even notice him for the longest time. Which was fine with everybody living in Alec.

# Avoid Exploitation

ONCE, A LONG WHILE AGO (as other storytellers have more cleverly said), Farnsley Sheepwater had an idea. If a person wanted to be mayor of a village that had no mayor, and in fact had *never* had a mayor, maybe a person could just go around to everyone else living in the place and ask their *permission.* That way, there would be no need to prepare ballots for an election, no search for a suitable polling place, no hard-earned cash wasted on campaigns. And the job of *mayor* would have no real responsibilities, only the title. It couldn't hurt to ask around. Plus, if anyone didn't want him to be mayor, why, they could just say so when he asked, and that would be that. A single objection and it would be all over, for Farnsley would never want to be anyone's mayor against their will. When it came to exploitation, neither exploiting nor being exploited appealed to him. All he wanted was to be of service to a place that had taken him in, given him a chance to belong. To Farnsley the concept of asking to be mayor seemed simple enough. Besides, as far as he knew no one else had ever mentioned wanting to be mayor. *Which is probably,* he thought, *why we've never had one.*

Where Farnsley had gotten his notions about becoming mayor, none of us knew, not even Farnsley himself. He was one of those who had been in SLANT so long that no one could remember when he'd arrived. Folks'd be able to tell you how he came about his name, though. That's a good one; a scrap of the well-worn fabric of SLANT lore.

Long-and-lanky Farnsley had wandered uphill from the creek bottom and into the yard of the big house one warm day in SLANT's early years —probably 1968, '69, maybe '70—like he'd been conjured up out of the vapor. One day he was just there, pitching in and helping out. *Name's Rick Farnsley,* he'd said. *I been hitching all over creation looking for a place exactly like this. Have ye room for one more?*

It was almost as if The Jimmies had managed to grow all six-foot-four of him out of the ground themselves, for the willow-whip of a boy was just a natural hand to garden.

Didn't know much about animals, though.

Jimi'd hollered to him across what was then the old barnlot one workday. "Hey, Rick! Save me a step or two, will you, hon? Kindly pour three or four buckets of water into the sheep's trough while you're over their way, could you?" (In the early days, SLANT had tried raising livestock on a small scale. Suffice to say, that didn't last long.)

Anyway.

By now, you who are too clever by half are way ahead of this story. After that old ram got finished telling off young Rick Farnsley for wearing the U.S. flag stitched (fashionably, he'd thought) to the seat of his pants—using its horned head to drive the point home ... twice—nobody could even look at the poor fellow again without thinking of him sputtering and splashing and nearly drowning himself getting out of the sheep's water trough. It's hard to keep a straight face when I think about it even now. Needless to say, he was never *Rick* again, which actually suited him fine since he'd been intentionally searching all over the country for a whole new identity for himself.

For a month or so after the incident, we all called him *Sheepswaters Farnsley*. He liked the general ring of it—at least he liked that it was a name that *meant* something real enough to have actually happened—but somehow it didn't quite rhythm itself out right; sort of took a downward turn when it fell out of the mouth, the *Sheepswaters* all in a higher register, like breathing in, and the *Farnsley* pronounced in a dead-end lower tone, like breathing out, that pulled the head downward and allowed the word to fall out like an old medicine ball hitting the floor with a barely-bounce.

On or about the twenty-third night of trying out his new name, Farnsley sat beneath the big tree behind The Jimmies' house. That tree was his favorite, a very old male ginko that someone had planted by the pump house years and years before The Jimmies found (and founded) the place. He smoked a bowl, pondered, and began to roll his new name around in his mind. He thought perhaps the unfamiliarity he felt was because he hadn't had the name long and so hadn't spoken or written it often enough for it to feel like his own—the course of a lifetime being how long most people spend wearing and sharing a name.

So, he began repeating his relatively new name in an endless, looping monotone (*Sheepswaters-Farnsley-Sheepswaters-Farnsley-Sheepswaters-Farnsley...*) with no beginning and no end, no first name and no last, no tone shift, no emphasis anywhere. He took a breath, and when he opened his mouth again, trying to remember where he left off in the cycle, *Farnsley-Sheepswaters* fell out in a first *up* and then *down* tone of voice. The name sounded much improved turned that way round. To be precise, it felt near perfect!

He began that very minute forgetting that he'd ever even heard of a Rick Farnsley. This new Farnsley Sheepswaters had a whole new lease on life, and that seemed fortifying and exhilarating enough to make him talk himself out of hanging onto the suicide-backup pistol he had hidden in the rafters of the corncrib just minutes before he'd stepped into sight on that first day he'd shown up on The Jimmies' place. He resolved then and there to throw that sidearm into the middle of Fidelity Creek, vowed he'd do so the very next chance he got to carry out the act unseen. And so he did.

Now, hang on here, because I'm about to explain something about the evolution of Farnsley's last name that might seem confusing. But that'll only last a minute. You'll be able to follow it. I trust you.

See, over a short period of time two *esses* were removed from *Sheepswaters*, primarily because Farnsley, realizing that anyone who wasn't privy to the name's origin might think that he (or, theoretically, one of his entirely-invented forebears—those pseudo-historic figures of the mythological Sheepwater clan—of whom, in his imaginary realm, he'd become quite fond and mostly proud) knew no better than to pluralize sheep by adding an "s." It would have been a misunderstanding, he surmised, that would stem from the hearer not considering the possibility of "sheep's" as some-how *possessive*, instead of strangely *plural* like its irregular partner "waters." Not to mention that he had never written the name with an apostrophe, obviously. He wondered if that'd been his first (or second) mistake. Thus, for accuracy—and thoughtfully, if he did think so himself, for ease of pronunciation on dear Wet Willie's impedimental behalf—Farnsley dropped those middle and last *esses* from his newly designated surname. I'm pretty sure he did this immediately upon realizing that he was embroiled in a rather traumatic spelling dilemma. Spelling dilemmas had always been traumatic for Farnsley. Debilitating, really.

All this attention to language would lead one to believe that Farnsley Sheepwater was bright enough to reason out this whole process—to know proper spelling, grammar, punctuation and usage rules, and to understand his position in the evolution of language. But if you bought into this line of thought you'd be wrong, for the reality of the situation was precisely the opposite. Farnsley had always, in fact, been so confused by such rules and knowledge and practices that he wasn't really sure whether it was right or wrong to insert or delete the apostrophe, not to mention pluralizing *water*, which seemed to him to beg instead for some sort of bulk singular spelling (like *milk* instead of *milks*, for instance), although he'd not known how to articulate the concept.

The one thing he *knew* that he knew was this: he didn't want to be *perceived* as stupid simply because maybe he *was*.

So, he solved it in his own way. He did what he'd done throughout his twenty-two years of living (up to then) and further, what he'd done during all those years slipping through school with most of his illiteracy intact: he hid his insecurities, lack of skills and outright ignorance by hedging, shifting, dodging, re-spelling or whatever else it took to stay under the radar of those who actually *do* know such things. The last thing he needed was for anyone to notice a red flag and question him about it. All he knew for sure to do was to remove the confusing parts, and fast; so this he did. Everybody is smart somehow, and *that* is how Farnsley was smart (and kind too, in a way, for he'd had that fleeting thought of good old, lisping Wet Willie and how these simple changes would benefit that sweet fellow).

And so, for the following decades, Farnsley Sheepwater lived in SLANT, his limited mind working up to this, the grandest event of his life, the biggest idea he'd ever had: Why shouldn't SLANT have a mayor? And why, since this was *his* Big Idea, shouldn't he *become* said mayor? Be SLANT's *first* mayor, at least. (He didn't envision himself as a career politician or anything like that. What if he didn't like the job?)

And in reality, it wouldn't even *be* a job, per se. SLANT had no city hall—hell, SLANT didn't have a charter, wasn't organized as a township or corporation or anything remotely like that. To fall into those Establishment traps would have missed the point, would have been utterly apart from the main purpose of the place. SLANT was off the culture grid by design. It governed itself *by not governing.* Thus, in the absence of a proper village council, SLANT had so far worked just fine, mayor or no.

Well, beginning in his fortieth April in SLANT, Farnsley Sheepwater started going around talking to people about his becoming mayor. He first approached The Jimmies, who approved. Most of SLANT's residents thought it was cute. Others thought it was far out. And it was. Both.

"I just wanted to talk to ye one-on-one about a recent idear of mine," Farnsley offered as his opening line to each person in SLANT. He talked to them individually, and he found that nobody disagreed with his proposal, not even the children, whose permission he also asked. (Apparently all living humans in SLANT figured equally in Farnsley's process, so any Terrible-Two or Surly Adolescent could have vetoed the whole thing—breaking Farnsley's heart and mayoral aspirations in the process—just by ignoring his question or saying *NO* out of habit, as Terrible and Surly children are wont to do by instinct and without a moment's thought.)

But as it turned out, everyone in SLANT rightly reasoned that since they weren't being asked to *organize* anything or *take action* to back up this entertaining illusion of "gubmint," well, such an exercise in electoral parody was no skin off their noses. Anyway, *mayor* would be no more than an honorary title, after all. And, most important, certainly none of them wanted the job. So it was that they agreed, to the last toddler and geriatric, that SLANT would definitely be an even better place with a kind and helpful neighbor named Farnsley Sheepwater as its civic figurehead.

In a few months, during which time he had conversed with every single human resident *and* kept his section of the community garden clean of weeds, the deed was done-and-done.

Let it be noted for the record that to this day Mayor Sheepwater is, officially, the only "Un-Official" that SLANT has ever had. And until the day one Terrible, Surly child raises objection, his "job" is secure. Long live the unelected, unpaid, inaugurated-by-consensus Mayor-For-Life.

# Be Kind

MEADOWLARK NIGHTENGALE LEFT A TRAIL of stemware
everywhere she went. She didn't mean to. Farnsley believed that on some
subconscious level Meddy needed to leave something behind to prove
she'd been there.

This pattern had been recurring for the past year. At first, she began
to miss, one by one, her favorite hand-blown wine glasses—a fascinating
screenwriter friend from long ago had given them to her on a special occasion. There had been six in the set originally, all of them peacock colored,
and then, suddenly, there were only three. Then two, and that's when she
realized that she had been taking her favorite wine glasses with her on
walks into the woods, down by the creek, to visits on neighbors' porches.
Right quick she packed away the remaining pair of her best glasses so
she wouldn't forget and carry them outside anymore. In their place on the
shelf, she lined up the cheapest little pieces of stemware she could find
from an online glassware outlet. These she proceeded to abandon frequently,
as well, but the loss was not emotional, at least. Some things, after all, are
easily replaceable. Others, not so much.

Over time she might leave one glass on a stump, another next to a
set of porch steps, several at the edges of the community garden plots.
SLANT and the woods around it were prettily decorated with both lovely
and homely glass goblets. When she'd realize she'd done it again, she
made herself feel better by imagining shafts of sunlight catching each
forgotten glass one by one as the earth rotated through its day. Sometimes
she conjured images of a moment—shattered glass sprinkling the ground
during a windstorm, perhaps, or a tiny wren bathing in rainwater caught
the night before in a piece of Meddy's forgotten stemware.

The mayor brought one of these unbroken, gone-to-seed goblets back
to her one early evening after he had noticed it reflecting sunlight among
weeds and wildflowers that grew near the little SLANT sign out by the
paved road. He wasn't positive the glass was hers, but he was pretty sure.
For one thing, it was standing upright behind one of the stumps that
folks used for sitting while waiting for a ride, or for Eddy the mail carrier,

or for the UPS truck. This was also where the SLANT kids waited each morning for the yellow bus to carry them down to their school off knob. Meddy had taken to sitting there for long periods in the middle of the day sometimes when she couldn't think what else to do. Her neighbors took turns checking on her from a distance, but she wasn't aware of that. She did know that she was blessed with good people all about, people who loved her, though she really had no idea just how much.

Farnsley walked into the edge of Meddy's yard, glass in hand, to find her bent well over, attempting to pull some exceptionally tough weeds from around one of the stilts that held up her porch.

"When I found this I said to myself, I said, 'Now, that looks like something Meddy might like to have,'" said he, diplomatically. He offered Meddy the glass with a gentlemanly bow. The goblet had a design blown into it that was reminiscent of a peacock feather. Meddy took it, held it aloft, turned it against the afternoon light. She did like it, very much. And it looked oddly familiar, though in this moment she couldn't quite place why.

"Why, thank you, Mister Mayor. It's lovely."

"I was just about to stop up at The General for a cuppa. D'ye wanna come with?"

"Another time," she said with a brief smile. "Nooner and I have"— and here she paused, her eyes careening in an intense memory search— "a supper date?" she finally said. She held out the underside of her left wrist where the mayor read the reminder she'd written to herself with a ballpoint pen.

*NOONER SUPPER*, her wrist said. *SUNDAY.*

Farnsley had noticed that Meddy (famously the most animated, passionate and outspoken person in SLANT) had of late become just a bit flatter in her facial expressions when she talked. Not all the time, but sometimes. She still displayed a sense of humor, but that *Meddy edge*, it seemed to the mayor, was gradually beginning to leave his old friend, mostly in fits and starts. Farnsley, who had carefully been picking up cues and was concerned, had no idea whether anyone else had noticed a difference. Still, she looked pretty good today. A bit more like her usual old self. That relieved him, and his relief was a surprise. Apparently, he'd been more worried than he knew.

"Okay then, Meddy," he finally said. "I'll catch ye around the milk bowl."

She lifted her hand, nodded her head once, looked vaguely about for a moment. Then she stooped over to continue wrestling the pull-resistant weed.

Farnsley watched her a second or two more, then turned, stepped into the spiraling one-lane gravel road and headed back uphill toward SLANT-center to The General, the community's common core.

# Enjoy Sunshine & Be Grateful for Shade

IF EVER A PLACE OF WHIMSY & MIRACLE could exist unnoticed, SLANT is it. It's a satisfying dichotomy: being the middle of nowhere and the middle of somewhere simultaneously.

The little gravel road that The Jimmies had turned down that bright long-ago day is easy to miss if you're whizzing by on the paved road that runs up and down the knob in curves both lazy and tight. There is the wide pull-off, true, but the gravel road leading from it into the woods isn't particularly inviting. The entrance to the SLANT property wasn't in the early '60s (and to this day still isn't) well-groomed or set off by stone pillars or anything so noticeable. It's unremarkable, really, except for the handmade SLANT sign, and even that is modest—blue letters on a plain white background, no border. A bank of bland rural mailboxes at the edge of the wide pull-off suggests several dwellings somewhere nearby, but not a one can be seen through the trees lining the paved road. It looks like every other little dead-end private road along that stretch of blacktop. SLANT did not and does not call attention to itself, and that is both by design and by custom.

SLANTers hold dear their live-and-let-live ways. At the same time, there's a sense of belonging and of neighbor-helping-neighbor that quiet-ly pervades the place. Oddly, no one feels obligated to spend time with anyone else, but no one feels offended if another SLANTer approaches, needing a hand or a tool or a talk. Schedules don't mean much in SLANT and neither do rules. The one thing that everyone originally had to agree on was that SLANT itself, meaning both the place and the carefully woven personalities that animate it, must never be compromised or overrun. And to that we all still agree, including those who came much later. Our community tradition holds. Anything less could mean calling attention to our odd little village to an extent that would create disturbances or discomfort for any of our residents. It could also mean doing something that made local or state law enforcement notice the place. Low key, under the radar—whatever slang or metaphor or trite platitude each person calls it—is deemed very important to keeping SLANT the free-spirited place it has always been.

Not to mention that we might be overrun by the curious, the selfish, the cowardly or the mean ... if everyone in SLANT isn't careful about who we invite in to live amongst us. Visitors aren't frowned upon, obviously, but no one is invited to move into the community unless everyone agrees. That's just the way The Jimmies had set it up, and everybody likes that one simple rule because it seems to us to epitomize the place's unspoken utopian slant.

Anyone who operates a business from their cottage, shelter, hut, house, RV, treehouse, cabin, camper or whatever they use for a home is obliged to meet elsewhere with clients or customers. The people who live in SLANT do not want a steady stream of consumers traipsing through our peaceful communal property. Nooner, for example, has his technology thing, which is all in virtual space, so only his computers are physically present in SLANT.

The General is the most public building in SLANT, and it's really only there to serve insiders and maybe a few close neighbors who live nearby out on the paved road. SLANT businesses don't advertise their location with road signs or newspaper ads or radio spots or online. If you know SLANT is here, then you probably belong. Even when a lost somebody wanders in, nothing changes. Kindness and courtesy are always the catch of the day at The General. Some of those wandering folks, like Juny, have been welcomed into the fold for good. Others enjoy a free cup of coffee and maybe a good conversation before going on their way up or down the knob.

Coming into this womb-of-a-place is like stepping through a gauzy curtain of green that seems to obscure the world beyond it. Our little gravel road, a one-laner, parts from the wide pull-off beside the mailboxes out at the blacktop and then meanders in a very nondescript fashion through a fringe of woods, young and old hardwoods mixed into an abundance of cedars. From the paved thoroughfare, you might not even notice the graveled slit insinuating itself into those trees nearest the paved public road; that's because of the lane's angle. The gravel enters the woods with a gentle rightward curve as soon as the tree line is passed, and the daylight immediately changes under that canopy, the world switching as if by magic from blue (or gray, depending on the weather that day) to vivid evergreens and russets. There is shade, lots of it, with occasional splotch-es of sky peeking through. The little road wanders several tenths of a mile before the first building can be seen, even in winter when the hard-woods are without leaves.

And then little homes and businesses start to reveal themselves, singularly. They're spaced out so well among the dense foliage that few of them are within sight of each other—one here, another there, with plenty of space and trees around, and a driveway for each. Some are small permanent buildings; a half-dozen others are campers or motor homes. Tiny sheds squat handily near most homesites.

Farther in, SLANT-center sits. The General (previously the old juke joint) with its wide covered porch is the village's anchor. From there, several small cabins and buildings—maybe ten, maybe a dozen—can be partially seen radiating outward and downward along a series of spoke-like cedar-needle-coated foot paths in a more functionally cleared section of woods. Benches and brief flower beds and the sunny community vegetable plots are everywhere, tidy and well-groomed, as are selected shade trees, some of them old growth. SLANTers who live in these more centrally located homes park their cars and trucks and motorcycles in common parking lots, small and graveled and well placed in wooded cut-outs near The General so as to be integrated perfectly into the community's random, organic design. There is Heart-Headed (a funky little head shop), plus a few tiny craft workshops and artist studios. SLANT isn't really about commerce at all. Whatever is made there is marketed elsewhere. Next door to The General is the L-shaped Craft Cabin, and inside that is plenty of communal workshop space, as well as just about any tool anyone would need to borrow for a project.

And then, as the gravel lane spirals downhill and out of the village center, the woods become thicker again, and the narrow lane winds through to the mouths of driveways and to house-seats where more little homes sit in perfect spaces, each delicately and respectfully apart from its neighbors. Homes in SLANT often don't even bother to face the road, but sit at whatever angle allows each a maximum amount of privacy and pleasant view.

Down in the bottom land beside Fidelity Creek, the gravel ends in a generous turn-around where a handful of vehicles can park. From there, a row of several tiny but widely-spaced cabins sit on stilts overlooking the water, joined only by a mulch-and-pebble foot path through the fringe of trees. One of these belongs to Meadowlark Nightengale, one to bonsai farmer Tractor Girl, another to Mayor-For-Life Farnsley Sheepwater, and yet another belongs to Joy DuPre, our brainy non-denominational Resident Philosopreacher whose open-minded experimental approach to spirituality is welcomed by all. Oh, and one of those little creekside houses is mine. People call it The Bard's house, but I don't own it. I just have the great good fortune to occupy it while I am living. Maybe the next bard who'll replace me some day will live here after I'm dead. It's a good little home.

In general, SLANT appears sort of dream-like, and it functions that way too. As I said, not a soul lives in SLANT without consensual agreement from all residents. This is truly an intentional community (though it has, by no means, anything at all in common with those haughty "gated"

subdivisions you've heard tell about). SLANT has always operated on consensus rather than exclusivity. The land is private, and it's owned by the
entire cooperative as originally endowed by The Jimmies. However a few
of the structures are the property of their inhabitants. The cooperative
has always been well-managed by The Jimmies and by rotating commit-
tees of residents, so the occasional re-graveling of the road and other
such matters are easily attended to and afforded from good management
of the land trust. Everyone pitches in, as their abilities allow, and everyone appreciates whatever contributions are made—whether that's making
workers sandwiches and lemonade, or watering plants, or heavy lifting
and gravel spreading, or bench building. Landscaping is a common effort
in the common spaces along the creekside homes and in SLANT-center,
and no one shirks the work or sees it as a dirty duty. We all believe in
pride of place.

Folks who've been invited to live in SLANT have to demonstrate a
commitment to community by embracing that sweet concoction of the
*laissez faire* combined with total respect and support for their neighbors
—*all* of their neighbors, humans and four-leggers and birds and trees
alike. Privacy is cherished. Age and disability and race and ethnicity and
poverty and personality oddness—these are not factors. We think of
SLANT as sort of a commune of autonomous individuality, and we don't
see any irony or contradiction in that. See, there's no such thing as a leader
who requires loyalty or directs action, so nothing here resembles a cult.
We're more like family.

Those few who have left SLANT for one reason or another are
responsible for their relatives or friends—folks they petition the community to welcome temporarily into their former houses. Most people who
come to SLANT, however, have no desire to leave—ever—for it's a place
where quiet belonging matters more than it seems to matter in most human places.

When people don't want more than they really need, and don't care
about acquisition or competition, and don't shy from working or helping,
then such a community will thrive. The Jimmies' philosophy and vision
are alive-and-well after decades of practical application. And in the
broadest sense, SLANT's inhabitants live better lives for it, come drizzle
or beam.

# What You See Isn't Always What You Get

IF YOU SAW BARREL CHUTE KNOB from the perspective of an aerial-view photo, you'd notice an irony that I must insist should not pass unnoted.

Simply put, if you were told that there were both a church camp and a tiny village up there, and if you'd been asked to guess which is which, you might be surprised to learn that The Rising Son *isn't* the settlement laid out according to "sacred geometry."

No, it is SLANT that has developed like a glorious Fibonacci spiral, reflecting a pattern akin to what some religious scholars say is the mathematics God used to create the universe.

The church camp, on the other hand, is rigidly designed, almost torturous in its finite layout, comprising a spirit-breaking physical structure. A severe grid.

But SLANT curves gracefully out of its own center, the way a chambered nautilus will (although with a less precise algorithm), even sending out additional curving radial arms, making the community resemble a quirky little galaxy with infinite possibility.

Indeed, I chalk it up to irony. The sacred and the profane aren't so predictable after all, no matter what the assholier-than-thous shout continually at us. But you know that already, don't you?

# Share

SO, AS YOU CAN SEE, SLANT isn't like any ordinary village, exactly. Not in the sense of a village that has actual streets on which actual stores or offices do actual business with the actual public.

SLANT is more like a big, happy, productive camp meeting, minus the organized, cultist religion. In certain ways it may have more in common with its upstream neighbor, The Rising Son, than it ever has realized. As previously described, SLANT's hub sits in a flat-ish space along a ridgetop gravel road cleared through the woods; it's populated by structures of varying sizes that sit along paths and connectors; and it draws to itself like-minded people who feel safely encircled by their shared imaginary "moat" of forest. Also, similar to the Bible-based Rising Son, SLANT has a mythology, it has its odd rituals, and it has a creed.

In less superficial ways, though, these two neighboring communities are poles apart. The most obvious difference between the two places, as you now know, is that SLANT's shape is organic, its paths formed naturally as people move back and forth among themselves, uphill and down, while The Rising Son's severe grid layout is regimented to an extreme.

Above all, it's hard to overlook the two communities' vast political differences.

But let me further describe SLANT's physical presence as a way to help you envision our little corner of Kentucky. Established buildings and dwellings that are closest to the old Seven Lanterns Tavern are considered to be SLANT-center, the historic juke joint being the common organ from which the community's life emanates. That building has had quite a history, as far as I've been able to research it. First it was an illegal juke hidden in the woods, lit only by coal-oil lanterns (this was during Prohibition); later a roadhouse, until the actions of a rowdy public became a source of constant violence and sorrow. The tavern had long sagged vacant and idle when The Jimmies found the land, and the juke was used for years after that only to warehouse discarded, dusty things.

Once Turk arrived, though, that old tomb found new life.

Turk had come from the west, Oklahoma to be exact, around 1980.

He had brought with him one young son, Turner, and he had brought his savvy as a seasoned shopkeeper. His twenty-five-year font of knowledge had been filled by working since childhood for his grandfather, a grocer back in Tahlequah. Shortly after Turk's much younger wife died in an armed hold-up at their store out there, his emotional pain forced him to leave the Sooner State for good.

He and little Turner had traveled first to the Grand Canyon, on up to the Black Hills, and then they had come to Kentucky to visit Turk's cousin, Wilma Carl Benbow, who had originally moved to SLANT with a boyfriend from Kansas City. Unfortunately for Wilma Carl, the boyfriend had turned out to be a big dumbass who was afraid of everything, didn't have the strength of a little bird, and whined about the lack of hamburger joints and bars throughout the duration of his time living on the knob. Wilma Carl was a big girl, all six feet of her, and she had a big heart. She had loved Dervish as much as she could, but when that long, tall, complaining drink of water decided to depart for what he called "next stop: civilization station," she wasn't altogether unhappy about it. Too, she figured Dervish had a right to be wherever made him feel good, same as she did. For her, that place was this cool little commune in the Kentucky woods; for him it was a concrete jungle in the Midwest.

It still kind of irked her, though, that she had to be attached by previous association to one of the scant few SLANT residents who had ever voluntarily left and was all-too-happy to do so.

With Wilma Carl's abandonment and Turk's widowerhood coming so close together, the consolation they offered each other seemed comforting to them both. Back in Oklahoma, they had grown up more like brother and sister than cousins, each of them having been an only child … and the only two children in their extended Cherokee family, as well. In fact, they called each other "sister" and "brother." Only a few SLANTers are aware that they're actually cousins instead of siblings.

Like a good brother would, Turk had come east to see if Wilma Carl was doing all right after her break up. Like a good sister, Wilma Carl took in Turk and his son because they had lost-soul eyes and might have dried up and blown away from grief had they stayed on the road much longer. Turk needed to work and to heal. Wilma Carl needed to earn a living. Turner needed a home. SLANT needed a store. Thus, once the community agreed to Turk and Turner's residency, The General was established inside the old Seven Lanterns Tavern building.

The General (as in 'general store') had a little of everything in it, and plenty of SLANTers buy goods from it every week because they don't like to leave the knob if they don't have to. Turk decided from the start to be sure to stock canned, dried, frozen and fresh foods—*your basic milk, meat, veg, bread and fruit* is what he called his meager stock—not a wide variety,

but staples that could keep a body together. In addition to food, Turk
put in a supply of thread, buckets, nails and screws, tools like hoes, rakes
and hammers, flashlights and batteries, a few cables and extension cords,
snacks, gum, fan belts, razors, rope and the like. The usual flotsam and
jetsam of daily living, with a smattering of camping and gardening and
survival items useful for living on forested land, which is what SLANTers do.

SLANT-center's small clearing is perhaps a couple hundred yards in
diameter, surrounded by light forest. The farther away from SLANT-center
one moves along the spiraling paths, the denser the woods. The General, in
alignment with its distant history, is considered the center of the center.
A row of five or six unmatched wooden rocking chairs on its porch always
gave out a welcoming vibe. And those rockers were used nearly every day
in decent weather.

Turk had set a precedent from the first day he opened The General's
doors. By leaving an entire front corner of the old tavern undisturbed and
open for use by the community as it saw fit (we quickly dubbed our corner
space the Shroom Room), he soon had groups of people sitting around
talking to one another on a regular basis—they generally gathered in
a group, sitting on stools and milk crates, in folding chairs around the
wooden table that someone had brought back from a library discard sale
off-knob.

SLANTers have never been tentative in our occupation of that common
space inside The General's northeast corner; once offered, we moved right
in. It was in this corner that card games were played, community decisions
made, potlucks spread—and it was in this corner that The SLANT Code
had developed over time.

After Jimi had handwritten on the wall a piece of advice her most
beloved uncle had given her decades ago—*Start small. Show growth.*—others
added more words of wisdom. And The Code grew from there.

Cutesy or too-silly-for-smart-people platitudes never, not ever, showed
up on those walls. The Code, from the very first and without anyone even
talking about it, evolved as the place to leave well-thought-out comments
that might be useful to others. Not rules, exactly, and certainly not
enforceable laws; more, they were ideas to apply to living individually
and collectively. The Code is our creed.

It took a while for the first wall to fill up; the written words that
spilled across the corner to the adjoining wall expanded down from near
ceiling level to about chair rail height. The Code was amazing to gaze
upon. A wall of wisdom, yet not at all stuffy. Some of the statements were
written with markers, others were painted on, and two or three written
with the heavy lead of a carpenter's pencil had to be touched up from time
to time to keep them from being smudged and lost. The only order was
time, based on when people thought to add things. There was no etiquette

other than an unspoken *no overlapping*. Some entries were sideways. Some observed capitalization conventions, others did not. Some of the more hastily handwritten tenets were a bit difficult to read. The Code became a symbiotic study in controlled chaos, kind of like SLANT itself: a social phenomenon made of the leftover parts of something larger that was going extinct.

The Code expanded randomly, steadily for going on forty years, so it became possible to see a whole system, to recognize patterns, to feel how its rhythms had drawn together into a modern folk dance of sorts, somehow both choreographed and improvised.

It was all good stuff on both walls—none of it graffiti, no silly *Stones-are-better-than-Beatles* type of nonsense. No, these were strong, simple words to live by:

| | | |
|---|---|---|
| Start small. Show growth. | Practice Generosity | Respect Truth |
| Don't diminish or disparage | Reduce, Reuse, Recycle | Curiosity Now! |
| Exemplify the Golden Rule | B R E A T H E | Contribute |
| deflect judgment & don't judge | keep your own counsel | BE VIGILANT |
| temper unrequited longings | Appreciate Your Place | stifle stinginess |
| Envision the Big Picture | Deserve What You Get | Before can be too late |
| Meditate toward solutions | Mediate All Madness | Look for good |
| don't mistake ego for self-respect | Manage Temptations | Cultivate goodwill |
| To EXPERIENCE IS TO UNDERSTAND | Stand up after a stumble | Embody Equity |
| If it ain't broke, don't fix it. | Make Lying Wrong Again | Be Here Now |
| *CARPE FUCKING DIEM!* | Open your MIND; Your HEART will follow | |
| Welcome Every Challenge | Turn Struggle & Strife into Love & Life | |
| When all else fails, compromise | Consider Justice, Mercy, Compassion | |
| Define what you value & defend it | sow seeds that address needs | |
| Do less. BE more. | Seek Understanding & Enlightenment | |
| Embrace Responsibility | BETRAYAL IS ONE THING; REJECTION ANOTHER | |
| Never misplace your sense of humor | Hope for the Best; Prepare for the Worst | |
| Nature = Communion | What You See Isn't Always What You Get | |
| Be steadfast, loyal & true | In the Absence of Strength, Try Courage | |
| Expel Manipulation & Humiliation | Cultivate Wisdom & Embrace It | |

Own yourself—be LOUD, PROUD and UNBOWED!

*when one strand is plucked, the whole web vibrates*

MAKE ORWELL + HUXLEY + ATWOOD FICTION AGAIN!!

| | | |
|---|---|---|
| feast at the common table | Celebrate The Familiar | do no harm |
| Recognize Collective Guilt | Eliminate Pettiness | Let People Be |
| Do Your Best ... Always | Listen, Think, Learn | Play fair! |
| Embrace What Matters Most | It will reveal itself | Prepare |
| Nobody believes in Everything | Lay weapons aside | BE WISE |
| Cultivate Healthy Alliances | Love Laughter | Don't panic! |
| To THINE OWN MIND BE TRUE | Expect Consequences | BE KIND |
| Apply common sense liberally | From Many, One | think ahead |
| Whenever possible, provide | Avoid exploitation | Be Ready |
| RESPECT IS ALL | Thank your Lucky Stars | SHARE |
| Resist the Big Damned Lie! | Change is a Teacher | Live & let live |
| Selfishness & Love Cannot Co-exist | Honor those who got you here | Guard your trust |
| SINCLAIR LEWIS *WARNED US!* | Enjoy Sunshine & Be Grateful for Shade | |
| a tender smile is a benediction | Remember your people kindly, fondly, well | |

These usually showed up when no one was paying particular attention. We could often tell who had contributed to The Code strictly by the style of the wording or by the handwriting. Sometimes people added statements that were inspired by previous deposits. A few of the entries were artistically adorned with little curlicues or with tiny illustrations—a flower here, a fern there, a sketch of some four-legger's vigilant eyes or unique ears—while others were of the straightforward, 'nuff-said variety, allowing minimal words alone to do the work.

So it was that Turk watched The Code grow over the years, as did Wilma Carl, from behind the cash register across the big room. Once young Turner got old enough to help out in the family business, he developed an unbridled fascination with The Code, which was well into an advanced stage of development by then. As often as he could get away with it, the boy busied himself in that corner of the store (having secretly named it Code Corner, as if it were one of those old beatnik coffee houses and he had sneaked in to soak up the ambiance). Turner especially loved watching the many different people of SLANT come in and make deposits on those walls.

*They think deep thoughts!* he would marvel to himself. *They aren't afraid of thinking them! They aren't ashamed to share their thoughts in public!*

Turner was inspired, not just by the phrases themselves but by the unique existence of The Code as a whole. The very fact that people had worked out their individual ideas and then generously shared them with the community in this extraordinary but silent give-and-take conversation was what most impressed him. *They embrace intelligence! They trust one another.*

These were striking observations that informed the boy's interior life. He marveled at the flexibility of purpose demonstrated by that sturdy old library table, was astounded at the trust left in the bookshelves through which SLANTers traded reading material, felt sentimental about the patient coffee urn that welcomed all and sundry, making sure no one ever had to pay for a cup of coffee in SLANT (donations to the coffee fund always welcomed, of course).

But, most of all, Turner found his young mind blown at the brilliance of The SLANT Code in its entirety. And because of his attraction to it as a living thing that organically evolved, he thought long and deeply about the fact that all those contributions were anonymous. This for-the-greater-good generosity and its requisite personal humility made a significant impression on both the boy he was and the man he would become.

When Turk and Wilma Carl both got old enough to retire—he to piddle around in the model-building hobby studio he had constructed in his shed, she to lounge around her house most afternoons, listening to NPR and reading books and eating nuts encased in dark chocolate— Turner, having grown into a quiet and stable young man, was left to carry on the family business. By that time he had added to The Code a tenet or two himself ... his favorite being his first.

He had studied for a long time to find the most succinct wording by which to encapsulate the priceless lessons he had been learning from the evolution of those walls running into and out of that single corner of the Shroom Room. When he was satisfied and ready, he had stepped over to Code Corner, picked up a wide-tip blue marker someone had helpfully left balanced across the top of an empty coffee can, and removed its cap.

For his very first contribution, he wrote one word: *SHARE.*

# Be Here Now

FOREST. DAY. SHAFTS OF LIGHT KNIFE THEIR WAY through branches, needle past needles, stab between sticks, linger on leaves, twist past twigs. The slant of sunlight is dramatic in this environment. Cedar needles and leaf mulch carpet the ground. Here an insect scuttles. There birdsong hangs. Expectation is everywhere—either that, or the complete lack of it, which can also feel sublime.

Nooner walks softly, unconscious of the measure of Catawba blood his system carries. Capillaries, veins, arteries. Genetic memory and historical grief in every part of his being: muscle, gristle, marrow and bone. Even his straight black hair knows it, but Nooner isn't particularly aware. He knows only that he can trust his body to find its way on any terrain. He can sense direction with an inner knowledge as accurate as a pocket compass. His instincts are good.

Nooner walks in and out of light, in and out of shadow. It's all the same to him, in much the same way that it's all the same to the deer who cross here, or the salamander or wild rabbit. In like fashion, his own eyes adjust with precision to light or its absence. Automatic. Autonomous. Anonymous. Anyman. Everyman. Everything. Ever after.

Nooner loves SLANT, and Nooner loves the land upstream too. That's the land of judgment and dogma and narrow-minded creed. Nooner knows this, but he isn't intimidated by it. To him, it's all the same *land*, the same knob. It's all Barrel Chute, in this slice of time.

Even so, this land has endured many names. Nooner knows it only as Earth. And from Earth's fibrous elements, Mother Nature knits life.

Today, Nooner does not walk with a purpose. He takes his time. He's come only to check in, see how things are, envision how things might one day be. Is there reason to worry, impetus to act? Is the land safe and caring for itself in a healthy manner? Are people making this difficult? He's come to read it and find out.

He wonders, more practically, whether the wild goats that were once Top Notch Annie's are controlling the poison ivy and kudzu farther up along the woods' edges, where ditches demarcate clearing from forest, where vague old fence lines faintly emerge from undergrowth.

The walk uphill is always slower than the return. He relishes this. He does not rush.

# Instress Redux

PLACE NAMES ARE NOT THE WORK OF THE LORD. Places are
named by people, some of whom claim to speak for the Almighty, though
their self-proclaimed rights and motives in doing so are nearly always
suspect.

The property on which the church camp called The Rising Son is
situated had once been a good old-fashioned gospel camp meeting ground
known as Beulah Land. As long as White folks can remember, it has been
a place where the strictest kinds of Christian religion rule. In this place,
families of a sect of old-time fundamentalist evangelicals had spent summers
in a compound developed over many generations dating back into the
1800s. But the site finally had to close down about the time the 20th century
ended, because of money: fewer and fewer families were returning annually—
the post-post-modern age brings everything, including preaching, to
people by way of TV and Internet, rather than people having to travel to
experience those things anymore. The last Beulah Land die-hards were
so sad that they called the region's largest newspaper and TV station and
asked them to cover the demise of this spiritual phenomenon. And in this
notch of the nation's Bible Belt, they got their media coverage. Of course.
As if religion is actual news.

"I have relied on the song of that old dinner bell since I was a girl,"
one of the elderly Beulah Land women told a reporter. There had been
a photo of her in the newspaper; in it, she chatted with Bible-carrying
friends under a large, open-air pavilion on the camp meeting ground.
"That bell's tongue has called us to services three times every day," she
said. "It called us to our daily bread. We have awakened to it in the mornings, and allowed its sonorous peal to carry us drifting into sleep at night.
Its toll has marked each believer's return to his heavenly home. And we
have rung it to punctuate our shouts of celebration when a new soul was
brought to the Lord or when a brother or sister achieved a spiritual break-
through. I will miss that bell, for it always brought us joyfully together."

It was unknown whether this speech had been carefully worded and
memorized in advance, or whether these people who had perpetuated

community traditions (many that were well more than a hundred years old) naturally talked this way. Perhaps they had preserved antiquated speech patterns in much the same way they had protected those old religious ways they held dear. I can't say for sure, but in either case their sincerity was beyond question. They loved this place, holy to them—it had been an entire universe for the "chosen" among them, and it had meant the world to them.

After the old camp meeting ground had closed, a Pentecostal association bought the compound to create a summer Bible camp for children under twelve, changing the name from Beulah Land to Gloryland, which became its second identity. Over time, the emphasis at Gloryland shifted from being a camp for kids to being a summer gathering place for the slightly more mature thirteen-to-eighteen age group, in hopes of saving the teenagers from fornication, smoking and other carnal and worldly temptations. A few years passed in that iteration, during which the Pentecostal youth camp struggled, then failed.

Besides summer camp, Christian school groups had traditionally held week-long or weekend retreats at the Gloryland property, even during the school year, and there were times during late fall and winter when individual clergy had been allowed to schedule time there to pray, write, read, meditate or relax from pastoral duties for a few days. Rumor on the knob had it that many pastoral nervous breakdowns had either occurred or been recovered from up there, back when it had been Gloryland. And someone said that in deep winter at least one pastoral indiscretion had repeatedly taken place—an ongoing pastor-on-pastor tryst that was an open secret among the camp's neighbors along the little road that trickled around the peak and down both sides of the ridge. "The sun ain't the only thing rising up there," Rachel, who called herself The Postmistress, had overheard on a chilly February morning—one flatlander wryly remarking to another while standing in a short line of folks awaiting their turns at the counter of her tiny post office off-knob. The tactful Rachel never learned how the source of the comment knew this to be true, but considering how connected and locally established the speaker was, she'd had no doubt that it must have been so.

But all of that was history. More recently, the region's ultra-conservative, non-denominational, cosmopolitan mega-church, *Streets of Gold!*, came into surrogate possession of the place with an eye toward developing it into an upscale, elitist Christian summer camp for privileged high school students who lived in the nearby city. For the property's third life, they changed its name yet again—this time to The Rising Son. Fornication as mortal sin, while briefly mentioned by counselors on occasion, was no longer the camp's primary focus; instead, its new mission was to condition a next generation of wealthy patrons who would financially support the mega-church itself. Immediately after the mega-church took over, the compound's physical face began to change, as well.

*Streets of Gold!*, indeed.

When this new management moved in, the very first thing to go was that beloved old dinner bell. Its rust and streaks of age and its rotting braided-hemp rope were judged ill-fitting with the camp's contemporary renovation, so the cedar post on which the bell was mounted was chainsawed off at ground level, and the whole thing—bell, post, rope and all—was dragged to a trash heap that had been established behind the tree line down at edge of the creek that bordered the property. *Nobody ever goes down there anyway,* was their rationale for creating their gigantic mound of refuse. Over the years, as it grew, this illegal trash heap saved the church camp from having to pay thousands in dump fees at the county landfill. No thought was given to how this dumping might affect Fidelity Creek itself or the neighbors living downstream at SLANT and even beyond. When one sees oneself as the entitled center of the universe, it stands to reason that one has no capacity whatsoever for realizing that any blithely-dismissed *down there* might have a whole different perspective if seen from the worldview of the neighbors who actually *live* down there, below and beyond said borderline. Shit rolls downhill, after all. But all of that was out of sight, out of mind—from the self-righteous view *up here,* anyway.

So-called improvements abounded at the brand-spanking-newly-named camp, and modernization occurred rapidly. *Streets of Gold!* had money aplenty, after all. On the roof of the administration building, right next to a spiffy satellite dish, a loudspeaker was placed. From it, a faux-ethereal electronic tone, among other things, would be broadcast via computer control—this tone was a 21st century signal for calling campers together for meals or gatherings. A dinner bell would have been too simple. A dinner bell isn't sexy enough for an urban mega-church's elitist teen camp in what they considered the middle of nowhere. Never mind that to folks actually living on the knob, it was most definitely the middle of somewhere.

Next on the makeover agenda, the grand old open-air pavilion was tightly enclosed and air-conditioned. So much for gathering together in the natural world they claim God created just for them. The remodeled canteen was (cleverly, they thought) renamed The Tea Party.

Off county road 111 was a lane that entered the TRS property. This lane was renamed American Way. Signs posted at the new guard shack near the entrance warned trespassers that they were not allowed to travel the American Way without permission. Apparently, this American Way was limited only to those whose beliefs were aligned with the propaganda of the mega-church. Pretty typical in an era when religion is co-opted and used as a political weapon.

Shortly thereafter, a dozer began to cut four new roads on the property. These roads, each the width of a two-lane street, were laid out in a grid. Many grand old-growth trees were lost. And then a spindly row of non-native saplings were planted along the grid's new roads. People on the knob, those who were watching anyway, thought the placement and length of those new roads odd, but they just assumed more cabins and dormitories would eventually be built along them—either that, or they were going to be the widest, straightest "hiking" trails of any forested camp on the face of the planet. However, once those paths were cut, there seemed to be no further road work for a long time, even though buried electric cables and water/sewer pipes had been run handily alongside each in orderly trenches. Oh, yes, and a significant number of small clearings had been cut-in at regular intervals, appearing more like a large subdivision in the making than the natural surroundings of a summer camp for kids. But nobody on Barrel Chute Knob pursued this beyond idle neighborhood gossip. They, respectfully, didn't feel they had a right to do anything about it, being neighbors of the live-and-let-live variety.

During the off season, multiple people witnessed rapid changes at the camp. These included hikers traversing the knobs at random, people who spent time hunting on adjacent forested slopes, and curious neighbors who poked around the site after hours when workers had gone home— trespassers, yes, but walking the woods was an old tradition on the knob, an activity driven by respect for natural curiosity. These close observations occurred in seasons when no children were on the premises, of course, for during the summer camp term people kept their distance, which is why hardly anyone really knew what went on then. But the facts that were known were discussed at the off-knob post office, at The General in SLANT, and in other places alongside the main paved road that crawled up and down and around Barrel Chute.

Let it be noted that Speculation is Fact's first cousin thrice-removed.

# Welcome Every Challenge

NOONER WOULD NEVER FORGET the day he had first encountered
the bad news. I've heard him tell the story many a time, beginning with
that first moment.

*The Rising Son*, the newly-erected billboard had read. There was a
great big illustration showing a robed Jesus from his chest up. His hands,
palms outward, were visible on either side of his shoulders, and the
suggestion of light beams radiated in a sunrise-like glow, arching over
his head from thumb to thumb. *Summer Camp, Christian Boys & Girls,
Ages 13-17. Under New Management.*

"You have got to be fuckin' kiddin' me!" Nooner wasn't having any of
it. "As if they don't have enough of those little mini-me-Falwells runnin'
around up there already."

Meddy, eyes closed against the wind, had yelled from outside the pickup's passenger window, "What's up your ass now?" She'd stuck her head
out there to get some air after Nooner's old beagle, Boogle, had passed gas
… again. Poor old dog had been at it all day. "What did you feed this guy,
Nooner? Cabbage kibbles and methane bits?"

Since her insult was directed not at him but at his dog, Nooner ignored
it. For that matter, so did Boogle.

"I *said*," he said, "that Christianazi outfit upstream from us has now
started advertisin' along the Interstate highway system." He hollered loud
enough for her to hear over the wind.

"No fooling?" she shouted back. Her eyes remained closed.

"Get ready," he said, loudly enough for her to hear. "We're about to
be invaded by hordes more of their little shit machines." No wonder their
billboard Jesus was posed in a *hands-up-don't-shoot* posture of surrender.
He must be feeling pretty powerless these days. Couldn't blame him for
wanting to just give up on those who in his name did so much that was
hateful and selfish and wrong. They had overlooked the *judge not* passage
in their Book, apparently.

Meddy pulled her head back inside the cab; the rough wind had made
her look like someone wearing a wig backwards. She turned to face the

side of Nooner's head. "And people wonder why I'm such a curmudgeon," she said.

"Beside the Interstate!" Nooner grumbled. "For the whole world to see." In those days, Nooner had been harboring a hope that Gloryland would eventually have to close altogether, since the number of young campers declined year upon year. He knew that very few people off-knob realized the old private camp was even up there, and if that kept traffic down on county road 111 (the road locals called "hunnerd-n-lebm"), it suited him just fine if they never knew.

But now this.

"Six Flags Over Jesus must have bought out that old camp," Nooner surmised, referring to the mega-church in question by its common local nickname. The church's real moniker was *Streets of Gold!* (as in "the streets of heaven are paved with purest gold," from an old hymn), but that branding was so stupid by itself, with its ridiculous trademark italics and exclamation point, that no one except members ever called it by its real name.

Meddy and Nooner had, in fact, driven past *Streets of Gold!* just before they crossed the county line on the outskirts of the city twenty miles back. "That place is a blight on Mother Nature's landscape. Its opulence and girth alone are enough to make you want to throw up," Meddy'd said then.

The mega-church lusted to be seen as an upscale "campus," though it didn't run a school. Besides an obscenely gargantuan church building, it had constructed itself a gigantic gym, a fully-equipped theatre, a lighted ball-field, an arena complete with bleacher seats and sky boxes, a Bible-study complex, a bookstore, a cafeteria, a retail store, a coffeeshop. It was enormous. Made Meddy feel both sad and angry.

"They 'invest' all their wealth back into *themselves*, instead of into helping folks who so desperately need it. Some mission," she complained.

Nooner, always a farmboy at heart, had once peered at the huge church buildings and said, "You could stack a lot of hay in there."

"Every time we pass that place, I see at least one homeless person panhandling at their exit ramp," Meddy said. "I always wish I could stop right there in the Interstate and take a picture of that to show the world: some poor victim of this so-called 'Christian nation' those hypocrites are so hot to own and control, and this guy's reduced to begging for coins to feed his family while that monument to greed sits right behind him, proclaiming itself an example of the lessons of the humble Christ."

"No shit," said Nooner.

"It's the portrait of 21st century America, I'm afraid," Meddy told him. "You know what John Wesley wrote, and this was a long, long time ago: *The rich in general have so little sympathy for the poor because they so seldom visit them."*

Nooner nodded and continued to fume.

"Believers who are struggling and uneducated," Meddy added, "they're easy targets for wealthy religious predators who see them as suckers and have no shame about manipulating them and then betraying their trust. It seems that those who get used are then taught to refer to their plight as 'God's will.' But that's only because they'd feel guilty if they rightfully called it 'God's fault.' Or more accurately God's leaders' fault. To me, it's all the same thing … and not sacrilege at all. I call it 'factrilege.'"

Thanks to *Streets of Gold!*, the upscaling of the church camp on SLANT's bordering creek was a done deal. That billboard had sealed it, in Nooner's mind (and he didn't even yet know about the impending property development up there). The little Bible-thumpers-in-training weren't going away after all. In fact, with the clout of *Streets of Gold!*, they were about to swell into a radical and snobbish horde.

"Bet you anything they bought the place off of what's left of the Holiness people," Nooner said, "and're gettin' ready to unleash their nasty mind-control on more kids than ever before."

"As good a guess as any. They've probably already started figuring out how they can grow it into another of their money-makers," Meddy said. "*Fund* being the operative syllable of 'fundamentalist.'"

Nooner couldn't stand the hypocrisy of the fundamentalists who apparently now ran the camp (he liked to call them "fundies" because it sounded more like "fungus"—which they were, his opinion), but he actually loved that campground … when it was deserted. Sometimes on days in deep winter, particularly cold days when there was not much snow on the ground, Nooner hiked up to the church camp, crossing its boundary line opposite the creek and up the hill from Meddy's little creekside house on stilts and then past Alec's treehouse straddling Fidelity. There was no year-round caretaker at The Rising Son. One guy drove up to check on things every two or three weeks during the months when the camp was closed. Other than that, it sat locked up tight, empty as a kettle drum, pipes drained, power off. *POSTED KEEP OUT* signs and *NOT RESPONSIBLE FOR ACCIDENTS* signs and *NO TRESPASSING* signs were all over the place, on fences and buildings and gates and trees. But Nooner walked wherever he pleased. And every time he entered the camp's commons area, he would turn and nod toward the front of the main building, which Nooner would soon dub *Mother-House of The Rising Son.* That property could be so cool. If it were his, he'd transform it into something wonderful.

"If I had this place," he'd say to his daydreaming self. "If I did."

The old camp meeting compound felt like sacred ground to his young environmentalist heart. It just about killed Nooner that fundamentalists were using it to corrupt America's youth—teaching them to judge instead of teaching them to love. It was the brain twisters, the adult masterminds, the so-called "spiritual leaders" that he despised, though, and not the campground itself. Nooner likened his feeling to a Bible story he'd learned as a child in Sunday School: Jesus cast out the money-lenders because he was opposed to *them*, not to the temple they were using for their own greedy schemes. Nooner saw the center of the campground, especially under the ethereal sunlight of the leafy dome covering its commons area, as being very like a temple or a cathedral or what he imagined the inside of a large mosque might look like.

He was saddened that the poor old place wasn't allowed to live up to its natural potential—as a *secular* camp it could be a splendid launch pad into a lifelong exploration of possibility. If kids came through a place like that to learn about the evolutions and symbioses that nature comprises, they could parlay that excitement, commitment and basic knowledge into an adulthood focused on healing the earth rather than exploiting it.

Exploitation in general was what their corporate church and herd-worshiping parents were all about. Kids are good at heart, he believed, so if they knew what one person's greed really cost so many people who lived lower on the food chain, they might become even "richer" than their parents—morally speaking, that is. If kids were allowed to know the real meanings behind the words that were used to control them, they might be inspired to become fairer than their parents. If kids could be shown that cooperation is better than competition, they might be able to save the human race from the self-destructive course their parents and grandparents had set it on.

Nooner fantasized about a camp where those positive things were possible. It could be a place where kids bought in to the community concept because they were well informed and had decided to factor respect for others into their choices. That would be a radical contrast to what this camp had illogically become, which was a place where kids were forced to participate, were suckered in, were taught elitist attitudes and exclusionary acts and, as a result, were compelled to act out frequently against "inferior" peers of their choosing who were outside their narrow little circle. In his opinion, places like *Streets of Gold!* and The Rising Son raised entitlement-oriented bullies. Period.

When Nooner had once tried to explain these thoughts to Meddy, who was a good listener and possibly the most intelligent person in all of SLANT, he'd worried that he'd not have enough words of his own to express what he really meant. Fortunately for him, Meddy seemed to possess a skill he'd not known she had—she could fathom his mind.

"What you're talking about is that some people never seem to leave the sandbox. Their sandboxes just get larger, that's all," Meddy said.

"But they never grow up. They act like selfish children all their lives."

*Right on the money,* Nooner thought. "How'd you get so smart?" said he.

"And the bigger they get ..." she said.

"Six Flags Sandbox," he mused.

"... the meaner they are about who they allow to play with them. Everyone not 'in' is condemned. Cast out. It's all led by adults condoning bad politics and modeling playground bullying at its worst."

How many lonesome little kids, Nooner wondered, are standing around needing to be welcomed into a sandbox? Where was the really great super-fun sandbox for sweet-natured and good-hearted kids? There ought to be a place for them that banned the poisonous elitism that The Rising Son and *Streets of Gold!* and such places perpetuated. Nooner envisioned a wide-open "sandbox" *right there*, in place of that brain laundry passing as a summer church camp.

He sighed big, just thinking about it.

But the annoying billboard was miles behind him now. He glanced over at Meddy, peacefully enjoying the view out her side window. She was absent-mindedly scratching Boogle's ears. He lay stretched across the seat between them, drowsy and satisfied.

"How you doin'?" he asked. She shrugged.

He and Meddy had gone to the city for her regular doctor visit and a liquor store run, SLANT being situated in a neighboring dry county—one of its only drawbacks, but a tradeoff worth a little inconvenience. The irony wasn't lost on him that the ghost of the Seven Lanterns Tavern (left over from the old days, before the dry vote) was now The General, with their BYOB community Shroom Room inside. The dry vote had been a result of what Meddy called "the peer fear influence" propagated by the mega-church's predecessor long ago. SLANT's metro-adjacent county and all its rural neighbors had all gone dry many years back (although the city had, wisely, remained wet), and that politically-motivated shift had been the end of the old tavern.

During the day's outing, Nooner and Meddy had also taken in a movie matinee at the art film house in one of the city's funkier neighborhoods. Because of his unfolding friendship with Meddy over the past few years, Nooner had learned to enjoy, among other things, the work of brilliant, if obscure, filmmakers. The soundtrack for Meddy's life was jazz, which he hadn't known he'd like, but he did! His friendship with her was unlike his usual pattern of experience. For a while, he had wondered at it; finally he realized that he was comfortable with the organic way she nurtured and taught. She didn't seem to know she was doing that. He hadn't even noticed for a long time that she was both mentor and friend. He could ask her anything and not feel embarrassed, in spite of the fact she was thirty years his senior. He felt lucky to have found her and knew his mother would like Meddy too, regardless of their very different backgrounds, for these two women, beloved by him, were roughly the same age. They weren't much alike though. His mommy wasn't argumentative, for one thing. Meddy was unique in other ways too, because while her mind regularly traveled to high altitudes, her feet never left the ground.

Nooner was the only person in SLANT who knew for sure that Meddy's health was fading. It was a confidence he was honored to keep, for he knew Meddy would absolutely and without question do the same for him, were tables turned. They were an odd pair of friends, but they were true blue, certain of their bond.

She hadn't told him what was going on at the first signs of her decline, but he had guessed anyway, for he'd noticed that her ability to stay up late waned, that she'd started taking naps in the daytime (something she insisted she'd not been able to do since she was a baby), that she sometimes forgot things or had to organize her head in order to recall something she'd known all her life. She had become sort of defensive and would speak sharply toward him on occasion too, which was very unlike her. By now, her memory was so intermittently bad that she had to write down every single thing, even the simplest. So, he had figured out that something was awry, and when she finally told him that she had been diagnosed with early onset dementia, he was heartbroken for her ... and for himself. He knew how much a keen mind meant to this lifelong learner, this role model, this older-sister-figure that he loved and deeply respected.

He determined then and there to do what he could to keep her mind active and engaged, and he knew this would not be a burden, for he enjoyed his time with Meddy precisely because she had always been so vigorously engaged in life's curiosities. She had made him understand that her condition was just the next step on the path that most people call Life. To her, being alive was and always had been a quest. In this sense, it was Living, not mere "life," that mattered to her. Many options, many directions, many choices, many questions: all possibilities.

Meddy was known for her tendency to complain loud and long about general injustice and unfairness in the world, but she'd not complained at all about her own illness, and Nooner knew she wouldn't. He might not know many things, but Nooner knew he was an important element in this part of Meddy's journey. He took seriously his role as her main link with the reality of her recent past and present, even as she moved slowly toward a new reality, one mostly foreign to her. "It's just the next adventure," she had told Nooner last time they were making this ride home, "and you know me—always up for an adventure." Her grin was genuine, he'd noticed then; it told him she wasn't afraid to forge ahead along her own road and see what things were like in that unknown territory around the next bend.

Yes, the tables were definitely turning for this pair. Now she occasionally had to ask him for clarification or help—and not be embarrassed to do so. She'd already had some days that were difficult, but most days were still pretty good. "Today," he thought, "is a good one."

They left the Interstate, traveling now up the knob on the much smaller county road. They neared the last big upward curve on hunnerd-n-lebm before the turn-off to SLANT. Home was right here, right now, and that last big curve always felt good because it was taking Nooner to his favorite, most personal and familiar place.

Suddenly, it occurred to him to wonder what *home* would mean to Meddy, say, a year from now.

# God's Grandeur

"I WANT TO BE CLOSER TO GOD," a snob of a girl named Marilyn
or Marigold or Maryann declared to the assembled circle of teens, most
of whom were gazing at her in varying states of what they hoped would
be read as quasi-blissful expectation. She started to sit back down on the
bark-stripped log, then hesitated abruptly like a child who has forgotten
a line in a school play but recovers just in time. "Oh! And I want to sing
His praises." Then she sat, smug and satisfied with herself that she had
remembered to say all the right things.

The small campfire in the circle's rock-rimmed fire ring crackled in
a contented manner, as fires will do. Something deep in it burned with a
lovely blue jet for a few seconds, and everyone waited in the pleasantly
smoky June night for the next teenager to stand and speak. It was quiet at
the church camp, the other campers having been worn out with their day's
labors. These newcomers were going around the circle, answering the
question that Coop, the Spiritual Teen Leader, had asked each to respond
to on this their first night at camp: *Why have you chosen to spend your summer
at The Rising Son?*

*Chosen* was a word that had nothing to do with Nick's being there,
but now it was his turn to speak. He knew he was supposed to tell the
truth, and he also knew which "truth" these people expected him to tell.
If he told his true truth, he'd have to admit that he found himself a church
camper this year solely because of some trouble he'd gotten himself into.
It had left him in the uncomfortable position of choosing between the
two alternatives his father had laid out: spend a few weeks in exile at The
Rising Son or go to work in the basement of his father's company in the
city—eight full hours a day, six days a week, with Sundays spent at *Streets
of Gold!*, the mega-church his father supported. Nick hated the thought of
both choices, but since he preferred to be (A) outdoors and (B) as far from
his father as possible, he had reluctantly come to TRS. At least it was in
natural surroundings, unlike that windowless underground chamber in his
father's place of business. Being in the sunshine felt less unhealthy, even
here among these desperate and deluded misfits. Already, though, he had

missed most of First Term at camp because of the court-ordered hours of community service he'd had to work off. Well, he'd be far away from the old man for these next six weeks anyway. And from that distance, even the new school year seemed blissfully far, far away.

Sitting in this ridiculous circle with other late-comers, looking around at the seasoned church campers, most of whom had carefully arranged their smug White faces in what they considered to be appropriately beatific expressions, he wondered if he'd made the right choice. This wasn't going to be easy.

"I'm Nick," he said, rising from his log perch. Here he stopped so he could decide how to state a truth that would work both for him and to the satisfaction of everyone else. The circle waited. He toed the earth absently. "I'm here because I thought it was the right choice for me," he finally said, making a lame attempt at diplomacy. In spite of the fact that Spiritual Teen Leader Cooper and the other kids clearly wanted and expected more, he let it go at that and took his seat. They seemed to decide to accept his ambiguous statement as one that favored their collective biases.

The circle continued, but after Nick sat down he barely heard anything. He didn't care enough to engage. Mostly, the voices were just murmurs— a series of blah-blah-blah sprinkled with predictable comments such as "to praise the Lord with all my soul and all my might," "to learn how Jesus wants me to live" or "to finish memorizing Leviticus." Whatever penetrated Nick's wall of disconnect was random, for it was all the same old Jesus this and God that and sanctimonious whatever.

"To experience God's grandeur in the wilderness," the next one, a stout girl, said. She offered only this, and then she sat.

This last comment with its phrase "God's grandeur" gave Nick a spark of interest. His head jerked to attention in the direction of the girl who had just spoken. Perhaps she had read the words of the unlikely Victorian poet whose work Nick had embraced during the school year just ended? His brain thudded against itself; it was an awkward lurch of unexpected hope. Could this be someone he might talk to? Someone who cared about ideas? Who had common sense? Who actually read books? Maybe so. That would be nice. Someone he could trust? *Don't get carried away*, he thought. While it was true that anyone who called this place "wilderness" was a little off base, the reference to his current favorite poet, Gerard Manley Hopkins, was encouraging. Intriguing, even. It possessed potential. He felt himself hoping the phrase that had perked his ear wasn't just a coincidental choice of words.

But *wilderness?* He hadn't seen much of it yet, but he thought the frighteningly-structured and overly-manicured confines of the church camp were far from wild. The camp's center was more like a cultivated park than anything truly natural. Still, it did beat spending the rest of the summer in a fluorescent corporate dungeon back in that stone, glass and steel heat-island of a city.

Because he hadn't cared about what—up until that sudden *to experience God's grandeur* moment—was being parroted with little variation by the dozen or so teenagers gathered around the circle, he hadn't really been listening. And because he wasn't listening, he hadn't caught the girl's name. Now, as he watched her across the fire pit, even through mirage-like heat waves and dim light, he thought he could see her switch off her ears and slip into a reverie of her own as soon as she sat down so the skinny girl next to her could stand to proclaim her own "holy" purpose there.

*I am invisible if I want to be,* the stout girl's demeanor indicated. She just sat there, it seemed to Nick, absorbed in her own thoughts, apart from her insipidly pious peers.

*This is good,* Nick thought. *This is very good.*

# The Wisdom of Top-Notch Annie, Part 1

"WHEN I WAS DYIN', I HEARD VOICES. Meddy. Nooner. The preacher, Joy DuPre. Too, I heard one ghost-like whisper from that church camp. And dear Alec ... even that unquiet soul vocalized somethin' in my general direction, and he used a soothin' tone, though I couldn't discern his words. These people weren't there, you understand, but I heard 'em just the same. They each called me by my name, seemed like. *Annie*, I thought I heard 'em say, but I did not reply ... because, in a matter of minutes, I could no longer reply to anyone, ever again.

"There was the smell of honeysuckle, too, and a feelin' that I was fallin' off the world. No, let me see—not fallin'. Floatin'. Well, not that, either. More that the world was floatin' out from under me—that I was fixed in space and the world receded, movin' from beneath me to some distance away. Felt like ... I didn't leave the world; it left me.

"Well, it was fast, this sensation, so I didn't have time to analyze the whole thang. I was dyin'. Thangs blew by in a hurry.

"But this is what I experienced, dyin'. It's all I have by way of explanation. As with most thangs, words are incapable of capturin' true truth. There's a thang you might not know yet, but maybe someday you will. It's just this: if you think long enough, you can think yourself into a kind of *knowin'* without language. And finally you'll find that the more you've read, the less sense anythang ever written makes.

"When I was dyin', I watched ever'thang happen as if it wadn't happenin' to me. I didn't feel it. I didn't grieve it. I watched. Fascinated. I wadn't afraid.

"In those last bits—which could have been minutes or months—puzzles solved theirselves, mysteries untangled. I felt a little foolish when I was dyin', the insides of truths and the knots of a painful lifetime revealin' themselves at last in simplest terms. Easy to see ... *then!*

"Those earlier years of carin' too much and tryin' too hard had depleted my energy and endangered my spirit far beyond any pitiful potential to enrich. Yes, I had known it while it was happenin' but was powerless to stop myself from that particular intellectual decline. I had b'lieved in goodness too much. I'd b'lieved that fairness was a real thang. But as worldly people in general proved theirselves incapable of goodness, of fairness, of generosity, I had to admit that I had harmed myself with those old beliefs. I'd held onto them too tight. And they had failed me.

"Observin' became the only activity of value in those last years of my life, all else havin' been proved false, empty, disappointin'. I gave up on opining, threw away social interaction as a daily activity. Too, I learned how little I valued companionship because of the pain and betrayal it inevitably causes. Companionship is entirely over-rated. It wadn't so much that I preferred my own company; in fact, I came to believe that my company wadn't worth keepin' either, as bitter rejections and past betrayals had convinced me. More, it was that I'd finally accepted the reality of my invisibility. One of the best lessons I learned in all my too-long short life is that if a person can manage to support theirself in solitude and by needin' less, then invisibility is invincibility.

"My best advice to those still alive? Prepare to take care of yourself pretty much alone. Then, get thee under the radar.

"I learned, at last, that what I had to offer was of little value and less consequence to ever'bidy. Once I saw how terrible I was at bein' with people (and how little I liked it), well, I stopped doin' that ... and was immediately happier. Ain't nothin' fulfillin' about tryin' to please others who tire of your eager and pathetic tryin'; nothin' more disappointin' than learnin' that one's own intense level of commitment is frightenin'ly out of balance with those who are firmly indifferent; nothin' less humiliatin' than expressin' noticeable enthusiasm toward a person who can muster only lukewarm tolerance of you. And there damn sure is nothin' worse than practicin' patience with a person you think is worth savin', only to have them reject you, lie to you, lie about you and leave. The world turns on an axis of betrayal, and betrayal is a mean-spirited bastard. How could such a world be anythang less than devastatin'?

"My inability to bounce, to forget, to 'move on' (as idiots often say) was cripplin'. I landed with a thud every time. And perpetually I recalled all of my griefs, even in dreams.

"I mired in my own splat.

"And after I left the stuck world and moved entirely alone to Top Notch— above SLANT, above the church camp, invisible to nearly ever'bidy else on Barrel Chute Knob—there were some years of findin' how to exist, and then some more of findin' how to go on about livin'. All of this directly contradicted the ways in which the world has brainwashed us about expectations. Finally, after all that un-learnin', I had to re-learn how to see and listen and think. Never did I miss people and all their dismissive, scornful, disinterested, bored, self-involved, indignant, desperate, false, mean, destructive, ego-driven, shallow ways. Human bein's are all of that and more. Yet I s'pose I must admit that *I* was self-turned, too, in light of my self-invented hermitage. Well, at least I wadn't hurtin' anybidy from within my revised version of existence.

"In my tiny cabin in a cozy clearin' carved from the cedar woods, I kept to myself so that I might keep myself. And that turned out to be all right. Turned out to be just about the most right thang I ever did.

"My life in the Notch was a good one; certainly my best years were lived here. I stayed alive by keepin' to myself. I appreciated the *quiet* most of all. I observed many thangs, not the least of which was how Mother Nature valiantly heals herself and, in the process, healed me. She's a good best friend, the old Mother. A teacher, a mentor, a parent. This is far too easy to forget in places where she's been scraped dry, asphalted over, manicured into little boxes, chemicalized to the point of bein' unrecognizable. She's all we need; but in the world we and our most recent forebears have created, that's a forgotten bit of wisdom, ain't it?

"And what will happen to the good Mother when healin' herself is somethin' that cain't be accomplished no more? Well. The greedy won't answer that question, and the rest of us cain't bear to.

"So, for a while, I lived. I found Top Notch, and the old Mother met me there. She helped me, and I did what I could, with puny efforts, to protect her. My lived life—talkin' about my *real* life, which only began up here in the Notch—turned out to be a relatively short one, but it was full and suited me. I recall readin' that Frank Lloyd Wright said he believed in God only he spelled it *nature*. Well, I believe in Nature.

"And then I was dyin'. And when I was, I heard their voices: Farnsley and Juny, The Jimmies and the rest—my neighbors, though these few barely knew me as such, and the rest not at all. That was my choice and I don't regret it. I was the eccentric, the fool on the hill. They respected me in my hermitage, and I 'preciate 'em for that. By respectin' my solitude, they earned my respect in turn.

"I wrote no book durin' my allotment of time here. I painted no image, cooked no exotic cuisine, played no instrument, practiced no commerce. I gardened a little, food for my own consumption. I hunted some. I walked far, to steady my heart. Beneath the last of the dyin' hemlock and ash trees and the abundance of healthy red cedars I sat long, to soothe my troubled soul by connectin' with their own.

"Oh, and I read. I read and read and read. And sometimes (if I was damn sure no one was around) I sang!

"I didn't bother the SLANTers nor the church campers, and in turn those who knew I was up here pretty much left me be. When our paths did cross, I nearly always saw them comin' first and dodged 'em, avoided havin' to put myself or them through the silly niceties of awkward conversation, so vapid and difficult.

"And so it was. In my distant observin's, I may've known these neigh-bors somewhat better than they knew me—and that was all right too. I preferred it. Prefer it even now ... in spite of the fact that I'm dead, so don't nothin' matter no more.

"Dead, but not a quitter.

"When I was in the throes of dyin', though, I felt energized. Now what I feel is exhausted from havin' completed that task.

"I wish I could be dyin' again, just to experience that clarity, that hope, that glorious enlightenin' energy one more time."

## Sow Seeds That Address Needs

"WELL, YOU CAN SOW THEM LIKE SEEDS or you can surrender them like chaff. Whatever meaning you place on them, that's their identity and their purpose." Meddy had tried to be patient when Tractor Girl'd asked her to explain what she'd just witnessed. Keeping it simple seemed best. "Their power is yours to decide."

Only two people knew where Tractor Girl had picked up the habit of using coins to invest symbolically in something much more meaningful than money for its own sake, and she herself is one of them. Meddy, who had taught her, was the other. People in SLANT, like people everywhere, have some crazy personal rituals, but this coin thing was something no one had seen before. Tractor Girl certainly didn't invent it—she'd just happened upon it and wouldn't let it go until she got an explanation. Once told and heard, she saw its beauty and irony simultaneously.

"Seeds or chaff," Tractor Girl had repeated quietly a few times like a mantra while she tossed inside her mind the myriad ideas this concept inspired. After a few minutes, she'd understood the whole thing, crystal clear. "And sometimes both!" she said. "And other times neither—but waiting is part of growing, too."

Meddy had nodded and smiled. Up to that moment, she'd never thought another living soul would ever know or care about or grasp the self-realized concepts that inspired her coin rituals. She'd always done them in secret because she was sure she couldn't explain—and because she didn't want to have to. It was private, after all.

The moment Tractor Girl had first spoken to her about it from beneath the creek bank on that day long past, well, that was the first time anyone had ever seen Meddy doing it.

"Did you just throw a handful of pennies into the woods?" Tractor Girl had spoken it quietly, as the slow current carried her to work early one sunny morning.

A moment before, Tractor Girl's kayak had peeked around the first curve in an S-shaped bend in Fidelity, and she had noticed a woman on the highest part of the creek's far bank. It was Meddy, who was standing with her back to the water and had no idea anyone was approaching. She had thrown her cupped hands upward and outward in a gesture suggestive of tossing a bird into the air to release it into flight, scattering ten shiny pennies toward a young redbud grove beyond the fringe of sycamores that grew near the bank. Tractor Girl, floating by nearly under Meddy's heels, saw the sunlight catch each coin and throw ten little glints into space. She had never before in all her days seen anyone throw money away.

"Did you just throw a handful of pennies into the woods?"

Meddy startled so hard, she nearly stumbled backward off the little cliff she was perched upon. "Lord have mercy!" she cried, clutching her chest. "You scared the life out of me!"

Tractor Girl, in one fluid motion, ruddered Whisper over to the bank and grabbed hold of a tree root that was sticking out. The kayak bobbed patiently in place as Meddy found her feet. "You okay?" TG said.

"For the love of Mary Magdalene, *YES*, no thanks to you," said Meddy. "Were you spyin' on me?"

"No! Not on purpose, at least. I'm just on my way to work. *Well, did you?*"

"Maybe," said Meddy. Sheepishness and embarrassment were feelings that were foreign to her.

"*WHY?* I never saw anybody literally throw away money before. In. My. Life."

Meddy recovered immediately. "I wasn't throwing it away! I was making an investment in something imminently more important than mere money," she stated matter-of-factly. The meaning of this statement hadn't been immediately clear to Tractor Girl, but she trusted the *something* inside her that said, *Listen to this. Learn this. Use this for good.*

It was then that Meddy, sighing as if she'd misplaced something dear, had presented her seeds-or-chaff explanation. In her meticulous way that usually was off-putting because it took so damned long for her to yield the floor again once you got her started on one of her ideas, Meddy tried. She didn't expect to be understood, but Tractor Girl was quick and bright and ready, so this seed of thought put down its roots inside her good and fertile spirit.

"Is this like a wishing well thing?" Tractor Girl had asked.

"Goodness, no!" said Meddy. "For one thing, I'm not merely wishing. That's a superstition beyond even me. No, the coins have to land where they'll not be found. Otherwise, opportunity missed. It's got to be private." She cocked one eyebrow. "At least it has been 'til now."

Tractor Girl was so enamored of this new idea that she didn't care whether she was late for work or not. She sat there holding onto that tree root, bobbing on the water like a duck taking a breather between dives, listening to Meddy talk about this strange ritual.

Meddy sighed. "Okay. One night I was driving back across Cumberland Gap," she explained to Tractor Girl, "coming from the funeral of an old woman in Virginia who had been dear to me, a mentor from my youth. I knew my crossing back into Kentucky was a marker of sorts, and I wanted to observe this particular event in some meaningful way. But I hadn't planned for this moment. I hadn't had foresight of how terribly hard this trip would affect my heart, you see. Well, I looked around my truck for something that I could make spiritual use of, and there were a handful of pennies in the ashtray—one of them was brand new, and another happened to have been minted in the very same year I'd met this beloved mentor."

Tractor Girl had murmured, "That's so cool."

"Without thinking, really, I took the wad of gum I'd been chewing out of my mouth and used it as a sticky filler, making a sandwich of those two pennies, dates outward. Stuck together, they had heft and would fly farther. Just as I crossed the state line I launched them out the truck window into the wilderness of the Gap, hoping hard that they'd never be found by any human, and while they were in mid-air I said goodbye to a cherished period of my life. It felt wonderful and it felt painful, but it felt right. It was the dates stamped on those pennies that held meaning for me, not the insignificant monetary value of the coins themselves. They weren't money to me in that clarifying moment—were worth so much more than two useless government cents."

Tractor Girl, hanging on every word, had been captivated by this concept. "You just rock my world," she'd said. And Meddy had blushed. "Is that why you use coins?" Tractor Girl had asked. "Because the dates are connected to whatever it's about ... when you do this?"

"No, not usually. That just happened to be how I switched to using coins. Most of the time it's about other things. As I said, it's about whatever meaning I attach to them. And it's also about showing that I don't value or accept or embrace other people's definition of a thing. Ah, hell, this very well may be just one of the many ways I choose to rebel against a society that I have so little respect for. One that has so little respect for me."

"But it's money!" Tractor Girl had said.

"It's pennies," Meddy countered. "What can you buy with a penny? Hell, even gumball machines don't take anything less than a quarter these days."

"Yeah, but ..."

"Look, I read somewhere that it costs the government more to mint a penny than a penny is worth. Now how stupid is it that we live in a country that throws away money like that? *Really* throws it away."

"Okay, but if this is all symbolic anyway, then why coins—I mean, why not something less valuable, like, I don't know, pebbles?" Tractor Girl had asked.

"Well, before that time I was telling you about, I did use stones or pieces of driftwood or even dried up road apples for my spiritual seeds," Meddy had said, "but after the coins up on the Gap that night, I had an epiphany. Pebbles, stones, sticks—these already belong in nature, which is why most people don't value them much, don't even notice them most of the time. And, really, all I had been doing was just moving those things from one part of their natural space to another."

"Ah," said Tractor Girl, who loved a good revelation as much as anyone in SLANT.

"But coins are human-made," Meddy said, "and therefore deemed intrinsically 'valuable.' More, they specifically represent a *consumeritualistic* culture whose sole purpose pits itself, either sooner or later, in direct conflict with nature. When you think about it, metals are mined from nature in the first place. I'm just putting some of it back. In a different way."

Meddy had glanced down at the creek, checking to see if Tractor Girl was hanging in there with this line of thought. She was. And more, she didn't seem to be getting bored with it or weirded out by it.

"So I began to think about coins as little talismans into which I could imagine assigning values that were the exact opposite of their original purpose. If one wanted to devalue consumerism—if one wanted to repurpose a coin, for example—one could, theoretically at least, simply call a penny the seed of an idea and cast it outward in that way. If the idea took root, bore fruit, well, one cent is a pretty good price to pay for a yield of substance … or spiritual sustenance."

TG had nodded, but her brow was haunted with deep-thought creases.

Meddy had said, "None of this is literal—from the idea about the seed, to the 'seed' itself, to what happens next, see?"

Knowing Tractor Girl to be a visual learner, Meddy took a break then, to let the images seep in. TG was steeping in her thoughts. When Meddy saw a look of satisfaction and then epiphany slide across Tractor Girl's face, she continued.

"Conversely, if instead of *planting* an idea I need to *discard* one, then I just name the penny with whatever thought or period or activity I am finished with and toss it out. If I don't need something anymore, I go through the act of sowing it—metaphorically—as a seed that will grow into something that I do need. Or I scatter it like ashes to be put to rest. It's the act and the meaning I attach to it that matters. Well, that and the undermining of money-as-a-god, of course."

"Damn," said Tractor Girl. "That's so smart it hurts."

"The physical sowing or tossing, that's where the power translates from the conceptual to the real. There's something about physically sending things out into the lost unknown—where they are highly unlikely to be recalled by any second thoughts I might have—that makes dealing with them so much less hypothetical, so much more healing," Meddy had said. "It's more real if you can't take it back."

"Does it work every time?" Tractor Girl wanted to know.

It was a question Meddy wasn't prepared to answer, so she simply said, "When you know you can't get something back—well, you better be damned sure you want to chance tossing it into the lost unknown, consequences and all."

They'd been quiet for a couple minutes then, as both women pondered the real, the false, the imaginary, the improbable and the possible.

Meddy finally broke the silence with a half-chuckle. "Honey, don't ever pay too much attention to the ramblings of an old coot. Bottom line: this is just one more crazy thing I do."

Tractor Girl smiled, winked. "Better get on down the knob," she'd said. "Tiny trees to tend, you know." She pushed away from the bank. "You really are something, Miz Meadowlark Nightengale," she said. "One of a kind."

"Puh," Meddy had replied, waving her young neighbor downstream. Meddy, as always, felt uncomfortable with compliments. Nevertheless, her dismissive gesture was good-natured.

One stroke of the paddle. Two. A third. Tractor Girl and Whisper glided into the lazy current and let it do the work. Without looking back, TG raised one arm above her head in benediction, fingers forming the V-shaped peace sign.

And in no more than a whip-stitch, Tractor Girl left Meddy around the bend.

# The Wisdom of Top-Notch Annie, Part 2

"WHEN I WAS BEIN' BORN, I knew ever'thang. All that I needed to know. More than that, even.

"When I was bein' born, there was a double rainbow in the mornin' and a full moon that night.

"When I was bein' born, somebidy loved me, cherished me. Now, that seems rare. Seems impossible.

"When I was bein' born, there was no doubt in my little bones that thangs were about to change forever and for good.

"That didn't last long."

# Temper Unrequited Longings

GOD CREATED THE HORSE; MAN INVENTED THE HARNESS.
Juny understood that better than most; knew all about something wild
and free and powerful having its will broken, its spirit stolen by something humans made. He knew what being controlled by a force other than
his own felt like. How damaging that was. How endlessly deadly.

The station ID at the bottom of the hour was the signal that the
local TV news had ended; it was time for syndication. Juny grumbled and
made a series of awkward stabs toward the channel button on the remote,
jabbing at it furiously with the contraption some damn doctor or other
had hooked to his left stump. *Wheel of Fortune.* He hated that show. That
and *Luck of the Draw.* "Luck, hell! Don't remind me," he'd mutter to the
flickering screen. "Only kind of luck 'round here is bad."

Juny hadn't always been addicted to the TV. Was a time he just didn't
have any extra hours lying around to give to it. *He ain't the sharpest knife
in the drawer,* some who knew him would say—and oh how true that was;
why, he'd not deny it a minute. But even though he found that by now he
couldn't tear himself away from the TV, even when his eyes were as red as
mainland China, he'd always had sense enough to know that there's hardly
anything on it that competed with real life and, especially, with real live
music.

Still yet, Juny sat in a misshapen recliner and watched anything and
didn't care what it was—westerns, comedies, mysteries, cop capers, doctor
dramas, cartoons, love stories, even that unreal "reality" mess they had on
now. If he especially hated it, he punished himself by watching it anyway
(except for *Wheel of Fortune,* of course, the very idea of which he despised
more than even his TV addiction could balance out). Hell, he didn't even
*like* what he was looking at most of the time. If he'd been a thinking
man, he might have found himself wondering just what it was that he
was searching for in all those broadcast waves ... and why he worked so
hard at finding sense among the mystery. He might have searched his
own heart and found what he was looking for a whole lot quicker, but that
would have been too painful.

What it had to do with was music. And fate.

Juny'd started playing the six-string when he was seven—that was a full twenty years before the accident. About all he could say now, when he found himself thinking about it in rare, unguarded moments, was that those were the best twenty years he could ever have asked for. He had nearly convinced himself, after all these years of longing for those dear, lost days, that he was okay with trading the three decades that had since come and gone for those *two* when he was able to make his music his way, fingers flying, voice soaring above the strings. By now, he was so out-of-kilter that he couldn't even let himself be grateful that he hadn't bled to death that day in the field.

But what could he have done different, after all? Told his elderly daddy, out there sweating, screeching and wearing himself down to the eighty-seven-year-old nub he'd become, that he refused to help his old man unjam that old cornpicker? That his hands were valuable instruments he'd prefer not to jeopardize? That he had big plans for what they could do? Why, he'd have been ridiculed off the place! *Whatchoo think you are, jackass, a surgeon? Goddamn concert violinist?* His daddy'd have hooted at him. Might've sneered. *You best figure out where y'bread's buttered, fool.*

How do you tell anything to a scrawny little scrap of a man who'd outlived three wives and had fathered babies up into his late sixties? How do you get a man who has no patience for anything that he doesn't already understand to listen to something new, an idea beyond the tight little world he controlled? Juny's daddy was a tyrant who didn't have the time of day for any kind of work short of hard labor, for that's all he'd ever done and was, by default and by damned, all he placed value on. Anything else was laziness in his book, pure and simple. Laziness and craziness.

Juny'd known from past experience that he wouldn't be heard if he tried to talk to his daddy about his dreams. A man like that can't learn, for he already thinks he knows it all. The old man had six living sons, all named after him, but since he couldn't call them all the same name, he'd given each a nickname: Son, Short, Boy, Pee-low, Junior, Juny. The girls didn't register on his radar; he never called them by name, wasn't even sure how many of them he had, truth be told. Such a man, why, he thinks himself invincible, believes he's got the whole world under his control, and in a way he does—his narrow world, anyway. The family realm was a tiny dictatorship by design. His was abusive and imaginary power. But however misplaced, a tiny power it was nonetheless.

So, Juny never protested during that fateful minute. He wanted to, but he never. Instead he stepped up to that farm machine, tried to grab the blockage and yank it out of that broken-down old corn-picker. But his daddy hadn't shut down the mechanism, so the damned thing grabbed Juny's work gloves—tips of the two middle fingers of his right hand,

thumb on his left—and yanked his arms whole hog into the savage workings of the contraption. This was serious agricultural machinery, made to
rip cornstalks out of hardened ground, tear ears off the stalks, separate
the tough from the tougher. Its bite was fierce—like to've pulled Juny's
arms out of socket.

Wasn't anything could be done, it all happened so fast. His daddy'd hit
the shut-off, pulled him free somehow, dragged him into the truck, those
mangled arms hanging bloody, and drove like a demon to Doc Eli's office
in town. But what can a country doctor do with such a mess, not having
on hand the right facility, help, tools, medicine? Juny's daddy felt real
bad about it later, even kicked and cussed his own best hound for sniffing
around the bloody rags he tossed as he cleaned the gore out of his truck.

The whole affair seemed like yesterday, and it seemed a lifetime ago.
Juny's daddy long since dead, the days now stretched out dreadfully for
this middle-aged man with a half arm and no hands … and no way to do
the *one thing* he was made to do, create the art of song with a six-string
guitar humming under his long-lost fingers. His physical healing being
well over and no need for painkillers anymore, Juny'd turned to the TV
these last few decades for his round-the-clock emotional anesthesia.

He didn't know why he watched; he just watched.

TV is the great numbing factor, the mind-manipulator, the single
most responsible force that undid an entire culture in three generations'
time, and there's no denying that fact. Over his lifetime, Juny had watched
it happen: from black-and-white to color, from three dim channels in the
air to hundreds pouring in from cable and satellite, from educational and
commercial programming to pay-per-view. *Oh, I knowed it wadn't never no
good for me,* he'd admit, but he allowed himself to be addicted all the same
because the addiction eased him, replaced his painful memory, diverted
attention from his irreversible loss. Moreover, he'd come to understand
that almost everybody else in the culture was using it in exactly the same
way as he did, and for pretty much the same reasons, their lives being just
as unbearable, albeit in other ways.

Juny had spent years longing to have his hands back, longing to pick
up a guitar again, longing to make chords and pick out melodies. *Goddamn,*
he'd say, defeated. *They used to say I was a natural. I HAD something.* This
longing was excruciating and it led him to depression, which led him to
excessive drink, which led him to liver damage, which led him to the brink
of death in ten short years. Finally, he gave up the chemical crutch for a
visual one and, ever after, spent his empty hours letting his ears and his
eyes and his thoughts, such as they were, be saturated with the inanity of
TV, TV, TV—every minute of every day and night that he was home. The
thing ran even when he was sleeping, and it entered his dreams to push all
possibility of his own thoughts away. That's the way it had to be. That's

the way he wanted it.

Juny'd sit for hours looking at movies made in languages foreign to him, staring at the characters' mouths to see if he could match up anything with the English subtitles that lay at the bottom of the screen like snakes that had sneaked into a jam cellar where they didn't belong. But one thing he never watched was any kind of music programs. He had enough pressure on him battling the music that slithered into his head when he wasn't vigilant, music he had played those long years back, plus plenty more tunes that he imagined but knew he'd never be able to play now or ever. No, he never watched live music on the TV; the last thing he needed was to see people who still could hold a guitar handle it so much better or (more painfully) so much worse than he'd once been able to.

Losing his hands was just a technicality in most ways. He had adapted to daily life so well that he hardly missed them, didn't remember what his knuckles looked like, whether his fingers had been slender or stubby. Had his palms been smooth or calloused? The backs of his hands, were they once freckled or veined? No matter. It wasn't the hands themselves that he missed, for he'd now lived more years without them than he'd previously lived with them. No, it was the loss of the *music* in those hands, rather than the hands themselves, that he grieved and pined and sorrowed and longed for. And he couldn't get any of it under control in himself; there seemed no end of his yearning to play again, which is why the vapidity of TV was such a balm. *It wadn't my choice to get hooked like this*, he'd tell himself. *Never wanted to depend on this damned Idiot Box.* But addiction was in his personality, he reckoned. He acknowledged that music had been his earliest drug, after all.

Sometimes he would try to find a way out of his grief and depression, starting with reminding himself that at least he wasn't dead yet. But in the end for Juny—who had once tasted the creative gift of an innate, ineffable and thrilling ability—life after the accident was more bearable when it was deadened. Truth was, he had no skills for dealing with the loss of that best part of himself, he couldn't do a thing about it, and he couldn't afford to care. Caring cost him too much, and it wasn't like he had a stockpile of emotional security lying around to draw on. *Come right down to it*, he'd hear himself think, *not being dead yet ain't necessarily a plus.* If he were dead, he wouldn't have to know things that killed him to think of.

Understandably, then, it was so unlike Juny to have gotten up in the midst of *Days of Our Lives* one afternoon to take a drive. He had one of those vans equipped with a special steering apparatus adapted to his amputated limbs, his left arm gone at the elbow, the right just above the wrist. He could drive, but he didn't very often. The set-up felt cumbersome to him, even after all these years. But on that early fall afternoon, he had decided, out of the clear blue sky, to see what was up the road. He felt a quick temptation to be out of earshot of the TV. That damned box was suddenly irritating the living shit out of his heart's last raw spot. And since he had unlearned how to think or wonder about things in general, he followed this urge by instinct alone. At the time, he didn't know why.

About an hour west of the heart of the familiar farmland of Kentucky's Bluegrass region, Juny found himself in a stretch of the Knobs. Funny how those hills popped up out of the flats. As if he'd never noticed them before, he peered at them, these single hills lined up like soldiers marching in a ragged circle. Where they were thickest—on the eastern side of the region—they overlapped each other in depths or layers like the Appalachian mountain range behind them. But here in the west, each seemed to stand of its own accord, one right alongside the next, pretty much. And if he'd kept driving in a straight line, he'd have driven through a gap between the circling hills and gotten beyond them in short minutes, headed further westward where *flat* was pretty much all there was to see.

But Juny didn't keep driving outward; instead, he drove upward. Following that same unexpected instinct that had guided him away from the TV's familiar cool-blue glow, he turned the van onto a two-lane blacktop that acted like it wanted to climb. In minutes, Juny found himself traveling up a winding way into one of those knobs and wondering—*wondering!*—if it had a name. Juny hadn't pursued an original thought in years, but this one got hold of him. Like a field that had lain fallow, was his mind becoming fertile for growing ideas again? Juny didn't know if he was up to it, but on that sudden afternoon he decided to see.

There was something cleansing about that drive, Juny realized later. A thing that parted the cobwebs in his chest and opened his *mind's* eye, the one that could still see something besides the Idiot Box that he'd felt chained to for what felt like forever. Uncomfortable at first, Juny felt as if the terrible longing that had broken his heart and driven him into the hermitage of a small RV with just his TV for company was relaxing its grip, if only a little bit. It scared him some, but Juny kept on climbing, up and around. He couldn't believe the angle of this hill; it was steep and rocky, well-forested, but it revealed little solitary houses and barns tucked away here and there just within sight of the road, and here and there the view opened onto a terraced hayfield, pasture, garden or orchard. Most of the rest, though, was woods. What Juny saw higher up on the knob was a variety of facets of Mother Nature at her most beautiful. In the longevity of his mind having been deadened after years and years of being pounded by TV commercials—repetitive hymns that illuminate America's number one religion, Consumerism—he had been made to forget all about this kind of beauty.

As he rounded yet another of those kiss-your-ass curves he'd been navigating every few minutes, where there was no settlement visible at all, he saw it. *SLANT*, read a sign in the pull-off. *Population 203 (Not Counting the Four-Leggers).*

Juny stopped right there. What else could he do?

He turned off the van and sat looking about from his perch high in the driver's seat. Everything was quiet and still and clear as a bell. He spied a big old friendly-looking dog of uncertain lineage scratching itself in a grader ditch where one well-used gravel path turned off the paved road. "Okay," he said aloud to no one. "So, there's one of the four-leggers, but where are the 2-0-3?" And just then, without thinking it through, Juny did something else that surprised himself; he turned over the engine, put her in gear, and steered his van right onto that lane toward where the gravel bent gently into a forest.

*The People's Court*, or something just as stupid, was blaring away back in his RV, but Juny was up here on the side of a strange, gigantic hill, going toward some curiosity he knew nothing about to see 203 people he didn't know in a place he'd never heard of until half a minute ago. He might end up disappointed. He might find himself in territory where he was unwanted. He might regret going down this path. But even if it turned out there wasn't much there for him, there seemed one and only one reason for his going there, and it was this: any place so aptly named was worth getting a closer look at.

SLANT. Little did he know.

Since that day, Juny arranged to have his camper towed up the knob and back along that gravel lane. Without much hesitation, he had decided to take up residence in SLANT as soon as he'd met some of the people of this crazy little place and they had invited him into their fold. That didn't happen on Day One, of course, but after a few visits, the match was made.

The day Juny got his rig hooked up to power and water, Mayor Sheepwater walked out the gravel path to the little sign beside the paved road. He carried two brushes, one narrow and the other one wide, and two small cans of paint, one blue and the other one white. With the white, he brushed out the 3 in 203. With the blue, he painted in a 4.

Juny's new life is less reclusive than his old. He's developed tight friendships with a number of SLANTers, most notably Birdie, a twenty-something who seems to be regarded as the village's latest Resident Troubadour. Even if that informal title is as empty to outsiders as Farnsley's Mayor-By-Agreement arrangement is, Juny wondered who in their right mind *wouldn't* want to live in a place where Resident Troubadour is an esteemed position, valued by all the people who live there.

Birdie plays her mandolin just like Juny used to play guitar, with the same sensibility and the same feeling. He loves her syncopations from the inside out. He can usually anticipate her every musical move—and when he can't he delights in the twists and turns she throws out there as she improvises. Though it's been frustrating and plain old hard for Juny at times, he has talked her through a lot of new licks, somehow finding ways to describe in mere words how his own fingers would move on those strings if he still had fingers, watching her hands with a knowing eye as she tries what he tells. And Birdie, bless her young woman's heart, has helped Juny see that the music hasn't left him. *It just moved,* she tells him, *from your hands up to your voice. Sing, Juny!*

You ought to hear those two wail together. It's like they were made to do this: the two-handed mandolin girl playing for all she's worth and matching Juny's no-handed lead vocal with the prettiest harmony singing you ever heard. Birds and angels resting in the tops of trees, along with all the residents (two-leggers and four-) on SLANT's sacred ground, have been known nearly to weep when Juny and Birdie cut loose on "Long Black Veil." Oh, he has pondered more than once whether the yearning regret of that particular tune picked by this girl and her way with music is what called him out of that darkened, narrow place he was stuck in on such a pretty afternoon long time back. *Something* surely pulled him up here to SLANT that day, and there's no doubt in Juny's mind that it's the power of music that put the sand back in his hourglass.

He feels like a colt again.

Juny still struggles with his TV habit from time to time, and he goes on viewing binges when the withdrawal gets the best of him. But he wins that fight more often than not these days. Sometimes when he can't fight the pull to watch, he gives in to it until he's bleary-eyed; but even when that happens, Vanna and Pat don't piss him off anymore like they used to. "I've got me a new 'preciation," he'll tell you these days, "for games of chance."

# Appreciate Your Place

THE KNOBS ARE ANCIENT. Geologists call them escarpments—
hundreds of steep, solitary hills that form a ragged, hundred-mile-long
horseshoe, each end of which starts (or stops, if that's your worldview)
at or near the Ohio River. This peripheral band of oddly cone-shaped
hills, never more than thirty miles wide, completely encircles the large
Bluegrass region in Kentucky. At their *western* terminus near Louisville
and on across the river in southern Indiana, there is another little patch
of knobs. But because those on the *eastern* edge of Kentucky's knobs don't
extend over the river into southern Ohio, there aren't enough knobs on
the northern side of the river to close that **U** and make it a complete circle.
Hence the horseshoe, as Alec noted via his geometaphor lecture.

Though the Philosopreacher Joy DuPre calls them "mountains," they
aren't, not by a long shot. The chain of knobs curving around the southern
and western sides of this horseshoe sit a hundred miles and more from
those in the foothills of Kentucky's Appalachian range on the east where
you'll find little towns like Berea and Richmond. Besides, the vast majority
of any given knob elevates to no more than three or four hundred feet,
and though the tallest ones in both Indiana and Kentucky are less than a
thousand feet high, only a handful of them are anywhere near that tall.
Most are puny by comparison with real mountains, yet each knob is
unique.

In truth, at their relatively diminutive height and without differentiation in vegetation as they elevate (said differentiation would be one
defining characteristic of an actual mountain), the knobs are no more
mountains in the conventional sense than Joy is a conventional preacher.
Her ordination had been purchased from an ad in the back of *Rolling Stone*
magazine when she was a teenager in the 1980s, but she took it seriously
all the same and over time developed the sort of personalized theological
spirituality that is by now solid and definable. Her belief set is based
primarily on what Christian faiths call the Golden Rule because, as previously
mentioned, she had found that *every* major religion in the world has a
version that is worded similarly and teaches the same lesson: *always treat*

*people as you want to be treated.* This, Joy believes just as her friend Meddy believed, is the essence of the one thing she values most in the world—fairness.

As for Joy not knowing a mountain from Shinola, well, she had lived her whole life up until a few years ago in griddle-flat Kansas, so what could you expect?

By contrast, there are people in SLANT who do recognize the not-so-subtle differences in vertical landforms. For example, the Billings boys had grown up in the coalfields of central Appalachia—southwest Virginia, to be exact. They were acquainted on a first-name basis with several actual mountains: Big A, Mullins, Baldwin, Sugar Cove, Horn. Having grown up on a rocky creek deep in a narrow holler folded between peaks, they were well aware of what it meant to live in the shadow of several mountains at once. They understood how the lay of the land could delay full sunlight on a garden plot until ten or eleven each morning and then bring the end of direct rays when the sun slid behind the tip of the opposite ridge at two or three that afternoon. It was, quite literally, a narrow view on the workings of the world, but it was the view they had been born into, so it had comforted them as they grew up.

Later on, the eldest Billings brother, Earl, ventured as far west as Kansas City, where he'd served in the U.S. Army during two lost years of his youth. He'd been thunderstruck by the geographic difference he'd witnessed with his own two eyes out there. He wouldn't have had any way of knowing so, of course, but one of his old Army buddies to this day still tells of the sweet hillbilly who, waking against the bus window to view his first sun-up rolling across the vastness of the Great Plains, turned with complete shock on his face to proclaim a discovery: "Look yonder! I never before have seen a whole train all at once't!" Earl had stared in stunned wonderment into that endless vista, and he never quite got over the great, wide emptiness of it. But at his first opportunity, he had left that "squarshed" land, hoping to head for a place with the kind of elevatory variety his heart required. He transferred back east to Ft. Knox, barely outside the western edge of Kentucky's knobs. Once he got out of the service, and not wanting to go back to the hard life of the coalfields, Earl stopped when he stumbled across SLANT and there, as a compromise, he climbed up out of the flats and he stayed.

In time, he convinced two of his brothers—Early and Late (the twins)—to come to SLANT, too, and they put down new roots there with him. Together they ran the Fix-It out of a workshop in SLANT-center. It was the brothers' collective ability to assemble, dismantle, coerce and repair all manner of machinery, gadgets, appliances, engines and so forth that had kept everything in SLANT running for the past many years. If your car broke down, they made it run again. If your water heater busted, they rebuilt it or replaced it. If your septic system backed up, they could handle it. Individually, they have their talents. Together they possess all the skills needed to make everything work, operating collectively as if they themselves are one fine well-greased machine. Because they can fix anything imaginable that is used in the greater SLANT area (save Nooner's computers), the Billings brothers are easily more popular than any god.

But Joy doesn't give up on the idea of capital-G God or lower-case god or gods or goddess or dog or Mother Nature or anything else that SLANTers want to put their faith in, as long as it's the kind of faith that feeds their souls and makes them better people—and, therefore, better contributors in community with others. She knows that people who seek to be as good as people can possibly be will automatically create a good community … as long as they are sincere.

She'll have none of this fake "righteousness." Joy can spot fakery a mile away, and she always calls it like she sees it. This is probably because there were times in her past when she herself had been a creator and consumer of bullshit. (For a number of years before Joy's psyche was fully formed, she had been overly critical, putting down people and their actions almost cruelly just to build herself up—an action she now understands was immature and misguided.) Consequently, she can smell it burning off of a pile of anything. If the bullshit is synthetic, she can readily identify and dispense with it before it does too much harm. Make no mistake, Joy is a believer in many things—and not necessarily the kinds of things that organized religion demands. No, she finds value in what she calls the Organic or sometimes the Natural. For example, real bullshit is about as organic a substance as you could ask for. You can grow enough food to last all winter if you fertilize your summer garden with real bullshit. But synthetic bullshit—political double-talk, for example, or a televangelist guilting people into sending him money that obviously is going directly toward advancing his extravagant lifestyle—well, that just about drives Joy around the bend.

So, bullshit from a bull, no problem. But bullshit from a bully she will not tolerate.

Folks in SLANT nicknamed her simply The Preacher. She is a scholar rather than a minister (though she *is* ordained), but she doesn't mind this funny nickname, mostly because she knows it's meant as a term of endearment from folks who know that being preachy is the very last thing Joy DuPre could ever be. She reads, she listens, she discusses, she suggests, she questions, she considers; however, she never preaches toward anyone or about anything. It has something to do with the red thread of Rachel tied around her left wrist—with that as a reminder, she practices staying away from talking in negatives so there will be no space for negatives to be sent her direction. Kabbalah, she learned it is called, but that's just one of many pieces of the world's religions that she practices.

As noted, Joy is something of a collector of spiritual philosophies and rituals. Her life's work is tied up in finding the best in each of the world's belief systems. Her goal is to use all those bits to create something actually meaningful and practicably applicable, something that amounts to *a better way*. So, it makes sense that Joy is doing her work in SLANT because folks are open to it—not only tolerant, they're curious.

Joy, who grew up in the Black Church tradition (AME, to be exact), happens to be one of SLANT's Black villagers, and not the only one, either. (From its inception, SLANT has cultivated diversity less by being intentionally inclusive than by intentionally *not* being exclusive.) Joy feels fortunate to be living in a community where she can do her research and develop her philosophy and discuss her findings and theories in the midst of diverse, trustworthy, supportive, curious thinkers—and *great* conversationalists—some of whom (like her friend Meddy) challenge her beliefs relentlessly. But true to her cultural traditions (and to the whole reason SLANT exists), Joy always welcomes a good old intellectual challenge.

Shy, we ain't.

What our Resident Philosopreacher appreciates most about the knobs is not topography, it is history. The fact that these landforms are little more than remnants of erosion over eons of time is easily translated into symbolism that thrills her. "Just look around you," she often says to Knobs region newcomers. "We're what's left intact after all the weakness is washed clean away." (Like Meddy and Alec, Joy has always loved sinking her teeth into a meaty metaphor.)

You see, the knobs' hard capstone rock, often limestone or granite, remained long after glacier melt had eroded the softer shale and siltstone into the wide valleys. Agricultural specialists point out that soil in the knobs region isn't very good; it often "goes to pieces" when cultivated. Gardens are grown, of course, but the slopes of these knobs themselves are too steep to farm on any large scale, apart from the success of orchards that have been developed on some knobs' tops, as well as micro crops grown in relatively small tillable areas in creek bottoms and terraces here and there. The sturdy limestone cores of hills that were once surrounded by that crumbling shale are what remain to this day. Their jutting profiles and steep cliffs are evidence of glacial erosion and the runoff of melting which gradually rinsed the softer soils and substances away from the only rock with strength enough to stand up against the constant pressure of water wear.

So, knobs are pretty much just forested rock, not easily negotiated and not readily tamed. But they support an abundance of life, both the naturally wild and the humanly domesticated kinds. The fact that trees, with their long roots and heavy tops, grow enthusiastically in the Knobs

never ceases to amaze Joy. When you drive along cuts where roads come
through, you can plainly see that there isn't much more than a foot or two
of topsoil (much of it clay) resting on scores of yards of solid rock. Yet
these giants of nature thrive somehow, she supposes by thrusting their
arboreal roots into cracks and crevices and taking hold—a death grip, of
sorts. Trees love it here.

By severe contrast, in central Appalachia's coal country, some hundred
miles or more to the east (another place where negotiating and taming the
terrain is problematic), there is a valuable mineral inside those real mountains: coal that fuels electric power plants.

The Appalachians are said to be the oldest mountains in the world,
but for more than a century, men with greed on their minds and confusion
in their hearts have stopped at nothing to extract coal, one of the world's
most coveted resources, a compacted fossil fuel that is hard as rock. To
get at it, ruthless coal operators have blown to bits mountains that are
many times larger than any of these knobs that Joy has come to know.
Coal companies regularly take a third to a half of any given 2,000- to
3,000-foot-high mountain, dump the "spoil" into the source headwaters
and tributaries that join over the miles to become America's greatest
rivers, and then they scrape and haul away the coal. Foolish men have
done this over and over and over again in the coal-bearing mountains
of West Virginia, Kentucky, Virginia and Tennessee until much of the
midsection of the long Appalachian chain that stretches from Maine to
Alabama is irreversibly imperiled.

The very thought of it makes The Philosopreacher's pupils contract.

Men of greedy clarity and moral confusion have also looked to the
Knobs for ways—like the televangelists Joy is permanently weary of—to
line their pockets. Fossil fuel industries "own" some politicians outright,
so they can do whatever they please in Appalachia. Thankfully, the Knobs
have little such profit-mongering potential and so have been left largely
alone. Oh, there has been some quarrying of sandstone and limestone, but
these are used for building, not for burning. There is use of limited gas
pools in a small arc of the Knobs region. Shale oil was considered a viable
possibility for a time but, for the most part, was determined not cost-
effective or plentiful enough to amount to a major supply source. And so,
the human locusts moved on to devise some other profit-driven exploitation in some other place. But Joy knows they'll come back when they have
exhausted the easier targets. She can't trust them not to make all of rural
America one big energy colony for the urbanites. It's just a matter of
time. She says she hopes not to live long enough to see this horror come
nearer to SLANT.

Joy has, by now, come to understand that while the time-resilient
knobs were spared because of their lack of marketable mineral, those

real mountains to the east, the ones with coal in them, are hers to embrace too. This is in part because the *Rolling Stone* preacher has developed a spiritual understanding based on her favorite Native American saying: *when one strand is plucked, the whole web vibrates.* The very streams that feed the Ohio River—and smaller ones that feed its Knobs region tributary, the Kentucky River—originate in those Appalachian coalfields. So, whenever a thousand feet of rock is removed to get at a two-foot-thick coal seam, all that stone and debris has to go somewhere—and where it goes is into the hollers, covering, killing or polluting the streams that are the source of water that *millions* of people depend upon.

The Philosopreacher and Meadowlark Nightengale have had many conversations around this topic of stewardship and the lack of it. Even though each approached spiritual fulfillment and philosophical thought in unique ways, either would have been hard-pressed to take the "pro" side of mountaintop removal mining, even to play devil's advocate for the sake of healthy debate. In short, this is so bad that neither could quite believe it could still be going on.

"You know, don't you, that those coal men shove what they call 'spoil' off the side of the mountain because it's in their way?" Joy said. "They've even got a name for it: *overburden.* Can you believe that?"

"Arrogance," said Meddy.

"Yes?"

"Their arrogance, these coal men, is so … casual," Meddy explained. "They feel utterly free to cast their unwanted waste onto whatever lies beneath the naked new rims of those old hills they're murdering."

"And don't be fooled …" Joy began.

"I'm never fooled!" Meddy said.

"I well know that," Joy said. Meddy threw her a look. "I do know! But lots of people *are* fooled," the Philosopreacher clarified, "often because they hide their sin behind fringes of trees they leave alongside adjacent roadways, blocking the view of what they've done."

Meddy just shook her head in disgust.

Joy went on. "King Coal's minions are full well aware that the industry is slaughtering or poisoning the water supply of everyone living down-stream—the science has clearly told them so."

"Hell," said Meddy, "what do they care about science? Science is a gnat buzzing around their ears; little less than some puny annoyance. All they care about is profit—science be damned."

"And in their eagerness to profit," Joy put in, "they simply declare science invalid." They both shook their heads in disgust. "And to further complicate things, the so-called 'valley fills'…"

"You mean 'holler stoppers.'"

"Right. All that 'overburden,' as they blithely call it, completely eliminates natural rain-carrying watersheds," Joy said. "Gravity being what it is, water will find its way off a mountain. All that water has to go somewhere."

"So, where it goes now is, what, everywhere?"

"Yep. Repeated flooding, especially where the creeks are filled with that strip-mine waste. Devastates the poor landowners below those surface mines," Joy said. "When spiritual people point out that this flies in the face of stewardship—which the Bible condones, of course—those coal men counter that 'God put the coal there for man's use!'"

"So, God commands man to blow up His own mountains to get at coal?" Meddy's sarcasm was edging in.

"Therefore ..."

"According to their 'illogic' ..."

"Right, they claim they're only acting in accordance with God's wishes when they destroy God's creation."

"As Nooner frequently says, 'Shit rolls downhill,'" Meddy said, then asked (sarcastically, of course) how those coal men had the power to fathom the mind of God, and Joy said she did not know, for she was pretty sure such a thing was not possible.

"Still, that's their claim: God meant them to destroy His or Her creation for man's selfish 'needs,'" Joy said, and the very thought deflated her.

"*Needs?* 'Wants' is really what it is." Meddy used her trademark air-quotes.

"And all the people said, 'Amen,'" Joy replied. No air-quotes required.

The friends pondered separately until Meddy wondered aloud, "What kind of god would reward that behavior, now or ever? And who in the living hell *are* these men—without any ability to *recreate* the things they destroy—who are they to dismiss their own God?"

"They ransack the very earth that keeps them alive, I'm afraid," Joy said.

"The greed of the greedy," said Meddy, "always obscures the needs of the needy."

"I'm gonna use that," said Joy.

"Of course you are," Meddy said, "and I wouldn't have it any other way."

It was difficult, but Joy, thinking back on this conversation a few days later, tried to focus on not judging those men; rather, she set herself to worrying about the state of their spirituality, the unhealthy egos they worshiped within themselves, the untended gaps in their collective conscience. It soon became apparent, however, that she was more worried about their souls than they were, for in spite of a growing public outcry against the actions of these greedy energy corporations and the men who ran them, the culprits not only ignored pleas to stop doing damage, they continually refused to acknowledge the irreverence of their handiwork. And their pockets were deep enough to keep it that way. They even made up t-shirts that read, shockingly, on the front side *Earth First* ... but on the back, predictably, *we'll mine the other planets later.* Talk about arrogance!

"Do you really think," Joy asked Meddy one still afternoon when it was too hot to work and too early to sleep, "that people outside the coalfields are so entrenched that they have no conception of their own complicity in this? I mean, I find it alarming, really alarming, that this is happening right here in America and nobody seems to care. It's a travesty."

"Why?" Meddy said. "Why would the selfishness of Americans alarm you at this late date? Most of the urban ones no longer know where their food comes from, most of the rest don't know where their electricity comes from, none of them know where their health care has gone, the most crazed right-wingers among them don't recognize that their so-called leaders are intentionally shutting down democracy for personal gain—and they don't, for the most part, care."

"Maybe it's not the selfishness that worries me, or even the lack of knowledge, but the numbers," the Philosopreacher said. "That's what's alarming. The sheer number of utilities customers who run their appliances non-stop. They leave lights on while they sleep—even while they're gone, even in broad daylight! They don't seem to care that their selfish energy demand is a huge part of the problem."

"But what're you gonna do?" Meddy said. "Nearly everybody in America has bought into the nation's consumerism addiction. They jones for entertainment gadgets, gizmos, doohickeys and thingamajigs of their very own—all the useless crap that snarfs up electricity like there's no tomorrow. Those people are the demand that insists on the supply. And those greedy coal shareholders are getting rich off a national addiction they've intentionally encouraged."

"I'm guessing that the farther away from the devastation, the more, well, ignorant of just how much their demand for coal-fired energy matters," Joy said. "Hundreds, thousands of miles from where coal is mined, we just flip switches on without a thought."

"Americans are notorious for taking things for granted," Meddy said dryly.

"It's not even necessarily intentional, I don't think," Joy said. "These snowballing consumerism habits …."

"… taught by national TV addiction," Meddy finished. "Internet too."

"Could be," The Philosopreacher agreed. "Probably. Certainly, in fact. But it proves to me one sure, sad thing: in general, and *in spite of* all the religious fervor these days, we seem to be becoming a soulless nation."

"Everything always goes back to the one big troublesome tap root," Meddy declared. "A root that's as hard to pull as privet. A complex, metaphorical root system that spreads and spreads and spreads until it's out of control."

"The love of money? That root of all evil?"

"Nope. Power," said Meddy. "Power in any form. And in our capitalistic system, usually power is manifest in money, yes. Almost everybody wants power of some sort, but when it comes to 'cheap' electric power ..."

Joy finished the thought, "... practically nobody recognizes what it *really* costs—especially at the source. Health, safe water, that sort of thing."

Meddy sighed. Joy closed her eyes. They both knew there wasn't much more to say about this. Who among us doesn't feel powerless in the face of it?

Meanwhile, folks in those ruined coalfields, including the Billings brothers' relatives, and their relatives' neighbors, were suffering. The water quality was getting worse; the coal jobs were playing out. They felt powerless over their own lives, but they wanted to blame someone, so they blamed environmental conservationists—whose only sin was illumination.

The pain of people in the coalfields was economic, physical and psychological, but the longer that pain went ignored and untreated, the more completely they acclimated themselves to it. It seemed a particularly ironic form of suffering, too. These were, very generally speaking, people shell-shocked from having been kept in generational poverty and forced to live in an unnaturally ravaged homeland, yet they parroted the economic ideas that had been brainwashed into them for generations: *If not for Coal, we'd have no jobs at all. If not for Coal, we'd not be able to feed our families. If not for Coal, our churches and schools would have to close. If not for Coal, our communities would cease to exist.* These had become mantras, empty chants that surfaced by rote because there were none others in the generations-deep collective psyche.

*If not for Coal,* they seemed truly to believe, *we'd all die a horrible, lonely, painful death.* But the irony of that already being their unhealthy reality escaped them.

Joy realized that many residents of central Appalachia thought of Coal as Father—which is just what King Coal wanted them to think: *If not for Coal, we'd not even exist. King Coal made us; we owe it our very lives.* In that region, Coal is a whole different kind of fundamentalist religion.

Oh, but like most dictators, this King also perpetuated lies within lies: *The burning of Coal isn't responsible for damaging the planet's atmosphere. There's no such thing as global climate change. Scientists are ridiculous, egg-headed laboratory dwellers who don't know a thing about the real world. Climate activists are over-educated meddlers. Anything you hear on NPR is leftist Commie lies.*

"King Coal's message," the Philosopreacher found herself telling anyone who would listen, "is just about the worst example of synthetic bullshit ever spread. It'll not grow a thing but worse." Joy didn't mean this as judgment; to her, it was a simple statement of fact. King Coal had concocted—why not call it what it was?—the Big Damned Lie. She believed any neutral person looking at the situation would be able to see said fact in all its transparent horror. Trouble was, not everyone was neutral; most people were far from it.

True to form, she talked to the Billingses about this to see if she could more fully understand why the men who operated King Coal's industry were able, at their own whims, to blow up so many dear mountains (and entire living ecosystems that dwelled within them), regardless of the dangers and the suffering it caused people and creatures living right there. To her surprise, all three of the Billings brothers seemed automatically and passively indoctrinated to the "good" of the coal industry's presence, though it was literally ripping apart the place that had formed them.

However, when pressed, Late did admit that he was concerned about the destruction of land that he had witnessed back home in Virginia. "They've tore it up pretty bad," he remembered. "Wise County's nearly gone. I reckon maybe that was part of my reason for leaving the home-place. The hills I knew ain't even hardly there no more. You cain't find thangs that used to be, thangs I thought always would be. So, when I left there, didn't seem like I was leaving the same place I'd growed up in, nohow."

Early backed him up. "I seen some strip jobs, them gigantic MTR sites," he said. "The size of them draglines, man, you wouldn't believe!"

"I saw one," Late put in, "that was so huge, the cab alone of that dragline was big as the Haysi Tigers' gym—just that one machine!"

"Takes but a handful of men to operate it, drive them trucks and dozers and loaders, set charges to blast out the rock," Early said. "Hell, a dozen men can take down a whole mountain in a few months' time."

Joy was shocked. "No way!"

"Way!" said Late. "I seen it. Ever'bidy up home knows it, but ain't nobidy doin' nary thang about it."

"They got to work, got to feed their families," Earl chimed in, right on cue and just as King Coal had conditioned him to.

But it was a fallacy. As a result of those conversations—and especially once Joy (having read books and studied websites rich with verified information and hard data) learned that obscenely large machines run by a scant handful of "miners" were actually causing Appalachia to hemor-rhage jobs in the region's primary industry—she became more worried about King Coal's victims: the families who live in the very heart of the coalfields. She worried about both their future and the quality of life under which they currently live.

Meanwhile, The Big Damned Lie became more and more obvious to Meddy and Joy, who hadn't grown up being brainwashed by it. It was the brainwashing that fascinated Joy the most. She got to thinking about something she'd heard once—how hostages can bond with their captors, even defend them.

"Remember ever hearing about a psychological condition that hostages experience?" she asked Meddy one day. For reasons unknown to her, she knew it had a city's name attached to it but couldn't remember which city.

"Sounds familiar," Meddy said.

Joy pulled up the search app on her smartphone, typed in "hostage disorder." Up it popped: *Stockholm Syndrome.*

"Here it is!" She read through a number of explanations from various links, summarizing quickly for the benefit of her friend who listened intently, nodding along to indicate that she was taking it all in.

The descriptions were pretty much the same (as it turned out, the Philosopreacher could have stopped at plain old Wikipedia). Based on their research, experts from different links mostly agreed on the syndrome's definition. The criteria perfectly fit the pattern Joy thought she had anecdotally identified through observation and informal research: the coal industry (1) claimed to be in control of the victims' basic survival needs; (2) kept the victims dependent and isolated to carefully withhold, deny or deflect contrasting information; (3) threatened their lives (in this case by threatening their livelihoods and communities); and (4) wrapped itself in a "good guy" image through which it pretended to extend kindness, benevolence, aid and protection *to the very people it imperiled.*

"This is one hell of a mind game," Meddy said.

"It is," Joy agreed, "but it's worked for so many generations that, obviously, it's become a way of life in those coalfields communities. They don't question it."

"With a warped worldview like that," Meddy said, "how in the hell would you ever get victims to question it ... or break the cycle?"

"Well, that's exactly it, isn't it?"

Joy found King Coal's self-crafted image of "savior" especially unpalatable. Even an atheist would have cringed. It was difficult for her to imagine, especially in rural America, that self-proclaimed "Christians" could allow such an idea to develop, much less embrace it so vocally and whole-heartedly. *What a dirty little secret,* she thought, *hidden right here in plain view.*

The more she looked at the situation, the more she realized that it was bigger than anything she had previously understood.

"The damage goes far beyond mining," she said to Meddy one day. "It's larger than the environmental issue, larger than the poverty issue, larger than the health issue, larger than the selfish messaging from a patronistic past that still controls both modern mining and religion in Appalachia."

"Oh, you think?" Meddy was beginning to exhale emotional fumes. She was way past this point of logic. The Philosopreacher ignored the edge in her friend's tone.

"I'm saying that this goes much, much deeper—a metaphorical labyrinth fashioned after the old underground mine tunnels: below the surface, invisible to the eyes of most," Joy said. "It's a matter of massive and systematic corruption that amounts to the moral deception and cultural oppression of an entire people over generations—and all carried out in the name of 'good.'"

"I'll tell you what it is." Meddy's voice rose. "I'll tell you exactly what it is! It's kin to the tactics of Jim Jones' People's Temple or those notorious damned Nazi Brownshirt youth methods, those mass indoctrinations."

*It is,* The Philosopreacher realized. *This is brilliantly devious; the best of the worst.* It made her shudder. For a white-hot fuel, coal's harmful history left her cold.

When a few days later Joy explained her Stockholm-Syndrome-of-Central-Appalachia theory to the Billings boys (far from "boys," Earl's younger twin brothers were actually in their forties), they smiled and wagged their heads thoughtfully and said polite things like, "Hunh. Ain't that a trick. Well, now." But the Philosopreacher could tell that they didn't know what to do with this new knowledge. She could tell that they had been dragged too far into the Big Damned Lie to exhibit the immediate outrage she expected. The *revelation* that must precede the *revolution* just couldn't get a foothold in their thought paths. If, in their homeland, King Coal was the daddy-figure, well, they couldn't be expected to suddenly turn against *family*, after all. Their culture had pointedly taught them that, too.

After that conversation, Joy was left to ponder what exactly she had expected. People are proud and don't like to think they can be easily hornswoggled, she realized. Anyway, if there was one thing she had learned in all her years as a bona fide *Rolling Stone* preacher, it was this: you can lead a horse to water, but you can't make him drink if he's scared—not even if he's dying of thirst.

And what if, she thought to add, it's a person's own "daddy" who has fucked up the water supply ... but still insists that it's safe as a church-house baptismal font? That was a circumstance our Philosopreacher knew was risky for mind, body and soul.

It all seemed fairly grim and hopeless, albeit not in SLANT's immediate front or back yard. There wasn't much to feel good about, not much to joke about. But leave it to Meddy to find a way.

"There's one thing I just don't understand," Meddy said on a day when they had talked and talked about how it was mostly about polluting the sources of water, that sustenance of life. They had come to realize that the destruction of much of America's southeastern region's water supply—even for people so far downstream that they are well out of sight of those endless, ugly moonscapes left by surface mining—is the worst and most far-reaching consequence of all … especially since healthy water, for humans and other animals, isn't exactly an optional element in their survival. "Just one thing I can't seem to wrap my head around," she continued.

"What's that?"

"You'd think," said Meddy, "if the Billings brothers have no *other* reason to care about what's happening in the coalfields they once called home, they'd at very least look out for their own interests and the libational concerns of the rest of us."

"How so?" The Philosopreacher asked.

"Well, hell," Meddy said, her crooked grin sneaking up on Joy. "Those Billingses've got to consider all of us brother and sister SLANTers who depend on their liquid-refreshment import business." (This referred to the off-the-books enterprise centered on selling mountain-distilled spirits that the boys bring to SLANT after every trip back home.) "Don't those boys realize that without good water in the hills and hollers of their youth, *the quality of the moonshine will go completely to hell?* Doesn't that matter to 'em at all?"

Joy cracked up. "Meddy," she said, "have I ever told you how crazy I am about your mind? It keeps mine on its toes."

Meddy laughed then. "Mix metaphors much?" she said. "I mean, I've heard of 'tow-headed,' but never have I given much thought to 'toe-minded,'" she said.

Joy, rolled her eyes and tried in vain to put on a scolding face. Shaking her head slowly side-to-side she said, "Look, everybody in SLANT knows you love a pun like Stinkum loves rolling in fresh deer shit, but Meddy my friend, you might want to rethink that last one."

"I'm just *saying* what I'm *saying*."

Joy dropped pretense and tossed a great big grin skyward. "Sister-woman, that's *exactly* why you're you."

# Mediate All Madness

"WHAT YOU DO IS EVIDENCE of what you believe."

It was Alec's latest epiphany, although he thought he was quite convincing in presenting this concept *as if* he'd embraced it, absorbed it, shared it for years. He looked from the willow oak to the ash tree to the enormous limestone boulder that was tipped precariously close to tumbling off the bank and into Fidelity. He was pretty sure the three were buying his ruse. Plus of all (he hastened to remind himself), he was a gifted actor, so no wonder they were onboard.

"Yes, I'm talking to you," he said to the sudden breeze that moved into his face and past his sweat-plastered hair. "I'm talking to all of you. To everything. Listen."

In one of his most polished trademark moves, Alec angled his chin upward and paused—*tres dramatique*, he thought—so that his audience would have a moment to prepare to absorb the full import of his statement. Which they'd better do in a hurry, because he was about to blow their minds.

"What you *do*," he repeated, more emphatically than was necessary, "is clear evidence of what you *believe*.

"And, by extension, what you believe is evidence of what you *think*.

"And what you think is evidence of what your brain *perceives*.

"What you perceive is evidence of what you *experience* ... or *suspect* you experience.

"What you experience is evidence of what you *do*.

"And what you do ... well, there you are again. It's a closed circuit." Alec let that soak in. "And by the way ... it can short out."

He hesitated only slightly before heading toward home, leaving his unusual audience to internalize this cycle of wisdom. He could practically hear the circular pieces click into place inside the "minds" of his unlikely listeners. Oh, they got it all right—but their pointy heads had all but exploded in the getting!

Big stuff. Not for everybody.

Walking through woods lit by a calming moon glow, Alec reflected on situations that concerned themselves with the complicated relationships between and among the physical and the psychological aspects of existing. Of being alive. He reasoned that those examples were taste tests of the many gourmet stews made from assorted human characteristics—the advantages and limitations of the body finding itself in a mash-up with the psyche's spiritual and the mind's emotional and the brain's magical thinking capability.

Quite suddenly and aloud Alec asked *himself,* "What are *you* capable of?" He stopped mid-step, one foot raised, and froze that way for seconds, maybe half a minute, looking for all the normal world like a startled cartoon character. Both eyebrows clamped high and tight on his forehead. This was a new question, and it had an obvious place in the continual evolution of his complicated theories.

As he'd predicted, he short-circuited.

How on earth could one *know* what one is capable of?

"Further, how can you prove it? What might be *evidence* of what you are capable of?" he heard himself ask. "And is *every* action *always* evidence of belief?"

He'd be all night and most of next week working that one out. He'd need to remember to breathe. Often.

All he knew for sure is what Longfellow had once said. It was something like: *We judge ourselves by what we feel capable of doing, while others judge us by what we've actually done.*

"Better stock up on green onions," he said. It was to be his last practical thought for days.

# Feast At The Common Table

TO LIVE IN SLANT WAS *NOT* to live in the past. As I've already told
you, The Jimmies had been a mere twenty-something years old when
they founded SLANT. Born in 1940, just as the Great Depression was
winding down, though the nation's ear was attuned to the drums of
another world war (complete with rationing), The Jimmies had been
raised by parents, teachers and caretakers who would always be haunted
and influenced by that decade of scarcity and worry that had preceded their
births, as well as by Roosevelt's "fear itself" that followed. The Jimmies'
respective parents and grandparents, in spite of their relative affluence, had
known the impact of the Depression and the hellacious consequences that
waited close at hand for one fatal slip in judgment. War in both Europe
*and* the Pacific was just plain confusing to the entire culture, and further
fed their trepidation.

In one way or another, these crises entangled every family in the land.

The Jimmies themselves, along with other affluent segments of their
generation, however, had witnessed only prosperity for most of their lives.
Though they were too young to remember much of the bad firsthand,
the war had ushered in a new era of women at work, peak production in
factories and the development of new media and technologies. By the time
they were about ten, several years after the war of their youth had ended,
America entered the prosperous 1950s, a decade during which they were
completely aware of the larger world around them. The nation's highway
infrastructure exploded with new development, automobiles took on a
radical new look, air travel expanded, television was popping up in urban
places, Sputnik ushered in a brand new universal paradigm, and the
possibility of colonizing off-planet became real enough to elicit wonder
beyond science fiction. After the passing of another decade, the country
entered the 1960s, where possibilities seemed limitless. All eyes were
turned to the starry heavens as the U.S. space program blasted off
toward a single goal: to have its own humans reach the moon before
the Soviets did.

So, while the Jimmies' personal experiences had little in common with their parents' and grandparents' experiences, they admittedly were influenced by their elders' ideas of how people should behave. And even when the generations didn't understand each other at all, they still trusted each other—personally, at least. It was a strange dichotomy; one that will die with the Baby Boomers. We can only hope.

"I'm a Victorian in a lot of ways; it's mostly ingrained in me against my will," Jimi would explain years later. "And, as Arthur Godfrey used to say, I come from a line of long livers!"

Nooner, who has always loved hearing Jimi's life tales, has told me that he will sit with her anytime he can catch her in a talking mood.

"One of my grandfathers was born shortly after the end of the Civil War," Jimi once told him. "Think of it: that's just two generations removed from me. He lived a hundred years, witnessed two major economic depressions, both world wars and a whole lot more."

"Did he talk about it? Do you remember any of his stories?" Nooner asked. He refilled her glass of iced green tea sweetened with honey. He'd steeped it with a bit of ginseng and ginger root. It was crisp, just the way Jimi liked it.

"All too well, I'm afraid. We lived by his rules, and they were based on the Victorian-era 'norms' imposed on him in his youth." She sighed. "My father followed suit. Conducted himself as his father demanded. Wanted to be a good son, I s'pose, the only way he knew how." Here Jimi paused in a remembrance almost too personal to articulate. "Thought he knew how to be a good father, too. Poor man."

"And how'd that work out for you?" Nooner grinned as he asked this, for he knew Jimi fairly well by now. Knew too that the founders of SLANT had a vision that was altogether different from those held-over Victorian ways of their parents and grandparents.

"They tried to press their ideas on me but, you know…The '60s. That is, *NINETEEN*-Sixties." She shook her head. "Still, some of their century-old influence stuck. Now that I'm beyond my eighth decade of life, I can see value in some of it—manners in personal interactions, that sort of thing. *Civility*, they would call it." She smiled at this. Nooner loved her smile.

"But," he'd said, "how's it all fit? Ever'bidy that knows you at all knows how much you value, I don't know, *rebellion* is the word, I guess."

"And outrageous imagination, too! These are the two things that push those old Victorian notions back into their own time," Jimi said. "Rebellion, imagination—these scared my parents and grandparents to death. We were a generation that they had no context for understanding. The world just changed too fast for them. Threatened everything they knew. The shock alone scared 'em nearly to death." Her thoughts seemed far away. "I have witnessed the creation of a completely new world in a single lifetime. Not all good, but definitely all remarkable."

Any time Jimi sighed, Nooner felt her whole history exhale.

It would be a misrepresentation of life in SLANT to paint its portrait as an old-timey, back-to-the-land, agriculture-based commune. SLANT is, generally speaking, not a throwback. Over time, people acquired satellite dishes and Internet connections and cell phones. Nooner himself, of course, operates a web-based business out of an office he constructed by adding on to one of the original sharecropper cottages. Certainly, SLANTers embrace cutting-edge technologies when such innovations (A) help and (B) can be used responsibly.

What they don't buy into is those politically-motivated, consumer-driven social structures that have sucked in most of the rest of the country. In this regard, SLANTers are grateful to have been welcomed into a community of like-minded people, and they're happy to give back. More often than not, they barter among themselves for everything they can.

One thing that can accurately be said of SLANT is that besides our obvious liberal thinkers, there are many among us who are moderates too (the Billingses, for example, and Juny and Dick and Horse). But here's the overarching element that draws us together and makes us work so well: in SLANT, everybody feels good about contributing, everybody feels good about receiving, and everybody feels great about cutting out the middle man—for the chain of middle men is the real money drain in any capitalist society, and that kind of waste is something SLANTers like to avoid whenever possible

The lack of guilt that exists in SLANT is admirable, too. The community wasn't built on any models; it had begun with The Jimmies' smoky vision (they jokingly like to call it a "joint" vision), and it has evolved organically from there.

After only a few years, The Jimmies had welcomed enough like-minded people into SLANT that they didn't feel solely responsible for the place anymore. Those who joined them fully embraced the idea of giving and getting in equal measure, thereby embodying the true spirit of "community," just as The Jimmies had envisioned.

Growing older, SLANT's founders relaxed into the reality of the place they had dreamed up on that magical day in 1964—the pipe dream that revealed itself as they sat in repose against the windshield of that silly old car of their youth.

Eventually, The Jimmies put SLANT into a land trust to be administered by a revolving committee of residents made up of anyone in SLANT over age twenty-one who wants to participate. It is working beautifully so far. The idea of community ownership is far more appealing than private ownership to people in SLANT. They actually like the idea of sharing responsibility, and each eagerly pulls her or his or their weight. This is because SLANTers aren't shirkers. SLANTers deeply care both about each other individually and about the community as a whole.

Nooner will tell you that he is delighted with the arrangement. He says he feels no need to own anything himself, but he loves the idea of being part of some shared experience larger than his own little life.

Talking with Jimi always makes Nooner think.

"Rebellion and imagination," he repeated.

"Some eras are stagnant," Jimi said. "Stable, some would call that, but I say *stuck*. Other periods require something more. A different energy. Innovation. Vision. Whatever you want to call it. The '60 and '70s were that kind of era. I think we've come into the next of those cultural shifts now, don't you?"

Nooner tightened his lips and lifted his chin in thought. "Might be," he said. "I don't know if it's better or worse overall."

"Doesn't matter. What matters is that it's *your* time," Jimi said. "I don't have the energy for struggling anymore."

"But you blazed the trail!"

"No, dear one, that was a whole different trail," Jimi said. "I won't be around to travel on this new path. I'm already nearly at the end of my journey, which will stop right here in SLANT."

"Now ..." Nooner said.

"Oh, don't mistake what I'm saying. I'm fine with that. It's time. It's good! I've had a fine life, rebelling and innovating and imagining and carrying on. Dreaming of the better world we all want."

"Dreaming and *acting* on it!" Nooner put in.

"That's right," Jimi said simply. "But I don't have a future anymore; all I've got now is a past. So, I can't tell you how much pleasure it gives me to pass the torch to you younger folks. As Jimmy and I have always said, our younger SLANTers have never ceased to make us proud."

"But can you trust us not to screw up your vision?" Nooner asked.

"Honey, it's your vision now. Our time's come and gone. Over'n'done with. Thanks for the memories, and all that rot. You can't possibly screw up our vision because we already used that up—and we had a helluva good time in the process!"

But Nooner wasn't quite prepared to let the conversation move to its next phase. "I'm not sure I'm ready," he said.

"You are," Jimi said softly. "You're capable; you're perfect. And I trust you."

"But no pressure, right?" Nooner grinned.

Jimi reached over and patted Nooner's hand, then took hold of his strong young knuckles with her knotty fingers. Nooner looked down, noticing—more than he ever had before—the browning speckles and blotches on her skin. It alarmed him.

"No pressure from this old gal, at all," Jimi said. "I'm content to slip casually into my dotage. You want to make me feel okay about growing old? Tell me I don't have to worry about leaving SLANT until the very day I die."

"Not on your life, Jimi," Nooner said. "Not as long as I'm sheriff of this gol-danged, one-horse town."

Jimi grinned with glee at this, for it was an old routine of theirs. Nooner beamed because he'd made her smile and wished he knew how to show this elder how much of his heart she occupies.

"Not on your life," he repeated. "We need you."

"Even in my impending or perhaps *established* infirmity?" she asked. Her eyes betrayed mischief.

Nooner went serious on her again. "How will we do any of this without you?" he asked quietly.

"Oh, you will, my darlin' boy. You will."

"Don't make us, though. Okay?" Nooner said. "Just hang around, will you?"

"It'll be a long while yet," she said. "I'm a tough old bird."

Nooner looked everywhere but into Jimi's face.

"Hell, I'm not even sick! Look here, Nooner, honey," she said and turned his chin toward her with gentle fingertips. "You've got plenty of time to get ready. I'm just old—but I'm not yet at death's door!" She smiled. "Still, the day will come. You do need to know that."

His eyes brimmed, but they didn't spill. He was glad of that much. "I ..." He tried, but he choked.

"I know you love me, darlingest boy. I love you back. But can we not get all sentimental about it yet?" she said. "Let's just know it and show it, why don't we? Just see it and be it."

Jimi knew she had been something of a grandmother figure to this young man for the past few years, ever since the day he'd arrived at SLANT. He was a grandson to her, too. But from her perch many years higher in the tree of life than his own, she could warble the joy of this, while all he could feel was distance and a premonition of loss.

The idea broke his heart.

"Don't you start mourning too soon," she grumbled. "You'll steal the power of the real thing when it rolls around."

"I got you," Nooner said. "And I hear you."

"You better. When the time comes, I'll count on you most of all. Hmm?"

He looked right into her vivid green eyes (she always called her own eye color "green-godDAMmit" because they were so noticeably bright and bold), and he nodded. She gave him a single nod back, then lifted the tea glass to her lips and gazed up toward the crown of the tree line.

The last full shafts of sun were taking their time dissipating.

The day's dusk still awfully early in its threat, they sat a while longer, drinking in the leisurely waning of SLANT's own brand of light.

There was no hurry for these friends to part, an elder and a younger at home in their world.

# Be Vigilant

SLANT HAD A HOMELESS PROBLEM. It had been going on far too long, and it was making almost everybody uncomfortable.

The problem wasn't that Bocker had accepted no housing options. Ever since he'd arrived, nearly everyone in SLANT had tried to take him in. He flatly refused to settle down in any one place. He wasn't restless or unhappy, though. In fact, quite the opposite was true—he was so fond of everyone in SLANT that he made the circuit from one household and place of business (or pleasure) to the next, checking to make sure everyone was doing all right. So, while all the folks in Bocker's big SLANT-wide family had places to call home, Bocker himself was homeless … by choice. On the move all day long, nodding his hellos, stopping here and there to visit or witness something, or accept the offer of a meal or a snack—everybody loved old Bocker.

The 204 people living in SLANT thought they knew each other pretty well, but Bocker, who had enjoyed extended stays at every single home in the community, knew they had not seen everything. Not even close. He, however, had pretty much seen it all, yet he was discreet by nature and kept every bit of it to himself. But then, he didn't understand most of what he saw and heard, anyway.

Still, his SLANT family was worried about the way he was living.

"Hang on a minute, now. I reckon we ought to try to see this from Bocker's point of view," Mayor Farnsley Sheepwater reminded the handful of concerned citizens attending SLANT's monthly Community Rap Session, a longstanding event whose title was at once embarrassingly dated, endearingly reminiscent, and accurately reflective of SLANT's origins. "Way I see it, it ain't that Bocker don't live anywhere," the Mayor-By-Unanimous-Agreement pointed out. "He lives *every*where. Cain't we be all right with that?"

"Makes sense," they all agreed. "It takes a village," they said to each other. "Live and let live," someone suggested. And, to a person, they decided there and then to leave Bocker alone. After all, who were they to deny him the right to live amongst them in his own curious way? They realized that there was only one thing of interest and value: it wasn't possible to imagine SLANT without him, just the way he was.

As a self-appointed sentry, Bocker was unmatched; on that everyone in SLANT agreed. What had worried them was seeing him ramble about as if he had no home to go to, no one to love him. But from Bocker's point of view, he had so much love coming at him from so many directions that he'd have been crazy to limit himself to just one home. He needed to visit with one and the next and the next and the next, spreading himself around and soaking it all up.

So, the homeless "problem" persisted, in spite of the best eradication efforts on the part of those citizens of SLANT who were most dedicated to co-dependency. And in the end, as had always been his habit, night after blissful night Bocker lay on his belly, stretched to his full length and bulk—which was considerable since he was part Collie, part Lab, part Golden Retriever. By sundown every night, he lay parallel to a threshold just outside the front door of any house of his choosing.

He rested well through most nights, SLANT's nocturnal sounds and scents being easily identified from many angles. But occasionally, Bocker roused and lifted his head at a sound or smell unknown. If the strange sense persisted, he leapt to his feet and grumbled in a low voice. If the situation further felt that Whatever-It-Was might become a threat by entering SLANT uninvited and possibly with malice aforethought, he sprang into action toward the suspicious sound (or scent)—"Bock! Bock! BOCK-BOCK-BOCK!!!" Always that 1-1-3 pattern, firm and clear and resounding. He never hesitated to repeat the sequence several times if necessary. He intended to convince Whatever-It-Was that he meant business.

He would return to his chosen post only when he was satisfied that order and safety had been restored.

Bocker, who saw things in simplest terms, loved everything about his gig in SLANT—the life, the work, his loved ones, their thresholds. As far as he was concerned, there had never been a problem. But even if the two-leggers thought there was, he reckoned it to be a good problem to have.

# Contribute

GREEN. THE WORD KEPT POPPING into Alec's head. Not the color, the word. Not the word represented by five letters marked on a page or screen, but the *sound* of the color itself. Not sound as in the word *green* pronounced aloud in English, but the color of the sound of the green that had a name that was the word made up of four letters (one repeated) from the English alphabet—a sound that *didn't even approximate* greenness itself. Not even close.

Why couldn't they see this?

Even *word* is just a word made up of four different letters from the English alphabet. That's all *word* is, is a word.

But *green*. Green is more than a word; it's a concept. Alec had studied it for years, decades even, and he had mastered the *green*.

He thought about *green*, not as a color but as an idea, with all the implications around it. What it means culturally: Currency. Wealth. Envy. Jealousy. Luxury. Leisure. Environmental politics. Naïve. What it means biologically: New. Fresh. Growth. Verdant. Lush. Illness. Infection. Mold. Death. It's all there—the whole cycle and practice of living and dying, all in *green*.

He thought about *green* as a concept, as in how it made him feel emotionally, psychologically, artistically. This is where his synesthesia kicked in, big time. He listed all the names he could think of that belonged in his "green names" category: Evan, Lena, Leonard, Gretel, Earlene, Ferretface, and so forth. Sometimes he allowed his mind to play only *green* music on its soundtrack: "Fables of Faubus," "There's No Business Like Show Business," "Bartender's Blues." (I have no doubt that Alec got a kick out of a song that to him was so "green" having *blues* in its title.) Then he calculated simple sums using various combinations of only the "green numbers": 22, 6, 4, 2, 412, 660 ... and 8, of course. Of *course*.

Alec always wished for a world in which people could talk about these things openly. His feverish need to be able to explain to the whole thick-headed planet his intricate theories and simple solutions was palpable. They *needed* what he knew; they just didn't know it. He had answers, but no one bothered to ask him the questions. He wanted to contribute, but when he tried, people looked right through him like the dunces they are. There was a time when Alec had blamed himself for not having language enough to explain his tightly complex thoughts, but by now he had come to understand that it wasn't him but the rest of humanity who didn't have language enough to understand what he was saying. He was speaking as plainly as he was able.

In general, though, people didn't seem the least bit interested in what he found to be the most fascinating topics in the universe. He had always known he was different, that he didn't fit in and was unschooled in the social graces that seemed natural to other people. He'd had no idea during his youth how stupid most adult humans are and how little they concern themselves about things of any greater importance than their mindless, easily duplicated and insignificant routines.

People are pathetic. That's what Alec thought. That's what he believed.

This day, Alec was sitting atop Barrel Chute in a little clear spot called Top Notch, the knob's highest point. An old woman had lived up here until she died recently, Alec knew, but she had been a loner like him—he hadn't wanted to interrupt her solace, ever, or have her interrupt his, and so had never actually spent time with her. Alec looked out over treetops whose roots were sunk into soil far, far below an abrupt drop-off just beyond his dirty, dandling sneakers. He tried to keep his head from exploding. He did this by opening his mouth and tilting his head back to make his esophagus as vertically straight a pipe as he possibly could, which after a little practice he had perfectly perfected to perfect perfection. *You could lay a carpenter's level against my Adam's apple,* he thought, staring into dense white clouds overhead, *and that bubble'd be dead center of its lines every time.* He had taught himself to do this soon after he started noticing a fizzling behind the bridge of his nose just before each blackout.

When he was sure he had defused and averted this catastrophe (more for the world's loss of his genius than for his own fear of merely losing his arbitrary life), Alec lowered his chin slowly, bringing his eyes back to horizon level. He let his eyes play from background to foreground several times, measuring the height of this ridge on which he sat against that of the neighboring knob across the little valley. Yep, higher. Barrel Chute wasn't quite up there with Worry Wart Knob. Not that it mattered. But good to know, in case he had to fly again ....

He looked toward Worry Wart and beamed a thought over to it. *You know how it is. And I know you know. Prepare to shove over when I send you the signal.*

# The Wisdom of Top-Notch Annie, Part 3

"FOR A LONG TIME—so long, too long—I thought language was for talkin'. But it's for listenin'!

"I thought learnin' was for answerin' questions. It's for askin' 'em.

"Makin' music is not for bein' heard; it's for hearin'.

"But most folks just do not seem to grasp this. Do you?"

# Seek Understanding & Enlightenment

MEADOWLARK NIGHTENGALE WAS PISSED.

*Why do all these X-tians feel compelled to send their children away to be brainwashed?* She wanted to know. *And then they have the nerve to proclaim that as parents they should be Biblically honored by said exiled offspring, which they gratefully send into the wilderness where they are allowed to become their basest selves. Puh.*

Meadowlark Nightengale (born Gladys Shirley Fleischmann in Flatbush, New York, though no one in Kentucky knew that … nor ever would they, if she could help it) had just about had it with those church camp kids shitting gleefully in the creek that ran along the edge of SLANT nearest her shelter. (She never referred to her place as a shanty or a cabin or a cottage, as some in the community lovingly called their own little homes, but she never called it a house, either.)

"I step out of my shelter to enjoy the bounty of Mother Nature, and what do I see? Human turds floating downstream in little paper boats— little paper boats made out of church service bulletins, no less!" Mayor-For-Life Sheepwater heard Meddy shout this into a heavy morning mist permeating the tiny woods-lot situated between her place and his. She seemed to have awakened as her old self today.

"Well, glory be to fucking god," he heard her add, catching the staginess of her tone, though the more nuanced sound waves were probably muffled and disoriented by this unusually heavy morning fog. "The little X-tians are presenting their version of an offering, I suppose." Meddy was a wry one.

How she could see human turds, or anything else, through this lentil soup of a fog-infested morning was a mystery to Farnsley. He had barely been able to see the crooks of his elbows, much less his own hands holding his anatomical spout that was draining his bladder onto the ground (his routine this morning being no different than any other since the first dawn after he'd populated his peaceful little corner of SLANT).

"Are you *shitting* me, pun intended?!" she yelled uphill and across the creek. "Don't bother to answer—EXCEPT IN THE FORM OF A

WRITTEN APOLOGY! And *not* written in feces! You shitty little ...
*SHITS!*" And then Farnsley heard her door slam.

Meddy had only the vaguest idea what a church camp—or a church
camper, for that matter—really was, never having been inside such a place.
It was an irony of life that a "Christian" camp for elitist teenagers was
SLANT's nearest neighbor. Not that they could see each other. The trees
and the incline and the distance prevented that. But certain boys who
sneaked out of their cabins to wander at odd hours often found themselves
down at the edge of SLANT, whose fringe-dwellers had become legendary
in the stories older campers passed down annually to the newbies. Why in
the world pooping at the creek was the ritual of the seasoned kids, no one
could imagine. A way to mark territory of their puny, twisted "courage,"
perhaps? Sometimes Meddy had witnessed their turds come floating down
the creek in clear plastic bags, those kind that zipped closed at the top.
Leaving air inside with the turds is what made the bags float. Each summer,
the campers tried some new way to transport their bowel movements
downstream. It was part of the ritual, she supposed—always trying to
top the previous year's turd-fleet technique. They must have thought they
were hilarious.

How the church camp and SLANT became neighbors was something
that Meddy neither knew nor cared to research. She only knew she wasn't
happy about it. However, if she had cared to look into the Knobs region's
past, she'd at least have developed an understanding of why certain
groups of people, the intentional community of SLANT included, came
to congregate in these places. (Not that it would have solved her floating
turds issue.)

What it was because of was geography. The Knobs (A) were largely
incompatible with crop farming and so were originally seen as undesirable
places to settle, (B) had narrow, steep, winding "roads" that had historically
been mostly impassable at certain times of the year, and (C) were generally
inconvenient and inaccessible in the 18$^{th}$ through early 20$^{th}$ centuries.
That is why—as far as I've heard, anyway—certain outcasts, outlaws,
sects, carnival troupes, untouchables, religious fanatics, segregationists of
various stripes, and mysterious or vaguely infamous types had traditionally and habitually occupied these remote and hilly regions. Some original
Knobs residents were running *from*; others were running *to*. But they all
had certainly been running *off.* Here they built their hermitages or their
ramshackle compounds, whose strangeness ensured that they were left
alone to grow ever inward.

Then came the mid-1900s when convenience and wealth were plentiful
in off-knob civilizations. Caution took a backseat to the lure of a picturesque
and miniature-mountain-like beauty. Outsiders, exploitation-minded
people, discovered the Knobs' "little Switzerland" potential and began to

dream of grooming that image and selling it. They imagined themselves and their customers in chalets, and they didn't see the irony of that, even though they were in the American South, less than a thousand feet above sea level. Not exactly mountains (though SLANT's Resident Philosopreacher, Joy DuPre, liked to believe they were—but she was from the Great Plains, so what did she know from mountains anyhow?). The Knobs region increasingly became steadily infested with uninteresting people who, thinking they were fit for the quirkiness of the Knobs, immediately un-quirked the place. The spread of mediocrity was slow but impervious, and while this activity had somewhat reformed the fundamentalist camp meeting ground up the hill—changing it from a snake-handling revival pavilion into a white-bread church camp for petulant adolescents who thought the whole thing a joke—the seismic cultural shift toward the Knobs region in general had not yet corrupted SLANT proper.

Meadowlark Nightengale, had she known all this, would simply have said, "Well, whoop-tee-fucking-doo. Praise the Fates and pass the shotgun shells. I only care about one thing: I don't want any little X-tian turds dirtying up my goddamn creek!"

For a peace-loving, back-to-the-land hippie, Meddy packed a mean .38 revolver. The 20-gauge chaser she kept in the corner by the door was no slouch, either.

Meanwhile, Farnsley (none too bright a bulb himself) had for a long time wondered about his nearest neighbor's use of this odd term, *X-tian*. He yearned to ask her what she meant by it. Not wanting to incite her, and having no desire to launch her into one of her lengthy, loud and circular diatribes, he had once tried looking the word up in the dictionary, but to no avail, no matter how he spelled it. He should've known that it wasn't a word-word; it was a Meadowlark-Nightengale-word.

Finally, on the occasion of this uber-foggy morning—in which he was so baffled how Meddy could possibly *see* a floating turd pass down the creek—he decided to bite the proverbial bullet and ask her about it directly. Considering it his mayoral duty to follow up on any community distress, he picked his way half-blind through fog-shrouded trees, finally spotting a faint glow in her window at what seemed like a much greater distance than he knew it to be, and he stumbled through the cloud toward that weak marker.

"Everybody okay over here, Meddy?" he asked her closed shelter door. "Thought I heard hollering."

Meddy opened the door immediately, pistol in hand. "Yeah, everybody's okay so far," she said, "but only until this fog lifts and I can see what I'm aiming at. Then somebody's *not* gonna to be okay. Namely, some little turd-leaving X-tian somebody!"

Farnsley remained calm, as was, he thought, the mayoral thing to do.

"I was wondering," he began.

But she was grumbling. "Don't know who they think they are, but if they think they can out-think a thinker who actually *thinks*, they've got another think coming."

It occurred to Farnsley that she might be about to blow. She was usually a kind and caring neighbor with a strong sense of humor. But she was outspoken, to put it mildly, and anyone who had ever caught emotional shrapnel from one of Meadowlark Nightengale's explosions never wanted to suffer through it again. Yet this neighbor, SLANT's mayor, bravely faced the possibility of another rare charge about to be set off. He squared his shoulders, stiffened his resolve, straightened his jacket cuffs, ran the fingers of his right and left hands through his floppy hair, and took a deep breath. This was clearly a situation that needed to be diffused, and he (being Mayor, and all) was just the person for the job.

*A diversion*, he thought. *That's what we need here.* For an Un-Official, our Farnsley is savvy about personal-relations politics. He sensed that he needed to get her focused on something else before this fog dissipated and allowed her to see well enough to crash through the woods and weeds on the other side of the creek and shoot up the unsuspecting church camp in a straw-that-broke-the-camel's-back rage.

And then it came to him. The best Meddy diversion known to human-kind was to ask her about one of the many intelligent-if-crack-brained faux-philosophical tenets she had developed. It was commonly known that once she got to talking, explaining, teaching, preaching, coaching and convincing, everything else just fell away from her—anxiety, anger, whatever she had been on about or about to do, you name it. She forgot everything. Just talked herself into a blissful state; got high on her own ideas. Some who were less kind might say it was the sound of her own voice that intoxicated Meddy. Anyway, that's what Farnsley decided would be his approach. He'd diffuse her rage by asking her a simple question that only she could answer, and in so doing he'd also get an answer he'd wondered about for a long time.

He exhaled in one long whoosh, knowing once he got her wound up he'd probably be stuck here for hours ... at least two, maybe four.

"Hey, Meddy?" he said, his voice tentative but steady. "Just exactly what do you mean by 'EX-chun,' anyway?" With that simple question, he'd opened an anger-escape hatch for everyone in SLANT *and* the church camp, though no one else knew it or ever would. Just him. That was okay. What kind of mayor would he be if he couldn't hypothetically throw himself on a grenade for his village?

"Are you serial?" Meddy blurted—surprise, maybe shock coloring the edges of her typical wordplay.

"I've heard you say it before, but never thought to ask until now,"

Farnsley lied. Sheepishly.

She stared at him for a full minute, perplexed as to where to begin. Finally, she took a deep breath, ran the fingers of her left and right hands through her wavy hair, straightened the cuffs of her flannel shirt, stiffened her neck, squared her shoulders and spoke in a much softer voice, as if preparing to lead an innocent child patiently through the wilderness of some scary adult concept—like divorce or sexual intercourse or why income tax is actually illegal yet the government keeps insisting on stealing it from everybody every year. Something complex like that. To an imbecile.

It made her weary just thinking about the task at hand. However, for this she always found patience. People had to be led to enlightenment. She never wasn't a teacher, in spite of having left academia some twenty-plus years prior.

Her problem was that she didn't know where to start explaining this thing. It needed context.

She'd been under the assumption that everyone in SLANT had already heard this philosophical bit of hers and understood what she meant whenever she called someone an X-tian. Hell, Farnsley had been here longer than she had; it was hard to believe he'd never heard her expound on this very simple concept (among the many she'd developed, this was perhaps her favorite). Going all the way back to the beginning of it just for him would be a challenge, for she hadn't been back there in long years, but it excited and energized her to have a new potential convert to her way of thinking.

Where to begin?

"Well, mayor, you'll appreciate the first part of this, anyway," she said, finally, "because it involves politics. My grandmother once told me that she used a cleaning product called Bon Ami—which was an oven soap, I think—to mix up a temporary 'paint' that could be applied to the window of the county courthouse so local election tallies could be made public as the votes were counted. This was way-back-when. Everyone gathered on the main street of her town to follow this primitive tabulation reporting, and my grandmother would update the results as vote totals from each precinct came in. This stuff she used was soap-based, so it was easy to wash off and reapply. There were only a few polling places to tabulate in such a small county, so it didn't take all night. See, there was no television or radio station in that little place to broadcast the results."

*So far so good*, Farnsley thought. Meddy already seemed calmer, more focused.

"The larger towns in the region that did have radio stations with broadcast signals that could reach all the way to my grandmother's tiny village, they cared not a whit about local elections going on way out there.

The county's own weekly newspaper never came out until Thursday, which was two days after any election." She was on a roll now. "So, the choices were (A) stand on the main street on election night and stare at the courthouse window or (B) wait two days for the 'local media' to get around to announcing their county's results. By Thursday, the rain or some ambitious, maybe defeated, courthouse employee would have washed away those Bon Ami soap tallies by then anyway."

Because of the way she pronounced the product's name, Farnsley— who had a hobby of picturing words in his mind—wondered how something that sounded like "bahn-AM-ee" would have actually been spelled. He'd never seen anything close to that brand name on any store shelf. He didn't know French, so it never occurred to him that it could have been a corrupted foreign phrase, "bone-ah-MEE," which it was.

Without taking a breath, Meddy continued her rambling context-setting. "I later came to realize that something very like that Bon Ami mixture must have been what stores used to create those holiday scenes on their windows at Christmastime," she said. "They must have added red and green food coloring or tempera paint to the creamy Bon Ami, so as to make more colors that could be brushed on like paint. Then they realized that they could temporarily write enticing words and sales phrases on their windows anytime of the year. Or maybe that came first." Here she shook her head as if to clear it. "Okay, admittedly, the evolution of all this is speculation on my part, but you see where I'm going with it."

It wasn't a question; it was a statement. Farnsley, in fact, did NOT see any such thing, but since she hadn't really asked, he decided to nod and ride it out, hoping it would make sense eventually.

"Soon, in order to paint their advertising words larger," she said, "they found shorter words to use. Language like SALE instead of DISCOUNTS. CLOSING instead of GOING OUT OF BUSINESS. And at holiday time they came to use XMAS instead of CHRISTMAS; four letters instead of nine, see?"

Four instead of nine. That, he did see. So he said, "Sure," which satisfied her. She charged on.

"So, here's really the meat of this, and it's where I start—well, where my thinking on this topic starts."

Farnsley was confused. *We're not STARTED yet?* he wondered. *All of this, and we're not even STARTED?* But he kept the thought from escaping across his tongue and falling from his lips. Instead, he waited, looking into her eyes with kindness, as if preparing to patiently lead an innocent child through the wilderness of some scary adult concept, like divorce or sexual intercourse or why studying hard is important to a person's future even though sports celebrities get rich off of being overpaid for perfecting playground games.

Anyway.

"What happened was, people started raising hell about the term XMAS. There was a whole movement started up talkin' about 'Put the CHRIST back in CHRISTMAS.' Hell, that still goes on today," she said. "Never mind that Christmas has been materialized and cheapened into the least Christ-like holiday imaginable. No, these un-thinking, non-reading, intolerant religious nuts didn't notice or care that their holiest of days was being commercially exploited." As an aside she added, "Yeah, I know what you're thinking—Easter—but don't even get me started on that."

There was no way Farnsley was going to get her started on that. No way he desired interrupting her mighty flow. The back-up might cause a flood. Of Biblical proportions.

Meddy barreled on. "They don't even care that in their own front yards Santa and his reindeer are landing on the tops of crèches where the holy family greets wise men," she said. "They just demand that stores stop abbreviating the name of said consumer event, er, religious holy day ... d'y'see what I mean?"

She waited. Farnsley pursed his lips and tried to look interested. His poor little brain was working overtime to connect the dots, but the damned dots kept moving around.

"How out of touch are they?" she asked (*rhetorically*, he gratefully noticed). "They don't even know that the symbol X had been an early representation for what became the English word 'Christ.' Completely fail to realize, also, that the X is a type of cross, one of their holiest icons. And obviously overlook the conundrum that selling out their holy day is the *real* issue, not abbreviating said sell-out. You with me?"

"Go on," Farnsley thought to say, vaguely. He kept one eye on her now-tabled handgun throughout most of her rant.

"So, they're all 'put Christ back in Christmas, put Christ back in Christmas!' And now here we are, having come into the anti-truth/crazy-ass/god-guns-and-gays agenda of the contemporary so-called 'Christian' era. You notice I put air quotes around 'Christian'?"

Farnsley dared not blink. He didn't want to interrupt the diversion; it was working like a charm.

"That's because—and here's my point—"

Oh, thank god, a POINT.

"—they are the very ones who need to put the CHRIST back in *Christian!* For the everlovin' love of God! These mean, hateful, cruel, power-mongers and judgers who call themselves 'Christian' don't act like they HAVE EVER EVEN READ Christ's very words!"

Meddy was heated up now. Farnsley was worn out. He wondered if he'd done the right thing in flipping this particular switch to its ON position.

"These nuts are nothing but dirty politicians and snake oil salesmen in X-tian clothing!" she shouted, sounding a little off the deep end. "They're American fascists! They hate everybody except each other!"

Fuck it. Maybe he should have just let her willy-nilly shoot church campers.

"These hypocrites," she ranted, "go around claiming the name of a great teacher-philosopher, when everything they do is in DIRECT CONTRAST to that man's very teachings!" She paused, probably for effect, then added, "Are you kidding me??"

Another rhetorical, Farnsley decided to assume.

"They aren't CHRISTIANS. No fucking way. They're just X-TIANS. Okay?"

Oh, man, was she on a roll. She was loud, but she was clear.

"THEY'RE the ones took the CHRIST out of CHRISTIAN. Okay? These self-focused, greedy, meddling assholes—they've taken *Christ* RIGHT OUT of Christianity! Okay?? You follow?"

Oddly, he did. It had all come together at the end. He got it! And moreover (in his humble, if jumbled, opinion) ... she was exactly right.

"So, see, I don't care what they want to call themselves. I'm not even a believer, yet I refuse to give them the good name of Christ to drag through the mud any longer," she said. "Using their own so-called logic, those people are X-TIANS to me, and probably even to their own disappointed God, too. And they always will be—that is, unless they return to acting on the teachings of their *very NAMESAKE*: 'Love one another'; 'Love your neighbor'; 'Treat others as you'd want them to treat you.' Which DOESN'T, I submit, include shipping anonymous, annoying turds to your neighbors down the creek!"

Her wild eyes emphatically punctuated her logical argument. Clearly, this meant a great deal to her. "It's all in there in their book, the message of Jesus is very clear, but they don't follow it. So, clearly, they don't really follow Him. And if they aren't going to respect and honor their own Christ *after whom they named their whole entire religion,* then I have no obligation to respect and honor them ... those ... those ruinous fucking pseudo X-tian assholier-than-thous," she spat.

Farnsley shook his head like an animal clearing its ears of an oddly-pitched tone. He couldn't think of a thing to say, so he found his friend's face and peered into her eyes, marveling at the mind behind them. His was a grateful smile.

Meadowlark Nightengale relaxed then and gave him a calm, friendly smile in return, patted his shoulder and left his wheels to turn. She stepped easily across the narrow room to place her hefty pistol on her highest shelf.

Well, that's a relief. Removing that sidearm from her morning explosion had been his point. But, as usual, Meddy had also managed to give him a lot to think about.

"Now, would you care to wake-and-bake this fine morning?" she asked her neighbor, the self-proclaimed mayor of SLANT. But Farnsley seemed a thousand miles away. She tried to hand him the typically ugly, poorly-rolled joint she pulled from the breast pocket of her flannel lumberjack shirt. Getting no immediate response, she prompted him again, "Mister Mayor...?"

He took it and the Zippo she held out to him, lit up, and gazed outward through the window whose light had guided him here.

The fog had lifted.

# Revisionist Inscape

IN ITS LATEST INCARNATION, The Rising Son had already changed the old camp meeting grounds dramatically.

One of the first things the mega-church had done was to mandate that its teen-outreach program adopt the attitude that all of its young people would be required to do labor-intensive clean-up and landscaping work at the campground under the precept of "service to God." This labor, supplemented by discussions of (mostly Old Testament) scripturally-based topics, would be the entirety of their summer camp experience. Hence, June Term that first summer at the re-envisioned camp had begun very unlike "summer camp" as it is generally known. It was, from the get-go, more about cutting and hauling and dragging and burning and digging and chopping and pulling and various other versions of what camp operators liked to call "sweat equity" or "character building." The July and August terms, of course, would be the same.

Camp administrators had been explicitly directed by the mega-church CEO to make sure their naïve counselors and teen leaders pushed every possible labor-oriented scripture they could find in the Bible to keep campers focused on the "holy necessity" of their work. Each day campers— modern day teens, mind you—were treated to a new one. From Ecclesiastes: "There is nothing better for a person than to enjoy their work, because that is their lot." From Thessalonians this rather obvious threat: "We gave you this rule: 'The one who is unwilling to work shall not eat.'" From Proverbs: "All hard work brings a profit, but mere talk leads only to poverty." (When I later learned of this, my first thought was, *Oh, I get it—a Biblical greatest hits. On forced-labor instruction.* Which didn't make me feel any better.)

The obvious parallels to internment camp conditions were ignored, plus any and all comparisons to Depression-era "socialist" programs (CCC and WPA) were firmly squelched by those flag wavers who ran the country's right-wingnut religious arm of politics. This exploitation of child labor was cloaked in the disguise of "beautifying camp property for the glory of the Lord." Period. End of discussion.

Never a word was said, however, about a very important fact in the matter: this free teen labor did not actually earn the young workforce "equity" or anything resembling a cooperative interest in the ownership of the property. Thus, it was most definitely *NOT* socialism. But these improvements—made at the literal expense of their parents who had paid for their kids to go to "camp" that year—would immediately increase the value of the property for its owner. And what no one grasped, particularly the low-pay-grade on-site seasonal administrators and counselors at the camp, was that the mega-church itself did not even hold the deed to the place.

It was owned by one W. Regan Connelldon, a sticky and cunning career politician who, upon visiting an established, high-end residential development on a nearly identical knob across the Ohio River in southern Indiana, had imagined glorious dollar signs floating cartoon-like above the similar Kentucky terrain and swirling about his head.

Under a quickly-formed LLC named "Sun Rising," Connelldon had instructed an agent to purchase, anonymously, the Kentucky property from the Gloryland folks as soon as it was conveniently forced onto the market. That same afternoon, he leased the land to the mega-church *Streets of Gold!* for three years, at a symbolic cost of one dollar per year … plus the stipulation that certain improvements would be made by the tenant during the lease period.

The public story was simply that *Streets of Gold!* had acquired use of some available land for its hot new summer camp for teens: The Rising Son. By design, the Connelldon connection to the property was glossed over entirely. The thinking among those who had executed this deal was that if anyone ever noticed, they could simply make a grand unveiling of the heretofore unknown one-dollar-per-year lease agreement (without mention of the improvements clause, obviously), which would make Connelldon look like a generous soul, rather than the greed-inspired politician and schemer he indeed is. This card was intentionally held in reserve, to be played only if some annoying journalist or lawsuit forced the mega-church's hand in the matter. Until then, *Streets of Gold!* would protect its "generous benefactor," no matter what.

Connelldon's larger plan, meanwhile, was efficient. He envisioned that within three short years he would improve his financial standing, ratcheting his status from multi-millionaire to billionaire simply by selling the improved property to a developer. Or perhaps he would partner with one of the developers who had contributed tens of thousands to his re-election campaigns. Either way, he'd come out richer.

Now, this particular politician isn't interested in the game of chess, and he had carefully managed to avoid military service in his youth during the height of the Vietnam War draft. In other words, he has no formal training in tactics. What he has is instinct, and relying solely on what he considers his raw "talent," W. Regan Connelldon has never strategized or executed anything without certain knowledge of what his next several moves will be ... and how they will benefit him. Usually he does whatever he wants, but always he does it while wrapping himself in the flag and standing in the darkest shadow of the cross. Sadly for our nation, he knows from experience that his go-to tactic is stubborn obstruction, the best weapon in his political arsenal is the Old Testament, and his most effective camouflage is red, white and blue. Until now, those have never failed him.

Most voters don't observe closely. Many swallow lies. Some don't want to be *informed* by their "news" sources; they want to be *affirmed* by them. Others feel powerless to do anything. Politics and religion are now co-dependent bedfellows. (Gay bedfellows, I assume. After all, it's mostly men running politics and religion both, you know? So, does this make those judgmental assholier-than-thous hypocrites, or what?) It's all designed to incite anger and fuel emotion around elections.

The whole thing is fascinating. And maddening. Also, it demonstrates the accelerated rate by which the myth and legend of the United States show divisive rot at its capitalistic core. In fact, this sort of arrangement is the next logical step in the sad devolution of a culture that has deluded itself nearly out of business in two short, greedy centuries. Ancient cultures in Europe, Africa and Asia find themselves watching astonished while a self-righteous and dim-witted minority of Americans smugly underwrite their own culture's demise via the damaged artificial heart of democracy: *the ballot box*. Or, more accurately, the screwy Electoral College, which is a joke that's not at all funny.

This situation is, of course, the inevitable outcome of a broken system that stretches itself out of shape in an effort to first *ignore* and then *deny* a clear separation of church and state; to first *manipulate* and then *disable* Constitutional separation of powers. Well, that ... plus glaring incompetence, undeniable corruption and blatant criminality that can (theoretically, we'll say) emerge during and after an election. Are these the evil seeds of a corrupted world of Connelldon's making?

It is unthinkable to many who consider ourselves devoted amateur political analysts that an astonishing horror show could ever preempt the U.S. Executive branch, Supreme Court, Department of Justice, State Department and Congress ... all at once! That surely can't happen here, right? And we'd never make the poor choices of turning away from NATO and our traditional foreign allies, while allowing our adversaries to get away with all manner of brash nastiness, could we? Widespread evidence of personal debt, influence peddling and blackmail among our leaders? *Here?* Really?

Check out this hypothetical: let's say we all witness overwhelming chaos and hypocrisy and the decline of ethics in our federal government—what happens next? Would our republic be doomed? It's unimaginable that *everything* could so easily be thrown out of balance and into a tailspin rigged with promise of a death spiral. Are our institutions of government too weak to hold? *Surely* we have learned that every hard-won protection is fragile—in voting, immigration, health care, policing, individual civil rights, privacy, national security, climate science, education, public lands, economics, employment, trade, agriculture, you name it. *Surely* we can't imagine any good coming from, say, neutering the Postal Service and the CDC *in the middle of* both a bungled pandemic response *and* a sabotaged national election.

*In America? Get outta here,* some might say. *Never happen. No fuckin' way.* Way.

Consider a time of great crisis in our land. A dark time. A scary time. An odious time. It boggles. As bad as bad "reality" TV is, aren't these scenarios far, far worse? Could the tentacles of negative consequences ever be untangled? If our very democracy were at risk from the top down—if, for example, the justice system fails—what does coping look like?

We'd all be wondering whether we were having a nightmare, hoping we'd wake up before we asphyxiate. Fixing whatever disaster we might find ourselves up against would take time. We'd hope and pray that we'd have enough of it.

As Jimmy once said about such a debacle, "It'll either end us, or else we'll be digging our way out from under this stinkin' pile of crap for a damned long time."

To which Jimi added, "I think we'll make it, but it's gonna take an army of patriots, every last one of us with shit shovels in both hands."

You know that in the early 21st century the U.S. political system (mostly reduced to theatre) became a virtual train wreck, with the rest of the world unable to tear its eyes away. You've seen evidence too of the localized version of such dirty politics. And so it came to pass that because of the crooked and the profane operating close to home, one of the numerous anonymous boxcars in that ill-destined pile-up might turn out to be an old camp meeting ground hidden in a forest beside a creek called Fidelity on a knob called Barrel Chute in the very American heart of the Ohio River Valley.

# Cultivate Healthy Alliances

NICK TRIED TO STAY UNDER THE RADAR at The Rising Son. The young Hopkins fan knew exactly why he had landed there, and it had little to do with the messaging, the property improvement or the spiritually-disguised manipulation that surrounded him. Nick had never been one to cave in to peer pressure. He was his own boy, and he fully accepted his place as an outsider, no matter where he landed.

At TRS, Nick did what was asked of him but little more. If he'd been a believer in whatever was going on in this puzzling place where he'd unceremoniously landed, he'd have been a more enthusiastic participant. As it was, he just wanted to soak up sweet solitude as often as the camp's schedule allowed that to happen for him.

Most afternoons there was a bit of free time. This was when, Nick later told me, he would wander off into the woods to contemplate whatever was on his mind. Sometimes it was girls, sometimes music. Occasionally he'd allow his thoughts to filter all the indoctrination the camp leaders were handing out, although usually this meant trying to unravel the uncomfortable, nagging feelings he had about why the whole message didn't sit well with him. Like any teenager with a good and open mind, Nick wasn't one to open up and swallow everything that was thrust upon him. He questioned. He especially questioned anything stinking of propaganda that was designed to twist religion into something ugly.

On a Wednesday mid-afternoon, he had his first one-on-one encounter with the stout girl he'd noticed at his first night's fire circle. Today, Nick was sitting on a fallen log next to an untended footpath far from the center of The Rising Son, thinking or not thinking. From the other direction came the girl. He hadn't seen her since that evening a few nights before when she'd made her "God's grandeur in the wilderness" comment at the fire circle, and he was, to his surprise, really glad to notice her walking toward him. But he could see in her eyes that she wasn't particularly glad to see him sitting along her own path of solitude. At the same time, she wasn't necessarily not glad either. It was just that his presence interrupted her own thoughts.

He spoke first. "Hey," he said. And she said "hey" back and would have walked right past him. But he didn't want her to. He hadn't spoken to anyone about anything real for days. And so he said, "I really liked your Gerard Manley Hopkins reference at the fire circle the other night." That got her attention. For, like Nick, she had thought she was the only sane and well-read teenager on the place.

"You know Hopkins?" she said.

"Read him in school last spring. Awesome dude, for a religious thinker."

"Well," she said. Pause. "Okay," she said. Sigh. "Who are you, anyway?"

"Nick. You?"

"I'm Samantha, but my friends call me Sam. You my friend, you think?"

"Could be. Up to you."

This made Sam smile. He might be all right, this Nick. He wasn't like most boys her age. They usually either ignored her or made gentle fun of her or even tormented her outright. She wasn't a skeptic for no reason. Life had taught her to be cautious, to protect her emotional self, to stay pretty much apart.

"So, what's your connection to Hopkins?" Nick wanted to know.

"My library card, I guess," she said. "I mean he's been dead too long for me to know him personally or anything."

Now Nick grinned. She might be all right, this Sam. She was smart and quick and seemed to have a dry humor. Wouldn't it be nice to find an ally among these stepford kids up here on this godforsaken knob?

"Wanna sit?" he asked. "Or are you in a hurry to get back?"

She sat. There were lots of things Sam liked about herself, but her thighs when she sat wasn't one of them. She tried to remind herself not to focus on what she perceived to be their enormity.

"What's your favorite Hopkins poem?" Nick said, evidently not judging her one way or the other.

Sam didn't even have to think. "Pied Beauty, no doubt," she said.

"That's a good one," said Nick. "Whatcha like about it?"

"It lifts up weird and flawed things, finds beauty in them, don't you think?" she said. "All that talk about what's dappled and brindled and freckled, what's strangely patterned. Makes me wonder if there's hope for someone as flawed as I am." She glanced at her thighs, got a shot of embarrassment, then quickly looked away and added, "I guess."

But Nick wasn't paying attention to her thighs, hadn't picked up on her own insecurity. He was gazing off in a listening posture. "I get that," Nick said, "about Pied Beauty. Makes me hopeful about myself too."

He too was self-conscious? About what? He was so normal looking! But her carefully composed face didn't belie her insecurities, didn't register blatant amazement. Cool as any teenager needs to be, she just said, "Yours?"

"I found myself drawn to God's Grandeur. Maybe it's all that alliteration, you know?" he said. "The 'shining from shook foil,' the 'smudge' and 'smell'. Then, too, there's something I like about the repetition. 'Have trod, have trod, have trod.' It's like a heartbeat, you know? Like the heartbeat of Time."

Sam thought Nick himself was shook foil shining. Spectacular. Not merely sexy. Smart. Smart was the best kind of sexy, her opinion.

"So, when you said 'God's grandeur' that night, I was impressed," he said.

"Sweet! I can't believe you know Hopkins!" she said. Then she got shy. "I always feel like such a nerd."

"I know. Nerd-dom is a weird place to live," Nick said. "So, it's cool to find a kindred nerd spirit up here." He tossed out a grin and caught one coming back in his direction.

"I thought I was going to expire when my moms told me I had to come. I don't know anyone here," she said. "And we're not particularly churchy, either. I mean, to tell you the absolute truth, I'm agnostic. Maybe even an atheist. But at least I'm *real*. These kids all seem like robots or something. And don't even get me started on these counselors!"

"My dad too," he said, grumbling. "Made me come to this place, I mean. I had two choices, and believe it or not this one wasn't the worst."

"Look," said Sam, "as long as we're both stuck here, d'ya think we can get each others' backs?"

In spite of her natural shyness and her perceived insecurity, Sam was a take-charge kind of girl. Nick would learn that this was just one of many things he'd grow to like about his new friend.

"Make me feel a lot better," Nick said. "I'm in. Pass the Pied Beauty with a side of Binsey Poplars, please."

"Or just a lukewarm can of Falls City beer would do," said Sam. She punched him in the arm, not too hard but not wimpy either.

Yep, a community of two was salvation enough. This, Nick thought, was going to work out for them both.

# The Wisdom of Top-Notch Annie, Part 4

"THESE PEOPLE WHO ALL THE TIME WORRY about Heaven and Salvation and Judgment Day and the like—I don't understand 'em. Reason I don't understand 'em is 'cause they are so blamed *fixated* on their notion of afterlife that they mostly don't do right by anybidy, themselves included, in *this very* life. This life is the only one they for sure have, but you cain't get through to 'em long enough to mention it.

"They used to tell me, 'Annie, I'm a believer. Ain't you?'

"Naw. I ain't.

"They b'lieve in myths. They even b'lieve in outright lies! That's a piss poor way to live the only life you know for sure you're gonna get. I mean, they cain't consider the possibility that they could be wrong about the so-called afterlife. But ain't no empirical proof it exists. Just stories people've passed on for so long that they're taken for actual. Unshakable belief in *any kind of Maybe* is how people get manipulated, used, discarded. Yet they have these myths, so they keep on b'lievin'! Keep on blindly followin'! It's a peculiar kind of insanity, if you ask me.

"My 'pinion? These people are so rooted in the *literal* that once they've heard a story, well, out of habit they assume it's true. 'Specially if they don't have confidence in their own common sense. Oh, and they're so self-centered they'll put themselves in that questionable story too! I feel deeply sorry for 'em. I do. Because when I was dyin', the only whatnots in that whole experience were just memories floatin' in and out from the life I'd done lived. Right here. On earth.

"And, yeah, I saw a light. But turns out it was just my brain flaming out when the oxygen dried up! Just neuron fireworks. Nothin' more or less than that.

"Look-a-here, I think there's a mighty big difference between Life and Livin'. One's a concept, but th'other'n's an action—somethin' that happens for real and true, better or worse. I nearly erased the word Life from my vocabulary. Nobidy knows what that is, precisely because ever'bidy *very differently* thinks they *do* know. You could go on and on all day about Life-this and Life-that. It's a vague thang— big, broad, theoretical. As in

*The Meaning Of....* you follow?

"But Livin'—now that's an act, a verb. It's one person puttin' one foot in front of th'other in whatever one place and time and circumstance they find theirself. In the moment. Livin's a unique *action* that takes place for each person; it's differ'nt for ever' single one of us. What's wrong with that? Livin' ain't about the herd or even about Time passing; it's an individual, biological experience that's gonna happen either in isolation or in community—but, hey, even a community is finite. For sure, it's the individual that's got to do the livin', and we don't always do it well, though 'ccasionally we manage to get it close to right.

"Life? Well, that's just a noun. A concept ... and, like I said, a vague one at that. Life, you see, spreads ever outward, with or without each of us, and definitely without respect for whatever's goin' on in our individual experience.

"Livin's what's real. The act of Livin' is as personal and unique as it gets."

# Think Ahead

THE LOG WHERE THEY FIRST officially met and talked was Nick and Sam's favorite spot secluded within woods on The Rising Son property. It had become their meet-up place. It was on a looped path less traveled, hardly used in fact and quite distant from the campground's center, so they accurately figured it was unlikely they'd ever be discovered or interrupted there. It was in this place that they eventually started to put together the pieces of what was really going on at TRS.

Now, the only way I know any of this to tell it to you is that Nick has been talking about it ever since. Yeah, we got to know him, and he's stayed in touch with us. He's talked a lot about it, mostly to clarify his own thoughts, I think.

"Seems like people who talk loudest often don't know what they're talking about," he said to me one time, "but that doesn't keep 'em from talking."

"Reminds me of what the Scarecrow said to Dorothy," I'd said. Nick had looked a bit confused at that, so I explained. "Said, 'Some people without brains do an awful lot of talking, don't they.' To which Dorothy replied, 'I guess you're right.'"

"Could be," Nick had said. "I think sometimes the crooked ones talk because they have an agenda, sometimes 'cause they're ignorant, sometimes 'cause they've got a false story to spread for reasons that make sense only to them. Sometimes because they broke trust and caused major trouble … and then refuse to own what *they* did."

"Live and learn. Well, now you know how people can be," I told him.

"Sad but true," said he. "Sad. But true."

So, anyway, that log. Him and Sam back then. And so forth …

"I mean, come on," Nick said to Sam one still, sticky afternoon, "what's with all the weeding and hauling and shit? Some summer camp! I never worked so hard in my life." On this day, he was nearly too exhausted to speak.

"Right?" Sam said. "And these Bible verses. Every day a new one, always about toiling and laboring. Never a word about love or kindness or compassion or joy. Or Jesus, even! This is the weirdest church thing I ever heard of." She shook her head. "But it's the only one I've ever been to, so what do I know."

"Today's," Nick said. "The one about 'whoever is slack in his work is the same as a person who destroys.' What a load! And that one from, I think, Ecclesiastes yesterday: 'Work hard because you're gonna die, and after you're dead you won't have the opportunity to work at all.' Hmph."

"Is this the way these camp things usually go?" Sam asked. "I'm clueless here, except I know it's no fun. At all. And I hate it. And I wish I'd never heard of this place or that Golden-whatever church that owns it."

"*Streets of Gold!* And don't forget the trademarked exclamation point at the end of their name. My dad sure doesn't," Nick said. "As for the way of all camps, I don't know, really. But something about this one doesn't smell right to me."

They discussed the work, the fact that all the kids seemed unclear of its purpose. It made no sense in terms of what they'd heard about summer camp activities, but they began to wonder if maybe it made sense on some other level … in some realm that had *nothing* to do with kids or camp or possibly even Jesus.

"Bet if we drew a map of this place, we'd see something. Maybe a pattern. I'm not sure of that, but it's something to do besides work, work, work all the time…at hard labor…like in prison camp." She stopped talking just long enough to take a bite of apple. "Anyway," she went on, chewing, "I'm one of those nerds who like maps. And I like drawing better than weed-whacking, for damn sure."

"And you like puzzles." Nick had learned a lot more about Sam that week.

"I do like puzzles," she said, smiling because he remembered something important that she'd told him about herself.

Nick fished a nubby Ikea pencil and his tiny blue Moleskine notebook out of his hip pocket. He opened to a spread of two blank pages. "Yeah," he said. "And this might just be a killer puzzle."

For the next half hour, if we could've seen them, we'd have seen little more than the tops of two studious heads bent together over one very small notebook. Because Nick's notebook was so miniature, they had to make tiny marks. Starting with just a dot at the center of camp (where that cherished old dinner bell had once perched atop its post, though these children couldn't have known that), they put little squares for the buildings (dining hall, cottages, cabins, administration building, and so forth), and then they drew single lines for the paths that connected everything, as far as they knew. They drew a squiggly line for the creek bordering the property, though they believed no campers other than the two of them realized there was a creek down there. (They weren't yet aware of the boys who had been busy perpetuating the tradition of sending turds downstream to terrorize SLANT.)

Once they had the layout of the camp drawn, disagreeing here and there about the placement of one element or another, taking turns with the pencil, they started to map out areas where their work was going on—this was work the campers spent doing almost every waking hour, except for rest and meal breaks. Suddenly, a regimented grid appeared in the form of four long lines representing the four bulldozed roads they had seen when they were working on newly-cleared paths that crossed these roads. The campers' work had been following men with chainsaws who got the big trees out of the way first. At regular intersections on their sketch, shorter lines crossed the four long lines, tying them together in even intervals.

"It looks like ... a town or something," Nick said.

"Oh, shit," Sam said. "It looks exactly like Howard Houses."

"Howard Houses?"

"The trite, tacky little subdivision where I live!"

They stared at the page. It *did* look like a subdivision. (They didn't know they'd been mapping only on Phase One of a much bigger project.) All their map was missing were squares representing future houses lined up within the blocks on the fresh roads. Last, Nick added a perpendicular dotted line across the far end of the four longest roads to indicate a lane that would tie them together, forming a shared terminus on the south end. He stabbed at the dotted line with his pencil. "Whatcha bet they'll have us clearing a new path right across there next?"

Sam felt something she hadn't experienced in a long time, or possibly ever: speechless. And then a question formed. The only question that mattered: "Who in the hell is behind this diabolical bullshit scheme?"

The woods knew the answer, but being silent types, not one single tree said one single word.

# Look for Good

"IF THE CHRISTIANS WOULD STOP YELLING, maybe I could hear God!"

Meadowlark Nightengale had been trying to explain to Joy why she was "off" religion. It had nothing to do with a belief system or a level of spirituality or anything remotely related to those things. It had to do with *NOISE*—the judgmental cacophony that extreme right-wing, nationalistic religion has, unfortunately, become.

Joy pointed out that Christianity has been co-opted by *neo-christians* whose practice is far removed from the original intent. Meddy didn't disagree.

Religions such as the Judeo-Christian combo that Meddy had grown up in (more Jewish than protestant, for sure, but not observant) had been corrupted, bastardized, deformed beyond recognition. Not that the same thing hadn't happened in other denominations. It seemed to Meddy that every version of every religion had suffered the same fate over the past forty years or so. Anymore, religion in general seemed more about hatred than love—less unity, more division. People seemed so easily eager to disregard God, creation, others. She didn't understand it, and she found it frustrating beyond toleration. It made her sick, sad and dismayed.

Spirituality Meddy understood. She was a spiritual person. When it came to contemporary organized religion, however, she had consciously thrown out the baby and the bathwater both. The whole business had become too much to bear.

Joy DuPre, on the other hand, took a different approach. Rather than focus on what was wrong with the world's religions, she chose to identify any of their particular parts that made positive sense for her. She was engaged in a quest to find the best elements from many religions and form them into one that actually worked. She and Meddy often had these philosophical discussions, though they didn't always agree.

"Why, Meddy," Joy said, a twinkle in her eye and a chuckle in her voice, "I hardly ever hear you say the C-word."

"I know it, I know it," Meddy said in a matter-of-fact tone. "And let me be clear: *I have no problem with Jesus Christ.* I admire the words and messages attributed to him. Truly admire them!" Here her level tone changed. "But when it comes to far too many of his so-called followers, I lose all respect for those fools. This isn't about who they *claim* to be; it's about who we *know* them to be. Fake-religious charlatans calling themselves 'Christians' … and then all they do is act like heathens—they judge, they scream, they bully, they manipulate, they lie. *They ignore their own teachings!* It's maddening!"

"My friend, not all Christians are narrow-minded," Joy said, gently.

"Well, I wish the broad-minded ones would speak up, then," said Meddy.

"You can't always tell by the loudest few what an entire group is like."

"Yes, you can," Meddy insisted, "and here's why: those who take charge *unchallenged* are, by default, sanctioned by the rest. They're allowed to become representative of the group because those who don't resist, or who silently separate themselves from those big, bossy voices, are complicit by their silence. And that's true for as long as the silent stay silent while retaining their identity to that group."

"I think you must feel deeply hurt by the church," Joy said. "From your past?"

"I'm not the only one," said Meddy. "Too much damage. For too long. Way beyond repair." She gazed off toward the creek. Her expression was not placid. "Damage of Biblical proportions, pun intended."

Joy said, "I'm so sorry." Her voice swelled with empathy. She was sincere.

"One big problem I have with X-tianity is that whole *love your enemies* idea," Meddy said. "What bullshit. I have to tell you, I'm very revenge-oriented. When someone wrongs me, I want them held accountable. I want them to pay a price that is equal to what their words or deeds cost me. And I want to *see* them punished—in *this* lifetime. I'm not satisfied with an empty promise of accountability happening at some pearly gate in some impossible future." Then she added, "Never happens, though."

Meddy had decided when she turned fifty-years-old (could that have been *ten years ago* by now?) that she had the right to muscle past whatever didn't sit right with her. *I've been a 'good girl' for five damned decades,* she had declared on that long-ago fiftieth birthday, *but fuck it—I'm done.* By now, at age sixty, she was sure she had made the right call.

But back then, she'd not previously thought this through, had never planned that fifty years would be "enough, by god." It just suddenly dawned on her the week she had turned fifty that she'd lived by other people's expectations as long as she was willing to. In one sudden moment, she sloughed off a burden she'd carried on her back all her life, and from that point on Meddy decided she was *through*—she wasn't going to play by anybody's ridiculous rules but her own, not ever again. She was as good as her promise to herself, too. And she knew this new direction wasn't a bad thing because she trusted her personal credo, her gut and her good gumption.

For one thing, Meadowlark Nightengale was not interested in the prominent notions that most people claim to care about—doing something heroic, leaving a personal legacy, that sort of egotistical crap. She just didn't care about individual glory all that much. Some folks are "more for me" types, and some are "greater good" types. Those of us who have been fortunate enough to know her are well aware that Meddy has always thought foremost about the greater good. She decided to agree with whoever'd said that it's wise to remember we're living in an entire universe and each of us is only one trifling speck of dust in it.

Meddy had learned somewhere along the way that neither education nor intelligence are the same as wisdom. At all. She kept a quote from a book called *Hagakure* (she didn't know it was an ancient warrior text; the quote, tacked above the window over her little sink, was there when she'd moved into her shelter): *When your thinking rises above concern for your own welfare, wisdom which is independent of thought appears.* That was sort of what she strove for, to be wise enough to act for the greatest good without even thinking about it. In other words, Meddy was big on doing the right thing no matter what, *even if it didn't profit her personally.* This had been a lifelong quest, but for years and years she'd collected ideas and developed many of her own, not really fathoming what it was all leading up to. Then at fifty, the dam inside her heart had burst, and she'd realized that being honest was as much about being true to herself as it was about unconsciously practicing the Golden Rule.

"I was thinking about you just the other day," said Joy. "About how much I admire what you did, how you decided to change yourself, how brave that is. Most people wouldn't think to change after developing fifty-year-long habits."

"Oh, hell, Joy," Meddy said. "You just aren't old enough yet. When you hit fifty—then sixty!—you'll see. You're paying attention now because you're closing in on the half-century, but that milestone is ten years gone for me now. I'm frying bigger fish these days. More old habits to quit; more new ones to start." She threw a slug of her drink down her throat, took a quick breath and finished her point. "And anyway, expressing those beliefs in newly outrageous ways didn't mean I'd picked up a new belief system all of a sudden. I just finally quit holding myself back, is all. I quit fitting in, dropped my social camouflage. I let my own self rip."

Meddy bent to pick up the stick that Bocker had lain across her right foot. Bocker knew that old people could learn new tricks. He was patient but persistent. Like everyone in SLANT, Meddy knew that he'd sit there staring at that stick and drooling on her sandal until she tossed it for him to fetch. The older he got, the less he remembered that playing with sticks was fun. For this reason, whenever he asked, his neighbors were always pleased to oblige. His politeness was so endearing.

Bocker's eyes were riveted to his "toy" as Meddy cocked her arm above the back of the Adirondack chair and stabbed the stick into the air, giving it a quick sling up and out. It was a good one, and he galloped off happily toward the trees to find it. But then a ground squirrel ran across his path and made him instantly forget his original purpose. It didn't matter at all, for little critters were fun to fetch, too, when he could catch them. The last they saw of Bocker that day was the tip of his attentive tail slipping into tall weeds at the edge of the rawer woods.

"I'm beginning to work on the Gnostics next week," Joy said. "Less sin, more enlightenment." Then she added, "Just finished that comparative piece on all the many versions of the Golden Rule." Joy was working on her thesis for a Master's degree in comparative religions, but that was just a means to an end—what she wanted was to define a whole new religion or faith or practice, or whatever it might turn out to be.

"Bet that was fun," Meddy said.

"It was. I found several more versions that I wasn't aware of when I started writing the chapter," Joy said. "If there's one constant in all of the religions of the world, that's got to be it—Golden Rule. Strange name. They don't all call it that."

"And yet," said Meddy, "though the pseudo X-tians claim it, it's the very thing they mostly ignore in practice anymore."

"Sometimes seems that way," said Joy.

"When, really, it's all we need."

"Funny you should say that," Joy said. "I think the Golden Rule is going to be the primary centerpiece of the hybrid theology I'm trying to develop ... you know ... theoretically."

"Well, duh," Meddy said.

"I know, I know."

"No-brainer."

"No argument."

"What happened to the X-tians using it as *their* centerpiece?" Meddy asked. "That's what I'd like to know. That's what's so aggravating."

"The problem seems to be that the Golden Rule is generally seen as little more than one of the first lessons taught to children," Joy said. "In practice, it gets lost by adults, I think, because they consider its meaning diminished by its association with childhood."

"You say that in your chapter?"

"Oh, you bet. That and a lot more."

"Good on ya, old gal."

The friends sat, listening to the sound of cicadas calling, doves cooing.

Friends can sit together like that without talking, if both of them are secure within themselves. A lull in conversation isn't uncomfortable when folks know each other's rhythms and, most importantly, know themselves very well.

After savoring long minutes of individual thought, Meddy spoke. "If you need someone to read that piece, offer feedback, I'd be happy to do that. If you like."

"I'll keep that in mind," Joy said, smiling. "You'd be the perfect reader, that's for sure, with your commitment to fairness, reciprocity. If you're nothing else, Meadowlark Nightengale, you're the Golden Rule's most famous promoter in SLANT."

This made Meddy smile. Two grey squirrels chattered irritably above them. A lone caducous leaf twirled in a lazy spiral toward the forest floor. Joy shifted her considerable weight in her webbed lawn chair, causing the frame to squeak out a small protest.

"Know what I think?" Meddy asked.

"Meddy, dear, you know I would never deign to impede any profound pronouncement of yours," said Joy, taking another sip of her rum drink. She ran the tip of her tongue around her lips because she didn't want to miss a single drop. It was so good.

"I think," said Meddy, "the Golden Rule gets 'lost' by most people because they don't want to be held accountable for its consequences. I mean, if people really made themselves measure everything they do against the Golden Rule, they'd be afraid of coming up short every time." She looked to Joy, then faced forward and gazed into some distant decision. "So to them, the Golden Rule is inconvenient, is what I think."

"That's about the size of it."

"Yet it's absolutely *crucial*," Meddy said, for this tenet was essential in her.

"I think so too," said Joy. "I think, in fact, that it's everything."

"And again I say, it's all we need. Well, that and *Be Honest*. But really, honesty is wrapped up in the Golden Rule already. I mean, who wants to be lied to? So, how can anyone lie?" Meddy said. "*Do unto others*. Can't be any simpler than that. If people—all people—would hold themselves account-able only to the Golden Rule, they could throw out the entire rest of that Book of theirs."

"Well put," Joy said. "The Golden Rule is indeed all we need."

"Exactly. What. I'm. Saying."

They sat again in mutual contemplation. You could have heard grass grow.

"On second thought," said Joy, "I'd add one more thing we need: to sit here in SLANT underneath these gorgeous cedars and hardwoods, sipping away an afternoon with this delectable coconut rum and pineapple-pomegranate juice concoction of yours."

Joy lifted her glass and Meddy responded in kind. They sipped, then Meddy pulled one of her trademark raggedly-rolled joints out of a shirt pocket and held it up for Joy to behold. "Only one more thing could make it better," she said, eyes twinkling with mischief. "Of all His plants, this could be God's greatest herbal creation."

"Ah," said Joy. "The peace that passeth among us, bringing further clarity to the somewhat enlightened."

"The misunderstood are always with us," Meddy said.

She lit up, drew deeply, and passed the peace.

# Be Steadfast, Loyal & True

NOONER WAS FIT TO BE TIED. "Them damn church campers," he grumbled on the drive back up the knob. "Think they're so much better than ever'bidy."

It never failed that whenever any of us SLANTers encountered church campers (who never went anywhere without their famous arrogance), it left a bad kind of aftertaste. They were different, the church campers were. And yet they were all the same. For one thing, (unlike SLANT) there wasn't a Black or Brown face in all of TRS.

This day, Nooner had run into three of the church campers down in the flats. The kids had gone off-knob for a mail run on behalf of the rest of the camp. Nooner was in the post office at the same time, preparing to send a little box containing a half-dozen half-pint jars of his homemade pear preserves to his mommy in Carolina. The fruit trees on the knobs, Nooner had found to his eternal delight, bore even better than his mommy's trees back home in Polk County, so he immediately set out to make the best better, just as she had always taught him. *Don't dwell*, she'd said countless times. *Turn your lemons into lemonade. And turn your lemonade into whiskey sours!* Always the food metaphors with Mommy, which was one of so many reasons why Nooner, a self-identified taste-aholic, loved her so much.

Nooner Rio Wayman knew his own story. He had been conceived in the middle of the day, because his young parents had both a sexual propensity for "nooners" ... and a sense of humor. His conception happened while they were traveling through Rio (rye-oh), Florida. Coincidentally, his father's people lived in Rio (rye-oh), Illinois, and his maternal grandparents were from Rio (rye-oh), West Virginia. These little places were not very well known, so Nooner had spent his whole life correcting people who—if they knew his middle name at all (a situation he tried to avoid)—stubbornly insisted on pronouncing it *ree-oh*, like the Rio Grande.

Now grown and out in the world on his own, Nooner had only been gone from his home in western North Carolina for a few years. He had kicked around a few months when he first struck out, catching rides with friendly truckers and motorists, sort of checking out the eastern half of the U.S. It had been a better education than the community technical college would have been, he was certain of that, and he had picked up many of the same skills through practical (which he thought was better) life-experience. At any rate, he'd landed up here in SLANT and by now had stayed put through a number of apple and pear pickings.

Winding down the narrow road today on his way to the P.O. off-knob, Nooner had crossed the little creek bridge and it had given him a flash memory of landing in SLANT several summers back. They'd taken him in, made him one of their own, the SLANTers had. SLANT was the puzzle piece that fit, snapped right into place in that soul hole that had felt empty and a little bit raw and had made him hit the road in the first place. After a few years, he was perfectly contented among this chosen family that Fate had brought him to, but he still missed his mommy something terrible. Still yet, having some of her best recipes kept him close to her in spirit. She'd mail them to him, and he'd try them out and mail the results back to her to test, if they were something that wouldn't spoil en route. From Kentucky, he sent her all kinds of things he'd make: peanut brittle, green tomato ketchup, pickled beets or okra, mayonnaise cake. Once he'd tried to mail her some sausages he'd herbed and stuffed himself, just the way she liked them, but by the time they arrived back home at the Tryon post office they were going bad, even though he fried them AND froze them before he packed them to mail.

Whenever she'd send him a letter saying she got a kick out of him fixing her the same foods that she used to cook up for him, it made him happy and less lonesome for her. They both knew he needed to live his own life, but growing up and cutting the apron strings when a mommy is all you've ever really had is harder for some than it is for others. Still, it was time. And she was as happy for him as he was for himself to have landed in such a magical place as SLANT.

At the P.O., Nooner stepped up to the little window and greeted Rachel. She was her usual chatty, friendly self. Everyone liked her. It was said that if you couldn't get along with Rachel, it was *you* who had the problem.

Even though they were off-knob, places like the big mercantile and the post office were considered in community with SLANT.

"How's things up on the knob, Nooner?" Rachel asked. It was just something to say. One of those niceties exchanged by rural people. They'd rather say, for example, "Y'all come go home with us" instead of just plain old "Goodbye," but they didn't really mean they wanted you to. Every humble body understood this informal code; it was a way of showing goodwill to your neighbors.

Anyway, Nooner hadn't felt required to give her any details about the most recent turd incident. Someone had somehow avoided Bocker long enough to deposit graffiti made of smeared shit on the side of SLANT's original namesake tavern, the building now known as The General. He liked Rachel too much to spoil her day, so he didn't. Plus, he really wanted to get to know her daughter a lot better, so he didn't think it would be smart to bring up unseemly subjects like turds; might tarnish the solidly-okay image she currently had of him. So, he just said, "Everything's copacetic, I reckon, Rachel," and let it go at that. She'd given a quick nod and flashed that comforting smile of hers, satisfied to move on to the next thing, which was mailing the package he'd brought to her counter this bright morning.

As Rachel was weighing the box of small preserve jars he'd carefully packed with plenty of newspapers and cedar needles for stuffing, the church campers entered. Since the front door to the tiny P.O. was directly behind him, Nooner hadn't seen them, but as soon as he heard their talk, he knew for certain they were camp kids. The arrogance in their voices gave them away. If you'd said to that bunch, *Y'all come go home with us*, they probably would jump up, grab their jackets and say, *Sure hope you got plenty of cold beer in your fridge!* Dumbasses.

They had come in talking, as usual. Them church campers, they were always *freakin' TALKIN'*—except when they were rolling their eyes or sneakily shitting in the creek or painting turds on your community center. What was it with church campers and shit? They seemed obsessed with it. *Prob'ly full of it, too,* Nooner thought. Better not to express every notion that enters one's head, he knew, so when the church campers came into the P.O. rattling their incestuous gossip, Nooner never turned around. He'd just as soon ignore them and hope they were quickly in and out of there. Maybe they had a key to one of the boxes or drawers so they could pull out the church camp mail and soon be gone. Nooner wanted privacy so he could find a way to bring up the subject of Rachel's daughter (the lovely Maureen) and get The Postmistress talking about the secret object of his affection.

That could have happened. But it didn't. Apparently, there was no P.O. box for the church camp. Apparently, they'd be standing there waiting to ask Rachel for the church camp's mail so she could hand a big rubber-banded bundle over the counter. And, apparently, they were going to continue the fairly rude conversation they'd been having since before they walked through the door.

Not ten o'clock in the morning, and already church campers were on his last goddamn nerve. Would winter ever come back so SLANT could be rid of these cretins for the cold months, at least? Wasn't it enough that they were *everywhere* a quarter of every year? *Jesus, Mary, Joseph and the donkey,* he thought.

Then he heard what they were gossiping about.

"And did you see all that white foamy crap in the corners of his mouth?" one church camper was saying. "Gross!"

"Well, if *you* spit every time *you* talked, you'd probably foam at the mouth too," another church camper said. Everybody in their clique cracked up.

Then the third church camper started a routine whereby he was clearly mocking whomever they were talking about. Every time he came to "z" or "s" or "sh" or "ch" or a soft "c" in a word, he slurred the letter, pinning his tongue to the roof of his mouth and sloshing saliva-laden air from the back of his molars as he pronounced those letters in a sloppy whoosh around the outside of his back teeth and along his cheeks.

"Sssomebody'sss gonna hafta ansssswer for thisss messss!" he mocked, with all the intended sound effect he could muster. "It ssstinksss!" The other two laughed at his impression. "I'm sssseriouss!" They laughed harder at this fake speech impediment. "Ssshut up, you sssonsssabitchesss! Thisss isss sssome sssseriouss ssshit!" This one he had stage-whispered angrily for greater effect, every sibilance over-emphasized, spit spewing every which way. All three of them collapsed into hysterics.

Nooner and Rachel, obviously unable to avoid overhearing in the tiny public space, had given each other glances, their eyebrows adding emphasis. The church campers were oblivious, wrapped so tightly, as assholier-than-thou teenagers usual are, in their own little judgmental and ego-centric world.

Rachel's face had become uncharacteristically stoic, and it was clear that she immediately resolved to be professional, courteous and all business as long as the church campers were present in her P.O. She tried to hurry with Nooner's mailing, so as to move on to this pack of silly teenagers, get whatever they wanted over-and-done-with, and move them out of there forthwith.

Nooner, simultaneously, was in the midst of a revelation: *They're mockin' Wet Willie!* The little assholes had been spying, waiting to see who would find their shitful masterpiece and witness what the reaction would be. It had been Wet Willie, Nooner remembered, who yesterday had alerted the rest of SLANT to the abstract turd "art" on The General's siding.

Wet Willie was everyone's mascot and teammate. He was a little guy, maybe four-foot-ten, his growth having been stunted by disease that he'd fought off just as he was entering puberty. Now thirty-five, he looked not like a child but like the petite man he was. He kept a scruffily scant beard so no one would confuse him for a boy. And *damn*, that man could play some mean keyboards! Funky from the ground up. From time to time, Wet kept a girlfriend too. Currently, it was Iwana. No one knew where he'd met her, but she was tall, blonde and European, you could tell by her accent. Iwana Bonet. She pronounced it *Ee-VAH-nah Bo-NAY*, but her friends lovingly called her I Wanna Bone It. She genuinely laughed and laughed when they said that. She wasn't so haughty-European that she didn't enjoy a *good-ole-Amurkin-joke-like.*

Besides being a small-stature man, Willie had a very strong, overly-sibilant lisp. Juicy, it was. All his life, starting with kids on the playground, people had made fun of the way he talked, and it had been painful for him. As a boy, he had cried at night, begging his mom not to make him go back to school. What she'd *wanted* to do was go to school with him and beat hell out of those little snots, but what she did instead was to help him understand that the best way to take out the sting was to face the problem head-on instead of hiding from it. She assured him that if he made it known on the playground that he was aware that his speech was different *but so what,* then they couldn't hurt him with it. Together, Willie and his mom devised a plan whereby he would embrace his lisp and even put on little performances for the other kids. He thought maybe he could be a sort of schoolyard comedian, a local celeb. To cap off the plan, he added one spark of genius: his stage name would be Wet Willie! *Because when I talk it sounds kind of WET,* Willie told his mom. *Try it and see,* his mom had said, *starting tomorrow.* So he did. And he became an instant hit and made many friends.

Now, when he introduced himself to people in his adult world, he told them, "Name'sss Willie. But my friendsss call me Wet."

*Nothing like owning the very thing other people wish they could steal and use against you,* his mom had always said. *If they don't have the power to get their hands on it, they can't do meanness with it. Language is power,* she'd told him. *Don't forget that, son.* And Willie never did.

So, here came these church camp turd-floating shit-smearing punks making fun of Nooner's friend like they owned the right to do so. First they harass, then they trespass, then they deface, *and then* they lurk around spying to see some reaction to their handiwork. But worst of all, they are stupid and insensitive enough to go out in public ridiculing a member of the very community they have injured.

Nooner could have reacted then and there. He could have whirled around and let them know that *he* was a SLANTer too. That he was going to walk out of the P.O. and head right over to the sheriff's office to report them for their crimes of the bowel. Or he could have swung his big left-handed powerhouse around and knocked one or two of them into the wall of keyed mailboxes. He could have called them hypocritical little snobs. He even could have blessed them and made the sign of the cross and then humiliated them by kneeling before them, praying aloud with theatrical passion and asking their God to forgive them for their hateful actions, carried out both in the dark and in the light of day.

He did none of these. Instead, Nooner Rio Wayman took the high road. He paid for his postage, bid a cordial farewell to Rachel (intentionally slipping in a request that she pass along his best to the lovely Maureen), and walked out of the P.O. without so much as a glance at the church campers. It was as if—he hoped they noticed—they did not even exist. Of course, they didn't recognize him as a SLANTer, and he knew Rachel wouldn't say a word to them about that.

But Nooner vowed this wasn't over—not by a long shot. By the time he had finished all his errands and guided his truck into the climb up the knob toward SLANT, he was, indeed, fit to be tied. Nooner had pacifist tendencies, but he wasn't your classical pacifist. He'd rather patiently persuade, as a rule, but he'd also cut the head off an aggressive poisonous snake without hesitation. He was practical in that way—a man of words first who didn't shy from action when action was required.

The more he thought about it, the more worked-up he got. *Smear turds on The General and then laugh about it all over town, huh? Go around in public makin' fun of one of the coolest dudes in all of SLANT, will you?* Oh, he'd show them the high road, all right—the dangerous, intellectual high road: a one-laner with switchbacks, kiss-your-ass curves, a rock wall of solidarity on one side and a drop-off into a hell-pit of Biblical proportions on the other. He'd show them what it's like to find yourself lonely and trapped in a scary emotional place with the psychological equivalent of a D9 dozer bearing steadily upon you from one direction and an out-of-control, fully-loaded two-ton dually of visceral fear roaring down at you from the other. (When it came to imagining metaphor and revenge, Nooner was a singular genius.)

And he ~~thought~~ knew just who to recruit to help him teach these creepy little conservatives-in-training the lesson of their lives.

Now to figure out exactly what kind of squeeze-play they deserved.

## Eliminate Pettiness

NOONER STOPPED BY THE BONSAI FARM on his way home. It was already morphing into a steamy day and Tractor Girl welcomed the break, suggesting they move into the shade. Nooner had just been heatedly explaining to her the whole turd brigade confession that he had overheard down at the P.O. "So, can you help?" he asked her.

"Help do what?" Tractor Girl said. "It's an interesting development, but I can't see how it involves me personally."

"Well, sure it does! It hits all of us. We *are* SLANT, and this turd-based defacement is a slam on us all."

"But revenge? Against kids? I mean jeez, Nooner. You really tryin' to work up revenge on a bunch of immature teenagers? First, that's kind of a dangerous direction to take, don't you think? Them being minors and all? You being a legal adult?"

Nooner hadn't really considered any ramifications bookending his search for revenge of the turds.

"Number Two (no pun intended), what exactly are you going to do? Trespass on their property and smear Bocker's doo-doo all over their footpaths and benches?" She looked him straight in the eyes. "I mean, listen to yourself, man."

As Nooner listened to her logic, the heat began to drain away from his temples. He heard the absurdity of his emotional reaction for the first time. Damn. TG was good.

"And third of all," she said, "I don't do revenge. Not that I haven't wanted to. Not that people who hurt me bad haven't deserved my revenge. But I just don't know how. I don't know how to defend myself. I don't know how to turn the tables on mean, motherfucking shit-asses. I never have had that talent—though I'll admit I've wished for it many a time. But in every circumstance where I've gotten angry enough to try revenge, it always backfires and makes me feel worse about myself than ever. So, I've given up on that crap. I'd rather just let assholes be assholes. I don't have to join them in their assholery. You know?"

Nooner knew. He was starting to feel embarrassed that he'd brought this whole thing up. Ashamed that he'd come to TG expecting … what … that together they'd execute a perfectly vengeful plan? And how in the world, he now saw, could that even happen?

"I love ye like a brother, but I'm solely into peace these days, buddy," said Tractor Girl. "You know me. I can't protect myself emotionally. Never learned. So, I finally figured out that the best thing I can do is stay the hell away from conflict altogether. So far, it's worked." She clunked her fist against her head a couple times and added, "Knock wood." This made Nooner smile a bit for the first time since overhearing those little shits down at the P.O. "And I damn sure *don't go looking* for trouble," she added. "Don't want to tempt fate."

"Yeah, okay, I get you," Nooner said. He felt a bit sheepish in the face of TG's emotional maturity. Nearly all his fire for revenge had sputtered out for now. He knew her cooler head had bettered him on this topic. "Dammit. You're right. I'm wrong. It was stupid."

"Nuh-uh. Not wrong to want to defend Willie. Not wrong to want to keep SLANT safe from vandals," she said. "But maybe a little off track on planning a revenge-fueled raid on TRS. I'll help you with almost anything you ask, and you know that. But not something like this, brother-man. Not this."

Nooner smiled at his friend. He realized she'd just saved his butt from doing something really stupid that could've gotten him locked up if he'd been caught in the act. "No need to lower ourselves to their shitty level, I reckon," said he.

"That's my two-cents," Tractor Girl said.

"That's a *lot* of sense," said Nooner, "and worth a fortune. Thanks for talkin' me down."

Tractor Girl shrugged and reached into the ice chest that rested in the shade under a big hickory. "Beer?"

"You bet."

The bottles chilled their hands; icy shards and water dripped off the glass bottoms. Tractor Girl pressed hers against her sunburned cheek. They twisted off the caps, clinked their bottles' necks together, and quaffed deeply in communion with one another.

Nooner, it must be said, felt like himself again. A lot could be learned over an ice cold beer with a warm-hearted friend.

# Betrayal is One Thing; Rejection Another

SOME OF OUR STORIES ARE HARDER TO TELL than others. Tractor Girl's personal pain falls into this category. It seems easier to tell it from the perspective of two different times—the *Before* and the *After*. This should help you understand how profoundly betrayal and rejection have changed her ... and will forevermore.

But first, let me note that Tractor Girl and I, while always friends and neighbors, became close only after the initial worst of her suffering was already behind her. I had no clue what a journaler she is! I came to understand that she chose to approach me with the story of her own splintering and recovery because she determined that what we have in common is writing. I am honored that she trusted me with this part of her story.

TG isn't much to talk, so one day she handed me a few notebooks, saying only that they would explain. These journals were difficult to read. That's an understatement. Not because of her writing ability—she's good—but because the pain she recorded in them is *so damned raw.*

I'm not sure why Tractor Girl wanted me to read and interpret her journals. Could be that she was tired of suffering in silence. Perhaps she knows from experience that each SLANTer is a small part of the whole history of our place, and she didn't want to hold anything back from the archive that is us. Most likely, however, after so many years she simply gave up on processing her pain alone in brave silence. In the end, maybe she just wanted someone here to know what she had suffered ... and that she strives to survive.

Don't we all reach a point of needing to share our pain in hopes that the empathy we long for will come to our rescue? TG didn't know how to talk about it. Neither did she know whom to talk to. So, she wrote it down. She wrote and wrote and wrote. I imagine she cried and railed and shouted, too, but not where any of us could hear. I imagine now, having read her journals, that her tears still occasionally water the bonsais while she does her solitary work downstream, day upon day, year upon year.

Honestly, we had no notion of what she went through ... or how long it lasted. How very long. It must have been exhausting. It must have been excruciating. Yet she went ahead with living in the way that she wished to. She did her work. She contributed to her community. She never let on. We truly had no idea. Until she shared, that is. Now we know, and I for one feel a great deal of sadness that she went through this hurt all alone.

It's a lot, but you can handle it. I trust you with it, just as Tractor Girl trusts me.

Maybe this story exists to teach us to look more closely, to be more present in our awareness of our loved ones. I'm heartbroken that she didn't feel safe.

Or maybe it's a lesson about sharing our experiences as a means of mitigating our own suffering.

Maybe it's both.

As for Tractor Girl's motive in her sharing, she told me this: "I'm hoping it'll help somebody else, Bard. Help them handle their worst suffering. Maybe give them hope to keep hanging in there until the hurt starts to ease. 'Til it's manageable, at least."

I agree. When grief feels so damned lonely, how could sharing it not help?

# In the Absence of Strength, Try Courage

IT IS POSSIBLE TO TRUST TOO MUCH. Tractor Girl had learned
this the hard way, and it was a lesson filled with pain, then sorrow, then
abject and inconsolable grief. And after that, she realized she will be
haunted with this new knowledge for the rest of her days. Her inner life
was utterly ruined for a long time, only because once she trusted too much.

These days, during her luxurious kayak commute along Fidelity to
and from her work at the bonsai farm, Tractor Girl is usually as blissful
as any human alive. Some days in her reverie, though, she suddenly relives
the commitment ceremony she and Gazelle had years back, alongside the
waters of Fidelity Creek, and the thought almost makes her smile—but
then comes the emotional whiplash. Even though in her memory she and
Gazelle will always be young and in love, wrapped in that breeze lifting
off the water, now she is forced to know something that's too painful to
bear. Someday, maybe, she'll fully recover—but that will be then, and *then*
hasn't come yet. This part is about the *Before*. And sometimes *before* is
already *too late*, whether we know it or not.

How could she have known, gliding through that beautiful era long
ago, that in time a dark future would arrive, one in which Gazelle, the
darling little thing who was the love of her life—who *was* in fact her
life—would horribly betray Tractor Girl and then shrug those seductive
shoulders and slither away without accepting one iota of responsibility
for the destruction of a precious life that she had held solely in her hands?
How could Tractor Girl have guessed that Gazelle would successfully
refuse to be held accountable—or that virtually everyone else in their lives
would let the betrayal slide down, down, ever downward into oblivion,
only because Gazelle was so adorable and petite and able to entertain and
deceive them so cleverly? Oh, she seemed sweet and innocent. Everyone
said so, and their confusion kept them from doing the necessary thing. No
one came to Tractor Girl's aid, because no one questioned the lies Gazelle
told about what happened and why. Not a single mutual friend considered
it their place to confront Gazelle. And Gazelle, it turned out, was far too
deep in self-serving denial to face responsibility on her own. How *tedious.*

Accountability—what a drag *that* would be for an artiste. So beneath her.

She was a musical storyteller by profession, Gazelle was. Therefore, apparently, she just felt entitled to create any narrative she chose.

So the betrayal, the infliction of unbearable pain, happened to our Tractor Girl. The abandonment. The intentional killing of something that mattered so much. Six years went by. Then ten. Tractor Girl suffered a sting for every tick of the clock through each of the minutes, hours, days, weeks to follow. Tractor Girl was alone with the fallout for months, years on end, even when she experienced a rare little joy, an occasional small success, the kind attention of someone—surrogates, as far as Tractor Girl was concerned.

By halfway through the first decade, it was all *ancient* history to the victimizer, Gazelle, who isn't made like Tractor Girl.

Gazelle always controls how much she allows herself to believe, to what degree she decides to feel, and what version of "truth" she will tell. Is it the performer in her that makes every situation merely a singular opportunity for her to *perform*? To invent *false* reality? To imagine a *so-called* truth, one that suits her urges and whims? To see how good she is at playing a role, at fooling people? That was Gazelle's sole strategy—her own self preservation. She didn't give Tractor Girl's suffering one thought in this world. She can face sizeable audiences, but she cannot face what she did to Tractor Girl. In short, Gazelle cannot face herself. And so she lied. She lied about what happened, invented a role for herself, played it to the hilt.

But Tractor Girl's very real wounds remained open, her heart and nerves raw as afterbirth through all those years, the intensity of that initial blinding burst of pain never subsiding. She didn't want to, but she oozed sorrow. The only truth she knew was what really did happen— because it had happened to her and she couldn't escape a single degree of it. Pain was her payback for having trusted another human completely for the first time in her life ... and for having been entirely betrayed, with the additional insult of character assassination thrown in for good measure.

The cheating was bad, but Gazelle's lies were the cruelest cut of all.

When it was over, and when time had passed and she could allow herself to look back upon it, Tractor Girl saw that because she'd had no help from anyone (and no choice in Gazelle's power to ruin Tractor Girl's life), she would have to learn to pretend that she was all right—got pretty good at it too, convincing everyone but herself that she was fine, past it, carrying on. Somehow she found just enough emotional muscle to fake all of that, though faking anything is unnatural to TG. But she came to believe she *had* to fake it in order to make other people comfortable, to save them from her overwhelming sorrow. Something in her was convinced that nobody wanted to witness her pain.

It was cruel and untimely, but Gazelle spun the false narrative about what happened, a lie that allowed her to live with herself quite without guilt. Her strategy—*never look back*—was shallow, but one can't deny its absolute effectiveness. Such a way is perfect for the self-serving nature of users like Gazelle. It is how they live with themselves, guilt-free.

*After* Gazelle, Tractor Girl was alone, even though people were all around her. These people seemed to notice nothing in her demeanor that they should be particularly concerned about. She had trouble breathing, but no one heard that. She lost her focus, lost her place, lost her thoughts because reminders were continual and cruel—numerous times every day for years and years this awful reality slammed into her ribcage, and bright streaks of red lightning flashed through her brain, often at the most inopportune times. Anxiety attacks were steady stalkers. Too much of her energy was siphoned off to this grief. But she worked hard to hide it all, and mostly she succeeded. No one connected the dots. At times, Tractor Girl considered herself lucky that people in general don't really give a shit about the emotional suffering of those around them. Most often, humans make an unconscious effort *not* to notice the immediate and crippling pain of others—yet they do this while pretending (is that a fair word?) to befriend. Her tactic was superficial, yes. But it kept her under their radar and kept scrutiny away. She was unable to talk about it anyway.

Most of all, she became obsessed with trying to understand how she could have mistaken Gazelle for the kind of person who was safe to love, the kind of woman who would mutually protect Tractor Girl from jeopardy. The kind of partner who could be trusted. And Tractor Girl, over and over, asked herself, *How could I have been so goddamn stupid?*

Eleven. Fourteen. The years of hurting and the years of pretending and the years of emotional isolation from passion and trust and safety became heavier and harder to carry. The compromises felt like necklaces of horseshoes, like hats of hot coals. Each heartbeat was another nip of the blacksmith's tongs, and each breath like a kick in the gut from a stout mule who refuses to go gently where the good farrier asks him to go. Even the sound of her former lover's name abraded the thin membrane off Tractor Girl's heart, unnaturally reshaping the organ every single time that rasp skimmed over it. News of her former lover—whom she had once known with an intimacy she'd not previously dreamed possible—was like bellows wind, whipping up such a fire as might *consume* her rather than forge her in some useful way, and sometimes she wished with fervor that it would just go ahead and burn her to ashes once and for all, putting her out of this misery. (Yes, she considered the worst option, but she hung on.)

Ah, but she has been known, too, to place her hand purposefully into that fire. The pain, as years went by, became familiar, after all. Pain was the only remaining connection to that lost love. And Time was no damn good as a healer.

Pain and Time twined about Tractor Girl, nearly squeezing the life out of her. She tried so hard to process it entirely alone, always turning back to her journals:

> *What no one else is able to see, because it is inconceivable to them, is that Gazelle is mean. She's good at things, and she has talent and an engaging personality. But her mean streak is as wide as the Ohio River. She eagerly carried out her role as Troubadour-in-Residence during her time here in SLANT. I loved her for these things and more, but there was always that underlying truth that Gazelle has a dangerous mean streak in her.*

It was a fact that Tractor Girl eventually was *forced* to acknowledge —although back then, in the *Before*, she'd thought they were happy; back then she intentionally ignored the myriad hints of this hideous truth whenever they showed themselves. And they did show themselves. Often. But in the *Before*, Tractor Girl wouldn't let herself see.

Years later, however, in the *After*, all the shadows re-emerged—like all the little touches that tint and shade and texture a photographic print, fixing the permanent memory as it develops in Time's darkroom. Gazelle materialized from that chemical soup as the wolf in sheep's clothing you've heard tell about.

> *She knows how to work it. And, damn, does she know how to disguise it.*

Tractor Girl vividly recounted in writing that Gazelle had called her a terrible, disgusting name, had hurled that glass bowl at her head one night in a fury of wholly-imagined jealousy. She relived—in the vulnerability of her journal—the memory of kneeling in shattered shards next to the wall where the bowl had smashed. She had wept and bled because she had nowhere else to go and because Gazelle was all Tractor Girl knew of home and all she had thought she would ever need to know. *I'm a foolish old thing* is what our dear Tractor Girl wrote of herself. But later she figured it out.

> *I see it now. She was determined to get rid of me, even way back then. Why didn't she just admit she never loved me? Why torture me? Is she that much a coward?*

TG journaled, too, about how scared she had been when she learned that Gazelle had come home from a week-long gig that had involved an indiscretion that Tractor Girl made herself pretend she didn't know about—because she couldn't bear that it was true. She later recalled the night she witnessed Gazelle and the Other Woman—that much younger, thinner woman—welded in an embrace, and how the Other Woman had held Gazelle much too long for a mere friendship hug. Remembered so painfully how the Other Woman had *closed her eyes* blissfully while holding Tractor Girl's wife. That had been the moment when Tractor Girl really knew, in spite of Gazelle's denials. And still our Tractor Girl had waited a year—waited and tried and hoped and asked the right questions ... and was rebuked and ridiculed for asking.

Our friend suffered alone—foolishly, yes, foolishly believing that Gazelle was capable of doing the right thing; insanely holding to that little liar and her lying lies because being a terrible a judge of character was something Tractor Girl hadn't previously realized herself guilty of.

TG looked back later with the knowledge that Gazelle hadn't meant *any* of the promises she'd made to the "us" of them, didn't consider those promises to be forever, as Tractor Girl believed them to be with all her heart, just as much now as she had on the day she'd spoken her vows to that liar, Gazelle, beside our lovely little creek.

Time passed. It passed. It passed. Tractor Girl even tried, after days and weeks and years and great stabs of emotional effort, to be in Gazelle's presence again on occasion, but she ended up with nausea and diarrhea every time, and pains shooting through her legs until she had to moan face down into a pillow to keep anyone from hearing her suffer. Not much of a talker, our TG. If anyone had heard this agony, they'd have asked. And she didn't want to answer. She, in fact, couldn't.

Her left arm and hand went numb sometimes. Her heart leapt and banged painfully, ricocheted with irregularity. It was very physical, this grief. It lasted for too much of Tractor Girl's life. And until she handed over her journals, no one knew its extent. Her public pretense was that good.

When her pain did call attention to itself, Tractor Girl always said it was something else—something she ate, maybe, or low blood sugar, or a lack of sleep, or an aching back. And she believes people accepted this because they wanted to; because it was easier to accept the deflection than to see that Tractor Girl needed their help fixing it ... and might not survive without their participation. But she protected her friends by downplaying what was really wrong and to what extent. The last thing she needed was to drive them away.

> *They'll be all I've got, in the end, but I fear that if they knew the ugly, unbearable depths of my pain, they'd run. And I wouldn't blame them.*

She believed that if she expressed her legitimate pain, she'd be unlovable and easy to discard. So, against her very nature, she deflected, faked it. She ate her pain. And it, of course, ate her.

Turns out, the Other Woman became just another fling in Gazelle's past, probably like Tractor Girl herself was a fling, truth be told.

Anyway, Gazelle moved out and "moved on" (a phrase TG hates to this very day, because a devastating trauma goes with you wherever you try to go). Gazelle allowed herself to assume that Tractor Girl must needs have done likewise with the same ease … and lack of consciousness. Gazelle was willfully ignorant to the fact that, after those affairs and after her temper tantrums, maintaining a friendship with the Other Woman but not with Tractor Girl was hurtful. Gazelle certainly never even thought about how thoroughly she had devastated Tractor Girl. Was it worth all that damage—worth tearing up a good person who had loved Gazelle too much, and worth murdering the "us" of them? In the end, and after all it had cost our dear, dear TG, that Other Woman wasn't even worth making a life with! If the two cheaters had stayed together, then at least there would have been *something* Tractor Girl could have understood about the *why why why why why why why* that pounded her jugular with every heartbeat for too many of the years that followed. It would have killed Tractor Girl, but it would have made some modicum of sense.

> *Nothing may ever again make sense. Not one cursed thing. Still, I will be required to stay alive, and so will have to find a way to keep from losing my mind. This is a daily struggle —worse some days, more manageable others—but always there is that essential something missing in this ravaged, empty pit where my heart once, and once only, rested.*

Tractor Girl even faced a day, after those first few years, when she steeled herself for a visit to the home of Gazelle and her latest new lover. Tractor Girl worked very hard for several weeks to talk herself into being able to try doing this, and many tears were shed in the process. The fear, while never overcome, was temporarily contained for the occasion, in the interest of finding "closure" at last.

On the way there however, a couple hours into the long drive, she received a cellphone message from Gazelle. The Other Woman, it seemed, had also come for a "friendly" visit, was already there, in fact—something that Gazelle hadn't mentioned in the negotiations leading up to Tractor Girl's deeply disturbing decision to visit. "But that will be all right," Gazelle's message said. Her breezy tone proved how insensitive she is. "We're all adults, after all."

Tractor Girl pulled her truck to the side of the road, and for the next half-hour she wept and moaned with grief and screamed her anger and beat the steering wheel and thought over this new development. She just couldn't do it. Couldn't put herself through it. She kept hearing Gazelle's voice: "We're all adults, after all."

*Really?* Tractor Girl was stunned.

Later, she'd journaled about this.

*And when, exactly, were we ALL adults? Was it when I sat in our home entirely alone night after night for more than a year? I sat panicked in your scratchy, hideous turquoise platform rocker, the one with the carved swans' heads for armrests and the ugly matching ottoman. Is THAT when we were all adults? Was it during those nights—so many of them there were—when I waited up late for you to come home from a part-time job at a place that I knew had closed hours before? Is that when?*

*Or was it when I went to that orchestra concert at the park in the city and stumbled into a date in which you and the Other Woman were sprawled on a blanket, cozied up together. I crashed my own wife's date with another woman! Just one of many trysts that you'd been having behind my back. Was THAT when we were all adults, Gazelle? Really? My memory is vivid of the look on the Other Woman's face when I appeared at blanket's edge. Her plans for the evening were ruined; she cared not that my whole life was! And neither, apparently, did you. So why can I still not understand that, yes, you were actually capable of that level of betrayal? It goes so far beyond being insensitive. It reveals the cruelty at your core.*

*But tell me, Gazelle, when were we ALL adults? When you cheated on me? When you lied to me? When you lied ABOUT me to our friends and family, telling them that I was the one who was the cheater and liar—in order to protect your fabricated image as a defenseless little thing? When you, The Perpetrator, cast yourself instead as Victim in your little homegrown drama—was that when we were all adults?*

*Or was it when you left all the worries about money in my lap, claiming that working at just any old job was beneath you? Was that when we were ALL adults, Gazelle?*

*Or was it when you were manipulating me with your insidious passive-aggressive techniques?*

*Or was it when you always knew you would leave me, yet you let me make a fool of myself by stupidly proclaiming all those years we were together that I'd never desert you?*

*When, goddamn it, Gazelle? When exactly were we ALL adults? Was it when you broke the vows you made to me at our ceremony beside Fidelity Creek? Was it "adult" that you were being when you kissed the Other Woman, let her take you in her arms, made love to her in our bed while I was away visiting my mother, a trip you'd calculatedly refused to take with me? Yes, I knew about that too. Then, perhaps? Then is when we ALL were adults? Seriously.*

*Or maybe it was "adult" of you to lie to me repeatedly when I begged you to talk to me about what was going on—begged … so that we might have had a chance to work through it. And even if you didn't want me, you might have been honest about that, might have allowed me the dignity of some small bit of closure. But you decided that you didn't need to respect me enough to allow that. 'Nothing is going on,' you said every single time. 'There's nothing to talk about. You're just being paranoid.' You said that to me.*

*You refused then, and have ever since, to tell me ANY-THING—why you turned against me; at what point you decided to dump me; why you had pretended to love me after you chased me and caught me, though clearly you never had loved me at all. Why you needed to make me out to be 'paranoid' when I WASN'T WRONG about what you were doing. Why did our vows mean so little to you? Why did you turn cold-bloodedly against me; strike like a goddamned copperhead? This poison that sickens and im-pairs me still—is that the most "adult" part of yourself that you could offer me? I who gave up things I loved to make sure you got what you wanted. Is that the best you could give the woman you proclaimed to love and with whom you exchanged vows, planned a life?*

*You fucking gaslighter. You sick liar.*

On the day of that ridiculously insensitive phone message—like many other insulting fragment-days to follow—Tractor Girl learned more about the breathtaking disrespect of which Gazelle is capable, and so TG turned her truck around, retraced the hundred miles toward "home" (whatever that might be anymore) rather than put herself into emotional danger again.

Plus, TG knew if she went back instead of forward, she wouldn't be arrested for assault. Because if she had walked into that mess, she wouldn't have trusted herself not to punch somebody's, everybody's lights out. Even for a pacifist like Tractor Girl, purposefully inflicted pain can be that maddening.

*I'll never jeopardize us.* Tractor Girl's journal revealed that she had always promised Gazelle this, with urgency. Many times she'd said it.

But she learned that she should have vowed more fiercely to protect *herself* from jeopardy all those years ago. Gazelle, it was obvious, had her own self-protection perfected and didn't need anyone's help in that regard.

Tractor Girl would yearn to say things to Gazelle, but would never be given the chance, for Gazelle always weaseled out of every conversation she'd agreed to, every request for closure TG asked her for. There were things she needed to ask Gazelle; things she needed to say to her face. But Gazelle refused such a hearing, every time—no doubt because she'd've had to face TG's truth and grief.

So, in service of her own healing, Tractor Girl wrote them down.

> *The weapon you used for killing me wasn't loaded with bullets. Nonetheless, here I am, riddled with holes. How I am still on my feet, I do not know. Well fucking done, Annie Oakley. Could you please stop shooting me now?*

The vulnerable little Hannaleigh, who still lives deep inside Tractor Girl, cried constantly for comfort that no one could give, and that impairment made pain even harder for Tractor Girl to bear. But though Tractor Girl may *think* she is not strong, she *knows* she is by-god brave. She looked this cruelty in its eye, spit on the ground at its feet. She stood tall and waited for whatever the end would be. *The end*, she wrote in her journal, *can't be any worse than living through this horror.*

Worst of all, there was this truth: Gazelle blatantly chose *not to fight* for their "us." Rather, Gazelle turned the whole thing against Tractor Girl—as if TG was the cause of the problem, was the one having an affair, was the one who broke their vows, was the one who lied about every fucking thing.

Anyway, Gazelle accomplished her secret plan for escape, eagerly packed up her stuff, and promptly moved in with the Other Woman off knob, staying there for a surprisingly short while before leaving Kentucky entirely. And alone.

And still our wounded Tractor Girl hoped for resolution. For years. She irrationally hoped that Gazelle would decide to fight for the "us" of them.

At the very beginning of the break-up, and hoping for a civil period of temporary separation, Tractor Girl had arranged for her beloved wife to go to the Blue Ridge and live in a place that had been so healing for Tractor Girl many years before, a place that was a hometown of her heart. She had once believed in the healing quality of that community. TG expected that, after some time spent there among people whom Tractor Girl loved and trusted to help fix this, Gazelle might return to her right mind, might remember love, might yearn to rebuild their life together. But it was all revealed as a lie. The vows. The "love." The healing place. The friends there. All a lie. And that knowledge compounded Tractor Girl's loss exponentially. For Gazelle went there and immediately stole the place from Tractor Girl; stole Tractor Girl's friends and loved ones too with her lies; played her role as "the grieving widow," as one of these friends years later described it to Tractor Girl. And what Tractor Girl will not understand, ever, is that those dear folks so easily accepted Gazelle's lies without *once* asking to hear Tractor Girl's side of the story. Tractor Girl, who had been their friend first. Tractor Girl, who is the only reason Gazelle was living among them at all.

In the early years, remarkably, she even trusted that Gazelle would miss her. Foolish? Oh my, yes. Because truth is truth.

> *Gazelle has proven herself incapable of anything sustainable, refused being pulled from the spotlight, is not mature enough to offer admissions, apologies, responsibility, remorse.*

The betrayals piled one on top of the next until our beloved TG was barely able to breathe. And that acute sensation born of all those losses and all those realizations would not leave her for a long, long time.

That magical place in the Blue Ridge that had once been TG's retreat from the world, just as toxin-free as SLANT now is, was suddenly no longer Tractor Girl's. Nearly two decades on, she's still waiting for Gazelle to do right by her, give her closure, apologize for the damage, admit the truths that Tractor Girl has needed to hear for so long. *Just a miniscule touch of sincere contrition would be nice. Is that too much to ask?*

Foolish, foolish Tractor Girl. Her busted heart, on the whole, meant nothing. She might as well have been struck by a truck on the highway; life as she knew it was that entirely over. Yet her injuries and the chronic pain they cause may very well linger for the rest of her days. She'll not let herself believe in romance again, that's for sure. Love, to our beloved TG, means Pain ... and little else.

> *Gazelle, ever the queen of denial, will never acknowledge any of this, especially not the premeditated parts of her actions, including with the Other Woman. (Oh, say her name: Lynelle. Lynelle the whore, the home-wrecker, the bitch, the selfish and cruel murderer of hope.) No, Gazelle will never look back now. She will survive, not needing to heal because she rejoices in her escape. After all, I had probably become testy and annoying during that last year when I knew I was being betrayed but was suffering as quietly as I could, trying to wait Gazelle out, hoping our life together wouldn't end, believing in her love in spite of all evidence to the contrary.*

Everything broke when Gazelle left. Eventually, seventeen years crawled miserably by. Eighteen. Somewhere along the way, as her journals reveal, Tractor Girl found a mantra: *She's never coming home. Gazelle is never coming home.* She wrote of repeating this thousands of times, attempting to convince herself. And she wrote that she forced herself to believe it as much as she could, even though she can never believe it at all.

> *'Gazelle is never coming home.' I silently chant it in the kayak, at work with the bonsais, walking the paths at SLANT. What else can I do? Gazelle is never going to apologize. Accept it! She'll never ask forgiveness for betraying me, splintering me. She'll never admit that she ruined my inner life in every permanent way. Won't confess that she destroyed me—me!—who sacrificed for her, who adjusted to her, who, frankly, dumbed myself down for her. More to the point, she doesn't care that she did this. She belittles me, derides what she calls my 'victim shit,' refuses to see that if I react like a victim, it is only because I AM HER GODAMMED VICTIM.*

> *'Gazelle is never coming home.' It'll be a long time before that feels like truth, but truth it will nonetheless be.*

Into what old age will Tractor Girl survive carrying this emotional burden? It's of some concern, for she had loyally tended the (false, as it turned out) fires of love and permanence that those singular creekside promises represented to her. Had kept her vows even in the *After* of the betrayal and the lies. When TG commits, she commits fully—to the bonsai farm, to SLANT, and to her marriage. Will she ever legitimately accept that Gazelle hadn't honored those same vows, hadn't helped her keep those fires lit and, worse, had never intended to?

One gnawing question (*Could I really have been that poor a judge of character?*) have ever since kept her from trusting, from believing in Love.

Finally, she forced herself to face the truth of truths:

> *Gazelle never loved me at all! She used me up and never did love me. She fooled me because it was easy. I saw what I wanted to see because I wanted love and a life with her too much. But I was just her checkbook, her fan. And I am an utter fool who thought I was loved when I never was. I fooled myself! But here's the reality: the Gazelle I fell in love with NEVER EXISTED. From the day we met, I fell in love with a role she was playing. I fell in love with a lie. I'm honest, so how in the hell could I have known she isn't?*

This helped some. So, Tractor Girl bucked up, pretended recovery, and she did a good job of pretending. She now knows that she will grow old and eventually die with many loving people around her; yet she also knows that she will be lonesome. And though her recovery has finally become more real, she worries that she will one day die in a state of confusion, wondering why Gazelle isn't there tending to her as she had promised to be when she'd sealed her vow on that sacred wedding day by cupping a handful of the waters of Fidelity to pour into Tractor Girl's hand.

> *But Gazelle won't be there at the end because her vow was a lie. Instead, I will age and someday die in a chronic state of confusion and loss. It will not be within the marriage I entered, willingly and forever. Gazelle tore that from me and threw it away. Threw me away.*

Poor thing. In the *Before*, Tractor Girl hadn't a clue that any of this hard and horrible stuff was coming, much less the lengthy suffering it would cause, and so she'd been as happy as can be every time she thought of her "sweet" Gazelle. Back then, in that long-ago present—and though she wouldn't know it until after hell descended in the form of the Lying Lover Lynelle, and all the other women in the Series Of Betrayals—an unknowing Tractor Girl was entirely happy for the very last time. Happy and innocent. She didn't yet know she'd already been played for a fool. She believed she'd been blessed to have found "the real thing" at last. God love her foolish, tender soul. For in that long-ago innocence, just another series of damn fine days paddling Whisper down Fidelity, with Gazelle in her home and love in her heart, all was well and good with Tractor Girl. She was still comfortably in life's flow and had not yet been left behind by it.

> *I have to get back to that—minus the lying cheater, of course. Do I deserve peace? That, I do not know. But I'm sure that I have earned peace. And that I need it. That's a goal worth pursuing. And I'm getting there. Maybe I'm worthy after all?*

Now, in the *After*, TG is still naïve, bless her shredded heart. She's ours. We love her, and now that we know this part of her story, we'll pay better attention. We'll do what we can to help her put the past *in* the past so she can quit hauling that putrified burden into her future. She's on her way. And she's obviously made a plethora of progress toward that end. I'm proud of her for that.

But what I think is that TG still doesn't intuit that so many people—and especially dishonest users like Gazelle—operate as if the past, as a concept, is just as fluid as the future.

# The Wisdom of Top-Notch Annie, Part 5

"YEARS BEFORE I DIED, I made a long-overdue decision:
"No one that I care for is allowed to hurt me anymore. That's over."

# Hope for the Best; Prepare for the Worst

"DAD? WHAT ARE YOU DOING up here?" The last person Nick expected to see walking toward him in the center of The Rising Son was his father. It was, after all, the middle of the work week.

Bobby Lee, just turning around after beeping the lock remote on his BMW, seemed confused at running into Nick, almost as if not only was he surprised to see his son at the church camp, but also that he'd forgotten he'd been the very one to mandate Nick's presence here. He recovered and stammered out a greeting of sorts. "How's it going, son? Working hard up here this summer?"

"That's just about all we're doing. Work. And pray. And pray about work. Can't say this camp's much fun."

"Fun's not what life's about, Nick. Time you learned that, dammit. You're nearly a grown man. You've had enough fun."

As if he'd been jolted by an electric shock collar, the uncomfortable reality of Nick's existence came back to him. Everything about his life, his peculiar father, their emotional distance from one another—these came crashing in. But Nick had had a lifetime of practice with those things, so he didn't lose his handle. He remembered to breathe, brushed off his old man's gruff greeting, kept his balance. Maybe that's what growing up was—finding balance, not freaking out when something unexpected or mean struck you in the gut.

Nick would do anything to keep from turning out like his old man, who never seemed to have a kind word for those closest to him. All the old man ever got excited about was that mega-church he belonged to, his business deals, and his drinking and poker and golf buddies. "So, you came all this way just to check up on me?" Nick asked, politely. Why else would his father show up here out of the blue?

"You've got sunburn, looks like. Bulked up those biceps some, too. Glad to see you in better shape," his father said, begrudgingly, and Nick thought, *Better than what?*

"It's only been three weeks, but yeah, I'm okay. They feed us pretty well, I guess." Nick never had known how to talk with his father. They always seemed miles apart, even when they weren't.

"Seen Con around here today?" Bobby Lee asked abruptly. He was looking everywhere except at his son. Con was a friend and business associate of Nick's father—some kind of politician and land development specialty lawyer. Nick didn't like him much. Con was an arrogant asshole, as far as Nick was concerned, which is probably why he and Nick's dad got along so well. They weren't exactly business partners, but as bourbon-drinking buddies they had done some land deals together over the years that always ended up making a ton of money for them both.

"Con? Up here?" Nick was confused by the question. "No, sir. But I heard there's some kind of meeting going on in the admin building. They've closed it off today. Maybe he's in there."

So that's why Nick's father had driven up to TRS—not at all to see him but to meet up with Con. Typical. But why here, of all places?

"All right then, boy. Good to see you've been hard at it. Keep up the good work for the Lord. *Streets of Gold!* is proud of what you kids are doing up here."

And with that, Bobby Lee was gone, striding full sail toward the camp's administration building.

Nick was left to wonder exactly what the hell his father and Con had to talk about all the way up here. Then he remembered the map he and Sam had drawn.

Holy shit on a shingle. He had to find her—now.

# Apply Common Sense Liberally

"HEY, JOY! YOU AROUND?" The voice belonged to Meddy. When Joy heard it through her open window, she saved the document she was editing and closed the screen on her laptop.

"Meddy!" said she, exiting her cottage, tea cup in hand. "I'm glad you stopped by."

"Not distracting you, am I?" As if it would have mattered. Meddy was clearly there to talk. Joy could always tell when Meddy had something pressing on her mind.

"I was at a stopping place anyway," Joy said. "Cuppa?"

Meddy held up her wine goblet *du jour.* "I'm all set," she said. "Just have a religious question for you. Curiosity, more than anything else."

Now, we've all known for a long time that Joy's fascination with religion is not emotional; it's academic. Meddy, on the other hand, had come to look at religion through a political lens, which was very emotional to her. *Been that way ever since the late '70s when Newt got himself coronated because the hard right turned churches into a conservative political tool,* she'd tell you. *A.G. (that's After Gingrich), it doesn't seem to me there's any other way to look at it. They're the ones who changed the rules! I'm just an avid follower of the game. Sorta like a rabid sports fan. I won't lose to cheaters without a fight.*

"You up for a busman's holiday?" Meddy asked. "Or union break, anyway?"

Joy lumbered down the four risers from her porch to join her friend under a friendly cedar in the yard. They had a favorite spot there, and Meddy had already folded herself into one of the chairs that had taken up permanent residence beneath its branches.

"Shoot," Joy said, collapsing into the other chair. As usual, it complained beneath her. "Though I never claim to have all the answers to anything—religious, spiritual or otherwise. If I *did* have answers, I could stop digging for them already. But naw."

Meddy giggled hoarsely. There were sparks in her eyes today. Joy was glad to see this. It meant Meddy was having a good day, was more herself than the shadow she was gradually becoming. "I just wondered if you know," said Meddy, sly countenance giving clue to what she was up to, "whether the X-tians believe in dragons."

This topic wasn't anywhere close to what Joy was expecting. "Dragons?" she said, momentarily stunned into that unmoored brain feeling. She actually felt her eyes blink. "Dragons, you say."

"I came across this delightful piece of unexpected trivia about an hour ago," she said, "and couldn't wait to see if you could verify it, although the Holy Bible already did that for me, to tell you the truth."

"Bible? Meddy, what in the world has come over you, reading the Bible?"

"Only for research," Meddy said, waving a dismissive hand in Joy's general direction. "I went over to The General and found an old King James Version on the bookshelf."

"I have to admit," said Joy, "that I don't have any idea how you put mythological dragons and the Bible together. Explain?"

"Myth is myth," said Meddy simply. "And this one's a doozy."

"Go on," said Joy.

"Well, it's just this." Meddy took a generous sip from her glass, ran the tip of her tongue around her lips, closed her eyes and angled her face toward the branches overhead. "What it was, was Reeds and Rushes."

"Okay." Like all of us, Joy had learned that when Meddy wanted to tell a tale, you might as well just let her tell it in her own way and in her own time.

"I was thinking about a family I knew growing up. A big extended family," Meddy said. "They all lived within two blocks of each other in several different houses."

"And where was this?" Joy couldn't resist the opportunity to try prying Meddy's origins out of her. She was hoping to catch her friend off-guard. No one had ever been able to get Meddy to say exactly where she'd grown up. *Back east* was the most anyone had ever gotten by way of information.

"Back east, you know," Meddy said and hurried on with her story. "As I recall, one side of the family was called Reed. The other side, Rush. Everybody called them The Reeds and The Rushes."

"Reeds and Rushes, okay," Joy said, cultivating patience.

"Right. The Reeds and The Rushes. I went to school with some of those kids, and there were a ton of 'em, I tell ya." She paused for another sip, short one this time.

"And this was where?" Joy slipped in again.

"Back east! Stay with me here. So, I'm listening to this interview on the radio today, and I hear 'reeds and rushes,' all one phrase, in reference to some discussion of the Middle East. Someone was quoting it from some ancient Hebrew religious text, I think. So, I thought how funny that was, that we'd had these Reeds and Rushes up and down my street all those years and nobody'd ever connected it to anything like that."

"Sounds like something to do with the baby Moses, doesn't it?" Joy said. "Oh, wait. Moses was bulrushes. Never mind."

"Yeah, well, I looked it up by doing an online search—'reeds and rushes scripture.' Guess what I found!" She didn't pause. "It's from Isaiah in the Old Testament. So, okay, next I went to The General, cracked open that old KJV to Isaiah and found the actual verse. And you'll not believe what it said. Here." She handed Joy a scrap of paper. "I wrote it down."

Joy put down her cup and began to read aloud from the scrap. As she read, her eyes widened. "Isaiah chapter thirty-five, verse seven. 'And the parched ground shall become a pool, and the thirsty land springs of water: in the habitation of dragons, where each lay, shall be grass with reeds and rushes.'"

Meddy burst out one great, "Ha!" and added, "What do you think of that!"

"Hmm. I've not come across this particular verse before," Joy said, head down, rereading the passage.

"Ha!" said Meddy again. "If this doesn't show that those old X-tians were just eaten up with garden variety mythology, I don't know what does! Dragons! The very idea. Right there in the King James Version of their Book! No wonder every bit of their storybook myth is open to doubt."

"Amazing," Joy said, staring at the quote. "You sure this is right?"

"Word for word!" said Meddy. She cackled, unkindly. "Makes you wonder what else they make up out of thin air, am I right?"

"Let me get a different version," Joy said, and she scurried inside for a chapter-and-verse comparison. Coming back down the porch steps with a Revised Standard Version in hand, she said, "Here it says 'jackals' instead of dragons. Interesting—shifting the threat from an imaginary reptile to an existing mammal."

"Aw, they change things whenever they need to, to keep luring in 'believers,'" Meddy said, dismissively.

"But I'd be most eager to find out what the KJV enthusiasts have to say about their version's reference to 'dragons,'" said Joy. "I do have to agree with you that it's an odd word choice."

"All I'm sure of, from living here in the South for so many years now and listening to people argue about the Bible," said Meddy, "is that the most fundamentalist, the most Pentecostal, the most narrow-minded of them, they all claim that the King James is the only 'real' Bible, and all the others are fakes."

"Oh, but surely they understand," said Joy, "that *all* Bibles in English are translations—from the original texts written in Greek, Hebrew, Aramaic ... Latin!"

"Hand that idea to them," Meddy said, "and see if you draw back a bloody nub. I'll bet if you asked somebody up there at that church camp, they'd say, 'It's gotta be *divinely inspired!*' They'd say, *'It's the King James or none at all.'*"

"Well, faith's personal," Joy said. "Surely you ..."

"But religion's illogical!" said Meddy. "Myth-illogical, that is! Ha!"

"Sometimes seems so," Joy said. "But, you know, we have to allow for individual choice. To say otherwise just doesn't seem like you, Meddy my dear."

Meddy thought about that for a few seconds. Then she said, "When it comes to organized religion—which is *not* the same thing as spirituality or goodness, mind you!—it sounds *exactly* like me. And I'll own that."

About that time Nooner came walking along the creekside path nearest Joy's house. He was headed toward Fidelity, fishing tackle in hand and supper in mind, but he didn't appear to be in any kind of hurry—not that that would have made a dime's worth of difference to Meddy.

"Nooner! Get over here, buddy," Meddy shouted in his direction. "Help us clear up something, you old dyed-in-the-wool Southern boy, you."

"Ladies," Nooner said, stepping closer to where they sat. "Afternoon."

"Good to see you, Nooner," Joy said. His backward ball cap made her smile because he had a hunk of hair plunging wildly out through the loop and band settled against his forehead.

"Nooner, honey, what Bible version did your people use when you were growing up in the mountains of Carolina?"

Nooner grinned. He knew from the look on Meddy's face that she was stirring up something controversial, or at least sassy, and he was willing to take the ride. "Only version my granddaddy's people would have on the place was the King James," he said.

"See?" Meddy said toward Joy.

"Yep. My granddaddy's people originally came from the coal camps over in West Virginia, see. Somewhere 'round Beckley, I think," Nooner said. "I've heard him tell that the only schoolin' *his* granddaddy ever got was from the church. Some folks then couldn't read, so the preacher had to, what they call, line-out the hymns."

"Are you saying 'line out'?" Joy wanted to be sure she was clear in what she was learning. For her, this was a study—information about a whole different sect.

"Yeah, you know—preacher would sorta chant a line, congregation would sing it back."

Then he demonstrated with the first two lines from Amazing Grace. Both Joy and Meddy were rapt.

"Went through whole hymns a line at a time thataway. I've heard it done, when I was a kid," said Nooner. "They were what we call Old

Reg'lar Baptist. Brought those ways with 'em when they moved to Carolina way back when. Hell, they spoke in tongues, fell out on the floor, took up serpents—all that old stuff. You better bet, when it came to the gospel they were strict and they were tough."

"Sounds like it," Joy said.

"Too strict for my taste," said Nooner.

"Wonder if that's the same as what I've heard called 'Foot-Washing Baptists,'" Meddy said. "Or Hardshell Baptists."

"I thought handling snakes in church was against the law," Joy said.

"Oh, it is ... now," said Nooner. "But that never stopped 'em."

"Anybody ever get snakebit?" Meddy asked.

"Sure, ever' now and again. Some of 'em said gettin' bit was proof of a weak faith; others said dyin' from the bite was the proof. Suvivin' meant strength of faith."

Joy was becoming more fascinated by the minute, religious and spiritual anomalies outside the mainstream being one of her academic specialties. Too, she was still figuring out the Southern mindset, especially with regard to their sometimes gothic and bizarre practices of faith.

"They brought their strict ways with 'em to the Carolina hills," Nooner reiterated. "And yeah, that old King James was the alpha and the omega for them. I've heard 'em say so, many a time."

"Why was that, Nooner? Do you know?" Joy asked.

"Said the King James was 'the true Word of the Lord God Almighty, amen,'" Nooner declared, using the same rhythmic intonation he had heard his elders use all his life. "Wouldn't stand by any other versions of the Word. Called 'em blasphemous."

"Is that so?" Joy said.

"See?" said Meddy. "And it says right there," she pointed at the scrap of paper balancing on Joy's dimpled knee, "that in the King James they believed in *dragons*. Flying, fire-breathing lizards. Straight out of children's storybooks and fictional campfire tales of yore."

"Now, I never heard nothin' said about no dragons, now," Nooner said. "'Course, I didn't come up Old Reg'lar Baptist. Nor Missionary Baptist, nor your so-called Footwashin' nor Hardshell Baptist, neither. By the time I came along, we was just plain old white-bread Southern Baptist."

"Well, read this." Meddy thrust the scrap of paper into his hand, and Nooner read the quote silently.

"In the King James?" he said. "Dragons? Really?"

"What made the King James so important to your people, Nooner?" Joy asked, feeling a revised thesis topic coming on.

"It just never was any question," he said. "Why, I've heard 'em tell that one time, say forty-fifty years back, a Bible salesman, young man maybe in his twenties, come knockin' on my granny's door and asked to sell her a Bible. Said he was gettin' up enough commission to pay his way through seminary college."

Meddy noticed Nooner working to keep a grin off his face during the telling. Joy, on the other hand, was all wide-eyed innocence, hanging onto every word like the scholar she was. Nooner went on, acting out the voices as he went. "'We got all kinds of Bibles, ma'am,' that salesman told my granny. 'We got Revised Standard and Good News for Modern Man and The Living Bible. Whatever kind you want.' And my granny, she said to him, said, 'Young man, I think going to school to make a preacher is a wise and noble thing for you to do with your life. But honey, I don't need no Bible. I already got a Bible of my very own—belonged to my Aunt Sary before me, and to my Grandmother Stamper before her.'"

Nooner could feel all four eyes locked on him, which made him relish the telling even more. "'Well,' says the salesman, 'what kind of Bible is it, then?' 'King James!' says my granny with gusto. She was natur'lly proud of that family Bible. 'Oh,' says the young man, 'that version's old. Don't you want to try one of these new Bibles? *Easier to understand*,' he says, singsong-like. Thought he was talkin' to a feeble-minded old woman! Bad mistake on his part. My granny got real indignant real quick."

Nooner took a breath and looked at Joy, who was seriously hanging on every word. Meddy, meanwhile, had a twinkle in her eye. She, as usual, was on his beam.

"So, anyhow," Nooner went on, "there's my granny. Fit to be tied. This fella has, to her mind, just insulted the one and only Word of God. So, she points her finger and says to him, says, 'Boy, let me tell you one thing for certain-and-true: if the King James Version was good enough for Jesus Christ, it's good enough for me!' And she slams the door right in that poor guy's face."

Nooner leaned back and grinned to beat the band. Meddy brayed with laughter. Joy was still trying to process his story, to make sense of what it meant and why he and Meddy thought it was so funny.

Then it hit her.

"Oh, my heavens!" she said. She was too horrified to giggle, even. "Oh, my stars! But the King James Version is only 400 years old!"

Meddy was howling so hard that she could hardly get out a word. "'Good enough for Jesus!' Ha!" she spit out with a whoop.

"Where in heaven's name did she, they, ever get that idea?" Joy marveled. It seemed impossible to her. "It defies all logic. It denies history!"

"Those don't matter to them. You know that," Meddy said, still cachinnating. "But I reckon if their image is of a blond-headed, blue-eyed savior, like those framed portraits in White churches all over the South, it's not too much of a leap to assume the Middle Eastern Jesus spoke and read English, too!" She couldn't stop herself from laughing. Hard. She felt no shame. "'Course he'd only been dead 1,600 years by the time the KJV was created! *And* his own crucifixion is *in* it!" She gasped for breath and decided to get control over herself. But that fell apart when she spluttered again, "'Good enough for Jesus!'"

Nooner grinned. "That's just how they think," he said, shrugging.

"Makes about as much sense as dragons," said Meddy, collecting herself at last and wiping her eyes on her bandanna. "I haven't belly-laughed this hard in weeks. I thank you, good sir."

"My pleasure," said he, and he bowed gallantly, grinning all the while.

"And *dragons!*" said Joy, shaking her head. "In the Bible. Who knew?" Then she said something that she'd heard her own grandmother back in Kansas say frequently: *"Will wonders never cease!"*

To which Nooner, with a chuckle, immediately replied, "Hey! My Old Reg'lar Baptist granny back home used to say that all the time!"

# Envision the Big Picture

"'NATURE DOES NOTHING USELESSLY.' It was Aristotle said that."

Alec talked to the night sky as if he were speaking to freshmen in a huge theatre-style classroom.

"Imagine that you are at some fixed point above the earth." He imagined it and then described his vision to them. "High enough to see the state of Kentucky. You'll know it by its northern border. And what is Kentucky's northern border?"

He had always fantasized that his lectures, if delivered in one of those auditorium-style college halls, would someday become legendary. So, is it hard to imagine that he "received" student responses to his questions, too?

"Certainly. Yes," he said, in response to an answer he "heard" coming from his class. "The state's northern border is practically the *entire* Ohio River, actually."

He'd been role playing lately (though to him the scenarios he acted out were very real) that he was already a professor on sabbatical who hadn't thought he'd miss academia (and mostly didn't). But when Alec did feel the loss of his short life as a scholar (once in a great while), he'd take a notion to step into the clearing beyond the fringe of woods in an uphill radius from SLANT late in the night. There, where he thought no actual humans were within earshot, he'd deliver one of his lectures. What Alec didn't grasp is that his solitary teaching under the stars was becoming more frequent of late. His neighbors did notice, but they didn't intervene, thinking it best to let him lecture away, if that's what he wanted to do.

"All right, imagine you have the capacity to adjust the view."

Alec sometimes arrived at an idea new to him that he needed to expand and expound upon. The years he had spent participating as a student in academia had demonstrated that old adage: *the best way to learn something is to teach it.* So, Alec had taken to standing beneath the open sky in a clearing toward the top of Barrel Chute, lecturing to the myriad stars as if each were an impressionable young mind yearning to understand things as he did.

"Zoom in until just the center of the Commonwealth takes up your entire screen," he directed the trees, the stars, the creek, the boulders.

Sometimes Alec taught history lessons. Other times, literature. Often it was a topic related to one of the sciences, usually inspired by something he'd read or seen on Discovery Channel back in his old life at seminary. Once or twice his nighttime lecture topic had been *technoligion*, a particular favorite of his very own making. Occasionally, he taught on the topic of global climate change and its relationship to plagues and pandemics, which he called *climatagion*.

"Zoom closer. Closer. That's it," he instructed. "Now, what shape do you notice emerging in central relief?"

Tonight, Alec was lecturing on one of his old standards: *geometaphor*.

"Correct! You see that very distinct horseshoe shape, made of hills. Circular but open at the top. That, my good charges, is the arc of the Knobs region of Kentucky. Notice how it encircles the heart of the state, each of its ends connecting with the Ohio River."

Geometaphor was one of many academic topics born of Alec's own mind. He thought that if he developed the concept more fully, some college somewhere would recognize his organic brilliance and finally let him be a real professor, his life's ambition this year. Not that he held credentials. But still.

His lecture continued. "Let's hold that thought and introduce another pertinent question: what is Kentucky known for?"

He knew he was already smarter than anybody they had on their faculty, so there was obviously no need for him to have to take classes just to earn a piece of paper that "proved" to the rest of the world what he already knew. Those deans and regents and chairs needed only to listen thoroughly to his theories, just once; then they'd know he was way ahead of them. Maybe even realize that he and his intellect were indispensable to their educational mission!

Now Alec seemed to be fielding "responses" to his query. "*Bourbon whiskey*, yes, by all means. *Hillbillies*, okay, if you must. *Fried chicken*—well, there's one in every crowd. *Basketball*—true enough. Keep brainstorming, my brave scholars. You're not there quite yet."

He considered these starlight lectures to be little more than dress rehearsal for his real life that was out there somewhere waiting for him. He was already a professor in his heart, just waiting to be "discovered" by the right institution. But his patience was beginning to wear. No school had yet sent anyone to discover him and his innate brilliance.

And then came the correct "answer," which only he could hear. "Bingo! The *Kentucky Derby*, of course. And, by extension, the thoroughbred *horse industry*."

Alec considered his superior intelligence a curse as much as a blessing. This was no small burden, being Aristotle's equal.

"Horses are at the very heart of Kentucky's image! And what do horses wear on their hooves?" His pause was brief. "Right you are. Horseshoes, of course."

It was not easy being the best at anything he turned his hand or his mind to. It was, in fact, very difficult. Hard on Alec and hard, he knew, on the people who must be comparing themselves to him constantly and coming up lacking.

"It's kind of like a constellation, only on the ground. You see? A geologic *horseshoe* surrounding a region known for *horses*. 'Nature does nothing uselessly.' And that, my little engines that would, is geometaphor in a nutshell."

When he got there, to the actual auditorium-style classroom just like the ones he had seen in movies, he would be satisfied at last. He would finally fit. He just knew it.

"Envision the big picture, my lovelies. Patterns! Mother Nature designs. Her beauty is both pied and pious. It is up to us to open our minds to the messages and meanings that her images offer."

As usual, his lecture was a complete success. He envisioned his students shaking their heads, marveling at his brilliance. He expected nothing less than acclaim.

Then the horror hit him: When he did get there, to his lectern in the big hall, he didn't know what he would *wear*. He panicked at once, head pounding so hard that he had to tilt it back and to the left to keep his best ideas from bouncing to the ground and getting lost in the grass. It's *important* to know what to wear. After all, everyone would be looking at him. Everyone always was.

# Prepare

ABOUT A HALF HOUR BEFORE SUPPER, after the day's brush clearing and other work was done, Sam and Nick met at their log.

"You are NOT going to believe who showed up here today," Nick said. "My dad. Something's up."

"And hello to you, too," Sam said. "Yes, I had a good day in the goddamn steaming hot kitchen. Thank you for asking."

"Oh, sorry," Nick said. "I'm sorry, sorry, sorry. Really. I hate that you had to pull KP again. It's clearly—what do they call it?—sexist and gender-biased to make only the girls do that. And I'm also sorry I can't control my thoughts and my big mouth from racing away with me."

"Nick. It's okay," Sam said. She wasn't aggravated. She was exhausted. "Just, my day hasn't been all that great either, is all." She visibly shuddered, then let out a big *whoosh* of a breath. "So, give it up. What's with your dad?"

Nick pulled his little blue notebook out of his hip pocket and flipped to the map they had drawn the week before. "Remember this?"

Sam looked at him like he was an idiot. "So? *Tell.*"

"This, I think, is exactly what we thought it might be. My dad was up here today to meet with Con, this guy he does land development deals with."

"Your dad's a developer?"

"Well, sometimes a developer, kind of indirectly. Sometimes a speculator. Sometimes an investor. It's all about land deals. He even buys some buildings just to, uh, flip right away," Nick said, stumbling around the terms. "The deals are always big ones. Tell you the truth, I'm not exactly sure what he does, but it has to do with big parcels of land or buildings or something, and he makes a shit ton of money doing it. That's all I know for sure."

"His company's big?" Sam asked.

"Huge."

"And he's up here snooping around?"

"He damn sure didn't come to visit me," Nick said. "Seemed like it made him uncomfortable to run into me. Like he forgot I was up here."

"Okay." Sam was trying to assimilate all this information. She turned to a tried-and-true technique that usually worked for her—summarizing in list form. She ticked off each item by touching her fingertips one by one. "So, he's a developer or land speculator or something, he's up here scouting around, and he had a business meeting with some con man today. Right?"

"Not a con man. A man named Con—capital C. It's a nickname, I reckon. Connelldon's his last name. Keeps getting elected to something in government."

"Oh, my god!" said Sam. "W.R. Connelldon? The senator?"

"Yeah, that's the guy." Nick heard a grumble in his own voice.

"What a dirtbag!"

"He's so full of himself it would make you puke."

"I know! He's awful!"

"You've heard of him?"

"Do you ever watch the news?" Sam said. "Or do you just live in some kind of bubble?"

"I hate watching the news. Every time my dad turns it on, I have to leave the room. It's depressing."

"Nick! For a smart guy, you can be so dumb sometimes."

"Listen, my whole purpose is to ignore political horseshit. My dad is neck deep in what used to be the Tea Party. Now, I guess, it's whatever kind of weird-ass cult the whole Q-worshiping Fox News crowd's become. MAGAts, or something."

"Yeah, they're scary. No doubt about that," Sam said.

"Every time Dad starts ranting about politics or turns on that stupid, friggin' channel, I gotta leave the room."

"Fox? Shit. I'm sorry. That's got to be frustrating," Sam said. "I spell it F-A-U-X."

"It's really mean! And it's depressing. Listen, if that's what passes for so-called news then, yeah, I do hate it."

"But, Nick, anyone with an ounce of sense knows that Fox is not and never has been *news*. Not even close. It's just the most recent version of radical propaganda—like, you know, Orwell's Big Brother. No offense."

"That's all right," Nick said. "No wonder I hate it." They sat silently for a minute before Nick shifted his thoughts back to the matter at hand. "So, what are you thinking? About what we're up against, I mean. "

"What I think is that we've got a mess on our hands, that it's a big flaming secret, and that there's nothing we can do about it," Sam said.

"What I think," said Nick, "is that I'm pissed that my dad and Con and that so-called church are using us and every kid up here to improve this property."

"Improve it? For what?"

"For profit! Open your eyes," said Nick. He tapped their homemade map, to focus her.

Sam gave her brain a good workout. It only took a few seconds until she said, "Oh." Her discomfort ballooned. "Ohhh. If this is what we think it is—if it's really happening—what do we do?"

"That's the part I don't know. Yet."

Sam felt her anger well up. After too many blistering days clearing brush outdoors and more boiling days inside the camp kitchen, she wasn't in a mood to act the part of a nice Christian girl. "What I *do* know is that no fat cat politician—or rich capitalist either, for that matter, even if he *is* your dad—can use me anymore to do their dirty work. And all so they can barge in and make another fortune. Off our hard labor!"

"I get it," Nick said. "Totally. I'm with you."

"Bottom line? First thing I'm doing is getting the hell out of this place."

"Not without me, you're not," said Nick.

Clearly, it was time for a plan.

# Recognize Collective Guilt

THERE'S SOMETHING ABOUT DEVELOPING a point of view that narrows the mind. It can't be helped. Happens to all of us, and it'll bite us if we let it take us too far. We need to be wary of the dangers of going too narrow, lest we end up in a position that pinches, perhaps suffocates us.

Once we develop a point of view, it becomes a filter through which we judge everything and everyone we encounter. It's easy to know and easy to say why we disagree with someone else, why we dislike what they do and the ideas they espouse. Much harder to go deep and thorough, as an impartial scholar like Joy DuPre, who really wants to understand, will look and look and dig and dig until she uncovers one redeeming or human or common element in an otherwise unsavory story.

So, let's drop our filters and be like Joy for a few minutes. Let's try hard to understand something we don't—for example, a politician like Senator W. Regan Connelldon. What drives him to act the way he acts, to talk the way he talks, to value what he values? We need to understand why he feels he must always "win" ... and more, why he automatically sees everything as a contest. Why he falsifies virtually everything, including his own image, so he *can* win.

What drives people like him?

In order to coexist within some degree of sanity, we must try as hard as we can to fathom what inspires him to posture as he does; what makes him see everything as an opportunity he can exploit; what makes him listen only to other deeply twisted partisans, capitalists and greed-mongers; what makes him *forget* that he has a *duty* in the representative form of government he endorses (and benefits from); and why he refuses to give all points of view a fair hearing.

His frequent go-to is obstruction. Why is that? Is he that insecure?

And let's try not to call him a filthy politician, try not to reflexively label him as selfish or owned by the moneyed class in which he lives. Let's really find out whether we can uncover one nugget of commonality (other than being a human animal) between us and his ilk.

You may be thinking, "Bard, that won't be easy." I'll grant you that, but let's for a few minutes honestly try.

First, we could acknowledge that it is capitalism alone that shapes, informs, drives and corrupts men like W. Regan Connelldon. He doesn't seem to know any better. He doesn't appear to consider any other system in which he might function. Capitalism, after all, isn't about cooperation; it's about competition and comparison and ruthlessness. It's about judgment for self-serving reasons. Fairness obviously can't be part of his thinking when he believes everything's for sale. Perhaps capitalism's philosophical basis, in his mind, is not only about profit or about acquiring possessions or piles of money or power; perhaps he truly believes that capitalism serves the only positive purpose in a culture, one that enables any given person to have a chance to succeed financially. But what is that purpose? We should try to comprehend, for it is the primary system within which we live.

Too, we have to force ourselves to understand that his worldview truly does not in any way consider the possibility that a person might actually start life with *less* than nothing, might live with poor nutrition and health hazards that leave permanent, chronic debilitation, might have no shot at acquiring profitable educational credentials, might be socially ill-equipped to land gainful employment, might have no one to advise or to partner with toward business or financial success, might not inherit property or money, might have no means by which to amass the trappings of a simply comfortable life, much less an elaborate one, much less a worry-free retirement. No way, in fact, for an uber-partisan politician like him to accept as absolute proven fact that some people *begin* so deep in a hole that there is no hope of escape—especially not when that hole is sunk into the very bottom of a hyper-capitalistic economy in which they can't begin to compete.

A fortunate person like Senator W. Regan Connelldon—or any other short-sighted birth-righted ultra-conservative One Percenter—is simply ignorant of any kind of life other than his own, and just as uninterested in knowing more than he already doesn't. Like any of us, such people have filters within themselves. His filters preclude assimilating the possibility of an utterly hopeless life into their own understanding of what "Life" is. This is why partisans like him are so impatient and judgmental and dismissive toward those whose needs cannot be met by the limited resources and knowledge available to them. There is little that we can do to help a person like Connelldon set his entitlement mentality aside, though that simple adjustment would accomplish a more generous worldview for him. Might even make him humanly whole.

So, where can we find a scrap of common decency, a modicum of humanity in the W.R. Connelldons of this world? Not in hunger, for they don't know it. Not in law or fairness, for they purchase whatever laws and "fairness" they desire. Not in sharing, for sharing seems to be in short supply among die-hard conservatives who expect money or favors or other financial desirables to come into their hands with every interpersonal transaction. And not in faith, for their true religion is capitalism, not theologies of human kindness. He'll never check his privilege. He can't even see it.

The harder we look, the harder it gets, yes? But we must keep trying. We must ask ourselves, "What would Joy do?"

Perhaps it is in physical disease that we all are human together? Disease and illness affect the human organism with abandon, not caring whether the host is poor or rich, this ethnicity or that, stupid or smart. Perhaps disease is where we ordinary mortals intersect with the privileged few? But no. Even there, those with the best resources get the best prevention, the best treatment, the best information and advice, and the best chances for survival, *because they can afford it*—for it is well known that in a capitalist system health care resources come at a dear price, even when the stakes are life and death. Especially then.

Okay, so we're not alike when it comes to physical illness and treatment. There's got to be something else, some other kind of suffering or joy that brings us all closer to the same existence. (And if you're thinking Love is the answer, it's not. Too hard to define. Trust me on this. The Bard speaks from hard experience.)

These privileged people, they seem to be missing something essential. With a warped worldview, it's difficult for them to know Truth like the rest of us do. They're not experiencing what we're experiencing. Life and Living both have become so damned hard for the Have-Nots that we seem to be losing empathy even for one another. And for the most part, the Haves neither exhibit nor act on empathy. So, we're all just as screwed up as can be.

Here's a main divergent factor: *we do not have a common definition for Reality anymore!* Neither for *Truth*. Neither for *basic Facts*.

So, we could be getting closer to the answer we seek. Forgetting human kindness, forgetting how to live respectfully with one another—these may now be what all of humanity has in common, no matter where on the spectrum we fall. We're losing our heads; our hearts are broken and so are our backs; we're forgetting how to treat each other with respect; we're guarding what we think we've got and lusting after what we know we've not; we're afraid of each other.

Is that it? Could be.

What we all have in common is *fear*. We are lost in our irrational fear. Consumed by it. Fear of each other and fear of manipulation. Fear of not getting enough ... more ... the most. Fear of being perceived as weak. Fear of *not winning* (whatever that means now).

Lies (and lies about lies) are every-fucking-where we look these days.

Two versions of reality exist—at least two—and we've had a national nervous breakdown because we're too politically and civically damaged to function even at a minimal level anymore. We can't do the simplest silly things like deliver the mail on time. Or agree to debate rather than brawl. Or disagree with each other without name-calling and revenge plotting. We can't seem to go about our daily living with peace of mind anymore.

And why are we turning on each other? Fear. *Irrational* fear. I believe even someone as neutral as Joy would agree.

Our fears have crippled us all, both mighty and meek.

We misread fear as disgust. But it's just basic fear. It is.

Somewhere in our collective cultural mental illness is where we as a people are closest to the powerful, and they to us. The cold-hearted brokers who call the shots on behalf of us are head cases and, as a result of how their decisions affect us, so now are we—even if via different causes, different effects. We've become one big cultural split-personality. We're trying to operate in "parallel universes," yet because we can see from one universe into the other, we know all sanity barriers have been blown to bits. All lines are crossed. Everything is shorting out and melting down. The damage is not only catastrophic; it may well be permanent.

We have so little in common anymore as citizens of a formerly united country. We no longer have a single "strongest link" of principle in our American chain. In fact, *all* the links have been weakened. Our nation's strength once was legend; now it's only myth. And this has driven us to collective lunacy.

Maybe that's all there is: *fear-driven mental illness* is our sole common ground. You, me, SLANT, *Streets of Gold!*, TRS and all the Connelldon types in 21st century America—humanity's collective *fear-based collapse of civil reasoning* is the only connection we still have.

We're connected by decay.

We're all broken together.

What a world.

Were you warned? Yes. Yes, you were.

# Before Can Be Too Late

"LISTEN TO ME. You have to count down. If you don't count down, we both die. Do you understand? Look at me! *Do? You? Understand?*"

His local owl rolled out her moody call along the branches at her own owl feet, and soon enough it arrived at Alec's feet on Alec's branch. In Alec's opinion, this owl was acting even more paranoid than usual.

"I know it will be a slow death. Who knows that better than I? I ask you. Who? Who-o-o?

"Never forget: it will be slow only for those of you who are the destroyers. For your prey, though, death will come the sooner. You see this, no?

"So, I ask: which is better when things are the worst they can get, when hope has to be abandoned?"

A terrestrial musk, full of the floor of the forest, lifted through the same air that carried his words.

"Live long, they say. Live long? For what?"

Alec scooted to adjust his position. He was sitting on the braided-branch porchlet adjacent to his treehouse. When the big support limb moved, unbound branches and leaves brushed against one another. They made a rustle that was neither shush nor crackle, neither murmur nor scritch.

"We count down, and we do the thing…the…the…the ritual. We do it every day, right? Every night, eh? Or—*say it*—what happens?"

Alec listened to himself breathe. He listened for the owl to whisper but, as usual, she refused to speak to him at all. Besides that, she was coming across as half-hearted. (*What would 'half-hearted' look like in an illustrated medical journal?* he wondered. But that was a project for another night.)

"You gotta be *arma-fuckin-geddon*, my friend. Stay off the ground as much as possible. That's the only thing that has worked. For sure. So far. Agreed."

Just then, either a twig snapped or someone below the tree cracked a knuckle and broke Alec's concentration. It was one thing or another all the damned time.

# Define What You Value & Defend It

A BIRD DOESN'T SING because it has an answer. It sings because it has a song. This ancient Asian tenet was one of the most important lessons Meadowlark Nightengale had learned in all her sixty years. One does not have to have a reason to be happy. Being happy is reason enough in itself. Guilt is for the dogs. Birds, on the other hand—and since she had endowed herself with not one but two bird names, she noticed these things—were about the thrill of flight and the trill of song. Meddy was a natural at carrying a tune, literally and figuratively.

*Define What You Value & Defend It* was one of Meddy's several personal mantras. She had mottoes for every last one of her innumerable moods, and in this moment her mood was *determined.* Meddy had strong opinions about a number of things, not the least of which was defending herself. She had learned the hard way in the first three-quarters of her life that waiting for someone else to defend you is a waste of time. *A person is at great risk out there in the cold old world,* she thought. *It's important to make a safe space for yourself,* she told everyone who would listen, *and then keep it safe no matter what that takes.*

Oddly, though, she wasn't what you might call a "defensive" person. Quite the contrary; she was open to both criticism and constructive advice alike. She rarely reacted rashly to comments made in contrast to her positions, at least not until she'd taken a minute to think about it, for she loved to turn conflicting points of view over in her mind, considering their worth at some level beneath the surface. It was only when she had clearly outlined her position in the world and then was overtly threatened that she felt the physical and psychic need to defend herself. She wasn't defensive against intellectual ideas, only against ignorant ones. This had made her a cynic, but an easily forgiven one.

Meddy had moved around quite a bit in her life, nearly always by choice. When she was much younger, she gallivanted unattached wherever her heart led. She experienced the United States in all its glory and all its ugliness. She loved New York City and thought it got a terribly unjust wrap for rudeness. *Some of the nicest people I ever met are New Yorkers,* she'd say with indignation whenever anyone challenged that notion. *New Yorkers are always on the move!* she'd explain; *being in a hurry and being rude aren't the same things at all.*

The Florida Keys was a place she'd like to retire, but she realized that she'd have needed to save up a lot more money in a retirement account in order to afford to do it—and now that was a plan forty years too late to execute. Still, she had spent so much time there over the years that it was another of the homes of her heart; she had a scant handful of these "hometowns," a chosen few out of the countless places she'd visited or lived. She loved Kentucky that way, and North Carolina (which may be why she and Nooner had such a strong connection). Likewise, the mountains of Virginia, plus New Orleans and Cape Cod and New Mexico. Oh, and the beautiful northwest, northern California and Oregon in particular. She'd been plenty of other places too, so who knew why these particular places were the ones that spoke uniquely to her soul? Meddy didn't have to know why—it was simply the truth. When she was in these particular places, in fact or in memory, something in her sang ... just because.

Meadowlark Nightengale had also spent as much time as possible in places known specifically as LGBTQ destinations. She needed, like many of her gay, trans and queer siblings, to be in places that welcomed her *because* of who she was, not in spite of it.

Meddy didn't much like the term *tolerance*. *Tolerance* and *acceptance* are very different concepts, she thought. And beyond even acceptance there is *respect*, which should be the ultimate goal of all human beings toward one another.

Uniquely, Meddy had arranged her life so that she could move from one favorite place to another whenever she was inspired to do so. And that is how the Keys and P'Town and San Francisco became natural fits for her. She had spent time in the heart of Lesbian Nation for a few weeks each summer, too, working alongside hundreds of other women to build the temporary communities that hosted various "womyn's music" festivals, and then working to dismantle those sites afterward to let the land rest until the following year when the process would start over.

Men in particular, and some women as well, didn't understand why anyone would construct and then deconstruct the same places year after year. The deconstruction seemed to many a particular waste of energy, once the hard work of building had been invested. But Meddy and the other women who accomplished this feat knew that the unbuilding was just as energizing, precisely because it was a spiritual activity directed toward honoring the land, thanking it for its use, and preparing it for the well-earned slumber that would last for the next ten months. They did this knowing that next year there'd be another celebration on the land. They knew it was dreamy anthropomorphizing, but they hoped nevertheless that the land and Mother Nature somehow felt the same way they did.

It was all very fulfilling until the fight about who is a woman and who is not heated up to a point that made the whole exercise archaic and ironically out of step with the times it had helped to usher in. Since when does sisterhood pick and choose sisters? Great strides had been made in the "gender wars" nearly everywhere else in the culture *except in the Queer places where those wars had begun.* Those festivals, the old ones, anyway, seemed hellbent to protect their little provincial spot in the gender binary, but the binary itself had become obsolete while they weren't paying attention. An entire glorious spectrum had replaced simple-minded male/female structures in the intervening decades since the festivals had originally been needed so badly. Ironic but clear, to Meddy's mind. This artificial exclusion ruined the whole thing for her.

Anyway, after decades of living as a free spirit on the road, perching temporarily in one and then another of her favorite places, Meddy had landed in SLANT. She wasn't surprised at how much she loved the wooded land on Barrel Chute Knob, but her attachment to the people, most of whom were straight and gender-conforming, did surprise her. Having lived in SLANT since 1977 B.G. (*that's Before Gingrich,* she liked to say), she had come to think of her neighbors as family, and she was no longer inspired to move on to the next elsewhere that might await her out there in the world. This shift inside her was another surprise, one that had crept up on her. It seemed to her unlikely that she would ever be satisfied to put down roots, considering her history, but here she was and here, she realized, she'd stay—as long as she could remain upright. She suspected this had something to do with reaching "maturity" (commonly known as *aging*). Meddy knew she would have to die one day, as people do, and this was as good a place as any to have one's ashes returned to the good earth.

As you already know, except for Nooner, Meddy hadn't officially told her neighbors about her condition. Her life among them was so comfortable that she didn't want to upset the balance by weighing them down with bad news, so she had determined that she'd just wait until she couldn't wait any longer. It was so Meddy of her. She knew that when she needed them, they'd be there. She just didn't want to have to need anybody in that way. Not yet. The new millennium, after all, had barely begun.

Meddy wasn't much for pop culture; she didn't watch television, certainly didn't read *People* magazine. However, during the first few years of the new century she had followed Elizabeth Edwards' story, and when it came to handling her own illness, she had modeled herself after EE (as she had come to refer to this strong woman whom she would never meet). In public, the ever-courageous EE had handled her own terminal diagnosis with class and charm; whatever she did in private was something Meddy could only imagine. The absolute empathy Meddy felt toward EE wasn't about their respective illnesses, for they didn't share that specifically. Meddy, after all, didn't have terminal cancer. There was common ground, however—not the least of which was the fact that EE looked so well that she could have fooled everyone rather than reveal the truth about her impending and certain death. Meddy's understanding fell apart, however, when it came to the very rude and very public display of disloyalty that her famous politician husband had brought down on EE with his pecca-dilloes. And he did this right in the midst of the most outrageous news imaginable: EE was dealing with death—her own was imminent. The whole sordid thing turned out to be an end-life crisis stretched to fit the warped proportions of worldwide publicity.

*He ought to be horse-whipped in the public square*, Meddy thought of EE's disappointing husband. It was the kind of thing her father used to say, and it went, as usual, directly to the simplest, harshest solution. Humiliation of that sort still wouldn't have reached the magnitude of embarrassment and betrayal that EE must have felt. Yet Meddy understood that revenge wasn't highest on EE's priorities list at the end of her life.

To be honest, Meddy wasn't sure why EE had gone public with her terminal illness in the first place. She supposed it had something to do with being a politician's wife, having every part of one's existence under the microscope for absolute scrutiny. Someone would have leaked the news anyway, so it was probably better to have put it out there herself. But then Oprah and every other curiosity seeker with any clout at all had shown up wanting to ask EE hard questions that Meddy herself wouldn't have had answers for. EE did, though.

And Meddy was glad, for it helped her cope.

That gracious example helped her sing, too, and she decided that she, with her ornithological name, would keep singing like a bird as long as EE had, which was right until the very end.

# Expect Consequences

"WE WILL MEET ON THE BRIDGE, strangers to one another."

Alec explained this in the full moon's general direction. His treehouse roof flap was open. He lay on top of his sleeping bag. The night was warm; humidity, low.

"Here's how it will happen:

"1. You'll be the one in the rusty old Jeep with the driver-side headlight burned out. I'll be the one riding the largest Harley they make.

"2. It will be dark.

"3. I will read your Jeep's single beam as another motorcycle, giving it no further thought, and so won't realize you are actually a one-ton truck straddling the center line, approaching 77 miles per hour.

"4. My helmet, in hindsight, is ridiculous. It has provided me a false sense of security.

"5. Our meeting is finished instantly. If there is suffering, then there is, but I have no way of knowing now what form it will take.

"6. By the time they find what's left of the major parts of me (in the following day's light), you will be sobered up in the small holding room in a public building, the first of several cells that will serve as your home for the next sixteen years. You'll be filled with remorse, dread, self-loathing, disbelief. You'll attempt to will yourself to awaken.

"7. And so shall I, in vain.

"Since I won't be able to wonder these things then, I'll wonder them now: Had you been *celebrating* or *consoling yourself* with the evening's potion of choice? Was it worth it? Did you already know your headlight was burned out? Did you care?

"And more, will my little brother still rush to call out a victorious 'Popeye!' as he has always done when riding in a car that meets an oncoming vehicle with one blown headlight? And if he innocently perpetuates the childish game, will I know? Will I care?"

Seeing vividly in the darkness, intoxicated with its power, Alec obsessively recounts various versions of this tale of absolute loss before finally talking himself to sleep. He illuminates and emphasizes different elements in each telling: the approach, the light, the moment of impact, the bridge, the crossing over.

# The Wisdom of Top-Notch Annie, Part 6

"THINK ABOUT WHAT YOU THINK ABOUT when you think about thinkin'.

"Meta. Meta. Meta.

"Contemplation is sadly under-rated. Reflection may be a lost art.

"Die, and you'll know exactly what I'm gettin' at."

# Remember Your People Kindly, Fondly, Well

SOLSTICE CAME, and many SLANTers made their way down the knob, by land and by water, to Tractor Girl's bonsai farm. They rode in cars and trucks, they came on bicycles and motorcycles and golf carts, and Turner even drove down a long semi-wooded path on his riding lawnmower. A few hiked, and some paddled down the creek, knowing full well that they might have so much fun at the party they'd have to depend on the generosity and kindness of Nooner or someone else with a pickup truck to carry them and their little canoes and kayaks and bikes back up to SLANT by road. Knee-walking that far dragging a boat would be a bummer of epic magnitude. Paddling or peddling home uphill and under the influence might be impossible.

When Nooner and Tractor Girl had spoken of throwing a shindig down at the bonsai farm, they had forgotten that the timing would be perfect to make their party double as SLANT's annual Come Together. This was an all-day, all-night summer tradition that dated back to Year One on the property—Year One after the Jimmies bought it and established SLANT, that is. Over the decades, the annual Come Together had taken many forms. Some years it was mellow and cosmic and "all that woo-woo shit," as Nooner called it. But other years it was a riot of braying drunkenness and dancing and laughter and horseplay. There was no particular prescription for *what* it should be, only a certainty that it definitely should *be*.

Of the 204 people in SLANT, roughly 95 percent of them migrated down the knob for the Come Together. The rest who couldn't make it were working a shift or visiting some other place or maybe had a backache or a cold or the old-fashioned blues. A few just had something else to do, maybe had a program they wanted to listen to on the radio, or maybe were overloaded with people for the time being and just couldn't do crowds right then. Obligation isn't as big a thing in SLANT as it is in most communities. No one judges. The main thing is that the people who show up really want to be there.

Some folks from off-knob were invited too. They were friends of the

SLANT community and had been in and around there, most of them anyway, as long as the Jimmies themselves—some even longer. And then there were a scant few who, for various reasons, had left SLANT; those folks saw the annual Come Together as a perfect opportunity to return, reunite and reconnect for a day or two. *Back from the wars,* you might say.

"Where the hell've you been keeping, sister-woman?"

"Out amongst 'em, sad to say. Relieved to see nothing's changed 'round here though."

"Same old same old. What'd you expect?"

"Oh, I don't know. A good old-fashioned revolution, maybe?"

"And we'd revolt from what? Paradise?"

There were laughter and tears, back slapping and hugs, nods and winks. And songs! Anyone who had ever lived in SLANT was forever part of the place, the people. And they fell easily and eagerly back into that unique energy of the knob and the creek and the communal spirit they had known long and well. The Come Together was a homecoming.

Even among those who still lived in SLANT, the catching up with everyone, two-leggers and four-, was the best part, better even than the coming together—although maybe not better than the home grown, the home distilled, the home brewed party supplies. And the food! Mounds of it, of course.

That solstice potluck turned out to be a success in the main because there were very few duplications among the bowls and platters. Nooner had brought six or eight sawhorses down in his pickup, and he and Tractor Girl had set them up in a long row in the wide margin of meadow that bordered the working part of the bonsai farm. They covered the sawhorses with doors and planks and scraps of plywood for a long, continuous tabletop. As people arrived, they found places for whatever dishes they'd brought, and it seemed that the buffet organized itself according to categories: nibbles, breads, salads, mains, sides and sweets. No one was in charge, and no one wanted to be.

There was more food than even this large crowd could consume in one day and one night. When it came time to eat, people lined up with the plates and forks and spoons they had brought, digging in and filling up on as much or as little as they wanted. The young people piled their plates high; most of the older ones spooned out bird portions to pick at. A couple of the little kids swept by, cutting into the line with precision just at the place where they could surreptitiously swipe two fried chicken drumsticks, one for each hand. Then they shot back to their group games of tag or hide-and-seek or whatever interested them at the moment, biting and pulling long sections of meat off the leg bones as they trotted away, not caring that their hands were filthy, and certainly not giving a thought to the fact that they weren't eating any green or yellow vegetables. They would toss aside the bones once they had cleaned them of meat, and then they would wipe their greasy hands on their britches, usually while still on the run.

Bocker and most of his little posse came to the party, but the cats couldn't be bothered. Boogle and Stinkum and some of the other dogs, chasing first the children but soon each other, nearly knocked over the stand holding the dishwashing tubs. A couple of the dish towels fell onto the grass, but Juny, who was taking a smoke break with the other musicians and had been imagining that the friendly pack was doing a canine dance to honor sunshine, deftly snagged the cloths with his left hook and draped them back over the tree branch that was serving as an *ad hoc* towel rack.

Down at Fidelity, teenagers were cannonballing off the rope that hung from a perpendicular limb growing out of the biggest of the sycamores. And although little kids and dogs ran this way and that through the picnic, to a child (and to a pet) they managed to stay clear of the lengthy rows of little potted trees that were the beauty and gift of Tractor Girl's life's work here on the knob. She hadn't even thought to rope off the bonsais, but she wouldn't have had enough rope for an area that big, even if it had come to mind. She knew folks would be respectful. They always were.

The day was hot but partly cloudy and the humidity was mercifully low. Musicians started playing tunes in a copse of shade trees. Tractor Girl stood some distance off, watching them tune up and set off on a musical journey that they understood in a way quite different from those who merely listened with one ear and enjoyed the melodies in a disconnected sort of way. Tractor Girl's eyes were full of love for her people. Birdie was busy intertwining her voice and mandolin with Juny and the other voices, the other instruments. Wet Willie owned a boxy old food truck, emptied of all its shelving and appliances, and against one of the inside walls he had strapped an ancient upright piano. It was an ingenious way of making an incredibly heavy piece of furniture into a portable acoustic musical instrument. His habit was to back up his box truck to whatever outdoor gig was happening, open wide the back doors and the long horizontal serving windows, pull up a stool to the ivories, and cut loose on those broken, yellowed keys. Honky tonk, rock and roll, gospel, blues—whatever people were playing, he could make it better with that funky old almost-in-tune piano. The entire truck seemed to vibrate, amplifying the sound. Iwana, whipping and swaying like a lithe willow sapling, danced in the dirt with everyone else and blew Willie kisses.

From time to time, as one song ended, someone on a bench or in a beach chair would call out a request, and the troubadours would cut loose, doing their best to accommodate. This delighted the picnickers, for they liked the old familiar tunes and political protest songs that were sort of a tradition in their little culture. However, they weren't averse to the energy of new songs, so the musicians gladly peppered their set with both.

The Jimmies greeted everyone with warmth, though they didn't stand up each time they were approached. They were growing older, their yellow-white hair proof of it. But even if their get-up-and-go had got-up-and-went, they still hadn't lost their sizzle. It was evident by the sparkle in their eyes and the smiles on their faces that SLANT and all the creatures in it made them incredibly happy. And everyone was happy when The Jimmies were happy.

After people had visited a while and danced a while and eaten a lot and laughed 'til it hurt, Tractor Girl climbed up on an old bourbon barrel during a break in the music and gave a belated greeting to all, recognizing The Jimmies especially, which made the beloved old couple blush and caused everyone else to send up a jolly cheer on their behalf. Then Nooner thanked everyone for showing up at this year's Come Together, and though the party was far from over (they would eat again in a few hours), he asked Meddy to offer a grand toast—a blessing on those gathered—which she was more than happy to do.

Meddy lifted her cheap wine goblet in her right hand, offering it in a sweeping motion around the circle, outward from her left to her right. She did this slowly, so as to gain everyone's attention, and when they had quieted sufficiently, she began.

"In this circle, in this space," she said, "we gather for a simple reason: there is something here that we need."

Murmurs and nods all around. A couple of *hear-hears.* One *Oh HELL yes*, which evoked knowing laughter.

Meddy smiled and continued. "Someday, in a world you have not imagined, you'll experience a moment nearly identical to this one. It might be visual, might be visceral—might be literary. When it springs before you, you'll recognize it wholly, suddenly. And then you'll hear my voice saying"—here she lifted her stemmed glass high—"I have often thought of each of you … kindly, fondly and well.'"

Someone murmured an emphatic *Mmm-Hmm.*

Meddy went on. "It will feel so familiar, when you hear it again. And in that crystalline flash, my friends, you must stop to realize that I will have demonstrated Time Travel. Because, you see, I'll still be here, now—and I'll be there then, too. And listen: you'll be able to say, 'By god, she *did* travel in time. It's true. I was there. I am a witness.' So, expect to be amazed that this old girl planned so carefully and so far."

Well, it was Meddy. What else do you expect? Nothing short of theatrical.

She continued. "Now, reach back toward me with a grin … so I'll know it's you, huh?" She urged her glass toward her friends with a slight twist of her wrist, a subtle, outward motion.

"To goodness. To *us*," she said, unleashing a mighty proclamation.

And with that, Meddy brought her wine to her lips and drank so deeply that she emptied a nearly full glass in what looked like one long draw.

SLANTers exploded all over the bonsai farm's meadow in shouts and whoops. Then they drained their glasses, cups, bottles and cans, too. Even the children, with their sippy cups and straws, imbibed chocolate milk or juice or soda pop. Whatever was theirs to drink, they all, every last SLANTer, drank to Meddy's Time Travel toast. Its meaning would become clear by and by, but on that particular afternoon they were unaware exactly what impact it would someday have.

It was a cultural event, destined to enter the pantheon of SLANT lore. That toast, in that moment, on that creek bottom farm, at that Come Together was ever after revered by every SLANTer old enough to recall having witnessed it ... and even by a few who didn't. Nearly everyone told and retold the story of it over the years that followed.

And Meddy herself? She, needing a refill, folded gently into the talkative crowd, quietly accepting shoulder pats and winks and smiles from her neighbors as she passed in search of another bottle of that good Montepulciano she liked. Surely Nooner had stashed an extra underneath the food table, just for her.

# Deflect Judgment & Don't Judge

"I GET THE FEELING she won't be here long."

"Whaddya you mean by that?" Nooner asked. He reached under the makeshift table to pull out a new wine bottle for Meddy. They had been watching Tomlah work the crowd. Currently, she was dancing in slow circles around Dick, who didn't ever dance and didn't intend to learn. But he liked the attention he was getting from Tomlah, so he just stood there, grinning and swaying like a dolt in the middle of the crowd of dancers, while Tomlah danced seductively around and around him. He didn't seem to notice that she was winking and waving her long scarf at other men too.

"She's done nothing but move from place to place her whole life, to hear her tell it," said Meddy, watching the scene before them unfold. "Though, when it comes to moving place to place, I guess I'm not one to talk."

Nooner had opened the second bottle of Montepulciano and was pouring Meddy a refill. "Thanks, brother-man. Best red ever." She took a long sip and exhaled with pleasure. "What I mean is that every story I've heard out of her mouth would have us believe that she's been the solution to everyone else's problems, that she's been the organizer of everyone's fun, that she's been in demand everywhere she's ever gone, that she's got a string of best friends and lovers from coast to coast."

Nooner winced slightly, but Meddy didn't notice.

"I can't imagine how she's managed to make a living," she said, "what with all that whirlwind of merriment she claims she's constantly whipping up. Must be nice to be convinced you're the social star of the universe."

"Maybe it's all true."

"Maybe. But what are the odds? When you only get one side of a story, you sometimes forget to look into any other side. Know what I mean?"

Nooner didn't respond. He didn't react. He didn't reply. He just stood there, staring past the dancers, gazing idly at whatever the surface of the lazy creek was carrying downstream—insects, leaves, shadows.

"Well, she certainly has a rich fantasy life. I'll give her that." Meddy, for some reason that was unclear to herself, realized that she was attempting to be diplomatic. Generous, even. This inclination made her skin feel crawly, so she gave up the pretense immediately. "Oh, what the hell. The woman is bonkers, and we all know it."

"Oh, I don't know," Nooner said. "She seems okay ... to me."

"Of course she does!" Meddy flung it at him. She was beginning to feel the effects of the wine. "Because she's a bona-fide professional flirt! I mean, look at her right this very f'r'instance."

"I don't see that in her," Nooner said. He felt a bit sheepish in a way he couldn't explain to himself. But he wasn't lying. "I think she's, I don't know, friendly, I reckon." He averted his eyes from Meddy's gaze.

"Ever notice how many times she's gotten you to do her dirty work?"

"Now, hang on there ..."

"Oh, don't take it so personally. You're not the only one she's using," Meddy said, spitting a little. "The girl's an expert."

The fact that the "girl" in question was a middle-aged woman went noticeably unremarked. The image of *ingénue* clung to her, by design ... well, struggled to cling. It was apparently how she'd always manipulated people of all genders and orientations. She hadn't *quite* aged-out of that role just yet.

Big old Bocker ambled by on his rounds, but he patiently stopped and even stretched his neck a little when Nooner reached down to give him a back scratch. Seeing this, a jealous Boogle hustled up to get some loving too. Nooner obliged, though he had to bend over quite a bit farther to reach the little fellow's rump.

"The way I see it," Meddy was saying, "Tomlah's a charmer. Has probably gotten through her whole entire life by working people, pretending to be helpless, baking them cookies so they'll feel obligated to help whenever she calls on them to return a much bigger favor." Meddy didn't look directly at Nooner. "Think about it. What's she done for you? And then, what've you done for her?"

"Well, I ..." Nooner was interrupted by some gleeful Come Togetherer calling a greeting toward him. It was one of The Jimmies' grandkids. He flashed a thumbs-up back.

"Doesn't matter, the particulars," Meddy said, not slurring much. Yet. "The point is—I'm guessing you've never had a conversation with her about anything that really matters to you. I'm guessing all your encounters have consisted of her batting her eyes and complimenting you—or her offering to feed you a ham sandwich and then dropping like a dainty handkerchief the idea of your doing some heavy lifting, or hinting that you might use your pick-up to go get her a load of mulch. Something like that."

"She's not ..."

"Nooner, honey, you know I love you. You've become the little brother

I never had."

"I know that. We're family now."

"Exactly why I'm telling you this. Hon, you're being played."

"Aw, Meddy …"

"I know you don't want this to be true."

"It ain't!"

The Tomlah in question had come recently to SLANT, a lone guest tenant in the recently-vacated home of one of the original SLANTers, Cora, who had found that her time to live on her own had long since passed. Cora's long-time partner had died, and the elderly Cora had moved herself into assisted living in the nearby city. Although she knew there were no other options after her final hip-shattering and face-lacerating fall, she hated it there, as she told Meddy and Nooner every time they visited her. Her near-blindness, her perpetual dizziness and Parkinson's and diabetes were beyond even the help of protective neighbors anymore. Plus, her heart was iffy. She needed full-time, around-the-clock looking after. Well, when Cora had moved out, the SLANT community had cautiously agreed to give her great-niece-in-law, Tomlah, a limited trial run. Many of us were hesitant, but none could reject the favor Cora had asked of us. At least we'd been willing to give it a temporary try.

Slowly, Tomlah had gotten to know a few of the SLANTers, especially the men. She hadn't yet done much contributing to the community, though. Her stay would likely be brief, Meddy reckoned.

Realizing she might be over-stepping, Meddy decided to take a different tack with Nooner. "Let's us take an amble," she said, picking up the wine bottle and steering him toward the creek bank, away from the crowd. "Here's an idea, dear one. Try not to be yourself when you look at this."

"How the hell …?"

"Just try. Be someone else. Be me. Well, maybe that's not the best suggestion I ever made. Be … I don't know—be Jimmy, or Turk, or Juny. No, that won't work either. On third thought, be a woman when you look at this."

"Be a *woman?*"

"Look, Tomlah's used her ways and wiles on men all her life, so none of you can be objective. Try to be, say, Joy. She's objective. Pretend you're seeing this thing through Joy's eyes."

"I don't know how to do that." Nooner nearly whimpered as he said it.

"Step outside yourself for a moment. Pretend you are watching yourself, only it isn't you that's watching, it's Joy. What does she see when Tomlah talks to you? Does she see sincerity? Does she see manipulation? How would Joy describe what's going on?"

Nooner exploded. "How the hell should I know what Joy would see?"

Joy, hearing her name from across the way, hollered, "Hey, Nooner!"

He waved back, forcing a smile so she wouldn't know why she'd heard her name above the crowd of revelers and so out of context. "Hey yourself, Joy," he called back to her. "Havin' fun?" Joy nodded an enthusiastic *yes* just as Turk walked up to her and pulled her attention away.

"Tomlah, she somehow got herself stuck in 'little girl' mode," Meddy was saying. "My guess is that it happened a long time ago, yet she thinks that stupid act still works. At her age. It's embarrassing!"

"For who?"

"For all adult women who have a sliver of dignity or, for that matter, pride. And self-respect!"

"Bullshit, Meddy. Shut the fuck up! You're pissin' me off with this feminist world-view stuff. I never even knew it existed before you came along." Nooner wished he hadn't raised his voice to his friend, but she *was* pissing him off, talking shit about Tomlah.

"Well, first of all, it's not bullshit, Nooner!" Meddy was indignant. "And if you think feminism is *bullshit,* then we've got a problem here," she said, "because I thought you were a *fair*-minded person who understands that feminism is about the difference between equality and *oppression.*" She was more disappointed than hurt. "I can't believe you just said that."

He took a breath. "Okay, I know. I didn't mean it. You're right and you've taught me well … but you're drivin' me crazy right this minute with your theories and your judgments and how you constantly try to make ever'thing fit into your little mold of what kind of behavior is right and wrong and smart and stupid. Give it a goddamn rest for five fuckin' minutes, will you!" He kicked at nothing, though what he wanted to be doing was kicking at something. "Just … this isn't about feminism right now, okay? This is about friendship. God *damn.*"

They stood for an awkward moment. Neither of them spoke.

The musicians had taken a break. A cardinal tworped its silver song. The breeze moved a tufted seed through the air alongside the creek until it dropped in to ride the surface of the current.

Meddy broke the silence first. "Well," she said, "I can see I've upset you."

Nooner didn't respond.

"I can see that I've overstepped your boundaries here. Again. My opinionated pushiness is one of my worst traits; you're damn sure right about that."

Still nothing from him.

"The older I get, the more I still have to learn," she said, trying a little smile in his general direction, but he didn't take the bait.

He lowered his eyes to a place on the ground just to the left of his boot toe.

She put her hand on his forearm. "And yes, this *is* about friendship. I'm not sorry I care about you," she said. "I'm not sorry I don't want to see you used. But I *am* sorry that I said anything. I'm sorry I butted in."

"Why'd you bring this up?" Nooner finally asked. "Do you not want me to have any friends but you?"

"Where in the hell did that come from?" Now it was Meddy's turn to be annoyed. "You're friends with everybody up here, Nooner. I love that about you. And I'm not saying you shouldn't be friends with Tomlah. Be friends with whomever you like. Just know that things aren't always what they appear, especially when one is smitten."

"The woman," Nooner said in a deliberately even tone, "is nice to me. That's all. I don't mind helpin' her out ever' now and then."

"Fine," Meddy said. She heard the indignant tone rise in her own voice, but she was a teeny-tiny bit tipsy, so she barreled ahead anyway. "Fine. Dandy. If you want to be used, you've found a convenient user, so you're all set." She wasn't proud to be expressing that ugly, crusty side of her nature. She knew from experience that she ought to be mindful, not let it emerge enough to blot out everything else.

"And what's *that* supposed to mean?" Nooner practically growled.

"It means only this: just because *you* are a friend, doesn't mean your 'friend' is capable of being a friend back."

"Friends," Nooner said, "are friends! You think you use me when I do things to help you out?"

"No. I don't," Meddy said. "And that's precisely the point. You and I have a true give-and-take. We both help each other, don't we? You take me to town, I buy the gas, the lunch and the movie tickets. You need something proofread, I do it, and then you let me use your computer for a while. You help me in my garden, I feed you from it. We give each other different things, but their values are roughly equivalent. Agree? Or disagree?"

"Well, sure we do. So what? Can't Tomlah and I do that too, without you gettin' all jealous?"

"Jealous?" Meddy shook her head and chuckled. "Oh, my dear, sweet boy. Jealousy is the furthest from it. I am crazy about you, but jealous I'm not."

"Well, what then? What else could it be?"

Meddy realized that she needed to be patient and not patronizing. "It could be," she said, rather more carefully than before, "that I'm being too protective."

She sat down on the bank, patting the grass beside her. With reluctance, he sat. "All I'm saying is that you might want to compare our sort of give-and-take to the kinds of exchanges you and Tomlah have."

"All friendships aren't the same, Meddy," he said.

"How well I know that, Nooner, honey. I've learned it the hard way. I guess I'm just hoping you won't have to. I *do* want you to believe that's my only motive. Truly. But give-and-take has got to be more than someone else taking what they think you have to give. That's all I'm saying."

"She gives."

"What does she give you, little brother?"

"Cookies, sometimes."

"That's nice," Meddy said. She was really trying. "A whole batch of cookies just for you?"

"Usually four or five, maybe a half dozen, in a sandwich bag. Plus, sometimes she gives me some food she's made. She don't like leftovers."

Meddy didn't blurt out what she was thinking.

"And other things," he went on. "Stuff she's gettin' rid of, she leaves by my truck," he said. "You know, like that."

"Do you like the stuff she's getting rid of that she gives to you?"

"Not much. But I figure if I'm headed to town anyway, it don't pain me much to swing by and drop it off at the Goodwill for her, which is what she always says. 'If you don't need it or like it,' she says, 'feel free to give it to Goodwill,' she says. 'It won't hurt my feelings. I'm through with it anyway.' So, that's what I usually do. She's just tryin' to be generous."

"Okay, so that's what she does for you," Meddy said, priding herself on saying just that, nothing more, and with no judgmental tone of voice. "Give me some idea of things you do for her."

"Oh, she might ask me to pull up a stump or cut and haul some dead branches," he said.

"Uh-huh. What else?"

"Throw her garbage bags in my truck bed and take 'em out to the bin by the road, I reckon."

"Okay."

"Maybe I'll let her use my truck, like you said, or pound together a little sittin' deck out back her place, like I did this week. Maybe run to the hardware for parts if her toilet needs fixed."

"And do you fix it, too?"

"Sure, I don't mind to. She don't know how to do things much."

"Can you say why you do so much for someone who gives you leftover food and junk she's throwing out?"

Nooner threw a look her way, as if to gauge her intent.

"I'm not being sarcastic, hon, just asking. What draws you to her?" Meddy was really trying to understand. There truly was no *gotcha* in her tone. "What I'm asking, I guess, is what do you like about her?"

"She has a nice smile. She pays me compliments and makes me feel good. She's very friendly."

"And do you hope for more? Does she inspire you to hope for more?" Meddy said these words as gently as she knew how.

Nooner was quiet. Meddy let him think.

"Maybe," he finally said.

"Does she seem interested in you?"

"Well, of course she's interested in me. We're friends, ain't we?"

"I mean, does she indicate interest of the same type that you hope for?"

Again, a pause while Nooner gave this some thought.

"Not yet," he said. "Not really. But hope is hope, you know?" Finally, he pulled up his head and faced his companion in defiance. "You know, Meddy?"

Out of affection for her young friend, Meddy made a decision, and it was final. "Okay, Nooner," she said. She looked at him with genuine kindness and a little bit of resignation, both of which he picked up on. "I'm going to trust that you have a handle on this and can see it more clearly than I can, because you're on the inside of it and I'm not."

Having heard the imbalance of evidence come from his own mouth, however, Nooner's eyes betrayed a new bewilderment.

But Meddy just said, "It's your business, and I shouldn't have interfered," and she meant it, and he knew that. She patted him on the knee and refilled his cup from the wine bottle sitting on the bank between them. "Land's sake, it's hot out here this afternoon. Must be ninety degrees in the shade."

"Yeah," said Nooner. "Hot."

"But change being the one constant in the world," Meddy said, breaking into her embarrassingly corny version of a high-pitched and 'veddy-British' accent, "this uncomfortable patch of weather will doubtless run its merry course sooner or later. Yes? Relief *will* break through. We simply *must* believe it so. Tut-tut, old thing?"

But levity wasn't going to work. Nooner was in no mood to play.

"Yeah," he said, throwing the rest of his wine down his throat. He was glum. "Has to." He stood, stretched, ambled off toward Fidelity in a complete funk.

*Oh, dear*, Meddy thought. But what she whispered aloud to herself was, "Oh, fuck."

# Let People Be

"IT'S NOT THE NORM, I'll grant you that," Meddy said to Dick, "but so fuckin' what? Who is anybody to decide what 'the norm' is, anyhow?" Meddy (as we all know) is famous for her love of air-quotes. Few people noticed, however, that she switched the number of fingers she used between single and double air-quotes for correct usage. This was important to her even if no one else cared.

Hours had passed since she and Nooner had talked down by the creek. Supper had been eaten. A big, long tale had been told by yours truly, The Bard, and I was pleased that it was well received and loudly appreciated with great laughter and applause upon its conclusion. (Although now that I think about it, I wonder if the mere fact that it finally concluded was the inspiration for their enthusiasm!) A second round of dishes had been washed. People were chatting or making the rounds or napping on the grass.

Darkness threatened, so Tractor Girl and Nooner started moving from torch to torch, lighting the place with little bits of fire staked throughout the picnic area on the bonsai farm. Someone was starting a bonfire closer to the creek. Meddy and Dick watched as musicians and the more indestructible partiers trickled in that direction.

In spite of the long day, The Jimmies were hanging in there. Meddy noticed that two or three people were carrying The Jimmies' chairs and drinks for them, guiding the couple toward the bonfire and guarding against stumbles as the two elderly "grands" traversed the meadow's fringe.

All day, Pair Square had been having the best time that ever was. They had danced in every possible combination: the two couples danced together; the exes danced together; the exes danced with their exes' exes; and they all four danced in a circle. They were so happy that sometimes one of them would dance alone. Other times other dancers joined their tight circle, and that was fine too.

"Who is anybody to decide what 'the norm' is, anyhow?"

"I know, Meddy," Dick said. "I know that—the thing about the so-called norm. I realize it's not the SLANT way to make those judgments. But still, it's kindly odd, you know? Them livin' all together like that … and not kin? Never seen the like in all my days. It ain't exactly right, now is it?"

Dick really was trying to fathom this thing. He wanted it to be right, but there was nothing in his background that could find a compartment into which the Pair Square would fit. "Pair Square" is what most everyone in SLANT called the Hibberds and the Finkles as a unit, but those couples didn't know it. At least no one thought they did.

"They're an interesting set, I'll agree," Meddy said, "but I've never known them to be anything other than perfectly wonderful neighbors. You got any reason to doubt that about them?" Suddenly, she felt worried. Or maybe drunk. "Is there something you aren't telling me? Something that's happened over by y'all's place?"

"Not a thing in this world," Dick said. And this was true. Pair Square had always been fair with him. He liked them, especially those two fellows. Dick had just been pondering and wondering and trying to work it all out in his head lately.

"I … I shouldn't have brought it up."

"Now, Dick, you know you and I can talk about anything, all kinds of things," Meddy said. She hoped she wasn't slurring her words. "I hope we always will. Can."

"You know I 'preciate ye, Meddy. 'Druther talk to you than just about anybody up here."

"You too, buddy."

"And I can make room for difference; you damn well know I can," he said. In fact, as the very first Black SLANTer, but certainly not the last, he knew all about how SLANT was the most level and equitable place he'd ever lived, racially or otherwise. So, it certainly wasn't "difference" *of any kind* that was concerning him.

"I do know, Dick." Meddy smiled at him. He appeared a little fuzzy. No, wavy. Like gravy. Maybe. She looked around for her wine bottle and felt a bit panicky until her hand found it underneath her chair. "Well, then, maybe you just need to figure out what's the main thing bothering you about Pair Square," she finally said. "D'you know that much, at least?"

"I cain't figure out how they knew, is all."

"How they knew?"

"Yeah, you know … how they *knew*."

"I couldn't say, Dick," said Meddy, "but they did. They got lucky and they figured it out. So, *good for them*, I say. They're all happy, don't you think?"

Dick nodded and allowed as how that seemed true.

"That's good enough for me," Meddy said with a shrug.

"I reckon," Dick said. He gave it a few final seconds of thought, then stated, "Good for them. I reckon you're right." As far as he was concerned, that was that.

Now, Pair Square hadn't always been Pair Square. In fact, they didn't even know each other until they got to SLANT, the couples arriving within the same week, probably ten years back. The four of them became fast friends right away, but when their friendship later took a bizarre turn, they were as surprised as everyone else.

Nobody had to point out to them that they weren't the norm.

Tommy and Jill Hibberd were from the Missouri Bootheel. Tommy had grown up there, working in a huge family farming operation near Dorena, but Jill had originally moved to those Mississippi River bottoms from somewhere in western Iowa. She came to attend college at SEMO State, and then she had stayed to work in a clinic in Sikeston after she finished her nursing degree. They had met at a truck stop late one night. Jill had learned that it was the only place in a twenty-mile radius that stayed open and kept a fresh pot of coffee going after ten at night. She loved to sit at the counter by herself and unwind from her long day at the clinic. They usually finished up with patients around seven or eight, but since she was the manager of the place, she had to stay and take care of the books, order supplies, do payroll, deal with insurance issues, work out the marketing budget, and innumerable other tasks that the doctors didn't want to fool with. She didn't mind having extra, non-nursing work, and they did pay her well for her expanded responsibilities.

Tommy, meanwhile, had suffered from insomnia all his life. Even as a child, he had lain awake at night into the wee hours listening to the far-off signals that came in on his plastic clock radio with the big, lighted, circular dial. He felt so much more alive at night; yet the farmer's life was one of early-to-bed-and-early-to-rise. While he loved the land, the farm-ing life itself just wasn't a good fit. He'd sometimes find himself driving around at night, wishing he could be able to lie peacefully at rest, like his neighbors behind the dark windows of farmhouses he passed. Tommy was tortured, and he didn't know why. One sultry July midnight, he strode into the open-all-night truck stop up the road. He had decided that maybe a slice of pie and a glass of milk might help him sleep. There sat Jill at the counter—and his life, though he couldn't have predicted it in that first moment, would never be the same.

Griddle and Finkle, on the other hand, had grown up in a little village on a lake in west Tennessee (across the Mississippi River from the Hibberds but a million miles away).

Griddle got her nickname flipping burgers as a teenager; Teddy Finkle had been the first new employee she was allowed to "boss." Even though they were in the same class at the high school, she had nearly two years' job seniority on him when he came to work at the Dairy Dipper. Her promotion to manager of the after-school shift was Griddle's first real-world taste of success. She and Finkle ended up married, a move that surprised no one who knew them. At first, they lived in a tar-paper shack near a small ferryboat landing, worked at Dairy Dipper (and several other jobs as needed), planned and dreamed, saved and schemed toward a vision they shared.

Backing up their willingness to work with their natural-born talents and hard-earned expertise, they were able, one step at a time, to design and later create the perfect little ice cream and hamburger parlor of their own making; they called it The Dish. The old-fashioned sit-down parlor also offered a drive-up window and quick service, one of the early enterprises in independent "fast food" in the South. Soon The Dish was a regional chain with locations conveniently situated on the main roads and new Interstate highways in north Mississippi, Arkansas, southeast Missouri, and the western ends of Kentucky and Tennessee. The volume of business and customer loyalty they experienced took everyone except Finkle and Griddle by surprise. They already knew most people in rural areas craved conveniences they didn't have.

A few years later, the friendly hometown competition that his former employees had invented inspired the Dairy Dipper's aging owner to sell out to the Finkles, who considered things to have come full circle within a decade. Soon after that, at the ripe old age of 43, Finkle and Griddle sold the whole profitable company to a national chain developer. They were set for life. It was then that they decided to get a big, comfortable Airstream, a new truck to tow it and a gasoline credit card; they intended to live, as many Americans dream of someday doing, out on the open road. But a few months after they left Paris Landing, Tennessee, they pulled into SLANT. They never pulled out again.

The Airstream that Griddle and Finkle arrived in stayed in SLANT, but had long since been absorbed by additions and annexes over the years. They didn't live it in after their house was built. Dick had moved into it in exchange for labor; he'd helped to build the houses at Pair Square. Since Dick had been camping in a tent all summer and fall of that year, they offered him the Airstream as a winter home. Once in, neither he nor the Finkles ever mentioned it again.

And so it was that Dick had been living right there for nearly ten years. Every so often he would decide that he needed one more small room, so he'd just build it right next to the Airstream, or next to the last addition that had been constructed there. He'd added a porch, then made covered walkways from one of these sheds to the next. There was no rhyme and little reason attached to his expansion projects; consequently, Dick's compound had the look of a hideout for a Uni-Bomber type, although Dick was far from that. He just needed more and more places to store and display his growing collection of books, records and vintage posters. Dick's compound was Pair Square's nearest neighbor.

Pair Square itself (the name SLANTers gave the place) was fascinating. To appreciate it fully, one had to go all the way back to the beginning.

The Finkles and the Hibberds had found SLANT at about the same time, but in different ways. Griddle and Finkle had just happened upon the place through completely random wanderings. It was a total accident that they found it at all. The Hibberds, on the other hand, were quite intentional in their arrival; they had been acquaintances of a man called Dervish who had spent some time in SLANT with his ex-girlfriend (our beloved Wilma Carl, of course) and had spun many stories about it. Over a year's time, the Finkles had encountered Dervish at least once a month in a local bar back in Missouri. There they bought him drinks as long as he'd talk about our mythical place. And he could talk about SLANT for hours, they soon learned. The Hibberds came to understand that anything out of Dervish's mouth was to be taken with a grain of salt; still, if only half—only one-fourth!—of what he said was true, they knew they had to find a way to get to SLANT. They weren't deterred even by the negatives he described. It sounded to them like the adventure they dreamed of, the community they craved, the unfinished vision they shared. Finally, Dervish drew them a map, which they treated as if it would direct them to treasure.

In a way, that's exactly what it did.

By the time they all had arrived (the Finkles in their Airstream, the Hibberds as tent campers), SLANT was quite evolved. The Jimmies' own family had grown to include not only Daisy, Lily, Iris and Rose, but Johnny Jump (whose nickname was Pansy), and P. Onie too—The Jimmies referred to the kids as their *flower children.* In ensuing decades the family had also added five grandchildren to the tally: Jewel, Opal, Goldy, and the twins, Amber & Amethyst—this generation they called *the rock-ons.* During those first forty years, more of SLANT's small houses had been built; several tiny enterprises had sprung to life; the gravel roads and paths into and throughout the commune had been improved. But the charm of the original vision for SLANT remained intact; the place was pretty much off the cultural grid, and that's what those who came to SLANT to stay wanted more than anything. As I've told you, it's something SLANTers work intentionally to perpetuate, both as individuals and as a community.

The Hibberds already embraced this, knowing what they had learned of SLANT from Dervish. They knew he had left because he couldn't abide the quiet, the remoteness from urban life. They knew his girlfriend had let him leave precisely because she couldn't force herself to go back to living in a busy metropolis, didn't want the life that he missed so much.

They were on her side, but they didn't say that to Dervish directly.

The Finkles, too, wrapped themselves around the SLANT concept as soon as it was explained to them. By then, because they were people who could have everything, what they craved was nothing. They liked the anonymity, the detachedness, the languid pace of SLANT. They liked the absence of competition and the presence of cooperation. Nothing was expected; nothing was required; everything was possible.

Within days of their separate arrivals, both couples had decided to put down roots right there in SLANT. They were equally ecstatic about their newfound friendships and about the strong landscape and gentle nature of their new community. Too, each couple could not get enough of the other's company. In spite of differing backgrounds, levels of educa-tion and economic situations, it seemed to Meddy and to others who were there as it unfolded that the two couples loved each other immediately, as if they'd always known each other. They all four became best friends on the spot.

What transpired from that point was no real surprise, given the context and extremity to which the Finkles and the Hibberds felt connected from the very start.

One evening, the four of them sitting around the fire pit, Finkle said he'd had a recent dream about the house he and Griddle would build. "It's an old-fashioned shotgun house," he'd said. "Two stories; three rooms up and three down. But I'd set it sideways and put the front door in the long side—wide across the front but narrow from front to back. We'll make it large enough to have a hallway running along one whole side, both floors."

"Okay," Griddle said. She seemed unclear but not oppositional.

"Yeah," Finkle said, "and it'll have a big garage with a workshop extension hooked onto one end at a right angle."

Tommy said it sounded great, but added, "We're going to have to go back home for a while, I guess. Work and save up some money to build a house of our own up here—now that these good SLANT folks have invited us."

For reasons Finkle wasn't able to fully explain to himself, a pain shot through his stomach. "No!" he said. "I mean, you don't have to save up. My dream has two identical shotgun houses sitting end-to-end. I think I'm supposed to build them both, but I only dreamed Griddle and me living in one of them. My guess is that the other one is yours."

"You mean rent the other house from you?"

"I don't think so," Finkle said. He was looking around inside himself for the answer, peering backward into the memory of his dream as hard as he could. "I think I'm supposed to build the other house for you."

"Oh, we couldn't ... I mean, we just ..."

"It's not a gift," Finkle said decisively. "I don't know how to build a house, but I figure you do. Have you ever built anything?"

"Well, sure. We always built sheds or barns or pump houses or room additions or whatever we needed on the farm," Tommy said. "Plumbed and wired 'em too. I can sure enough build. Are you thinking you can hire me, or let me trade off my labor on this thing?"

"Trade off labor works for me."

"You kiddin' me? I build two houses, one for you and one for me, and you pay for 'em?"

"That's about the size of it. And if you'll teach me how, I'll help." Finkle realized it would be a bargain for them both, and that made him happy. And that's when he understood why SLANT was different from other places—this sort of thing could really happen here. And it didn't seem strange.

"Man, put me down for that barter!" Tommy hollered, and he picked up Jill and danced her around the campfire they'd shared in front of the Airstream for the previous few weeks. "Hey, Jilly, you hearin' this? Hot damn!" They danced like drunkards, and their joy was contagious.

Griddle stepped up behind Finkle's chair and leaned down to hug his chest from behind. "That's a pretty sight, isn't it?" she said to the top of his head.

"Damned if it's not," he answered, not able to tear his eyes from the scene and wanting, someway, to be in it himself.

Finkle wasn't one to waste opportunity, so he and Tommy jumped into one of the trucks and barreled down the knob early next day to find a lumberyard and make arrangements for delivery of basic building materials. He had spent the entire night drawing house plans according to his dream. Once done, he and Tommy easily calculated what they'd need to get the structures framed and finished. Finkle wasn't worried that he might come up a little short on materials; he could always order a second delivery. As it turned out, he'd ordered a bit more than what was needed, but that gave him another idea.

"Let's couple 'em," he said. Nobody didn't think that was a fine idea.

With Tommy leading the charge and Finkle helping out as he was able (which wasn't much, unfortunately), Griddle and Jill added their creative skills to the project. Besides Dick, they also hired Jorge, his sons Pedro and Joe, plus a couple of local Amish carpenters from off-knob who had done a lot of work in SLANT and knew most everyone up here.

The houses went up fast. The two structures sat in a straight line, the end of one was a mere twenty feet from the end of its twin. They were mirror-image identical in every way, right down to the color of paint and the style of knockers on the doors. With the extra materials he'd miscalculated but already paid for, Finkle and Tommy modified the design to include a many-windowed dogtrot sun room that connected the houses and created a commons room. They added doors that entered each house at either side of the greenhouse-style dogtrot. Suddenly, what had been two houses was now one. The two porches across the separate house-fronts were joined and expanded to one long gallery. And with the two garage-workshop wings jutting forward at right angles from the far ends of the main linear structure, a three-sided courtyard area suggested the appearance of a square, hence its nickname.

It was attractive, it was functional, and it was unifying—more and more, the Finkles and the Hibberds were becoming a single unit. Pair Square was officially born on the day the last nail was driven. Within a year, the double-shotgun abode was adorned with a giant screen porch across the back. They all moved around inside and outside the enormous house as they pleased. It was almost as if they were brothers and sisters who just never got around to leaving home.

So, what of it? What of these two couples sharing a single home? Why did they enjoy each other more together than with half of them apart? How did the concept of family extend to four adults sharing a house? What kinds of marriages could hold up in this kind of situation?

Finkle and Tommy didn't think about it; they just lived it. Jill and Griddle never worried about it; neither of them thought to fear that the other's husband would make unwanted and, therefore, uncomfortable advances. It wasn't possible. They all completely trusted each other.

Pair Square did nearly everything together: played cards and board games, hiked, cut and hauled firewood, worked around their place, pitched in to help neighbors. They talked to each other about almost everything, but there was one thing they never talked about as a group (not until years and years later). The Hibberds never mentioned to the Finkles something they had noticed: as soon as they had arrived in SLANT they'd stopped having sex. And the Finkles, who had noticed the very same thing about themselves, likewise never mentioned that to the Hibberds. As it turns out, not only did both couples stop having sex, they never started back up again. Ever. And even weirder, they didn't care, for all the other parts of their lives were so complete, felt so good and fulfilling, that they hardly noticed. And they forgot that other people might think it odd. The entire subject dropped simultaneously from the consciousness of all four. Life was too interesting for such a distraction.

The first year, Griddle and Jill taught each other things: play guitar, can vegetables, do leather-work, repair furniture, cultivate sunflowers. Candle- and soap-making were big that year, so they threw themselves into that. Tommy and Finkle put in a huge garden and maintained it; they kept the woods and the yard delineated. All four pitched in to landscape the courtyard formed by the mirrored L-shaped houses. In the second year, Tommy took a job off-knob; Finkle tried to get him not to, but

Tommy didn't want to be seen as a taker. By then, Tommy recognized that Finkle wouldn't ever have to go to a job again for the rest of his life unless he wanted to, but that didn't make Tommy rich by association. In need of cash flow, he found work down at the same lumberyard that had delivered the building materials for Pair Square.

By year three, Teddy Finkle suddenly realized he was in love with Tommy Hibberd.

It did not occur to Finkle, never having failed at finding a way to accomplish anything he was set on having, to keep this to himself. He declared it to his three housemates immediately, shocking Tommy but (interestingly) not Griddle. Jill didn't seem to care one way or the other; in fact, she was the one who suggested that the two boys go off somewhere and talk it out, which they readily did.

"Well?" Finkle said once the men were seated on a dead-fall log under a copse of willows near the creek's edge. "Say something!" But Tommy seemed to be elsewhere, occupying himself with heavy thought, as if trying to decipher a particularly challenging arithmetic problem.

"I love you," Finkle said again. "I. Love. You."

Tommy nodded, shook his head, moved his eyes side to side (Finkle tried to decipher this, worrying that it meant something negative). Tommy's gaze next focused downward (probably not a good sign, Finkle thought), then up (better), and through it all his brow furrowed more and more deeply. Finally, that Missouri farmboy looked right into Finkle's face and opened his mouth: "Well, I'll be damned—looks like I love you back." He sat very still for a full minute, stunned by having heard those particular words tumble out of his own mouth.

Then Finkle, being a man of action, swept Farmer Tom into his arms and showered his face and neck with kisses. Things progressed rather rapidly from there, to the confusion and delight of them both. They were shy, but they were brave.

The girls never spoke about what transpired between them while the boys were away sorting it out. All that's known for sure is that by the time the fellows walked out of the woods a couple hours later, Tommy's clothing had already been moved into Finkle's half of the house, and Griddle had happily brought her things over to Jill's side. Then everything went on exactly as before, with one distinct exception: sex was definitely being had again in both sides of Pair Square on a regular basis.

# Keep Your Own Counsel

AROUND MIDNIGHT, the party thinned. The Come Together slowly
came apart until next summer's reunion. There were die-hards of all ages
who would party down 'til sun-up at the bonsai farm, but most SLANTers
took their leave when the clock turned from Saturday to Sunday. Solstice
had come again with a big bang, and SLANT was well satisfied that
summer had been rung in with the style and energy it deserved.

Meddy made her way home on foot through SLANT-center along
the main path, passing The General with its porch full of rocking chairs
empty in the dim moonlight. She had caught a ride up the knob with Dick
and was now enjoying her night walk toward her shelter. A figure sitting
in the posture of a stargazer was seated on a bench near the community
gardens, smoking. It was Horse, and Meddy thought, *Good on ya, old boy.*

"Hey, Horse," she said when close enough to greet him in a low voice.

"Evenin', Miz Meadowlark Nightengale," Horse said. Nothing more.
Meddy knew Horse liked the peace of a night sky as much as she did, so
she didn't interrupt his quiet bliss. If you wanted to find Horse, outdoors
at night was always your best bet. Sometimes he sat, sometimes he walked,
but always on clear nights he was out.

Horse was a card-carrying wanderer (if there could be such a thing),
and he'd been one since he was a kid. In the vernacular of his youth, he
was a hobo. He had moved around a good deal, frequently by rail. "I like
the life," he's told me. "Got into it in the '40s. The '50s rolled in—better
times—but I kept right on. Livin' free. I was made for it, seems like."

He left home and school at thirteen, but at that time he, being an early
bloomer, already had the look of a grown man, eighteen at least. He'd
caught his first ride from a trucker who had stopped for a cup of coffee;
that driver dropped him off in Cincinnati two days later. After that, Horse
had thumbed, jumped trains, walked and walked and walked. He went
east to west, then up and down the west coast for a while. Like Meddy,
he knew the desert Southwest and the Great Plains. Knew the Missouri,
Ohio, Mississippi, Tennessee and Cumberland river valleys. The deep
South, New England, the Outer Banks and Cajun country. The wheat

basket of the plains and the ranch lands of the Rockies, too. Yet he never got past believing that he knew less than other people because he had never finished school. He considered himself uneducated. This always amazed me. Meddy too, who considered Horse one of the most well-traveled and well-read people she had ever known.

He went by Horse, though his given name actually had an additional syllable. Nobody had ever used it, though, and he was nine years old before he understood why his name wasn't spelled like it sounded. Every year at school, though, he'd have that terrible first-day moment when roll was called to start the year. A new teacher, attempting to put faces with all the students' names, would come to his on the list and sing out, "Horace?" The result was predictable, a scene repeated year upon year: the cringe; the slide down in his seat; the laughter of his classmates; the muttered, "Horse. Call me Horse. That's my name." Most teachers, especially if they were young and new on the job, looked blankly around the room, as if wondering whether calling a boy *Horse* was permissible.

So, that was one of the ways Horse felt like an outsider. When authority figures don't understand your very name, you consider yourself marginalized, and that becomes a big piece of your worldview.

As an adult, Horse never minded being called a hobo, for he thought it an honorable lifestyle. *Bum*, however, he never could stand. To him *bum* meant someone who wouldn't work, moved from handout to handout. That wasn't his way. Aside from the occasional soup line in the dead of winter when there was little work for an outdoor laborer, he shunned handouts.

"I pay my own way." He always spoke these words with pride. I once heard him say, "If I can't pay for what I need with money, I barter it with the sweat of my brow, the strength in my back, the dishwater on my hands!" Meddy thought he ought to add to that list the unique products of a mind that solved practical problems entirely organically. At any rate, pay his own way he did, for years and years. And still.

Horse rarely stayed in one place for long. But there was the unforgettable year when he spent *four entire months* in one place. It was the Ropers who took him in, put him to work, gave him shelter in their attic room because the barn was much too cold for a man to sleep out there all through a long winter's night. The Ropers weren't suspicious people. If a man needed a job and if they needed a worker, they hired him. And if a hand who was working for the Ropers needed a place to bed down, they would show their Christian charity and make sure he had a place of his own, even under their own roof with the family. They epitomized the label "good people."

That winter long, long ago, Horse had come to the Ropers' farm in central Tennessee at a time when they needed a hand with the milking.

Unlike a crop farm where the most intense work occurs during the planting, growing and harvest seasons, a dairy farm is a year-round operation. That particular winter, 1950, the eldest Roper boy had gotten married and joined the flight of Southerners to industrial centers up north. Without that son, Mr. Roper was short-handed. Lucky for them both, Horse had come up the lane at just the right time.

Mrs. Roper had arranged a cot for Horse in a cozy little corner of the attic; not as warm as the crowded downstairs, but a damn sight more comfy than the hayloft would have been. Since he worked from before sunrise until after sunset, he took his meals on the back porch or up in the attic alone. He was the only hired hand on the place that winter, and while his employers had offered to feed him at the family table, he politely deflected that kindness ("No, that's all right, but I thank ye ever so much for offering, ma'am") on the grounds that he was by nature a loner. Horse put in a good solid workday, Mr. Roper always said, but he wasn't much of a talker, that was for sure and certain. If he preferred to keep to himself, they respected that and let him organize his own life around the work they had hired him to do.

Horse spent all of his evening and nighttime hours in that attic. What he did up there, they couldn't have said, but he never disturbed anyone else or gave cause for suspicion. Sometimes he borrowed books. He was courteous and so quiet that they often forgot he was there until time to go back out the next morning to milk and feed the cattle.

In my imagination, it was the Roper children—the two younger ones, anyway, still living at home when Horse had been there—who put it all together. Much later, they compared notes and realized that all they had ever seen uncovered of him was his head. The time of year had dictated his wearing clothing that covered his entire body; the cold weather had prevented his ever having to roll up his sleeves, remove his gloves or unwrap the knitted scarf he wore around his neck.

A few years after Horse had left the Roper farm, those children were up in that attic, playing or looking for something or storing a small trunk or table for their mother, perhaps. One of them, James, got to poking around to see what else there was to see. He found himself in the corner under the rafters where Horse had once made his cozy little nest. James hadn't thought about Horse in a long time.

"Look here," he said to his sister. "Horse must've left it."

He was pointing to a handkerchief, folded like a little package and tucked into a tight space between a rafter and the decking of the roof's underside.

"What's in it?" said Lillian.

"Maybe it's money," said James, and he worked the folded handkerchief bundle free from its hiding place. "Maybe we're rich and we don't even know it."

"We're not rich. You're a dreamer."

James held the little bundle carefully on his open palm, slowly peeling open the handkerchief's folds—one, two, three. When he pulled back the last corner covering the contents, he recoiled a little. Then he looked closer, pushing the objects around with his index finger. He picked up one of the objects, then dropped it and held another to the light.

"What the dickens are these?" he said.

"Something all dried up," said Lillian. "Is it herbs? Leaves? Ooooo—dead bugs?"

"Scabs, looks like to me," James said.

"Scabs? They're too thick to be scabs. Besides, who keeps scabs in a little package like a gift?"

"Horse did, I'd say. But wonder why?"

"Wait, James. You don't think these could be ..."

"Lillian, don't you say a word to Momma. I mean it. Not a peep."

"But you touched them, James! You've got to tell!"

It was said that James did, indeed, contract smallpox, though how the virus could have remained active for so long in those dried up scabs, no one could explain. James was kept quarantined, and he survived. Could it be? Well, in this story it's real. But whatever had happened to Horse, no one in the family ever knew.

Decades later, after Mr. & Mrs. Roper were long since dead and their heirs decided it was finally time to let the old place go, those same children, now beyond grown, were cleaning out the attic and preparing for the sale of the property.

"You 'member old Horse and the 'gift' he left you in that corner under the roof?" Lillian said. Those days seemed a hundred years ago.

"Some gift," her graying brother said, poking through another dusty box. "Say, you want these old hats of Mother's? You'd look good in a net ... or in just about anything that covers your face."

Lillian grinned and gave him a swat. They went on with the task of dismantling their childhood home. *Remembering everything* meant they weren't really losing anything.

Meanwhile, on Barrel Chute Knob in Kentucky, a couple hundred miles away, an ancient man with a variety of interesting wrinkles and calluses, and a multitude of strange roundish scars, had once walked into SLANT looking for odd jobs. Said he needed honest work for honest wages because he liked to pay his own way. Said he wouldn't bother anybody and liked to keep to himself, always had.

At some point, Horse had become default overseer of SLANT's community vegetable gardens. He liked SLANT and we liked him. And so it was that after decades on the road, he had surprised himself and stopped wandering.

These days, SLANT's night sky belongs, most of all, to Horse.

Meddy well knew that.

Far past ready to sink into her bed and sleep like the dead, she arrived at the door of her shelter. *Good old Horse,* she thought as she unlatched her door, *taking in the night.* A line from the poet Hopkins came to her, but from where she couldn't have recalled: "Look at the stars! Look, look up at the skies! O look at all the fire-folk sitting in the air!"

Minutes later, Meddy closed her eyes to drift instantly off toward what would be tomorrow's ungentle hangover. Consciousness waning, she experienced one last flicker of memory: old Horse, that kind and solitary man, sitting so still and quiet on a bench under the starry sky. She knew Horse didn't have much, didn't want much, but she also knew he felt proud that, approaching the end of his long life, he still had his health ... scars and all.

# Listen, Think, Learn

THINGS WERE HEATING UP on Barrel Chute Knob, but they were heating up slowly. TRS (or, more accurately, the politician controlling the conversion from church camp to residential windfall) was secretly raising the stakes incrementally for everyone downhill, without the neighbors even noticing. That's probably because SLANT, as a community, stayed pretty much to itself most of the time. *Live and let live* was never a truer maxim than there.

Nooner, however, had noticed. Little things came to his attention in ways that he couldn't have articulated, even if he'd been pressured to try. He just knew things about the knob, knew when something felt shifted, knew when sounds didn't carry the same, when the air smelled unfamiliar, when the season didn't quite fit. Once he fully realized there was a mounting body of, not hard evidence exactly, maybe alterations, is when he started to worry. But he kept his concerns to himself until he was sure and could articulate whatever it was that he sensed. He and good old Boogle took their usual long hikes up and down. Both were vigilant ... and quiet about it.

Meddy, meanwhile, was more and more letting her anger and frustration overwhelm her sensibility. She was angry at a number of things: the turd incidents, her declining mental capacity, the sad state of politics mixed with religion in Kentucky and the nation and the world at large. Meddy was stuck in negativity, and she wouldn't free herself from that until, deeper into her journey, she came to a place of compassion or, at least, comprehension. More than anything, Meddy needed to stop railing against things over which she had no control. Not caring about the state of humanity, however, wasn't yet an instrument that could be found in Meddy's medicine bag. She had never quite known how to not-care.

Joy, on the other hand, was watching, learning, distilling, extrapolating, extracting, analyzing and generally keeping to her role as an interested and scholarly observer-philosopher. Unlike her friend Meddy, Joy worried less about finding something to be upset about and was more interested in mining for that perfect nugget of truth or that exquisite chunk of enlightenment in every situation or topic she encountered. It was hard work, this intellectual mining was, but true to her name she found bliss in the effort.

Alec, as usual and by choice, stayed to his ownself. In his way, he observed some of what was going on around him, but even when he formulated opinions about what he noticed, his interpretations would have seemed strange to anyone else, though they made perfect sense to him.

And Juny ... well, Juny just wanted, more than ever, to sing.

All SLANTers had simple desires: Horse wondered at the stars and Turner pondered The Code, and Tractor Girl lovingly shaped and encouraged her bonsais. Mayor Farnsley Sheepwater carried out his friendly mayoral and diplomatic duties as he saw fit. Pair Square went about their shared quotidian existence in peace and harmony.

In SLANT, things were quite Zen.

Meanwhile, big changes were apparent up at The Rising Son, not that the campers or counselors knew the difference, having just that summer arrived with the reopening of the site as a teen camp. If you had said "Zen" to anyone up there, you'd have been considered sacrilegious.

Besides the physical "improvements," there was a shift in both mood and tone at the church camp because of the change in management and, less perceptively, because of the different worldview of the younger generation of campers who didn't buy into the rather rigid priorities of their predecessors and elders. There is something fresher and smarter and more independent about a large percentage of teenagers these days. Maybe it's their dependence on screens, from which they get most of their information and through which they form their identities. Virtual isn't virtual to them. Virtual *is* their reality, and that's just as science fiction had long before predicted for our species' future. Having grown up in a world of so-called social media, young humans have no clear idea that "friend" means something entirely different to people older than they. As is their way, they collect virtual "friends" in large numbers, and this makes them feel rich—this is their meaningful currency. Ironically, face-to-face conversation is difficult for them, and not at all interesting—in fact, it makes many of them nervous. Face-to-face is a concept they participate in only as far as it takes to pacify their teachers and elder relatives. They can have love affairs and arguments and nearly everything else, including new forms of sexual interaction, by way of screens that are invisibly webbed together. People just a few generations back would have called it magic. To many of us, the definition of the word *social* has completely flipped to its opposite meaning.

The on-site leaders up at TRS were younger too. And less worried about money. And more savvy to the technologies their charges faithfully use. If one were not so jaded, one might assume that the *Streets of Gold!*

leadership adopted a policy of making sure the counselors they selected were very young (most in their early twenties) just so the teen-aged campers could better relate to them. Nothing could be further from the truth. What happened was that the mega-church realized, upon taking over the old church camp, that they could save a ton of money by hiring college students on the cheap to organize the daily workings of the camp.

Beyond that, there was one other criterion the mega-church's interviewers kept uppermost in their minds: hire only those young counselors *who demonstrate that they don't think independently.* In this way, *Streets of Gold!* and its partners in the development deal could be assured that nothing would be questioned or challenged, and everything would go according to plan ... under perfect camouflage.

## Cultivate Wisdom & Embrace It

"SCOTT BUCHANAN WAS WISE. *Who was he?* Who cares. Your own acquaintance with him isn't necessary to this lesson. I knew him well, and that should be enough. He was wise. Take my word for this."

Alec intoned his "irrefutable" truth to the patient group of trees that he had convened for the tour he was leading through the woods. The trees stood there, looking slightly nervous, clumped as they were in a breezy little grove, swathed in shadowy moonlight. They silently took in his message, which seemed urgent.

"Wise. That's what everybody said. But *how,* you may ask, was he wise? I will tell you." Alec gathered his patience and continued. "Scott Buchanan was wise precisely because he knew when to stop talking."

Here Alec paused for effect. As usual, his timing was impeccable. Not a tree moved. All seemed to be holding their collective breath.

"Scott Buchanan stopped talking when he found himself at the end of his rope. He stopped talking, and he took action instead." Again the well-timed pause, but only a slight one this time. "And if you don't understand that, then I don't know how to help you."

With this pronouncement, Alec spun, stepped off without another word and melded with the larger darkening woods, leaving his small tour group of trees to think on this. He knew they'd be there when he got back. Those trees did not know one single thing about getting around in the forest. Especially at night.

# Cultivate Goodwill

UP AT THE RISING SON, Sam's recent determination to flee was instantly infectious, and Nick couldn't stop thinking about the plan they were hatching. Whatever the hell his father and Senator Connelldon were plotting behind closed doors, Nick knew it had to have some darkness in it. There were designs on the church camp property that had nothing to do with Hopkins' take on God and Nature ... and everything to do with Money. The more Nick thought about it, the madder he got toward the kind of men (one of whom was his own father) who would (A) use kids to carry out their dirty work for free, (B) expect the parents of those kids to pay "summer camp" fees for their free labor on the land and (C) hide it all behind the name of God. The whole business was infuriating, and Nick decided he wasn't going to participate in the shameful charade anymore.

It was bad enough that the mega-church that "owned" TRS was clearly more a for-profit corporation than a spiritual center. The vibrations in that place had made Nick's skin crawl every time he'd entered it on Sunday mornings with his father, Bobby Lee—Sunday supposedly being the one commerce-free period of every week, by tradition anyway. But Nick knew his father considered the connections he made inside *Streets of Gold!* to be some of his most important business allies. In fact, lots of work was accomplished in the handshaking and back-slapping that went on in the aisles before and after every service—and certainly at any "fellowship" activities sponsored by the mega-church.

And Nick had noticed something else, too: men were the ones who carried out all of this; women were never included in the networking, unless food needed to be prepared and served or dishes needed to be washed. Nick was of a new generation of bright young men who were baffled by how archaic and unbalanced such a crazy gender-divided system seemed. He knew he could never, in good conscience, perpetuate it. Nick was deeply good, and he was inherently fair-minded. He recognized exclusion and oppression when he saw it, even if he didn't quite yet have the experience, language, thought processes and courage that would allow him to articulate how he felt about these things. He just knew on some

deep and certain level that almost everything about that place was "off."
Same held true for its church camp.

Now at some remove, Nick was able to stop suppressing his disgust and
fully face the trauma he'd felt at having to be in that so-called sanctuary.
The place was creepy. The messages from the pulpit were mean-spirited
toward anyone who wasn't part of that congregation. The fervor whipped
up among the mega-church's congregants seemed more like theatre than
faith, which felt all wrong because Nick had learned that prayer was
supposed to be personal and private. He had read the book of Matthew.
He knew what Jesus himself had taught: *go into your room and shut the door
and pray to God in private.* But that kind of humility was far removed from
the circus he'd witnessed inside *Streets of Gold!.*

Nick vowed to himself, under a glorious cedar high on Barrel Chute
Knob, that he would never enter the doors of that fucked up place again.
If there were consequences, he'd just have to face them until living with
his dad finally became unbearable—and if that happened then he might
be forced to leave everything behind and weather the world alone. He was
young. He was intelligent. He was confident he'd be up to that challenge.

But all of that was in his unknown future. Now what he had to do was
escape his known present: this so-called church camp. With all the pieces
of the puzzle in place, he was horrified at the picture he saw—and grateful
to have a friend like Sam as a safe collaborator.

While he waited for Sam to arrive at their log, Nick let his thoughts
wander freely. Words from his favorite poet slipped into his stream of
thought, and he remembered lines from a poem Hopkins had written
a century and a half ago about the cutting of trees. All Nick could
remember was a fragment, but he lingered on it. "Country is so tender
... even where we mean to mend her, we end her when we hew or delve:
after-comers cannot guess the beauty." *That's what's happening here,* Nick
thought. He remembered his teacher telling the class that Hopkins
considered God and Nature one and the same. *God made this knob and
all the nature on it,* Nick thought, *but here come greedy men, my dad being one
of them, and they hack away at nature until its original wonder will soon be
unrecognizable, maybe obliterated altogether. In the future, no one will ever know
what's been lost.* Being present as witness was bad enough; being an active
part of that transition was a step too far.

The entirety of his epiphany—the corruption of religion, the unethical
political element, the disregard for the environment, the exploitation for
profit, the misuse of youth for labor, the secrecy—it all fell upon him at
once. For the first time in years, since his mom died, Nick felt truly sad
and angry enough to cry, but he didn't. He couldn't. He'd either forgotten
how, or Bobby Lee had trained it out of him—or both. Probably both.

Sam arrived at their log in the middle of his reverie and rescued him from what was most likely a downward spiral in the making. "You ready?" she said.

Nick nodded. He wasn't ready to meet her gaze, but he was damn sure ready to leave this unholy ground. "I was sent to this church camp as *punishment*," he reminded her ... and himself. His voice betrayed utter shock. "It's been severe. And revealing. And I believe I'm worthy of better than this torture, no matter what my dad thinks of me." His voice wavered just a second on that last phrase, but it only made his resolve grow.

"You still okay with escape?" she asked. Again he nodded. All she could do was take his word for it. She looked him over with close attention. He seemed sad and overwhelmed, but he appeared resolute. *He'll make it*, she thought. "All right," she said. "Let's go."

The two struck out downhill toward Fidelity Creek, the TRS property's southwestern border. They didn't really have a clear lay of the land down that way, but they did know downhill was the general direction they needed to go toward home. They had also decided that avoiding the main road was best.

A couple hundred yards from the center of the church camp they followed a rough path that appeared to head down toward Fidelity. Under the crest of the hill they came upon a dumpsite. Stepping through a thick fringe of trees, they were shocked by an enormous swamp of refuse that spanned several hundred feet between them and the edge of the creek, and it was equally as wide. Some of the stuff that had been dumped there was spilling over into the water. It was a horrible sight, one of the ugliest things the kids had seen so far, and they could hardly believe that it was part of the otherwise well-manicured property that was The Rising Son. Obviously, anything this nasty would be obscured from public view. That would explain why a margin of trees had been left between the sloping meadow and the creek.

That dump held all kinds of garbage, from cans and bottles that should have gone to a recycling facility, to broken furniture, to treated wood and other hazardous construction material, to building insulation (who knows how old and dangerous?), to rotting food, to the type of organic matter that the campers had been clearing all month—limbs, brush and so forth. Some of the latter would decay eventually, but there was so much of it, and it was in huge pieces. It would take years and years to break down. These were the larger limbs that couldn't be run through the wood chipper they used in the uphill clearings where the kids had been working. Much of what could be chipped had already been spread on camp pathways as mulch, but this—well, the entire dump site boggled the mind. Especially the stuff that would never break down—plastic bags and forks and cafeteria plates, scrap metal, rusting pipes (*leaching lead?* the kids wondered), and so forth. It was disgraceful. Why was it here? Whose fault was this? Who cares so little?

For a time, Nick and Sam were too stunned to move. They stood and stared for ten minutes or so, unable to wrap their heads around all of the implications. When they started to walk again, they tried to skirt the lower edge of the dump, dodging hunks of metal and glass and other demolished building materials, trying not to step in decomposing icky waste. It was nasty. All of it. Nick was glad Sam had reminded him to wear his hiking boots for their escape.

They made their way to the edge of Fidelity. Sam noticed as they stood on the creek bank that some of the debris from that awful trash dump was floating in the water. Then they saw a bottleneck where a trash dam was starting to build. It was a god-awful mess.

The ancient dinner bell was thoughtlessly discarded there, too, but it was half-buried, so the kids didn't even notice it.

Soon, they noticed movement slightly downhill. Two boys were there, doing something at the edge of the creek. They saw Nick and Sam at about the same instant our refugees saw them. "Hey," one boy yelled, "what're you doing down here? Get the fuck outta here!"

Nick recognized both of the boys. They had bunked in the cabin next to his. The one who'd shouted was a squirrelly little guy named Mikey.

"Come on, Nick," Sam said quietly, "let's backtrack. We can circle around them and cross downstream."

"It's okay," Nick said. "I know them. Hey, Mikey. What's going on?"

"Piss off, man," Mikey said. "You don't want to be here."

Nick, who was standing a few yards closer to Mikey and the other boy (whose last name was something like Black or White or Greene, some color name was all Nick could remember), held out a hand behind him to signal Sam to stop where she was. Both Mikey and the other boy half stood from a squatting position in the weeds, bending over at the waist while hastily pulling up their jeans. Nick could see that behind each of them was a slab of scrap lumber, and on each slab was something that smelled like defecation. *Oh, my god*, Nick thought, *they're dropping their bowel movements onto these little shingles. As if they're communion plates to be served. What the …???*

"I'm telling you to get the hell out of here, Nick," Mikey said. "This is none of your business."

Nick was thoroughly confused, didn't understand at all what he was seeing. It didn't fit into any category that existed within his mind. Well, how could he know? How many of us play with our poop, use it as a weapon? What Nick was witnessing was a fraction of what Meddy and others at SLANT had been dealing with for years—the immature tormenting behavior of boys who have both too little and too much imagination regarding terroristic activity. In Mikey's case, his older brother had told him about the "old hippies" who lived down Fidelity at

SLANT and about the campers' tradition of sending turds downstream, sometimes to get caught in SLANT's weirs and brambles along the creek's edge. Mikey's brother had also told him that boys had long talks about how easy it would be to sneak into SLANT at night and smear shit on the side of that big store building in the middle of the village. All they had to do was lure the dogs into silence by bringing them food. The strange thing about boys who dream up this sort of thing is that they don't really know *why* they want to do it. They just do it. And then brag. Laugh about how hilarious it is.

But Nick, in that moment, was unaware of the turd tradition. He just knew this wasn't right ... and he knew he wanted nothing to do with it.

Mikey turned his face toward his buddy and said, "Launch 'em." The other boy picked up both small planks by their edges, carefully turned to place them on the surface of Fidelity Creek, and down the torpid current they began to float. Both boys burst out in raucous laughter, which made absolutely no sense to Nick.

"What's going on?" It was Sam, who had stayed put because she trusted Nick, but she wasn't happy about it. She started to move closer.

"For christsake, Mikey," Nick said. "What *is* this?"

Mikey looked at his accomplice and said, "That'll show those old hippie farts," which restarted the guffawing between them. Nick and, by this time, Sam just stood there staring at the two idiots. Without another word, they stepped around the boys and picked up their hike downhill. They trudged through woody brush and trees, slowly picking their way.

When they were finally out of earshot (they knew they were when they could no longer hear the boys' laughing), Sam said, "What the hell was that?"

"You don't want to know, Sam," Nick said. "You really don't. Trust me."

"Well, at least tell me what's wrong with that one kid, the one doing all the talking."

"Don't know him very well. Name's Mikey. At camp he's the one Cooper bullies the most. His favorite target," Nick said. "My guess, Mikey finds weird ways to get that anger out of his system, since Coop is bigger than everybody and a counselor besides."

"Something's wrong with that Coop," Sam said. "I've always thought so, since that first night I saw him at the fire circle. Something about his eyes."

"Got a mean streak in him, that's for sure. Takes it out on the bad boys."

"He's creepy. I've stayed clear of him."

"Well, he's got that preacher thing about him—thinks he's God's gift to the universe," Nick said. "Pumps himself up 'til he believes he's better than everybody. Then swaggers through the world like it's actually true."

"I don't know much about preachers, do you?"

"I know enough. From the preachers I do know, it seems that to be one you have to be arrogant and condescending. And I know that has nothing to do with what Jesus taught."

"You know the Bible pretty well, don't you?" Sam said.

"Not really. Just some of it. Mostly, New Testament. I just think people who call themselves 'Christians' ought to read and follow the words of Jesus Christ more often than they do. But they're stuck in that hateful Old Testament head space."

"See, I think that's why you're exactly the kind of person who should be in the ministry," Sam said. "You ever consider that?"

"No way," Nick said. "They'd eat me alive."

"Who would?"

"People in the God business! I'd never get out of seminary in one piece."

"Well, come on, Nick. Don't hold back. Tell us what you really think." Sam grinned and punched him in the arm.

"I think," said Nick, stopping and looking up at some trees whose branches arced across Fidelity, "that somebody's living up there."

They had arrived at Alec's treehouse. Thankfully, Alec was not at home. Otherwise there'd have been, without doubt, some sort of bizarre encounter.

Sam and Nick were mesmerized by the feat of engineering Alec had accomplished. Here was a little tarp shack, oddly-shaped but sturdy, and it looked like it would stay nice and dry on the inside. It was balanced atop flooring made from poles of irregular length which appeared to be cut branches with the bark still on them. The flooring was lashed to hefty limbs growing from two or three enormous trees that were so big they reached each other from opposite sides of the creek. There was a crudely-built ladder on one creek bank leading up to the treehouse's platform. On the other bank was a series of narrow log ramps winding up to the other end of the structure. Because the tarps were camouflage, you wouldn't necessarily notice the treehouse, hidden by the natural canopy of the big trees, unless you were looking right at it.

After they scrutinized it from their purview on the ground, Sam and Nick walked on down the creek. Soon enough, they came to a place where the creek was quite narrow and not too deep. Here, they waded across to what looked like a couple of stumps on which had been built some sort of simple wooden apparatus that would hold a bicycle, maybe, though that seemed out of place here in the woods.

"Oh, I know," said Nick. "It must be a rack for storing a canoe. Look here—straps to cinch something down." Good guess. It was, as you already well know, the place where Tractor Girl stowed her kayak, but she was at work downstream on the bonsai farm, so Whisper wasn't there when Nick and Sam wandered in.

Once across the creek, the kids kept walking downstream, and in minutes they came to the first of SLANT's creekside cabins, which happened
to be Meddy's shelter. They were walking and talking about which way to
go next, how to get off the knob, what they would do when that happened,
and they crossed the footpath that led to Meddy's door about the same
time she came around her shelter from the rear. Needless to say—but you
know I will—all three were jolted. The kids were shocked into silence.
Meddy went into a rant.

"Who in the hell are you, and what the hell are you doing here?" she
shouted. She looked directly at Nick, who was standing in front of Sam.
"Where do you think you *are*, son? And, more important, who do you
think *we* are?"

Sam stepped into fuller view.

"Are you any of those little SHITS from up in that god-forsaken
church camp?" Meddy said, her eyes squinting into a potentially much
bigger explosion. "Bunch of TERRORISTS is what they're creating up
there. If you're not sending your turds down the creek, you're smearing
shit all over our buildings! All over our mailboxes, for the love of all that's
holy! Who's in charge up there, anyway?"

The kids started to back away. Their eyes were as big as dinner plates.

"Don't you dare run from me!" Meddy said. "You stand right there and
answer for what you kids are doing to us."

At once, Nick understood what he'd seen with Mikey and that Brown
or Redd or whatever-his-name-was kid upstream. They had been preparing
fresh turd boats to send down past this old woman's house. *What fucktards!*
he thought

"Ma'am," Nick began. But Meddy cut him off.

"Don't you *ma'am* me, boy!"

Sam, who could read a situation instinctively, stepped forward and
stuck out her hand to shake Meddy's. "I'm Sam," she said. "Pleased to meet
you. We know those boys, a little bit anyway," for by now Sam had put it
together as well, "and we aren't part of whatever game they're playing at."

Meddy was a bit taken aback by the kindness in Sam's voice, and she
was impressed by the girl's straightforward greeting. Her squint released
like a spring.

"I apologize on behalf of The Rising Son," Sam added, "though I
don't know why I feel obligated to do that, since we're in the process of
running the hell away from that crazy place right now."

Impressive, indeed! Meddy's anger fell right away from her, and she
was instantly interested in getting to know this unusual young woman.
Smart. Sassy. Independent. A survivor in the making, clearly.

"Well. All right," said Meddy. "Sam." She took a few seconds to measure the motive of her trespassers. "I may be pleased to make your acquaintance, but let's wait and see whether I've jumped the gun on that tendency. Name's Meadowlark Nightengale, but my friends call me Meddy. Until you prove that you *aren't* my friend, you can call me Meddy too."

"Thank you, Miss Meddy."

"Oh, for the love of god, drop the 'Miss,' will ya?"

"Done," said Sam. "And this is my friend Nick." They both looked at Nick who seemed afraid to speak. "Nick, meet Meddy."

He finally came to his senses. "Pleasure," he said, as amicably as possible. "I'm sorry if we startled you."

"Mutual," Meddy said. As only she could do, she'd quite suddenly transitioned out of outrage mode and into matter-of-fact mode. "Now what's this about you two running away?"

# Whenever Possible, Provide

"NOONER, WE'VE GOT OURSELVES A SITUATION HERE," Meddy said into her cell phone. "Can you come down to my shelter, or are you currently caught up in the middle of something that can't wait?"

Nooner said he'd be down straightaway, and in a matter of five minutes he was at her porch. He couldn't remember when he'd gotten a call like that from Meddy, which is why he knew it must be important. He wasn't expecting anyone else to be with her, though. Yet there they were—two of the TRS kids sitting at her picnic table with glasses of lemonade and a bag of store-bought cookies in front of them. They had already torn through quite a few of the cookies, it looked like.

"Nick, Sam," said Meddy, "this is my good friend and neighbor, Nooner. He may be able to help us figure this thing out."

"Figure what out?" Nooner wanted to know. Seeing the two church campers dropped him into an immediate funk. He didn't know what to do, other than take his cues off of Meddy, all the while trying not to be defensive, which is what he felt like being. Nooner and church campers had never been a good mix, as Meddy well knew.

"Sam and Nick have been telling me a story that you'll want to hear. On top of that, they're refugees from House of the Rising Shit upstream," she said. "They're on the lam."

"What the hell does that even mean, Meddy?" he asked.

"They've run away, Nooner. They are conscientious objectors. Escaping that mess up there. You have no idea. Tell him what you told me," she instructed the kids.

And they did. They recounted the theory they had put together, complete with the hand-drawn map, about the probable housing development going on up at The Rising Son property—including Nick's dad's involvement with the senator, including the scripture-driven forced-labor camp that had been regimented uphill, including the horrible dump ... and including their disgust with the whole deal.

Nooner listened. When they had finished, he exchanged a long and troubled look with Meddy. Before he could decide whether to believe them or not, he had to determine whether they were really escapees or merely spies. He was leaning toward the latter. But Meddy seemed to believe them, and Nooner had long since learned not to doubt Meddy's judgment in these sorts of matters. He knew her intuition was good, but decided to proceed with caution nevertheless.

"You know anything about the vandalism we been gettin' down here?" he asked Nick.

"No, sir," Nick said. "Well, on the way down we saw some boys from camp doing something that wasn't right, but other than that, I had no idea."

Nooner gave him the stink eye and turned to Sam. "What about you?"

"Same," she said. "I couldn't believe it myself. And that toxic-looking dump up there is getting in the creek too."

True. Nooner and Boogle had noticed early stages of that mess during their off-season hikes up and down.

"Never been down here before today?" Nooner asked, somewhat severely.

"No, sir," Sam said. "I didn't even realize y'all were living down here. They don't let us off the leash up at TRS. It pretty much sucks."

"And you say your dad's hooked up with this land scheme?" he asked Nick.

"Looks like it, sir," Nick said.

"Please, for the love of all that is good and holy, don't *sir* me, son."

"Yes, sir," Nick said. And when Nooner groaned, Nick added, "I mean, okay. I'll try not to."

"Makes me feel a hundred years old. So stop it. Else I can't talk to you no more. Dig?"

"Gotcha," Nick said.

"So, what do you see in all this?" Meddy asked Nooner.

"Damned if I know," Nooner said, "but it cain't be anything good. Question is, what do we do with these young'uns?"

"Well, we can't keep them, but I don't feel right about sending them back up there either," Meddy said. "I guess they're free agents, after all. I mean, they walked in here of their own accord. They're not my kids, they're not your kids, and they're not hurt or lost or guilty of anything. Best I can tell, they're just out hiking, trying to get off the knob."

"True," said Nooner. "But the fact that they ran away from that camp is gonna bring down a world of hurt on them … and on us, too, if we shelter 'em."

Meddy couldn't argue with that. The kids sat quiet, waiting for whatever was next. Nick ate another cookie. Nobody said anything for a minute.

Finally, Sam spoke up. "Look," she said, "we had to leave that place."

Nick nodded his head vigorously in agreement.

"We'd had *enough*," he said.

"Maybe we didn't think through all the consequences," Sam went on, "but we can't turn around and go back up there and let them work us to death all summer. Especially knowing what we know. If you guys just let us hang out here tonight, we'll be on our way in the morning, I promise. We're not looking for trouble, but we're not the makers of trouble, either."

"They're worn out, Nooner, and they're scared and prob'ly hungry," Meddy said. Nick nodded his head at this last bit. "Help me figure this out. I'm thinking it'd be wrong to turn 'em away. It'll be dark long before they can get off-knob on foot."

"Goddammit, now. I don't know," Nooner said.

"Nobody's come looking for them so far," Meddy said. "And if they do, we'll just say they came hiking through and asked for shelter and we gave it to them. Which is every word true."

"Maybe," said Nooner.

"And, of course, we'll hand them right over."

"I guess," said Nooner.

"Meanwhile, though, maybe we can help them. Feed them, at least."

"I reckon so," said Nooner. He wasn't fully convinced, but he couldn't see what would be wrong with feeding hungry kids and finding each of them a bunk for the night. SLANT didn't turn folks away as a rule, not that people showed up like this, ever—just walked out of the woods, on the run from what they perceived to be a dangerous situation. But still. This circumstance was, indeed, a proper fit for everything SLANT was all about.

"Nooner," said Meddy, "maybe we ought not tell anyone else they're here. Keep everybody free and clear of any involvement. Plus, if somebody comes to The General asking about them, Turner won't be lying when he says he hasn't seen or heard of them. Same with everybody else."

"Jesus H. Christ on a stale saltine, Meddy," Nooner said. "What in hell have you gotten me into this time?"

*Frustrated* didn't begin to describe what Nooner was feeling.

"If you'll take Nick home with you tonight," Meddy said, "I'll make a pallet on the floor here for Sam."

"Dammit."

"But first, let's all eat and talk about it. I'll find something to fix. Might be canned tuna, but we'll make do." She turned and headed toward her shelter door.

"I swear I'm gonna kill you, Meadowlark Nightengale, if you don't get me killed first," Nooner said.

Meddy didn't miss a step. "I love you too, pal," she threw back at him over her shoulder.

In half an hour, they were sitting around Meddy's picnic table eating peanut butter and honey on toast, drinking tall glasses of cold milk, and talking about the problems up at The Rising Son—problems that could affect SLANT in ways that were just now occurring to them all.

# To Thine Own Mind Be True

"NOTHIN'—AND I MEAN NOTHIN'—happens in the absence of fear or threat." Nooner moved his head from side to side as he spoke. Meddy recognized this gesture. She'd seen him do it hundreds of times. Shaking his head slowly side to side, as if indicating a negative response, was how he double-checked himself. She knew that even if he were confident enough to make a big pronouncement, he still had to think it through again, several times, as if looking around for something he'd previously missed. She wondered what would happen if he ever caught a mistake in his logic after he'd already opened his mouth. Would he admit it or cover it up? He'd admit it; he'd have to. He was too genuine not to.

In this case, though, Nooner knew he was right. And Meddy—who was having a particularly good day, health-wise, and was thrilled with that fact—could tell that Nooner was confident because whatever was going on behind his eyes as his head wagged side to side didn't betray the theory he'd already worked out, even with the last-second scouring he was giving it.

The four of them—the two kids escaping that questionable mess of The Rising Son and the two SLANTers—had enjoyed their impromptu peanut butter feast and were relaxing into dusk outside Meddy's shelter. They had been discussing all the possibilities they could think of regarding the situation at hand, including what TRS seemed actually to be, including why it existed in its current form. From there, the little group had moved on to why humans separate themselves into various, vehement philosophical cadres. They had landed on a simple question: which of our human characteristics is our most primal, most basic. Which is our true driving force? It was a fine discussion, an honest back-and-forth, first one playing devil's advocate, then another. Sam was particularly good at this, although she did more observing than talking in this round. Perhaps this was because she intuited that Nick was on a path of intellectual discovery and she didn't want to get in the way of that. Meddy noticed, and she admired Sam for this and wished she'd been smart in that way back when she was Sam's age.

Nooner contended that *fear* is the strongest force in human nature.

Meddy knew Nooner was right in what he'd said, because she knew *she* was right and she agreed with him. But Nick wasn't ready to buy into Nooner's premise whole cloth just yet.

"Whatcha mean by that?" The kid was suspicious. "People organize things all the time around positive stuff, and they don't feel any threat."

Nooner took a sip from his lemonade glass and settled back into the ancient lawn chair. "Really?" he said. There was an air of calm about him now. "Like what?"

"Like pep rallies and church and parties. Stuff like that. They do it just to be doing it. Or because they like the idea of coming together for a common cause."

"But that makes Nooner's point," Sam said.

Nick's brow furrowed. "How does that make your point?" said the kid to Nooner. "It refutes your point. Those things have nothing to do with fear or threat or whatever."

Meddy loved that Nick used words like "refute" in casual conversation. He was a rare young man with a world of potential, and she hoped he'd get himself free from his intellectual bondage some soon day. If he did, he could put that big vocabulary of his to good use in this world. She almost hated that Nooner was going to have to blow the kid out of this water of complacency that he'd floated in during all of his seventeen years. But it had to be done. It could only help Nick in the long run. He'd need to know, soon, how to stop floating and start to swim against the current. Sam already knew this, as she had proven during the few hours she'd been at SLANT, Meddy noticed. And thankfully Nick, well, he wasn't swept away yet. There was still hope for him, if he started kicking and pulling right away. He was already in the intellectual swim, and he wasn't likely to drown in it.

"Okay. Pep rally," Nooner said. "It's organized for a purpose. What is that purpose?"

"Team spirit," said Nick. "School spirit, if everyone gets involved."

"And what's the threat?" Nooner asked.

"There's no threat. Like I said, it's just bringing people together in common cause."

"I'm not sayin' every threat is sinister," Nooner said. "But tell me, why do they need to be brought together? And why in that way?"

"Because of, say, a big game coming up. I don't know," said the kid.

"Oh, you mean, like, there's an impendin' competition?" Nooner said. His voice feigned innocence.

"Well, yeah, that's usually why we have pep rallies." The kid wondered if this old guy had a clue about the way things worked. Sam, on the other hand, just grinned. She was already way ahead of Nick on this one.

"And what're all the possible outcomes of said competition?" Nooner asked without much inflection or tone. He realized he sounded a lot like Meddy. This didn't bother him at all.

"Well," said Nick, "obviously our team could either win or lose ... or tie."

"Or," Sam put in, for the assist, "I guess, the game could be canceled at the last minute or something."

"So what's the purpose of rallyin' before a game?" Nooner asked.

"To get everyone pumped up," Nick said. "To give the team enough moral support to win. Hopefully."

"So," Nooner said. "Without the rally to pep the team, what's the threat?"

"If they don't have the right energy, they could lose."

"Bingo," said Nooner.

"Oh," said the kid.

Meddy was impressed that Nick paused to think, rather than forging ahead with some knee-jerk defensive argument. Yep, there was hope for this one. Meddy leaned back in her hammock, rested her eyes for a moment, and listened contentedly as Nooner schooled the kid.

"Church. What's the threat?" Nooner's tone was a little demanding, but it was serious enough to inspire the kid, make him think, drive the lesson home.

"Hell. Satan."

"Party?"

"Boredom, I guess."

"No shit," said Sam, grinning down at the top of her friend's head from her perch one riser higher than his on Meddy's front steps. She playfully punched him lightly on the shoulder.

"See? There's always a threat," said Nooner. "Sometimes it's innocuous, like a ballgame or boredom. It can seem awfully important at the time, but in the grand scheme of things, it really ain't. Not all that much. Agreed?"

"Yeah, I see that," said the kid. "But what about church? The threat of Hell's pretty big. I mean, that's about your salvation. Your everlasting life after death."

The propaganda of *Streets of Gold!*, it seemed, still had a significant part of him in its clutches, despite how much Nick claimed to dislike the place.

"Sometimes," said Nooner with a patient sigh, "the *architects* of an organization," he looked at Meddy for support and when she nodded her approval at him, he continued, "go beyond mere threat. They have to kick it up a notch or three in order to extend their reach, grab as much or as many as they can. But here's what I think: the more unlikely the story they're pushin', the more severe they'll insist the threat is. Its consequences are presented in worse and worse ways. And then it no longer seems like just a simple threat; it starts to feel bigger and scarier, and that fear of the mythological threat itself can even manifest as terror. Compare merely bein' temporarily grounded, for example, as opposed to bein' told you'll be flung into some eternal, flamin' Hell. See?"

Nick did see, sort of. Sam on the other hand, nodding vigorously, grasped the logic entirely.

"Look," Nooner said, "people deny themselves their own truths and adopt in their place the lies that people in authority tell 'em. Lives are co-opted! In real extreme situations, mass panic forms, wars are cooked up, elections are disrupted. At the very least, pack mentality takes hold."

Nooner exchanged a glance with his mentor, who nodded her support again.

"Like with church congregations that are rabid in their doctrine," Sam put in. "Or political groups that practice violence—or threaten it, anyway."

"Are you seriously calling church some kind of 'pack mentality'?" Nick asked, looking up at Sam.

Without hesitation Sam nodded in the affirmative. "I am," she calmly said.

"Don't matter what nobidy else calls it," Nooner said. "The only question you need to concern yourself with is what *you* call it. How *you* see it. I'm only raisin' the question. You have to look harder than they want you to—at ever'thang, not just religion—and determine what you see, what makes sense in your mind. Only then can you figure out how *you* define it."

"But why?"

"Just *think*, that's all. Think for yourself. Step away from their, I don't know," he looked at Meddy to check his vocabulary, "*rhetoric*, I reckon." Meddy nodded, and Nooner continued, renewed. "And get some perspective. What's logical? What's illogical? What's crazy as owl shit?"

"What do you really, really believe, Nick?" Sam said softly. She wasn't teasing him this time.

"Which few of your many priorities are most important to you?" Meddy added. It was impossible for her to withhold her urge to speak, even though she was so proud of the balanced and fair way Nooner was handling the conversation. "Ask yourself when you may have given those up, given your own opinions over to the priorities of people with an agenda to control you. That sort of thing," she explained.

Nick appeared calm and pensive now.

"Just *think*, is all I'm sayin'," Nooner said.

"I think," said the kid. "I do."

"I know you do. So, you also don't have to believe what I say about threats. Nor fear, neither," Nooner said. "But now that you've heard it, you might find yourself puttin' ever'thang to that test before you decide to tumble into somebidy else's vat of boilin' oil. Guard against ANYONE usin' your own fear against you."

At this, Meddy privately smiled her crooked smile. Her best student had now graduated to teacher. Into the semi-darkness and without opening her eyes, Meadowlark Nightengale smiled and she smiled and she smiled.

# Don't Panic

"I'M GOING BACK," Nick announced when the four convened next morning.

Sam's mouth fell open. "You're what?" she said.

"Going back up to TRS," he said.

Meddy and Nooner couldn't contain their surprise.

"What's this?" Meddy asked.

"They'll have missed us by now," Nick said. "They'll have called our folks. My dad'll be worried, and most of all he'll be mad as hell. But that's not why I'm going."

"Well, I'm *not* going back," said Sam.

"I get that. But I'm going to be eighteen in a couple months, and I need to finish high school so I can get as far away from home and *Streets of Gold!* and my ridiculous excuse for a life as possible. I've worked out the countdown, and I'm going to see it through. Just wish I didn't have to do this first part of it up *there*." Even though he was resolute, he didn't look happy about his decision.

"Nick, are you sure?" Sam asked.

"I am."

"You havin' second thoughts about what all we talked about last night?" Nooner said.

"Not at all. I'm more clear than I've ever been."

"Then, why?" Sam said. "Why go back to that place? Especially knowing what you know."

"I don't have any reason to volunteer to tell them what I know. Undercover, I can keep collecting info. I might be able to make a difference."

"How? How in the world do you…"

"Sam, I thought about it half the night, over at Nooner's place," Nick said. "I'd be willing to bet my college fund that Coop has no idea what's really going on."

"You think he's not privy to the backstory of this development deal?" Meddy asked. Nooner couldn't sort out what he was feeling, so he stayed silent.

"Right," said Nick. "I think he's a prole. Just following orders. Spiritual Teen Leader, my left ass cheek. He's no leader. He's not even that smart. This is just a summer job to him. I think ... I *hope* I can get through to him."

"Oh, please, Nick," Sam said, her tone dripping disgust. "Coop is one of *them.*"

"I'm not sure that's true, considering that he only punishes the most assholy of those kids. I'd like to find out. Either way, if this mess is to be exposed, I'm the one to do it. It's my dad and his crooked old frat buddy Con spearheading it, anyway. And what are they gonna do when I open up? They can't kill me. So, what the hell! Maybe I'll just take 'em on."

Finally Nooner spoke. "You up to this?"

"Not sure. But I'm up to trying. I can start the ball rolling."

"Damn," Nooner said. "Brave kid. You'll prob'ly get crushed, you know."

"Yeah, probably."

"But if that's what your gut's tellin' you to do, then maybe you're ready for whatever comes after."

"It is."

"Well, I'm not walking all the way home by myself," Sam said. "And I'm not going back up there. So, I guess that leaves calling home and asking my mom to come pick me up from here."

"Good choice," Meddy said. "Let's go get my phone. You know where to tell her to find you? Need some back up?"

Sam visibly shuddered, then bucked up. "I might," she said. Meddy gave Sam a comforting nod, and the two moved toward Meddy's shelter to make the call.

"Hey, Sam. You take care. I'll call you ... after," Nick said.

Sam nodded. "Do," she said. "And, hey, tell 'em that when I ran away you just came after me and helped me find a safe ride home. That ought to buy you some time while you're figuring out the rest." She gave him a weak smile, then up Meddy's steps she went, Meddy following.

Nooner was quiet for a moment. "You gonna be all right, buddy?" he asked.

"Not sure. But it's what I've decided, so here I go." Nick shouldered his backpack and stuck out his hand. "Thanks for everything."

"You bet," said Nooner. "Come see us sometime. Good luck, man."

They shook hands.

"And don't worry," Nick said. "I won't involve you and Meddy."

"Tell 'em whatever you need to," Nooner said. "All we did was feed you and keep you safe overnight."

"Well, here I go," Nick said again, but he didn't. Tears welled.

Nooner averted his eyes and waited while Nick collected himself. He could tell the kid was dreading not only the long walk back upstream but also his solitary arrival at TRS. God, there'd be hell to pay up there. Nooner dreaded it for him.

"I wish my dad was like you," Nick finally said, causing Nooner to blush. "I'll see you around. I promise."

"See ya, kid," Nooner said. "Be safe."

Just as Nick turned on his heel to start his slog up and out of SLANT, he slipped his phone out of his hip pocket, held it aloft and said, "You've got my number."

"We'll keep in touch," Nooner said. "Take good care."

Meddy came out of her shelter to say that Sam was still on the phone with her mom and everything seemed fine. The mother had been relieved to know that Sam was safe and well. "She'll be here in about an hour," Meddy said. "Poor kid."

"What the hell, Meddy?" Nooner said. "If those greedy bastards are tearin' up jack uphill, God only knows what that'll do to Fidelity Creek, to Barrel Chute, to all of us downstream."

Meddy felt suddenly exhausted and a little bit disoriented. "I'm going to have to nap on this," she said, "once we get Sam squared away. Let's try to wrap our minds around this thing and meet up later to make sense of it."

"Sense," Nooner said. "Wishful thinkin', if you ask me."

"Well, we can't just sit down here and do nothing. Can you imagine what construction of a massive subdivision would do to this little knob? Listen," she said, "it's gonna take more than just me and you to get a handle on this whole thing."

"All right. I'm all in. I'll be there. You know that."

"I do. I'm a lucky duck," said Meddy. But immediately she felt that odd tectonic slip that she sometimes noticed happening inside her head. She wasn't sure what would come next, but she was aware, at very least, that this might end up being more Nooner's project than her own. "Take Sam up to the road to wait for her mom, will you? And, please, stay with her 'til she gets here."

"How 'bout you? You all right?"

"As right as I can be. A nap should fix things. Let me give that a try."

Nooner didn't know what else to do, other than what Meddy had asked of him. He didn't realize it, but he was smack in the middle of that odd place known as The Sandwich Generation, simultaneously taking care of those older and younger than himself and wondering how in the world he was going to manage it all.

# Do No Harm

TWO DAYS PASSED and, after consulting with The Jimmies, Nooner called a community meeting in The General. At least ninety percent of adult SLANTers came. Unlike representative forms of governing, SLANT's decision-making gatherings are akin to the type Cherokees and other Native Peoples originated—every member of the tribe has a direct voice. It's not representative democracy; it's *direct* democracy. Live-and-in-the-moment, all expressions/opinions/votes are equally-weighted. No one is left out. Consensus is the goal. Farnsley knew this very well from his own "un-elected" experience.

Meddy herself wasn't feeling quite as well as she'd been during the crisis with the kids, so at the meeting she sat off to one side and tried to force herself to stay focused, with limited success. Still, she was determined to be present for Nooner, just as he had always been for her.

Meanwhile, Bocker and his posse gathered on The General's porch, lying around in their various states of panting repose, waiting for the silly two-leggers to finish whatever they were up to inside.

"Folks, there's a situation on the knob that y'all need to know about," Nooner told his neighbors, after the Shroom Room quieted. He explained as briefly as he could what was going on up at The Rising Son property, including the sketchy details of who was involved and the mystery surrounding the political connections and implications.

"Now, obviously, we don't own that property, and we have no say in what they do with it. *Unless* it has an impact on us down here. And it just might. Construction of a subdivision is a messy business. There's debris and dumpin' and run-off and erosion. We need to keep Fidelity clean and protected, and we need to keep an eye on what kind of damage this sort of activity might do to affect us and *our* property. We may," he added with emphasis, "have to get fairly active in our resistance before this is all over. I think it could be a struggle."

This caused murmurs of concern, agreement and alarm that passed among us all. The threat especially concerned Dick and Horse, who both lived on the upper end of the SLANT property, nearest the direction of

TRS. If Alec had been in the crowded room, which he would never in a thousand years be, he'd have had an immediate go-to-pieces. His treehouse home was actually closest of all to what was happening up there. To be entirely honest, we were all a little relieved, for his sake, that he didn't show up for the meeting. It would have been too much for him. He'd have short-circuited, for sure.

"What about the road?" Juny asked. "Can hunnerd-n-lebm handle traffic for a big development? Not to mention the trucks and equipment it'll take to get it built."

More murmurs; more agreement; more concern.

"Well, now, that's another good point, Juny. One more issue to add to our concerns, ain't it?" Nooner said. "Maybe first thang, we ort to make a list of what all we're concerned about, questions we need answers to."

At Nooner's suggestion, Turner had set up an easel with a big sheet of blank poster board clipped to it. Tractor Girl grabbed a marker from the coffee urn counter that sat under The Code. She started writing items on the poster board.

"Thanks, TG," Nooner said.

She wrote *Subdivision construction + ill effects.* She wrote *ROAD, too much traffic?* And she wrote *TOO MANY PEOPLE, can the knob sustain us all?*

As the meeting progressed, more items were added. Horse sat quietly near Meddy, but others had plenty to say. Jimmy brought up property values, and Tractor Girl added that to the list. Jimi, on the other hand, asked that they all consider how exactly they *defined* their values, graciously suggesting that *quality of life* was the greatest value of all. Tractor Girl added *Quality Of Life* to the growing list.

When the discussion became too enthusiastic and overlapping voices raised the volume to cacophony, Mayor Sheepwater stepped up to ask for a return to suitable decorum. "I know we're all upset and worried," he said. "Any unknown can do us like that. But let's keep cool heads so we can deal with this thing. Nooner here is tryin' to get us t'come together to figger out a plan." That helped for a few minutes.

Turk and Wilma Carl presented a united front on the issue of how much money SLANT would need to raise to fight this if it went to court. "Nooner," Wilma Carl asked, "will we need to hire a lawyer, do you think?"

Tractor Girl wrote *Legal fees???*

Nooner said next that he was most concerned about damage to the land itself, so Tractor Girl wrote *Land preservation.* Then she added *Protect Fidelity* and spoke a few words about the importance of keeping anything from happening to the waterway, ending softly with, "I'm not much of a speaker."

"That's right, though," Nooner said. "TG's bonsai farm is downstream from us, and we cain't afford to have it suffer neither."

"Not to mention that Fidelity is a tributary to Jaybird Run, which eventually feeds the Ohio River," Finkle said. Everyone nodded and made agreement noises.

Then Dick said, "Seems like to me there was a time when religion and politics were separate things, weren't they? Not no more, though. Once those two got tangled up, it made a big mess in this country that ain't got nothin' but worse."

"Strange bedfellows," somebody said. "That's really what this is about," said another. "Politics and religion mix about like motor oil and milk," a voice called out.

"Hey, Joy, what about any spiritual or religious connection?" Nooner asked. "You got any ideas how to connect what you know of that sorta thing with what TRS and *Streets of Gold!* are doin'? What I mean is ... could you help us appeal to 'em through any kind of scripture or such like?"

Joy allowed that there were certainly a number of statements and verses about stewardship and neighborliness in the Christian Bible, and she promised she'd be thinking about how to work up an appeal from that perspective. "There's a verse I recall from the Old Testament," said she. "It reads something like, 'I brought you into a plentiful land to enjoy its fruits and its good things. But when you came in, you defiled my land and made my heritage an abomination.'"

Folks nodded. They could relate.

"Another one off top of my head is from the New Testament," Joy added. "That one says 'it is required of stewards that they be found trust-worthy.'"

Jimi said, "Very smart, Joy."

Nooner said, "You're on the right track there, Joy."

Tractor Girl wrote *Religion angle—Joy.*

The brainstorming went on for another forty-five minutes. Some of it circled back through topics that had already been raised and posted on the list. As people had new ideas, they shared them.

The community discussed the possibility of eventual media coverage that would probably be necessary. One or two wondered aloud whether studies would be needed to determine maximum clean drinking water supplies on the knob. Jorge said they ought to find out where all the sewage from the big subdivision was supposed to go, because dumping it into Fidelity *must not* be an option.

Tractor Girl kept adding items to the list. Everyone had a chance to speak if they wanted to. SLANTers were good at brainstorming. And even those who didn't have a particular idea *yet*—like Wet Willie and Iwana and several other neighbors in attendance—said they were committed to helping the cause in any way they were needed. In other words, there were no dissenters. The whole of SLANT was willing to tackle this threat. Together.

By the end of the meeting, they'd collaborated to compile a pretty good list of questions, issues and ideas, which Tractor Girl said she'd type into her tablet and forward to everyone for reference.

"This is just the beginnin'," Nooner reminded them, "and they don't even know we're onto 'em yet, so let's keep this amongst us for the time bein'. We've been on this knob a lot longer than those developers have. We know it best. Just remember what SLANT has always stood for: people over profit."

*People Over Profit,* Tractor Girl added to the list.

"Now, let's all go give it some more thought," Nooner said. "Y'all put your big brains to work on this. We'll meet again in a week. By then we should know a lot more from our inside source up at TRS." He was, of course, referring to Nick.

Before everyone left, the mayor stood again and said, "'Preciate yer input, ever'bidy. Now, don't forget our main objective—we ain't tryin' to tell nobidy what to do with their land or water or, as Jimi has reminded us, quality of life; we just aim to protect our own. We got an equal right to do that."

Meddy, at last, spoke. "And thanks for caring," she said. It wasn't until then that they noticed her distinctive voice hadn't been heard all evening. Most of them realized how uncharacteristic this was. "We're all worried sick these days about our nation," she added, "and we rightly mistrust those who've chipped away at our liberties. I suggest we all commit to preserving the part of our dear world that's closest to home ... and we must do what we can to safeguard our rights ... while acting with civility. We're decent people, good-hearted," she reminded them, "and *smart.* So as we decide how to move ahead, let's not forget that."

*Be Civil,* Tractor Girl wrote. *Use Our Smarts.*

"Amen," said Joy.

"Amen," said the assembled, and everyone tumbled out into the night, conversing and conspiring and allowing the wheels of grassroots activism to churn within and among them in the time-honored American way.

The newest struggle for community and environmental rights had begun.

# When All Else Fails, Compromise

"WHAT DO YOU WANT?" Alec was having an old, old conversation between Alec and himself.

"What have you got?"

"I've got what you want."

"What is it that I want?"

"Whatever I've got."

"And what is that?"

"You tell me."

"No, *you* tell *me* what it is that you've got."

"I already told you. I've got what you want."

"I don't know *what* I want."

"Yes, you do."

"Yes-I-do what?"

"Know what you want."

"And what's that?"

"It's what I've got, dummy."

"But how do I know whether I want it until I *get* it?"

"You'll know."

"But what if it isn't what I want? At all."

"It will be."

"Why?"

"Because I've got it. And you want it."

"Maybe I *don't* want it."

"Maybe you don't *know* what you want."

"Maybe not."

"Then just shut up and try what I've got."

"Fine."

"Fine."

"Okay, fucking *fine*, goddammit!"

"Enough."

"Agreed."

"So, shut up."

"*You* shut up."

"You're almost there, dude. *So* close."

"You're fucking *killing* me, you know that?"

"That's the plan, my man."

# The Wisdom of Top-Notch Annie, Part 7

"LISTEN TO ME, LEADERS OF TRS! (Damn, I wish I wadn't dead so I could actually speak this to you!)

"The perversion in you has nothin' to do with your bein' believers or ignorant or vain or any other specific thang that you may or may not be. You are twisted because *you haughtily refuse to believe that you have a responsibility to listen earnestly while not talkin' at all*. You fail because you are unable to accept a Truth that may be many times greater than your own fiction. In fact, what *you* think of as Faith is actually part of events in which believers like you have done real damage to other people's lives— for centuries.

"Cain't you comprehend? This knob is a community. This whole world is a community! Justifyin' your bad behavior may work inside your own head or within your own congregation, but out here it looks ridiculous. You embarrass yourself, and you are much too foolish to know it. Bein' judgmental is counter-productive!

"AND YOU, OVER THERE—YOU SLANTers! (If only you could hear me!)

"The sweet weirdness in you has nothin' to do with your bein' old hippies or young liberals or smarter than the average bear. You embrace bein' outcast from the mainstream of society because *you haughtily refuse to believe that you have a responsibility to listen earnestly while pausin' yer talkin'*. And you have yet to learn exactly why it is that people who are less liberal or less schooled believe ... *whatever* it is that they believe. You don't have to agree, but you do need to know—you need to hear whatever they're *claimin'* they believe.

"Discountin' what people believe is a form of damage too. Don't be fooled into thinkin' you've no blame. Refusin' to respect anybidy's right to believe the mythology of their choice, well, that's counter-productive. Do you see? You are your own worst enemy, when it comes to findin' people where they live and usin' words they are capable of understandin'. Arrogance is unsavory. If you don't want to be judged then, damn it, don't judge!

*"EVER'BIDY, LISTEN!* (If I weren't dead, I'd come—reluctantly, yes—out of my old hermitage to speak, to halt, to untangle, to repair.)

"Ever' natural thang in existence has what the insightful poet Hopkins called its *inscape*—that quality which makes it unique, holds it together. We human bein's are no more all alike one to another than hemlocks are like maples! But they *are* all trees, and *we* are all people. So in this way when we recognize what individual things have *in common*, we see *instress* as a positive condition of simply *being*. Together. Instress is the value of respect, of recognition, of co-existence between each individual's unique inscape.

"Go read Thomas Merton. He lived just a stone's throw down this road from us, for heaven's sake! And read your Hopkins too, dammit! There's nothin' political about him. The monk and the poet—they can teach you about Nature; they can teach you about Faith; most important, they will show you respectful connections between the two. You don't have to be a religious believer or a political junkie or a literary geek to appreciate their work. It's useful!

"Get out of your little tribes! Find common ground! Do right by Nature! It's Nature that supports us all.

"Any of us perched on any given face of this multi-faceted thang that we generally agree to call *Life*—why do we so easily forget all the other facets? It's as if each group thinks its entire world is flat and singular, instead of bein' but *one of many* surfaces, part of a continuum belongin' to the same beautiful stone.

"If I call 'swing your partner' but you forge ahead and 'promenade,' we're all gonna crash into each other. Stop hearin' only what you expect to hear! All of you! And start noticin' instead that although the light gleams *differently* from Life's other facets, they all do gleam just as yours does.

"Watch and listen especially to those other facets that are in closest proximity to your own. They are your neighbors. They share a stone with you.

"Egocentric is as wrong-headed as god-centric is. *There is no useful center.* There is only human diaspora. We are no place and every place at once. And anytime we are actually *somewhere*, we gleam there in dyin' fragments only.

"Well, so do the stars. But those very same stars both make us out of their carbon and twinkle down on us all."

# The End Writ Large

THE FOLLOWING YEAR ON THE KNOB was a long one. A rough year, it was. One thing after another seemed to have conspired to undo SLANT and its people. First there was The General, then Meddy, then the battle against the corrupt senator and his minions in that so-called church.

Alec finally lost his own private struggle, which was infinitely sad but not altogether unexpected, considering his unstable state. Jorge and Nooner and I now hike up to Alec's treehouse a couple times a year, just to check on it. Sometimes we sit for a while, gazing down on Fidelity. Such a peaceful place. We don't have to do much maintenance; Alec did a great job constructing it. But we like to provide upkeep as necessary. We figure some other poor soul in trouble might need it someday, same as he did.

So, it was a year of losses and uncertainty, dismal reckonings and the good struggle toward uprightness.

What you want to know is whether SLANT survived. What I ask you (knowing what you now know about us) is how you could think otherwise?

Sometimes the good guys actually win. It doesn't happen often in the current version of the world, but that's the way it went down in the tale of this small place. Not without compromise, not without loss—but we did win, those of us who made it all the way to the end.

It was difficult and expensive, and it took a terrible emotional toll, but we saw it through, as we always have in our place up here on Barrel Chute Knob. And as we may, in fact, have to again in some future time—though harder years would be impossible to imagine.

In every war, there are casualties. Nothing casual about them, as you've probably heard me say before, but there you are. Thankfully, there are survivors here, too. I am among them, though I'm not at all sure why. The hard world often seems unworthy of the colossal amount of emotional effort it requires of us. Still, we carry on. And so, we know, do you.

I'll tell you all about that year, but it'll have to be the short version because the long version would take a year to tell.

# Stand Up After A Stumble

THE FIRE STARTED VERY EARLY on a winter Sunday. It was still dark outside and no one in SLANT, not even Horse, was awake. By sun-up, it was all over. The General was a heap of charred wood stabbing the sky, blackened glass shards littering the ground like glittering treasure, smoking ashes reminding every last SLANTer of their collective grief.

The beloved old community building and everything in it were total losses. Those seminal namesake characters—the carefully preserved S, LAN and T on its siding—would never be seen again, except in photographs. That is the bad news. The good news is that no other structures in SLANT, not even the gazebo, not even the Craft Cabin immediately next door, were damaged. And no one was injured while fighting to contain and extinguish that devilish blaze. And so, if loss had to happen, in the end the fire could be seen as a net win.

Nooner was convinced it was arson, given the recent unpleasantness with the church camp up Fidelity. Many of us, in fact, believed that to be true. But we were wrong. It was wiring, worn out or mouse-chewed, that sparked and shorted and erupted in a small flame that rapidly grew, feeding on the dry old lumber of the structure. In no time, the front windows were exploding outward from the intense heat. And soon after, the roof caved in—just dropped straight down onto its own footprint. It didn't take long. Yet the ruins smoked for two days.

Some four-legger, I believe it had to be Bocker, had first noticed the smell and then heard crackling sounds while the fire was still burning small inside The General. He frantically alerted the community that something was terribly wrong. People came running from every direction, yelling for more help, but all they could do was to point water hoses, shoot fire extinguishers and throw buckets of dirt at the flaming building and, more important, wet down the roofs and walls of all the structures nearby so as to keep them from attracting evil flames to themselves. In retrospect, though losing The General was heartbreaking to everyone in SLANT—particularly Turner, Turk and Wilma Carl, of course—we all know it could have been a tragedy of far greater proportions. The entire village center might have gone up, including the big house, that original farmhouse in which The Jimmies live. People might have been taken to hospitals. Or funeral homes.

When a home or barn or other beloved building burns, the event is simply terrorizing. What happens the following day, when one returns to the pungent and smoldering wreckage, is that the shock and excitement begin to wear off and a deep grief takes over.

Losing a home or any similar structure is like a death in the family. If you haven't been through a fire of this type, if it hasn't happened very close to you, these will just be words. But if you have, then you know that my saying *it's like a death in the family* is not an exaggeration. That one substantial part lost to us, filled with precious history and genuine affection and deep psychic devotion and our very origin, is gone forever.

We hardly knew what to do with ourselves for a long time after.

Put simply: we were traumatized.

The kind of loss you experience from a devastating fire manifests in different ways for different people. In the case of The General, the worst of it came in the month or two following the fire. For many of us, though, the effects of that trauma have lasted the rest of our lives. Some can't sleep with a nightlight on, because if we wake up in near-total darkness and see evidence of a glimmer across the room or down the hall, our first reaction is terror; our first thought is that the tiny bit of light is from a flame. For a long while, some among us hated returning to the scene because it brought that terrible night back in full force. Some, to this day, have a sudden negative reaction to the smell of smoke, even from a camp-fire or chimney or stovepipe. And then we remember where we are. The old General is gone, but we're still here. SLANT survived.

Some blocked out the whole fire event, couldn't seem to remember for weeks that The General was gone, so they'd absentmindedly head over to pick up a loaf of bread or a quart of milk or to grab a package of light bulbs. It's much the same when a person dear to you has died but you keep forgetting—you think, for example, you'll call and tell them a thing you just heard because you know they'll appreciate it better than anyone else you know. Trauma, especially when it's particularly severe, is a weird and lasting condition. In the case of The General, it was a collective loss— one that the whole of SLANT grieved together and for a long, long time. Historically, we'll forever grieve. But the passage of time provides us perspective.

It would be sentimental to say that the greatest loss of all was The Code. Sometimes I dream it's still there and I'm leaning against its wall, reading a good book. More often I dream that I'm inside the fire, watch-ing flames lick our words right off those precious walls. But The Code is a thing that is practiced, not just read or archived. It lives securely in the minds and hearts of every resident of SLANT. It shows up in our actions. It didn't die in the fire. A more perfect and literal example of a living document could never exist. It is more than mere words. The Code, by necessity, is action. The Code is us.

As humans do when any dear one dies, we in SLANT had to find ways to live with our loss after The General was gone. The Jimmies committed to replacing the structure as long as Turner was willing to reestablish the business. He was. They did.

You won't be surprised when I tell you there was no shortage of volunteers to help raise the roof.

## Selfishness & Love Cannot Co-exist

MEDDY'S FATE TOOK A STRANGE AND TERRIBLE TURN when cancer hit her that year. It smashed into her full on, in a hurry, out of the blue. With little more than a few months' warning, it did its worst.

For several weeks in autumn, she'd complained of a terrible pain in her back. This, she knew, had nothing to do with the mild dementia she'd been preoccupied with over the past year. Nagging, aching, horrific physical pain in the middle of her back—until finally she asked Nooner to drive her to a doctor to see what was what. In short order, tests revealed non-Hodgkin lymphoma in an advanced stage, which she, at first, refused to accept. But then pancreatic cancer showed up too. Her physical condition deteriorated so quickly that in a matter of six months, she knew the disease would win, and it would win sooner rather than later.

So, what to do? Meddy's decision was swift and final: she would take this last journey with as little struggle as possible, so as to maximize her energy for more important things. This meant not wasting time in hospitals suffering debilitating treatments that could only buy her a few extra weeks but would cost her what precious little strength she had left. Meddy wanted to die the same way she had lived: with dignity and in control.

Of course, illness of this kind quickly takes all control from the sufferer. But dignity, she decided, the illness could not be allowed to obliterate. It wasn't easy, but Meddy was used to hard. She didn't fight. Like a cork in water, she adopted a very Taoist manner so as to dodge collisions with the disease—ebbing and flowing to counterbalance surges. In this way, she had spurts of strength and energy for her old and dear friends, particularly Nooner and Joy and Farnsley and, of course, The Jimmies. She had what she considered "the important conversations" with each of them in those last weeks. They were all sad but realistic about what was happening, Meddy most of all. The fact that her friends and chosen family didn't shy from the truth of the matter made her feel respected.

For the most part, Meddy stayed home in SLANT during her illness.

As long as she had a bit of help—and there was plenty of that on hand—she did very well. Toward the end, she spent a few days in the hospital, getting some relief from the worst of the pain, but eventually she insisted on being sent back home to die. This was her wish and her plan. There was morphine, which Joy and Nooner took turns administering to her. There was Hospice, who sent someone every day to provide comfort and advice to her caretakers. By not fighting it, Meddy actually did enjoy her last days, in spite of the fact that she more frequently needed help.

But at the very end, there was a kind of bliss. She didn't waste a drop of energy explaining this to anyone, for she knew they couldn't understand ... until it was their turn to die. Anyway, these weren't her usual teachable moments; these were her private moments of preparing to cross over from living into oblivion. Having survived past the point of control over herself and what was happening to her, she longed for three things only: consciousness, dignity and grace. She achieved them all.

Her last private conversation with Nooner was lucid and insightful. She was having one of her good days, so they sat outside under her tree for a while. They chatted, riffed, agreed, disagreed and generally reveled in the sweetness of companionable presence—like the old days, before illness, dementia and drama.

"What am I gonna do?" Nooner said. He was using all of his strength not to break down in front of her. "When you.... Without you?"

"Well," said Meddy, "you're going to celebrate my sudden relief, I hope."

"*Sudden* relief? You're not thinkin' of doin' somethin' crazy, are you?"

"I'm not saying I'm gonna hurry it along," Meddy said, "but when old Death finally gets here, I'll be good and ready. I've not had much what you'd call 'joy' in this life. As good old Langston Hughes wrote: 'Life for me ain't been no crystal stair.' I've had happy times, sure. Friends. SLANT. You! But living inside this thing called *Me* has been pretty painful ... inwardly. I've hardly caught a decent breath because of this big hole in my chest, a perfect square, made that way by very precise and intentional cuts from people in my past who stole chunks of me while I wasn't looking. I'm just sick to death of betrayal as a human construct, and I've grieved up all my energy. Plus, I've learned at last that I'm irrelevant ... that we all are irrelevant. Eternal rest sounds beautiful to me, my brother. Living in this world is a whole lot of goddamn work."

He managed a sad smile. She took his hand. They sat quietly. A bee buzzed.

"Oh, hey," she said. "I finally figured out what Love is." She off-handedly dropped this into the lull in their conversation—it was time to change the subject anyway. "I've never really been able to believe in romantic Love because I couldn't define it, not in all these years of being a shade-tree philosopher. Turns out, it's so *simple!*"

"What Love is?" Nooner wasn't sure he'd heard her correctly.

She nodded. "Get this: Love is making sure you always look out for the other person with just as much care as you use when looking out for yourself. If *both* people in a relationship faithfully do that, without selfish motive or manipulation or agenda, everything works. Nooner, honey, when you find your mate ..."

"IF," said Nooner. He always tensed up around this topic.

"*IF*. Okay. I get it. You like your solitude as much as I do," Meddy said, flashing that old devilish grin of hers. "You take after me in that way."

All she got back from Nooner was a scowl. It was fake, and she appreciated his effort toward normalcy in this least normal of times.

"So ... when or *IF* you find your perfect mate," she said, "all you have to do is measure each of you by that standard. If you both pass that test, you'll be 'fine as wine from the summertime vine.'"

"That's not even a thing," he grumbled, then slyly grinned. She raised a single eyebrow.

But the lesson took. Nooner saw that love really is that simple. Just like the Golden Rule says.

He thought about Meddy's theory all that night, and what he concluded was that his dearest, truest, most brilliant friend had once again formulated a priceless universal truth. *Selfishness cannot co-exist with Love.* Real love, actual love, is too big—there's no space in it for selfishness, and vice versa. If each person in any loving relationship (romantic or otherwise) is selflessly, supportively, mutually, respectfully looking out for the other—and it has to be *both* of them doing this *in like measure*—that's Love.

That's all Love is.

# Embrace What Matters Most

IT WAS ON THE FIRST FRIDAY IN MAY—the day before the world famous run for the roses, the Kentucky Derby—that Meddy died. Oaks Day, we locals call it. The day at Churchill Downs when the fillies run for the lilies. Perfect. Meddy was no longer a filly herself, but she *was* a seasoned old mare who well remembered what being a feisty filly felt like.

She was alert and as pleased as could be that her friends were sitting and standing around her as she lay in a hammock on the porch of her little shelter in SLANT. Farnsley, sensing that the end was imminent, had made a batch of mint juleps. A day early, yes, but juleps are part of the entire three-week long Derby Festival in Louisville and central Kentucky, so it seemed right. If she made it to Derby Day, why, we'd be grateful for the excuse to do rerun juleps again tomorrow!

Farnsley, Joy, Nooner, Tractor Girl and I—and Meddy herself—raised a single gleeful toast: "To everything all at once, no matter who, what, when, where, why or how!" Meddy took one little sip, but could barely hold the cup with both hands. She was cycling in and out of comfort and discomfort and morphine, we could tell, but she insisted we stay. As if we would consider leaving her, possibly to die alone! At her request, we divided the rest of her julep in splashes among our cups in a way that felt a bit holy communion-ish.

Meddy well knew what was happening all that day. In her typically matter-of-fact manner, she even talked about the inevitable. "There is something that happens right *there*, between dying and death," she said, gesturing to illustrate her point. "I would like to know what that is." The very definition of *lifelong learner*, Meddy was.

The conversation that day ran a spectrum of topics. As usual, nothing was off limits. Before the afternoon was out, the juleps were all gone and so was Meddy. She was gone! Easy. Quick. Without fanfare.

That day, her friends had told her we loved her, and she had been agreeable enough, letting us say nice things about her, which was a rare thing for her to do. She did it for us, not for herself, I realized. And equally rare, she told us in as much detail as she could muster (which at that point wasn't much) how much we, each of us, meant to her. How fortunate she felt. How strong, she said, we'd helped her feel. We all made each other laugh too, which was important. It was a loving finale.

At some point, she closed her eyes and thought about how much she relished hearing familiar voices on her familiar porch, casually and intimately conversing with one another. "Here's what matters most," she murmured. "Right here is what it is." She smiled and listened and thanked her lucky stars … and then she simply, quietly went. Just like that.

It was so Meddy of her.

## Never Misplace Your Sense of Humor

MEDDY'S FUNERAL SERVICE was a simple one. The whole thing was
over in under an hour. It started at the gazebo in SLANT-center, where
folks gathered inside and outside the small structure to sing, led by Birdie,
Juny, Willie and the rest of SLANT's musicians. They sang "Going Up
Home" and "Give Yourself to Love" and "Willing" and "Don't Let Your
Deal Go Down," songs Meddy herself had chosen. Dick played "South-
wind" on the dulcimer. Jorge played "Ashokan Farewell" on the fiddle. Joy
said a few words of comfort. Meddy had strictly instructed Joy that she
was "not to deliver a lengthy or boring sermon," to which Joy had replied
that would be an easy enough wish to fulfill since she didn't know how
to deliver a sermon that was either lengthy *or* boring. They had laughed
together about that.

Joy's brief but uplifting words at the service were exactly what you
would expect one beloved and respected friend to say about another. And
then the whole crowd—oh, it was a big one; well more than two hundred
people, for everyone in SLANT was there, plus Nick (who read a Hopkins
poem) and Sam (who recited one) and several other non-SLANT friends—
walked second line, at The Jimmies' slow pace, behind Nooner and Joy
and the Mayor down the little lane toward Fidelity Creek. Beyond the
creekside row of tiny houses, they paraded (two-leggers and four-) past
Meddy's shelter and on to where Whisper rested, for there would be no
work today. They gathered around to watch Nooner empty the cardboard
box of Meddy's ashes into the languorous current of Fidelity.

Then Nooner stepped back to the path, and the mourners followed
him into Meddy's own lonesome yard. He pulled out a small sheet of
paper on which, in her handwriting, were words that Meddy'd asked him
to read. As he settled into his part, no one noticed Tractor Girl discreetly
sinking a handful of pennies into the water where the ashes had been
poured. That was just between her and Miz Meadowlark Nightengale.

Nooner offered up Meddy's own words in a strong voice. He already
knew they would sound familiar to her beloveds, because she had spoken
them in her toast at the Solstice Come Together down at the bonsai farm

the year before.

"These are Meddy's words to us," Nooner said, clearing his throat, reminding himself to breathe. "Here goes: 'In this circle, in this space, we gather for a simple reason: because there is somethin' here that we need,'" he read. "'I have often thought of each of you ... kindly, fondly and well. This final day comes to us all, but that should be a comfort to you, not a fear, you Time Travelers, for look at us: we're here now—and we were there then, too. Remember? I told you this would come to pass! Now, raise your faces and reach back toward me with a grin ... so I'll know it's you.'"

They did recognize those words, the SLANTers did. And they grinned through tears, and definitely remembered their Meddy—kindly, fondly and well.

Nooner wore a sterling key charm on a long, delicate silver chain around his neck. He'd been wearing it every day lately. Today he lifted the charm out of his shirt collar and dangled it in front of his chest. "Meddy gave me this little key about a month ago," he said. "It had belonged to her for years and years. She said I would someday soon find the meanin' that it could hold for me. I think I've found it here today. Thanks for one final lesson, Meddy, old girl." And here Nooner choked up, though he tried so hard not to because she had instructed him with absolute fierceness that he was not to cry at her funeral. *Buck up!* had been her exact words. But we all know, don't we, that strong pull of emotion that takes over whenever it wants to, especially when it's expressing grief and emptiness, *insisting* that we mark the utter permanence of loss. We have known it, and we can't stop it, and neither could Nooner. He released the tiny key, and its chain allowed it to come to rest onto his shirtfront, just at the level of his heart.

"Love you, Meddy," he said, through fat tears rolling off his beautiful high cheekbones. His voice was different now, for he was speaking his own words. "You, and SLANT, ever'thang and ever'one here—all of this ...." And here he paused to swallow, hard. "All of this is the key to so much that was locked up tight inside me, but I didn't even know I had any of it until landin' here. Now I'm a cage swung wide open. I'm free." In a whisper he added, "And so are you, my friend."

Here Nooner's head dropped and he broke down completely. Joy stepped over to him, rubbed his back with an open palm, took him in her big, loving arms, patted his neck, stroked his head, held him like a beloved child while he wept violently into the side of her pudgy neck. She held him tight and tenderly, rocking him almost imperceptibly side to side until he got hold of himself. We were all snotting, sobbing, weeping, wiping. I wasn't the only one who stole a glance at The Jimmies, wondering mournfully which of them would be the last hippie standing, for they both were getting up there in age. But for now, to our good fortune, we still have our Adam and our Eve.

Finally, when he was ready, Joy released Nooner so he could go and lean against a sturdy old cedar trunk to steady his breath. Then she turned and spoke simply to the gathering. "Amen and amen. Or as Meddy herself would have said, 'Roll 'em if you got 'em—there's never a better time than right this very minute!'"

Then Joy, with a big, mischievous, benevolent smile, pulled from beneath her vestment the last joint Meddy had ever rolled, a super long one. It was, as usual, just horrible looking—asymmetrical, simultaneously tight and loose, lumpy, ugly, too skinny in some places, too fat in others. Meddy's friends immediately recognized it as one of her trademark messes of a rolling job. The dripping, snotting, wiping crowd began to smile through our tears, then got to giggling out loud, converting our sobs to laughter, remembering our friend and all that she had been to us ... all that she still was and would ever and always be.

Joy fired up the medicine, then passed the peace. As it moved from one person to the next, each taking a hit—some firing up and passing their own joints to multiply the bounty like loaves and fishes—we began to talk and to tell our Meddy stories and to laugh and pound each other on our backs and hug and shake our heads in wonder. Meddy would have brayed her hearty laughter at the sight. And she would have been touched, too. Moved, even.

Most of all, she'd have known that Nooner and all the rest of us would eventually be just fine. And that is the one thing in this world or the next that Meddy had desired above all.

# Don't Mistake Ego for Self-Respect

YOU CAN TELL A LOT ABOUT A PERSON by watching him do a certain thing when he's in an intense exchange with someone. During that year when SLANT worked to protect itself from the mess going on upstream, there were a shit ton of intense exchanges. Nooner had his fair share, for sure.

Nooner has a particular way of stopping to think whenever a conversation gets revved. Some people don't stop and think; they just plow ahead and let unformed notions spill forth with no thought to consequences. Others stop talking but never break their gaze. Some show no emotion. Others avert their eyes, or they turn their bodies away from the conversation altogether for a moment. Some cover their faces, and others absolutely and memorably do not. Nooner's way is none of these. When he hits that better-to-think-before-speaking snag, he stops to think so thoroughly that you can practically see gears turning inside his skull, and every one of those gears moves a different facial muscle. As a range of reactions burn through his mind, his eyes rove in search of the specific information he needs to retrieve or discover. He winces; he frowns. He argues silently with himself.

He has no idea he's so transparent. He can't see what the person watching him sees. He can't even see that there *is* another person, in moments like these. He will be deep into his problem-solving head space, with no other awareness. This can last from a few seconds to a few minutes.

So, there we were one day, he and I, patiently waiting for the stoplight in front of the off-knob post office. (This was before the TRS conflict was resolved, of course.) TRS staff and parent volunteers were standing in the intersection with little plastic buckets, taking every nickel and dime and dollar bill anyone waiting for the traffic to move would give them. Nooner rolled down his window just to find out what kind of sales pitch the deacon walking his lane was spouting. That bucket came toward Nooner, the fellow rattling the change already deposited in it, as if this would entice him to add to its jingle. But Nooner had a different agenda.

He decided to make the guy work for it, at the same time knowing that he'd never, ever contribute one red cent to the questionable and shameful TRS "cause."

"Tell me why I should support your camp," he said in a carefully even tone, putting it as bluntly as he could.

"Why, friend, don't you love the Lord?" This didn't sound anything like an answer to the question Nooner had asked. But, of course, there was more to follow that out-of-context reply. Much more—nearly all of it platitudes, stitched together with vague threats and lures concerning "eternity" and "salvation" and "Hell."

When the arrogant TRS fellow with that assholier-than-thou mouth on him had launched his spiel that day, fronted by the all-too-familiar televangelist cadence and facial set, Nooner had gone into his internal thinking routine. A joy to witness.

I think as his brain's gears whirred, his interior reaction must have gone something like this:

*You think God is so small that She can fit into your narrow little mind? Are you on crack? Surely you don't expect me to accept the lies you tell yourself. You think God is so manageable that He can be defined by you? Quite an ego you've got there.*

*The height of arrogance is to believe yourself so significant that God is created in your image or you in His. God is a concept that you can't ever understand, no matter how long you ponder Her. If God exists, S/He is both male and female ... or neither. Or both. Humans limit themselves—but there's an incredibly fascinatin' spectrum that makes all binary concepts seem quaint and impotent and hurtful and sad. What kind of God would create humans and then confuse hell out of them about their most basic personal identities? A sadist, that's who.*

Of course, Nooner wasn't necessarily saying all these individual words in his head. He was just flashing through feelings and thoughts that, as best they could, allowed him to be one with his own knowledge and beliefs. It was almost as if his mind were channeling Meddy. Yet he'd still not spoken a word that I or the arrogant beggar could hear.

*You should know that the God you purport to acknowledge is way beyond such petty games. Oh, but you're not! You'd consider me a heretic sinner if I suggest God is a figment of the human imagination!*

More consciously Nooner thought, "She made me smarter, Meddy did. And goddamn, am I grateful that she's still with me every day." He missed her, but thinking of her made him more glad than sad.

*Yet what do we know of any god? What can we possibly know? Humans can only imagine, can only create myths that match our narrow agendas. How dare we make God fit human proportions. How very dare we.*

Nooner missed his Meddy—well, that's an understatement-and-a-half. I saw that he could practically feel Meddy in the truck cab with us. She'd have loved this. She'd have said, "It boggles the mind how those who consider themselves so God-like will act in ways that aren't even God-worthy."

Nooner knew that he knew what he knew because Meddy'd been so patient with him, helping him to find his own set of beliefs, to be fearless and secure in them, to understand that his beliefs and positions were just as valid as hers or the next person's. Well, she did that for all of us, didn't she?

*Anyone tries to tell me he understands the mind of God,* Nooner went on thinking, *that man's a liar. A liar! And I'll call him that to his face. A goddamned liar, and there's no blasphemy in that judgment, for it's truer than the lie you tell yourself about your mythological storybook. Yes, I said it! Religion is just one more set of myths in the long history of human storytellin', and one myth is no more real than another, one person's god no more valid than the next—for they're all created to entertain, to shame, to teach, to control by fear. What you base your entire world on is a myth, my opinion, and I'm the heretic who's callin' you out on it.*

All of this—the thoughts, Meddy's voice in his memory, all of it—had blown through his mind in a flash as he sat at that stoplight listening to the religious bile spewed by the man with the plastic bucket. And soon Meddy's voice seemed to merge with Nooner's own notions.

*And saints? Forget saints. Saints ain't holy and they ain't god-like. They're just people that're better at being human than the rest of us. How? By carin' as much about others as they do about themselves. In humanity, that's a rare quotient.*

All of this meaning just zoomed through Nooner's head. Thirty seconds, the lot. Maybe less.

*You are so small,* Nooner thought, coolly looking over this cocky little bucket-begging fool. *You are tiny. And so am I. We all are. You want us to think the maker of Everything lowers Itself to speak only to you? Get outta my face. You are a disgrace to the very idea of a lovin' God, you damaged little man. The only three-letter word correctly associated with you is not G-o-d; it's e-g-o.*

I imagine Nooner was kind of proud of that last bit, for it was a new idea, wholly his own. He appeared to be—silently, intellectually—on a roll.

*You are exactly like the unfaithful lover who victimizes a partner and then ridicules that same partner, belittling them for feeling victimized. Your way of manipulatin' people has nothin' to do with goodness, nothin' to do with honesty, nothin' to do with humility, nothin' to do with anything positive. Damn sure nothin' to do with the humble Christ you claim to follow.*

*You are a mistake. Not a mistake of God. A mistake of humanity. This is because you are not of God. Far from it. You are the negative of God. The reverse of holy. A dangerous hypocrite.*

Damn! He was thinking like Meddy! Finding the words! On his own! And he knew this new Nooner was a whole lot better than who he'd once been. The old Nooner was liable to cloud up and rain tooth, nail, fist, heel and blinding sweat all over that fool. But the new Nooner wisely uses his human head instead of his animal instinct.

*And by the way, an addiction can be quite simply defined: it's somethin' hurtful to yourself and to others that you cain't stop yourself from doing. Your public addiction is convincin' others that you seem to know what you're talkin' about. Your private—and more serious—addiction is that you continually convince yourself that you actually do know what in the hell you're talkin' about. Your "God" is just your lame-ass excuse for your warped ego. But if you could take responsibility for yourself, then you wouldn't need to blame "God's will" for your own losses and shortcomin's, wouldn't need to pray to Him to fix the messes you make because you lack control over your actions. You are pathetic, little man. It's a lazy evangelist who scares people with the Old Testament instead of inspirin' them with the New—which is where Christ's only words reside!*

These were Nooner's beliefs, although, like many of us, he couldn't have expressed them aloud in language quite as well-formed as the *ideas* that he fully understood in his innate way of feeling them and thinking them and hearing them and knowing them.

So, while his internal processes were complex and sophisticated and lightning fast, all he decided to say aloud to that fellow was this: "I know what you *say* you think of your God. But what I will always have to wonder—when your sales pitches and your demands and your imagined entitlement and your need for control and your fear mongering are all said and done—is this: what does *God* think of *you?*"

Nooner was a homespun genius at distilling the myriad thoughts that could run through his mind like a rushing river topping a dam. He had a gift for following thoughts in their initial flood, patiently waiting until they were a mere trickle of truth's essence. *What does your God think of you?*

It was the first time the arrogant fellow had been taken aback in years—maybe even for as long as he could remember. He stared at Nooner, his mouth hanging open a bit, his eyes drifting slowly down and to the right. He jingled the bucket of change again, but not very enthusiastically. His mouth was *empty* of platitudes now. Nooner, it seemed, was the cat who had finally gotten the demagogue's tongue. God, I loved seeing it happen!

So as to prolong the discomfort of this guy's rare speechless moment, Nooner, noticing that the traffic light had finally changed to green and that the "conversation" had come to an abrupt standstill, took his time reaching for the shifter. He genially said, "See you around, buddy. Have a good one." Then he deliberately put the truck in gear, turned left, and we headed up hunnerd-n-lebm, the winding county road running steadily up and around toward SLANT where truth and goodness and courage were always the order of the day.

# Nobody Believes In Everything

*IT DOES NO GOOD TO DIG A HOLE.* That's what the woman standing beside that stuck truck had said long ago. The voice, the stranger's face, the mud—it all came back in a burst.

Tractor Girl hadn't even been thinking about trucks or mud or the year some rough backwoods boys had rained nighttime gunshots over the land where the women's music festival had been held, back when that particular festival still existed. Tractor Girl wasn't anywhere close to that line of thought today, yet the statement came through as clear as the sound of a perfectly-tuned bell. This exquisite example of metaphor, was all the sweeter because it was birthed naturally and without manipulation.

That rain had *poured,* she now recalled. Poured. For days. The festival grounds had become saturated and soupy. When one of the women working transportation, or maybe one of the trash queens, had gotten a pickup stuck, eight or ten or a dozen of the women walking nearby put down whatever they were carrying and stepped in to help push the truck out of the soggy mess it was mired in. And because it was a camping festival, no one cared about getting a little dirty, or even a lot dirty. Good excuse to strip down and jump into the lake.

All the women helping were butches, of course. And each had an opinion—of course. A few of them even agreed with each other about how best to unstick the vehicle. First, they tried having the driver gun the engine while everybody rocked the truck forward, but that didn't work. It only succeeded in spraying copious amounts of mud off the tires. Then they tried sticking things under the rear tires in hopes of inspiring traction, but that was a no-go in the slick slop. While a few of the women were studying the situation—heads cocked at various angles, lots of hemming, hawing and whaddaya-reckon talk—the driver apparently decided to give it one rousing rev to see if a miracle might occur, might allow the truck to leap out of the muck and surprise them all. The roar of the engine was great; the flinging of mud, spectacular.

"Whoa! Whoa! Whoa!" yelled a woman who needed to be in charge more than any of the other women needed to, at that moment anyway.

The driver whoa'd.

"Does no good to dig a hole," the bossy woman said. She'd been standing aside, away from the spraying mud, the spinning tires. While others had shoved to no avail, she had been observing. She had been considering.

Everyone, noticing that the truck hadn't, in fact, leapt from the mud, instinctively turned their mud-spackled faces toward the rear tires to see what was now what.

"My daddy always said it does no damn good to dig a hole," the woman said again, muttering it mostly to herself this time. She was thinking toward a solution, but that solution might just have to be leaving that truck sit for a day or two and waiting for the earth to dry out some.

The thing was buried nearly up to its axle.

Does no good, indeed.

Tractor Girl hadn't thought about that in years, yet here it came again, this time out of a dry blue sky. And damned if it wasn't a perfect fit.

*It does no good to dig a hole.*

What Tractor Girl had been thinking about was her broken heart. She was constantly searching for a way to understand the cause of it, even just a little bit. She wanted to get away from the hurt that there seemed no end to. So great was her pain sometimes that she fully expected to die from it. But what the universe gave her was, "It does no good to dig a hole."

Actually, that made perfect, immediate sense. It explained so much about why she felt so heavy and bogged down all the time lately, why she hadn't been able to move her heart in any direction, why thinking this over and over and over wasn't working after months and years of trying. It was a mess, the kind that wasn't easy to get out of. Sometimes one has to wait, still and quiet, for time to pass so things can dry out. Digging one's way out of sludge or muck or quicksand may not be possible—and not only that, trying too hard often makes things worse.

*But can I stop digging now?* she wondered. *Can I stop needing to understand? Will I bury myself trying?*

Tractor Girl took inventory of what was left inside her. Truth be told, following the whole Gazelle thing, there wasn't much. Betrayal is betrayal. Abandonment is abandonment. Period. It's permanent torture. And it hurts like hell.

*Well,* she realized, *I don't believe in magic anymore. I am way past that. I guess my conscious mind just caught up, so please let my heart gain ground to match it.*

It didn't feel good to admit that she could feel so disappointed that she wanted to die, yet she oddly felt somehow freer inside that, all the same.

*Once you know something,* she thought, *you can't really unknow it.*

Suddenly, she realized how much like Meddy that sounded. It was
a comforting thought. If Tractor Girl had been able to smile in that
moment, she would have. But her friend Meddy was thoroughly dead. No
bluff. Sometimes Memory is a four-flushing bitch.

The emotional muck engulfing Tractor Girl was thick and gluey and
relentless for most of that shitty year of Meddy's dying and The General
burning and the TRS clash. All of which triggered Gazelle's long-ago
betrayal.

Tractor Girl was exhausted from struggling against her torment for
such a long time; she felt nearly dead from working to keep from being
sucked deeper into its darkness where finally, maybe, she wouldn't be able
to draw breath at all. Ever since The Betrayal, TG had to wake up every
fucking day and start over. It never got past the point of overwhelming
effort. No significant progress had so far been made. But she needed to let
it all go!

And there was now this sparkling truth: *it does no good to dig a hole.*
Nothing muddy about the meaning of that. Meddy would have loved it.

Tractor Girl had lost so much that mattered to her heart. Nearly
everything. Except the bonsai farm, that is. And SLANT, of course, which
had been her family, her place since long before Gazelle had come into
her life. She decided that if she had to bury herself in anything, these two
places were it. She wouldn't give up on them, mostly because they had
never given up on her. She hoped anyway that she'd have the strength to
keep the bonsai farm and her SLANT family close, for they, in reality, were
what had been keeping her propped upright. So far.

Gazelle refused to admit her sins and apologize for them, so there was
nothing for TG to do but find her own way to live.

Tractor Girl took to the water and the bonsais for blessed distraction.

Today, thinking about her losses and about not digging a hole and
about Meddy, Tractor Girl wiped snot and smeared tears. She spat. She
cussed. She rested her anguished heart for the first time in a long time,
and that felt good, though she knew this small relief might be only
temporary. Even so, she always felt grateful for any minute respite from
her wretched agony. Baby steps. But still.

And then she recalled that on the wall inside the gone General
someone had, not long before the fire, added this observation to the SLANT
Code: "Nobody believes in everything."

*Right,* thought Tractor Girl. *And sometimes, everybody believes in nothing
… if only because we can't fool ourselves forever.*

And that was the moment she knew she was going to make it.
Everything was going to be just fine.

# It Will Reveal Itself

WHAT IT CAME DOWN TO was the dump. Or, more specifically, the water.

For a solid year, the good people of SLANT tried all sorts of strategies to expose the shoddy development that was going on upstream at TRS. There was the initial, local door-to-door campaign to inform residents up and down the knob of the developers' plan—and that went pretty well, for *nobody* downstream wanted to see Fidelity or Barrel Chute defiled. There were the series of attempts to get regional news outlets to cover the political story, but that early effort was to little avail since too many people who control local media were tied into (A) the mega church or (B) the corrupt politician behind the development scam.

Even after the scandal was revealed and the dubious child labor situation was known and discussed, there were believers tied to TRS and *Streets of Gold!* who refused to accept the truth set directly before them. As members, they couldn't fathom being wrong about the mega-church. As conservative voters, they couldn't admit being wrong about a politician they had returned to office term upon term. As parents, they couldn't accept being wrong about the way they had carelessly allowed their children to be used. So, they clung to the fragile fabric of the lies they told themselves, tattered though it was, sheer as it seemed. They clutched the ravelings of their beliefs. For they couldn't possibly be wrong, could they? In what they fervently believed? In what they had been "taught" for decades, for generations? They were still swallowing the propaganda they'd become addicted to.

It was a struggle.

SLANT was committed to unfiltered rational thought. And most of the neighbors up and down hunnerd-n-lebm were onboard. But the majority of mega-church members and TRS supporters, who mostly lived elsewhere, wouldn't believe the truth. They just couldn't. And so, their irrational resistance struggled against SLANT through the seasons.

Then there were the county's zoning laws, which were revealed to have been ignored or defiled by the secretive development high on the knob, well out of sight of most residents and travelers. Sewerage systems up at TRS were entirely inadequate, and drinking water was determined to lack proper treatment for a project of its size. Local officials determined that they could not legally sign off on such a lack of adherence to basic public safety standards.

A cult-like component was revealed, as well. When the bigotry of who would and would not be "allowed" to purchase lots or live in the homes to be constructed became apparent, fair housing and anti-discrimination laws were tested. People—families who didn't adhere to fundamentalist religious practices, and more specifically didn't accept the strange and narrow beliefs of that particular mega-church behind the scheme—were found to have been black-balled from attempting to own any of the lots on the property. How, we SLANTers asked ourselves and each other, was this different from the racially-motivated housing discrimination that had fueled the Civil Rights movement more than a half century ago? In its essence, it was no different. Religious discrimination is just as dangerous and just as evil as any other kind of segregation or oppression. And so, suits were filed. Based on the evidence, and based on voiced fears that a cult situation such as this would get out of hand in the same way it had happened out west some decades back when a religious cult had taken over and destroyed a small rural town, the state's attorney general was compelled to get involved. Separation of church and state became a hot topic tied to the whole mess.

But this all came after the initial action that finally caught the general public's attention, thanks to good old Nooner.

You see, Nooner got the idea to ask Nick to come hike with him upstream that winter (when weeds were dead and didn't hide the horror). They went to photograph the huge illegal dump that spilled into Fidelity. The key solution revealed itself in that one simple idea ... and finally hit a public nerve. He and Nick posted and shared their photos as widely as they could on the Internet. As Resident Bard, my part was to compose text to accompany those images. Everyone pitched in whatever talents they had to offer. We based our case on clean water as essential to life and health. And that's when environmentalists got involved.

One particular group known as Our Common Wealth, a widely-respected organization that had successfully fought water pollution caused by mountaintop removal mining in coal producing sections of the state, threw their political-activism weight behind SLANT's effort. The ensuing broader exposure was widespread, and its effect was immediate. Suddenly, it seemed, the whole country was aware and watching and speaking up against this brand of pollution and exploitation. The *New York Times* and NPR even reported stories, mainly because Connelldon was a national political figure. The argument became irrefutable that those living

downstream would be adversely affected as the project proceeded and as
the horrid, illegal dumpsite grew. It was definitely David vs. Goliath, but we
all know how that story ended.

What Nooner and Nick had photographed was not only the expanse
of the dump but also closer looks at what was actually in it. More than
debris from the cutting and dragging away of trees and brush, there were
the flotsam and jetsam of new building materials and discarded chunks of
what had once been the older structures from the original camp meeting
grounds. And there was plain old garbage, lots of it, all uncovered and
being washed into Fidelity. Vermin and pests inhabited the mess. Worst
of all, discarded dangerous chemicals, asbestos and other nasty stuff was
leaching unhealthy crap into the water. But it was, in particular, Nick's
horrifyingly beautiful image of that discarded old dinner bell partially
obliterated by refuse that finally seemed to have the biggest emotional
impact on many of the mega-church's members, especially the older ones
and those who drove in from rural areas to attend its services. The
discarding and defacing of a beloved culture for a rich man's personal
gain unlocked a deeper meaning of the whole story for many people, even
the most stubborn. Ironic, but that emotional image of the old church bell
worked to awaken not only religious folks but also those who had the
political power to do the right thing. So, the cult would have to reckon
with both the law and public opinion. This would, in the end, swamp the
dirty development deal.

Once national media lit a flame of truth and revelation, local media
found itself unable to avoid the story. Con was challenged by reporters
and citizens alike; this even happened at public events where he made his
re-election campaign appearances. At first, his constituents saw him only
as their representative in government whom they expected to enforce civil
rights and environmental protection laws. His complicity in the development remained secret for a time. Before long, though, the focus shifted.
Rumors of his secretive involvement picked up steam.

The senator dealt with these allegations in exactly the way a Gandhi
scholar long ago summarized Gandhi's four-step understanding of bad
actors: at first Con *ignored* them; then he *laughed* the whole thing off as
minor and contrived; then, when the questions started to get under his
skin, he *fought* it (briefly).

Predictably, he started trying to control the reporting by refusing to
participate in question-and-answer sessions. If he had something to say,
he issued lopsided press releases but granted no interviews. He tweet-
ed vehemently, but he looked quite ridiculous doing so. Of course, none
of his prepared statements ever referenced his development project up at
TRS. However, in the end he couldn't control the growing outcry, the
public's right and demand to know. If he ever acknowledged to himself that

his greed-driven scheme had been bungled, he never allowed that to be known. Here was a man elected to protect the land and people, yet he was part of their destruction. Con tried hard to ignore conflict of interest allegations, in hopes they would fade away.

However, before too many months passed, and under pressure from constant media commentary and the barrage of letters and calls to his congressional office, he privately backed away from the TRS development deal, quietly placing his sole interest in the TRS property on the market. The Jimmies, in their wisdom and because of their long-standing network of both connections and inherited wealth, got wind of this and bought the old camp meeting grounds at the asking price. It would be a buffer zone against the possibility of any human-made threat harming SLANT or Fidelity Creek ever again. Too, the mega-church was court-ordered to clean that creekside dump—and were given a tight deadline to get it done.

It was a politician's greed combined with the corruption of those religious fundamentalist mega-churchers that got us into this mess. What got us clear of it was the "disinfectant" effect of "public sunlight," a notion described by a former U.S. Supreme Court Justice, Louis Brandeis (a brilliant but long-dead Kentuckian—highly progressive and regarded as a "Robin Hood of the law"). Corruption and greed are less likely to survive intense public scrutiny. So that, in a proverbial sense, was the end of that.

SLANT was at peace again, stronger and better than ever.

Acting as The Jimmies' designated proxy, Nooner knew how to protect the new property—he now refers to it as Upper SLANT. He's always been a land-loving dreamer, after all.

It was, indeed, a long and difficult year, that one. But like Fidelity Creek, everything flowed on and on, day and night. Balance, fairness and stewardship were restored. It was a hard period for us, a time of great losses, including the environmental/survival struggle, and Meddy's death (our core community's first—though Annie, who had lived high above TRS up at Top Notch, did precede her), and the fire that destroyed The General. However, on Time's bigger clock, that whole year was but a fleeting second.

In the SLANT vs. TRS debacle, the process and its resolution were the embodiment of Gandhi's notion of *satyagraha:* truth force.

And SLANT? Well, we got the last word! After having been (1) ignored and (2) ridiculed and (3) fought against, finally we prevailed. This was the only acceptable karma-based outcome, perfectly natural in that chain of events.

So, what's step four? The Mahatma's man was right. (4) We *won.*

# Deserve What You Get

SO LIFE, AS IT WILL, WENT ON. We the fortunate people of SLANT deepened our commitment to one another. Our shared memories increased manyfold.

Not the least example of this was the glorious event that inspired one of the biggest and best Summer Solstice Come Togethers that SLANT has ever experienced. It was the double wedding of the Pair Square couples. Much had happened in the culture at large over the previous few years, not the least of which was a long-awaited and, in civil rights terms, far overdue ruling handed down from the highest court in the land. It was the legal precedent that allows everyone of legal age to marry whomever they love. That Supreme Court marriage-equality ruling had made lesbian and gay people first class citizens at last. The entire "debate" around this issue had dissolved. Lo and behold, in proof of fairness, people's taxes went neither up nor down because of it, no straight people were forced to become gay, and the world kept right on spinning.

So, word coming out of Pair Square made it known to all that wedding plans were in the works. Everyone in SLANT—right down to Bocker, Stinkum, Boogle and the entire posse of four-leggers—seemed excited about the prospect.

The double wedding took place at Tractor Girl's bonsai farm on a perfect day in June—Pride month. The sun was bright; the breezes were light; the temperature and humidity levels were a delight. Twice as many people as the population of SLANT—including those from off-knob, some of whom didn't know Pair Square but wouldn't miss an annual Come Together—attended. This wedding was hugely celebrated because ... well, it was suddenly a big fucking deal that Finkle could legitimately marry Tommy and that Griddle could marry Jill. For some people, this wedding, like many others around the country in those first few years after the ruling, proved just how much of a big equality deal this particular unifying act of humans is. Even curmudgeonly old farts like me, who don't have any faith whatsoever in the so-called "institution of marriage," were impressed. The culture had indeed turned another important civil rights corner.

No one wanted to miss the wedding. The week before, Pair Square had lingered on the county courthouse steps, licenses in hand, to enjoy their fifteen minutes of fame in that one simple act—so small, yet so culturally significant.

And so their wedding happened on that last Saturday in June—a satisfying setting for a memorable Come Together ringed and tinged with perfect bliss. The Honorable Reverend Philosopreacher Joy DuPre performed the double wedding ceremony. Nick was the photographer. To everyone's delight, Nooner repeated Meddy's prophetic toast at the reception. Our new Resident Troubadour Wet Willie (Birdie having fallen in love and moved an ocean away!) joined with Juny and the rest of SLANT's fine music-makers to create sonic beauty. I offered an original wry poem about politics and love being strange bedfellows, pun fully intended. The Mayor spoke words of welcome and good wishes. Sam, her mom and her mom's partner were there. Meddy was sorely missed.

The event was informal, and it was rich with SLANT culture. Everyone danced and offered congratulations to their friends and smiled big-and-bigger at the shift we all felt because this double wedding was not only possible but legal to boot. Another sweet victory for the good guys … at long last.

Unions. Reunions. SLANT, that June, was still growing, still showing up for Life and for Living, still hoping, still embracing change. And, most of all, we were still believing in renewal—steadfastly practicing the knowledge that second chances earned are deserved.

On that double wedding day, SLANT in its pied beauty was just doing its thing. And so it still is to this day. And so it ever shall.

# The Wisdom of Top-Notch Annie, Part 8

"I BEEN TRYIN' to come up with an epitaph, now that my livin' is over. Not for my tombstone or memorial marker or eternal flame or any such of a thang. Just some sort of a summary 'bout what I've learned; somethin' for *me* to know.

"It's not been an easy challenge to conquer but, hell, I've all the time in the universe now! So, I been considering quotes that I'd encountered in my too-long short life.

"Thought about Shakespeare's line *One touch of nature makes the whole world kin*, for example—that idea's been proven a lie, though. The shenanigans of those damned fossil fuel barons being a case in point.

"For about one cosmic minute I thought Camus' *In the depth of winter, I finally learned that within me there lay an invincible summer* held merit. Now I know it's rubbish. Eternity ain't nothin' like a season on earth; eternity's a void. Take it from me. I'm dead, remember? I know some thangs.

"I do believe Willa Cather comes close with her *I like trees because they seem more resigned to the way they have to live than other things do*. Likewise with Montaigne's *Nature understands her business better than we do*.

"But just now I recollect that one day long ago I found somethin' even closer, prob'ly in an old Bartlett. It was spoken or written or somehow expressed by some Russian named Ouspensky, and that's all I know. But his words went somethin' like this: *It's only when we realize Life is taking us nowhere that it begins to have meaning*.

"Perhaps. If 'begins' is the operative.

"Ever'thang we know, we don't. The older we git, the clearer this becomes, 'til finally we cain't deny it any longer. All we can ever do is *attempt*. We begin and we begin, over and over and over again. That's all Livin' really is.

"And Death? Guess what? Dead is dead. For good. Which means dyin's just another beginnin': the start of the eternal phase—a *perpetual* beginnin' with no middle and certainly no end.

"Hell, maybe that's my epitaph. My own words: *We Are Forever Beginnin'*. Will that do?"

# A Tender Smile is a Benediction

THE REBUILT GENERAL, with its designated community corner sheltering its wood stove, is cozy and welcoming. For summer days, there's a heat-healing ceiling fan that wasn't there before. Turner makes sure the brand new coffee urn stays full and fresh. We're learning how to make the space our own. For one thing, instead of Shroom Room, we're now calling that spacious corner our Zoom Room, because we installed a wireless Internet connection in there. Handy for pulling off a virtual Come Together during a pandemic. Books are finding their way to the new swap shelf. We've contributed odd chairs and stools. From local red cedar, Jorge crafted a gorgeous new reading/game/potluck/shootin'-the-shit table. It's all coming along.

But I suddenly noticed that, other than a framed photo of the original General that now hangs revered above the coffee urn, the new painted walls seem too clean, too spare. As Resident Bard, I invoked my vocationally-endowed power to do something about that. So one recent day, in sacred honor of The Jimmies and our genesis, this is what I wrote on that blank wall (just as Jimi had when The Code was birthed): *Start small. Show growth.* Here's hoping it's a jumpstart. I expect most of the original Code plus new thoughts and epiphanies will appear at that intersection where walls from diverse compass points meet and meld. We've begun writing (living!) our next chapter.

Our braided resolve is strengthened. We're still creating sanctuary, still aim to protect and nurture what's right. We're open to what's to come. We've faith in each other. We offer each other tender smiles. Makes us feel strong, safe and loved.

All this I've told to you as best I can—warnings, warts and all! It's not a predictable ride, but it was *our* ride. Good of you to come along.

Every doctrine has its dogma, its scriptures, its sacred texts. Here in SLANT, The Code is our creed, our orthodoxy. We created it together out of wisdom, grit, intelligence, intention, practice and goodwill.

It is alive in us, is venerated among us. The Code inspires us. We animate it.

Metaphorically we are, each and all, palimpsest. Our founding (and evolving) parables progressively overwrite, intersect, amend a past. Illation builds upon (or supplants) illation. That's because SLANT is a perpetual work in progress, which is true for us all in this strange human world. We are delighted that our story is a *living* history. Still unfolding. Still teaching us—as are the lessons from our beloved prophets. You see that.

Like every doctrine, we revere our mythology. Now you know some of it. Perhaps when you remember us, you will think of us kindly, fondly, well.

And so, as SLANT's Resident Bard, I offer these humble intentions to you:

May our Code and our mythology sanctify and lift your own spirit.
May you learn, grow and embrace change all the days of your life.
May your struggles not swamp you, nor your losses paralyze you.
May you give and receive kindness every single day.
May you safeguard your own grace and do likewise for others.
May you encounter joy, reach peace, embody equity, think for good.
May you always assist the truth and resist the lie.

The turning world leaves us no choice but to do the very best we can. So, I reckon that's what we'll continue to do.

Oh, and *of course*—smoke 'em if you got 'em! For *that* is SLANT creed, dogma, mythology and ritual all rolled into one. (Get it? Yeah, you do.)

And all the people say ... *"Amen."*

www.ingramcontent.com/pod-product-compliance
Lightning Source LLC
Chambersburg PA
CBHW071426260626
47170CB00008B/2605